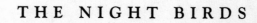

THE NIGHT BIRDS

THE NIGHT BIRDS

THOMAS MALTMAN

SOHO

Published by

Soho Press, Inc.
853 Broadway
New York, NY 10003

Library of Congress Cataloguing-in-Publication Data

Maltman, Thomas, 1971–
The night birds / Thomas Maltman.
p.cm.
ISBN: 978-1-56947-502-7
1. Teenage boys—Fiction. 2. Dakota Indians—Fiction.
3. Minnesota—Fiction. 4. Domestic fiction. I. Title.

PS3613.A524N54 2007
813'.6—dc22

2006052207

BOOK DESIGN BY PAULINE NEUWIRTH, NEUWIRTH & ASSOCIATES, INC.

10 9 8 7 6 5 4 3 2 1

For Melissa

And it shall come to pass afterward, that I will pour out my spirit upon all flesh; and your sons and daughters shall prophecy, your old men shall dream dreams, your young men shall see visions: And also upon the servants and handmaidens in those days I will pour out my spirit: And I shall shew wonders in the heavens and in the earth.

THE BOOK OF JOEL, CHAPTER TWO

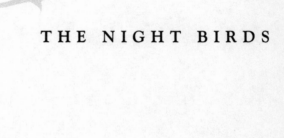

THE NIGHT BIRDS

KINGDOM TOWNSHIP,
MINNESOTA

1876

HOMECOMING

I GREW UP IN the shadow of the Great Sioux War which started here in Minnesota in 1862. Born four months after thirty-eight Dakota warriors were hanged en masse in Mankato the day after Christmas, I was named for an uncle, Asa, killed during the conflict. Sometimes, lying awake after the wicks were turned down, I listened to the wind outside and wondered what I inherited along with his name. I grew up mindful of the deep scars people carried from the war, but did not know the story behind them. My mother, Cassie, a slender, flaxen-haired woman, became pinch-mouthed if I asked her questions.

When my papa still attended church he never stepped forward to take communion and he told me he would beat me within an inch of my life if I pressed him on the matter. The second summer the locusts returned to our land, Papa stopped going to church entirely. He stood in his barren fields watching my mother and me ride away in the buckboard. Locusts sparked around him like hot specks of grease in a griddle. He stood in his infested fields, watching us ride to church as he crushed the insects in his clenched fists until the greenish-black blood ran down into his shirt sleeves.

I grew up with the past coursing under the surface of my family life like some dark underground river that I could sense but not touch. Against the dozens of pamphlets published far and wide about the conflict—A *Thrilling Tale of Captivity*, and *The Red Man's Revenge*—I had the measure of my parents' silence. Just under layers of topsoil I sensed the story waiting there and knew that it had something to do with sorrow, and that it made them afraid to this very day.

The year 1876 was the fourth year of the locusts. What I thought about that long ago afternoon as I scanned the prairies was that there is beauty in devastation. Passing clouds of locusts clothed the sun, on the move now that a new brood had hatched and eaten our countryside down to the bone. Their many wings were jeweled by the sunlight. A million scarabs of gold moved across parched ground and the land hummed with the song of their gathering hunger.

With no crop rows to harrow and tend, my papa and I passed time most days by climbing the Indian watchtower built in 1871 by Silas Easton, from which we could look out over the stripped farmlands and the oxbow of the Waraju River, a shallow stream in this dry season. Papa's duties as constable of Kingdom Township required him to spend a portion of his week scanning the frontier for hostiles, though no Dakota had raided this territory in over a decade. South and east, the land sloped away in rounded hills that sheltered ponds for cattle and sparse stands of burr oak and silver maple. North and west lay a sea of tallgrass prairie dotted with islands of wheat fields. If I followed the southern curve of the Waraju River, a caramel gleam in the late afternoon sun, I could catch a glimpse of smoke curling up from our cabin on the edge between hill country and grassland, just outside the township.

On a hot June day, with dust devils passing over barren earth, the first of two visitors who would alter the course of our family relations walked into our lives. He came across no-man's land abandoned by the Vajen family two years before, and something in the way he moved bothered me. A lone man moving at an easy trot. "Papa," I said, giving his shoulder a gentle shake. "There's something coming."

The stranger spoke no English and his lips were crusted with black blood from the locusts he had eaten to sustain him on his journey. Papa spoke to him a language I had never heard before, a rush of clicks and gutturals that brought a hesitant smile to the man's face. I knew him for an Indian only by the darkness of his skin, more sienna than the brick-red I had imagined, but otherwise he was dressed like a poor farmer: wool pants, a white cotton shirt partly eaten by locusts, and a bent slouch hat with the top cut out. An aquiline nose perched in the center of his weathered face and his broad features were framed by twin silver braids twined with strips of fur. He stood a head shorter than my father. I remember the keen sense of disappointment I felt on viewing my first specimen of the savage race. He didn't carry any weapons and there was a hint of senility in those black eyes shaded by the hat. I looked off to the north trying to imagine his journey across hundreds of miles of land his kind had been banished from a decade ago, his bare feet somehow unbloodied by the razor grass and stripped stubble of dead wheat fields. The hesitant smile the old man wore faded when Papa brought his half-stock prairie rifle up to his shoulder and cocked the hammer.

The township of Kingdom curved over the top of a series of hump-backed hills shaped like a dragon. Hedged by dark woodlands along the backside, the dragon's sleeping head opened out to an oceanic span of grasslands the Waraju River flooded in rainy years. From the grasslands came wolves and locusts and now this Indian.

While we were still a long ways off, my teacher, Mr. Simons, had spotted us with his looking glass and rang the bell of the church that also served as our schoolhouse, ensuring a large crowd when we came through town with our captive.

The higher you climbed the dragon-shaped hill the more prosperous things became. The floodplains were inhabited by immigrant farmers like the Ecksteins—Bohemians who adjusted to the plague by cooking the locusts in a buttery dish they called "fricassee." At the base of the dragon's tail, you passed the grist mill where farmers came to grind their grain. Here the road split a graveyard of leaning crosses bearing the names of German settlers killed during the Indian uprising. Up a small rise, the Schilling family had struck together some dour clapboard buildings that passed for the town's dry goods store and livery. My father was the constable and his single room jailhouse, which he said would blow down in a strong wind, squatted next to the livery barn and blacksmith shop. A rutted dusty road continued up the dragon's spine until you reached a brick hotel with ornate columns the Meyers had built in the hopeful days when they thought the railroad might pass through town, and onward to the whitewashed, country church from which the bell now resounded. Mr. Simons was fond of ringing that bell.

It seemed people had come from all over the county, summoned by the sound. Farmers abandoned their useless work in the fields at the promise of some new glimmer of entertainment. There were shop-keepers in soiled aprons and women in bonnets so deep only the beaks of their noses showed. All of them hovered around us, a low excited murmur rippling through the ranks when they saw what we had. Papa had taken the Indian's slouch hat and shirt, and the old man jogged behind us, his bare chest glistening, his wrists bound, a leather cord encircling his throat.

For a moment we all paused outside the jailhouse. In the distance there was the everpresent drone of the locust hordes taking flight now that dark had fallen. If the crowd was disappointed in our captive, the first prisoner my papa had captured since a group of horse thieves troubled the county two years before, they didn't show it. One woman, her voice hoarse, kept calling the Indian a *rot tuefel* in low, Germanic undertones that sounded like a person spitting. If the crowd hoped for a show they received some measure of it when the Indian raised his head and began to address us in his mother tongue.

I didn't know any of the words, but watched my father carefully. Papa's lips narrowed. The entire crowd froze and Myra Schilling would later claim that the Indian put a spell on us. At first he seemed to be speaking to all of us, but then his eyes found me standing beside my father and I stopped breathing entirely. He held my gaze for only a sec-ond. The dull, faintly senile luster was replaced by a dark, shining intelligence. Then the Indian's speech came to halt as my father jerked the end of his cord and choked off his words. He was dragged inside and locked in the one-room cell. All through the evening, people paraded through the jailhouse to admire the Indian and praise my father. While a few pitied the prisoner, most of the talk I heard was darkened by the memory of past events. *We did right to hire an old Indian fighter*, I heard them say. *I bet there is a bounty on this one's head. What do you reckon he was intending? Probably sent to scout us out. He's come to prepare the way. Don't take him to Fort Ridgely. We can deal with his kind here.*

As for me, I mostly figured that the Indian was guilty of poor timing. General Custer and the Seventh Cavalry had just been annihilated at Little Bighorn as the country was preparing to celebrate the first centennial. Our nation was reeling from the loss of this hero and three hundred soldiers. A few newspapers openly called for the "extermination of the entire treacherous red race." And while we were far from the Montana territory where this had happened, the people here had suffered greatly during the month of August 1862 and had long memories. They did not see a man before them. They saw a devil.

In the dark a thing turns on itself. As long as the locusts were here, the chickens had to be kept penned in their sour-smelling coop. Otherwise the hens devoured the locusts like gluttons until all you tasted and smelled when their eggs fried was the sulfurous, black taint of insect blood. That night I found another hen dead in the straw, pecked to death. The other hens huffed and ruffled out their feathers, a jury of malcontents, while I held up the kerosene lantern and inspected the mottled corpse. The body was already going stiff and I knew the meat was ruined. We were down to a dozen hens and a sickly rooster now. With the weather so hot and space tight and enclosed, the hens turned on one another. They were not so different from the locusts which cannibalized each other when nothing else was left to eat. They were not so different from human beings, as I would learn that summer.

I carried the dead pullet by the talons as I walked back to the cabin. Locusts crunched under my boot heels and some took flight and battered themselves like moths against the lantern. Crunch, crunch. Each step released a sour smell of innards and blood and I was grateful not to be barefoot like so many other country children. Think of every terrible sound you have heard—a saw on bone, a man grinding his teeth in anger—and you will know what I heard as I crossed that field every night between the cabin and the henhouse. The hen's broken neck flapped loosely against my pant leg. When I felt something crawling against my fingers, I knew the maggots had got to her. Rather than carry her back I flung her out into the dark, onto a moving carpet of insects.

Inside I skimmed a few dead locusts from the wash basin and splashed cool water on my face to erase the image of the dead pullet. Papa surprised me then, coming up behind me and lifting me in a great bear hug. "You did good today, boy," he said.

I felt the sinewy strength in his arms, smelled his sweat and the whisky on his breath. He had lean, hatchet features, a hawk's profile, and a mane of wheat gold hair. I was a dark, thin child, sparrow-boned and breakable in his grasp. Even as he crushed the air from my lungs with this hug, we shared a wheezy laugh. "Old Eagle Eye," he called me. He was sunburned, the skin on his long nose peeling. "We'll make a proper soldier of you yet."

Then Mother called from the table saying, "Set him down and come get your grub," and the moment was over too soon.

All through dinner, fried fish and buckwheat bread, they talked about the Indian and what his capture meant for us now.

"Do you think he's an important figure?" Ma asked.

Papa shrugged. "They paid that man from Hutchinson five hundred dollars for gunning down Little Crow in a field of raspberries. He didn't even know what he'd killed until they'd scalped the body and someone saw the corpse had a double-set of teeth and bent wristbones."

"Will they still pay a bounty after all these years?"

Papa didn't know. "But five hundred dollars," he said. "Imagine what we could do with just one hundred. I could buy back the percheron from the Schillings. We'd have enough to live on until the hoppers leave." A few stray locusts crawled over his dinner plate and he pinched them absentmindedly between his fingers.

"We'd have enough to buy passage out of this country for good."

"You know I won't ever leave here," he said.

From across the table, I saw her eyes glisten. Behind her a laundry line was strung from one end of the cabin to the other, clothes hung to dry over the stove where the locusts couldn't get to them and devour the fabric. The cabin was a simple two-room structure, not so different from the one Papa had grown up in with six siblings on this very same ground. That cabin burned to the ground with the rest of town in 1862. When all the ashes had settled and the war was done and every last Dakota chased out of Minnesota or strung up from the gallows, my father rebuilt over the old root cellar. Our cabin nestled in the crook of a low hill, sheltered from the north wind. A good place, if unlucky.

"Things are changing," Papa said. "I can feel it. Things are turning back to the good."

When I spoke they looked startled, they had been so absorbed in their own conversation. I was quiet enough as a child that my parents often forgot me. "What was his name, Papa? The Indian, didn't he tell you a name?"

"He called himself Hah-pahn, which means second born. I knew it for a lie, though. That was only his childhood name. An Indian will tell all sorts of lies to save his own skin."

"Did you know him from the before times?"

He shook his head. "Been a long time since I spoke Dakota. It come back to me, easy as sin."

Ma got up to tend to the dishes. "You don't think they'll lynch him before we can collect?"

His laugh came out like a low, rumbling cough. "That's only talk," he said. "That's all they're good for. Even liquored, I don't see a one of them killing a man. Not that it's a bad idea. It might have been easier if I had just shot him when I saw what he was." His voice lowered. "Must be two hundred miles between here and the reservation in the Dakotas. A long ways on foot."

"Why did he come here, Papa?"

"Said he was homesick. Imagine that. He said he was dying and wanted to see the place of two rivers one last time."

In the washbasin my mother let the dishes clatter together. "Don't you go getting sentimental," she said. "He's worth money to us."

"Don't worry," Papa said. "I pegged him for a liar from the first. I haven't forgotten how we suffered. Any trust I had for Indians died a long time back."

Lying atop my sheets that night I felt as uneasy as the locust legions preparing for their invasions northward. They left by morning in great glistening clouds, traveling as far as Polk County the papers would later report, almost to Pembina and the Canadian border. By now we knew not to celebrate. All that remained of our fields was chaff and dust. An inch below the ground ran a white, pulsating river of eggs waiting to hatch next spring.

I heard the locusts stirring, the scrape of their wings a rasping drone like a vast machine humming through the night. Here was a thing of wonder. That multitude of insects communicated as one great hive, one mind, while I lay there, one boy, with nobody in the world who knew his secret thoughts. I was stuck thinking on the Indian. He would have walked straight past our watchtower while my father dozed if I hadn't said anything. My stomach clenched when I remembered my father talking about the Indian's homeward journey. It wasn't right for me to feel sympathy for his kind, but I did.

A tallow candle made a circle of light on my nightstand. I picked up my Bible and turned to a page at random. This was a kind of divination I had heard about in school. You closed your eyes in prayer and then opened up the Bible to see what message God had for you. That night my fingers blindly found Hebrews, Chapter Thirteen. The first verse spoke of brotherly love, which didn't help me all that much since I was an only child. I started to close the book when something caught my eye. Verse two read: "Be not forgetful to entertain strangers; for thereby some have entertained angels unaware." I read over that verse three times, my spine tingling. What had we locked inside that jail cell? What was God trying to tell me now?

The same heat that spawned the dust devils we saw earlier now settled over the cabin. My loft room window was peeled open with a shirt tacked over it to keep out the hoppers. Moonlight flooded the room while I sat on the edge of my bed studying the back of my hands and the darkness of my skin. At school when we played Little Crow and the soldiers, I was always one of the Indians, while Franz Schilling, the storekeeper's son, got to be Colonel Sibley on account of the sideburns he could grow even though he was only fifteen. We reenacted the killing of whole families in Slaughter Slough, the girls fainting in their dresses and petticoats. After the massacre, Franz led his soldiers through the tallgrass to hunt down those of us unlucky enough to be Indians that day.

Once we even made a fake prison of woven willows and Franz brought a rope from home and showed us how to make a proper noose and sling it over a sturdy oak branch. Since I was Little Crow they sent me up to test it out, even though this was not how it happened in the books. I didn't protest. At that age I was eager to please and just as curious as the rest of them about death. You know what I felt? I felt guilty about things I hadn't even done. I felt that I had this coming. Made of horsehair, the rope itched around my throat. Then Franz kicked away the log. If Mr. Simons hadn't seen us in time and come running I might not be here now to tell this story.

Down by the grove a screech owl started up. It sounded like a catamount, like the shrieking of an old woman. They make that screech to scare up the mice and wrens, but it doesn't sound so nice to humans either. Normally the shrieking would have sent me under the covers to huddle for I was a cowardly child, but tonight it was too hot. I knew that I wouldn't get any sleep. The owl kept calling. I thought about how surprised I had been when the noose worked and cinched tight and my face swelled with trapped blood. Terrified, some of the children ran beneath me and tried to lift me up by my boot soles. By the time Mr. Simons cut me down I had voided my bladder and had to be sent home.

I thought about that old Indian and realized they would likely kill him when they discovered his true name, either here or at Fort Ridgely. That's what they did to Medicine Bottle and Shakopee after they captured them in Canada a year and a half after the uprising. I had read everything I could about Indians. I knew then that I didn't want him to die that way. For the longest time, I sat there thinking on the hopes for wealth he represented to my parents and what might happen to him in the following days. Without knowing it, my hands went up around my throat, touching skin that still remembered the burn of a rope.

Since I was a born insomniac, my parents allowed my nightly ramblings. On hot nights like this, I usually liked to go the springhouse, which was full of spiders but dark and cool. But tonight, dressed only in night-clothes and in my bare feet, I picked my way over a mile of moonlit ground swimming with sleepless locusts. I walked until I couldn't hear the owl anymore. Trees stripped of leaves unhitched their shadows in the moonlight and followed after me.

I pretended that I didn't know where I was going as I went past the graveyard and climbed the dragon's spine. The streets were bare, the shops shuttered. A horse nickered from within the livery stable, smelling me in the dark.

I told myself that I was bewitched and not in my right mind, but I had walked all this way carrying my father's brass circlet of keys in my fist.

The inside of the jailhouse was as dark as the bottom of a well. I didn't have a lantern, but I knew this room by heart, filled as it was with relics of another time. Human scalps as long as horsehair manes twisted from the rafters. The scalps danced in the breeze from the open door. I could hear them as they reached for one another in the night. In the newspapers it said that the thirty-eight Dakota held hands in the moment before the trapdoors opened beneath them and they dropped to their deaths. They held hands and sang their death songs. But these scalps weren't from that time; they were taken during the Devil's Lake Campaign of 1864. Yet that's what I thought about as I heard the whisper of their twisting.

Except for that sound it was silent in the jail. I listened for snores, the sound of a man breathing, and heard nothing. I told myself he must already be gone as I stepped forward and began to fuss with keys. A sudden pressure in my bladder. With my fingertips I followed along the wall until I felt the cool iron of the bars. On the other side of them I sensed him, there, watching. This gave me pause. He could have reached out and seized my hand through the bars. I shook so badly I dropped the keys; they rattled to the floor. After I picked them up, I tried a couple before I found one that worked. The lock mechanism whirred like the turning of a clock. I stepped back. The Indian spoke, his voice surging out and echoing all around me. His voice spoke in that same language, low and strangely birdlike. The hair raised on the nape of my neck.

Then I ran like Little Crow's warriors were after me in the dark. I ran until the air burned inside my lungs, the keys jingling in my fists. I didn't stop running until I passed the graveyard and paused to catch my breath near some desiccated plum bushes. When I was done I turned back and looked toward the town, the strange humpbacked dragon's spine and the moon hovering over the buildings. I saw the Indian in the very center of the street. He had retrieved his hat. He lifted it like a gentleman and then bowed. I never saw him again but it came to me that when he had spoken in that rush of clicks he might just have been telling me his true name.

By morning the news spread through town that the Indian had gotten away. People argued over whether he had been spirited out of the jail or let go on purpose. And even though I had crept so very carefully back inside our cabin that night, my father had been awake too. "You didn't go near that Indian, son?" he'd asked me. I could only stammer in answer, hoping the keys made no noise as I hung them again on the nail. I knew we would have another conversation when he returned from riding with the men he gathered for a posse.

The Indian's escape coincided with the departure of the locusts. The townspeople were hushed by the sight of them eclipsing the sun. Disappointment turned quickly to relief. Even if the hoppers came back again next year, there was a sense of something evil passing, a lifting of spirit.

Down below the hayloft in our barn I had made myself a secret hiding place that I shared with a few of our cats. Swallows dipped and dove in the little bit of light that sifted through the slats. It was quiet here now that our prize Jersey bull and the percheron had been sold to pay debts the summer before. I had a cigar box where I kept some much-thumbed Beadle dime novels Mr. Simons had been kind enough to loan me. Our pastor, Jarrel Henrickson, called dime novels the "ruination of the American moral fiber," and maybe that was part of my problem. My own papa only called reading them "loafing." Even though I had my favorite book, *Malaeska, the Indian Wife of the Great White Hunter*, I couldn't concentrate on the sentences because I kept thinking how cowardly I had become. I had betrayed my own kind and deserved any punishment I might get for it. Paging through the book, I wished I had been born in a different time, earlier, when things were still wild.

I stayed all day in that place, until Pa returned at twilight. He came into the cavernous barn at a time of long shadows, took off his hat, and held it against his chambray shirt. "Tell me one thing," he said. "Why'd you do it?"

I closed the book, placed it carefully within the cigar box, and hid it in a mound of hay. I wanted to tell him I was sorry but my throat felt as thick as if I had drunk a cup of molasses.

"I provided a place for you, kept you warm and fed and safe. I've raised you with all the love that I have left inside me even though some nights I felt as hollow and stripped as these fields. Don't you know that?"

I peeked around the corner of my stall. His hair was pasted to his skull, crushed down by the hat. He drew his finger along his brow, wiped away the sweat leaking into his eyes. I stayed frozen, unable to speak or move further. And the terrible thing was in that moment what I felt mostly was relief they hadn't caught the Indian. He had eluded hounds and men on horseback. Papa looked at me and my relief turned back to shame when our eyes met. His cheeks were sunken, his nose a hawk's beak. His shirt was soaked with sweat.

With a clenched fist he thumped his chest as though to loosen the words stopped up there. "Come here," he told me. "I don't have any patience left in me."

I followed him to the barn's entrance. When he took down a rawhide whip hanging next to a hay cradle, I went numb inside. "Take off your shirt and hold onto that beam," he said. Then I saw that he was crying and I felt a deepening of shame. "I heard you come in last night. I think I knew even then what you'd done. You won't be wandering at night anymore after this. If people in town knew, they would hate you the rest of your living days. If your mother knew the true reason for this whipping I am giving you now. . . . Don't you have anything to say for yourself?"

I shook my head, not understanding why I had done something that hurt the only people who loved me in this world.

Papa hit me three times while I clung to a beam that traveled up to the ceiling. Blue fire danced before my eyes. I didn't scream or holler the way I thought I would. Then my father collapsed to his knees, weeping, and didn't strike me again.

I kept my hands wrapped around the beam. Runnels of hot blood ran down my back. The muscles there felt raw and seared. I waited for him to hit me some more. The sound of his weeping spooked me beyond anything I had heard or seen before. I had done something that locusts and Indian wars and massacres couldn't. I had broken a man I'd thought invincible.

Still shirtless, I went to him and knelt and put my hand on the top of his head. I touched him hesitantly, the way a person touches something dangerous, a wounded wolf or grizzly bear. He didn't jerk away from my touch, didn't get angry. He took my hand and held it to his face, saying in a husky whisper, "You don't know what it cost me to keep you here. You don't even know what it cost." I didn't understand him then, but I felt something break inside me at those words.

My father never hit me again after that, not even after what happened later.

A SECOND
VISITOR

SCHOOL STARTED EARLY that summer since so little remained of our fields. The only thing that thrived were the bullheads—an ugly fish with a mean, wolfish snout—that prospered in summers when thick swarms of locusts drowned in the Waraju River. With the river running so low we could stand in the shallows and spear them from the muddy banks with pronged jigs. I spent mornings at school in Mr. Simons's classroom and afternoons fishing and trying to make up to my family for what I'd done.

Papa went alone to Silas Easton's Indian watchtower, but no more Dakota came through the county that year.

A week into school a letter arrived from the town of St. Peter. Papa was still away that day. I came home after a luckless fishing expedition to find Ma holding the envelope close to a candle, trying to fathom the contents. Her thin face looked crimped and worried. When I came through the door she set the letter down on the table and stepped away from it. "Asa, who in the world do you think your Papa knows in St. Peter?"

I shook my head. Papa had traveled east the two previous summers after the crops were destroyed to work as a hired hand on other men's land, those who had been spared by the locusts.

My mother had aged these past few years, the gold in her hair dimming to a muted straw color. The hands that held the letter were nut-brown and wrinkled. "Set yourself down," she told me. "I'll fetch us some sarsaparilla tea and then I want you to read me this letter. You don't think he'll mind, do you?"

"I don't know."

"No, he'll consider it a favor. Don't that handwriting look pretty to you? I do wonder who he knows in St. Peter." She ground sarsaparilla root into two bone china cups and poured hot water over this, her afternoon constitutional. Sometimes, she spooned a dose of laudanum into her own cup and passed a few hours rocking in a chair, her eyelids fluttering while she dreamed. I drank tea with her, though in the summertime a hot drink was the last thing I wanted. On school days she fixed a cup for each of us and then asked me to tell her about what I'd learned. Mr. Simons kept a map of our country with flags marking famous battles during the War Between the States. His lectures were dry recitations of battle movements, generals present, faceless numbers of the wounded and the dead. This history I carried back to my mother and sometimes embellished—spinning fibs about the men there, great and small, their secret fears and hopes—and because she had only two years of learning herself she would nod, saying, "Isn't that something?" She had learned just enough to cipher the city that an envelope came from, and guess that the hand that wrote it was either "educated" or "feminine."

The letter lay between us while we sipped our tea. I saw her continue to glance toward it, her blue eyes watery. Halfway into our ritual she reached for it with a trembling hand and said, "Why don't you open it now?"

"Ma'am? You think maybe you should be the one?"

"Oh no. We'll tell him you were practicing your ciphering."

I figured things couldn't get much worse with my papa and so used a long, dirty fingernail to hook open the envelope and shake the letter out on the table. Ma stood up, hands behind her back, and paced the room. "My, that's a passel of writing there," she said. "You go ahead now and read it."

Dear Sir,

I have located your name from the Brown County Census of 1874. To my knowledge you are the only Senger family in all of Minnesota. I am writing you on behalf of one of the patients here at the St. Peter Hospital for the Insane. According to our records she has been with us for over a decade because of a nervous condition called epilepsy. Her name is Hazel Senger and while she refuses to talk or cooperate with most of the medical staff, I believe she may be of some relation to you. The reason for my writing is first to inform you of recent medical advances pertaining to the treatment of seizures and fits of apoplexy. Namely, we have had some success with a powder called bromide and said patient has not suffered a seizure in over a year. Due to overcrowding at this facility, I believe the time has come to release her back into the world.

She seems to have developed a closeness with one of our staff doctors, a certain Alastor Wright, who has managed to get her speaking again and put her to work in the laundry department. While his methods have proven to be unorthodox, one cannot argue with results. In recent weeks he has begun to spend an inordinate amount of time in her presence—to the detriment, I fear, of his other duties.

I believe that his successes should now bear fruit. In light of our situation, Hazel Senger will be released from St. Peter on Wednesday June 19th with an ample supply of the bromide. The state has provided for her care for long enough. If you are indeed a relation of this woman and care about her well-being, you should be at the entrance of our hospital at nine in the morning when we will release her along with a number of other patients who no longer need our care. Such charity cases, after all, are the province of the family and not the state.

Cordially,
Dr. Wendell Frietz
Chief Medical Officer

"Why don't you hand me that letter, Asa?" she asked when I was done reading it. I gave it over without comment. She held it up in the greasy light coming through the window panes, her lips mouthing the words like a child. Then she walked over, opened up the wood stove, and tossed the letter inside. It happened so quickly. Without knowing what I was doing, I overturned the chair and sprang across the room. Tongues of fire licked at the edges of the letter. My mother stood there watching it burn. The oven door was open so I reached inside and plucked the letter out, singeing my fingertips. Black flakes came away. Ashes. But you could still read the heart of the letter. "You put that back in the fire," mother said. "Do as your mother tells you."

The front door opened. Papa was back from his time at the watchtower, the rifle slung over his shoulder.

I lay on the floor of the loft room that night listening to them argue with my ear pressed to the boards. My mother had not cooked any dinner and I knew that I wouldn't be getting any. Somehow that didn't matter.

"I won't have that woman in my house," she said.

"She's my blood relation."

"I'm your wife."

"Blood's thicker than water. I won't have that argument used against me in this lifetime. Once was enough."

A long silence. I knew she was crying now. "But your momma said she died. Your momma said she didn't survive childbirth." Her voice quavered.

"Ma never did or said a thing that wasn't in her own best interest. Truth only mattered if it suited her. No, she intended this to happen all along."

"It will change things if you bring her here. Our boy," she said. I pressed my ear closer, straining to catch the next words. What did I have to do with any of this? I was disappointed when she continued. "We barely have enough to feed the boy now. No crop in four years. How will I feed another mouth?"

"We'll find a way."

"Your mind is set, then?"

"By God, yes. We'll take the steamboat to New Ulm and walk from there."

"After all these years," my mother said. "And I thought that letter was from a sweetheart. Now I only wish to God you had a sweetheart."

"You're a curious woman." I moved again, straining for a better position near a knothole. The boards creaked. Papa, sensing me listening, shushed her. "This house has grown ears," he said. "We've said enough tonight."

Long after the wicks were turned down I lay awake thinking on this news. Aunt Hazel, who had shamed the family by getting pregnant while a captive of the Dakota, was alive. She was supposed to have died in Mankato, mourning her Indian lover who got hanged. She and the baby died in the following spring of 1863, and that was all I knew. My head spun with this news. And now she was coming here, released from an asylum.

When I was seven years old, a severe winter storm had barricaded us in the cabin. Howling winds piled drifts as high as the roof. While waiting for the snow to melt, Papa passed time drawing stories for me on a long ream of butcher paper he had left over because he spared the life of our aging sow the past harvest season. I sat for hours watching. I marveled that such large, gnarled hands could hold a pencil so lightly and summon shapes and shadows to fill the page. He set words down, too, though he was a poor speller. He did not speak and became agitated if I asked questions about the story. After three days the wind died down and Papa rolled the ream of butcher paper up, tied it with a leather cord, and handed it to me before stepping outside to dig his way to the barn. I have been puzzling over that story he drew for me ever since, for I kenned that he was telling me about the past in a way he couldn't out loud.

Papa's drawings illustrated a tale of two children, a boy and his baby sister, who are lost in the woods. Throughout, there are hints of something terrible that has happened to leave these children orphans.

They shelter in an oak tree hollowed out by lightning. Night after night they hide there, conjuring monsters out of ordinary things that pass their tree in the dark. The baby girl begins to starve. Just when the boy is losing hope, a talking crow tells him of a nearby farm. The boy makes a sling of his muslin shirt and carries the baby in it behind him, like a papoose. He journeys through the woods, following the crow as it flits from branch to branch. At a nearby farm they find a goat the boy milks to feed his sister.

My favorite illustration comes right before this scene, where the children first emerge out of the woods into the clearing of the farm. If you look closely, near a stump of an old tree you will make out the shape of a woman's horned feet as she lies prone in the grass. I knew with a child's prescience that the woman in the picture had died in some awful way my papa never bothered to explain. The story ends curiously; the boy finds his way to a town and hands the child he has carried for so long to a woman whose face is shadowed by a bonnet. Then Papa ran out of paper as well as patience. Who were the boy and girl of the story? I understood that Papa knew them and that the true ending had been too painful for him to tell.

There were other mysteries when you studied on the pictures closely. Now it occurred to me that questions I had wondered about for years might finally be answered. I lay back on my bed thinking these things over and didn't sleep a wink that night.

"You don't look crazy," were the first words my mother said to Aunt Hazel.

"It's good to see you, too," my aunt responded.

"What I mean is, you don't look how I thought you would." My mother was one of those people known for speaking her mind, which is what they usually say about people with bad manners. But it was true. You don't expect a woman who you thought was dead all these years— but really was just in an insane asylum undergoing torturous treatments—to look hale and hearty.

Nine days after Pa left to retrieve her from St. Peter, Aunt Hazel came to our house wearing a girlish yellow-print dress, her face freck-led from walking in the open sun. She had clear green eyes and dark brown hair. And there was something elfin in her smile.

"This is the one," she said to me. She was carrying a carpet bag that held all her worldly belongings. She set it down, saying, "Come closer."

I hesitated, thinking on the bits of information I'd managed to wheedle from my mother over the last nine days. That Aunt Hazel "knew things a Christian woman ought not to," her way of implying the woman was a witch. That Aunt Hazel hadn't resisted when taken cap-tive, had wanted it even. Now this woman stood before me and she was not the wispy, white-haired vision I had imagined. Not a woman with faraway eyes and long yellow fingernails, but one who looked you straight in the face and saw the fears you hid in your underbelly and smelled the regret on your skin. To tell the truth, she frightened me. But despite certain recent lapses, I was an obedient child and so went to her and let her put her hands on my cheeks until I looked up into her eyes and tried to still the quivering in my stomach. Only a woman does a thing like that: takes you into her hands like she held a sparrow and was divining its lifespan, the good and bad. Men are keen about other things, but not very often about people. Aunt Hazel didn't say anything about what she saw in my eyes, not at that time.

We cooked one of the pullets that had quit laying, the hen either sick or obstinate, and had a dinner of baked chicken and potatoes, a rare treat. The adults talked about the trip, and the territory west of St. Peter. "Did it surprise you to see the land?" Mother wanted to know. "It looks like the end of the world outside, the Lord have mercy."

"It did make me sad," Aunt Hazel said. "But I wasn't surprised. I read about the locusts in the paper. At St. Peter there's many a farm wife, worn out from her travails. This prairie never was all that fond of settlers." While she spoke she moved her food around the plate but didn't eat any.

"You think God is punishing us?" said Papa. "Reverend Henrickson said so from the pulpit." A scattering of fine bones lay picked clean on his plate.

"Maybe," Aunt Hazel said. "And maybe it's just the land itself speaking to us and our iron plows, our gelded bulls, and foreign seeds and threshing machines."

"You talk a lot," my mother said. "I remember a time when you didn't talk so much."

Aunt Hazel was quiet for a time and then she told a story in answer. "Listen," she began. "Once there lived an ancient king who believed all children were born with an innate language and he wished to discover whether it was Greek or Latin. For two months every child that was born in the kingdom was gathered in a single room in the castle. The nurses were forbidden to speak with the children while the king waited to hear what language would arise from them naturally. The babies were well fed and swaddled in warm blankets, but never a word was spoken to them."

Hazel paused and then she looked directly at me across the table. "All the children died," she said. "One by one, not hearing a name or a whisper, and the king came to understand our universal language, silence, and the price it demands in the end."

Mother brought her fork down with a clatter. "That's a terrible story," she said.

Father leaned forward in his chair. "Hazel," he said. "It would be better if you spoke more plainly around here. Save the stories for your book."

Still incensed, Mother said, "I don't know why any of those women would trust the king with their babies. If it was my baby I wouldn't let another soul handle it." Then she seemed to realize something and sank back in her chair. Her mouth opened and closed again and she got up and started gathering the dishes. "Well," she said, "Well."

For my own part I liked the story despite the consternation it caused my parents. Hazel's story cast a spell and not much else was discussed that evening. What I loved most about it is what it said about the silence I had grown up with. Both my parents had thought they were sheltering me with their secrets, protecting me from some awful truths only they knew. *I don't believe in dredging up the past*, Papa liked to say. Well, now the past was here with us in the flesh, and she spoke in stories that seemed to say the past mattered, and that silence would only cause more bad things to happen in the world.

After dinner, Mother threw Aunt Hazel's uneaten chicken out in the yard. When I came back from carrying water from the springhouse she still seemed angry, clattering the dishes around in the washbasin.

Aunt Hazel took out a mason jar of white powder from her carpet-bag. She set it on the table, unscrewed the lid, and dipped in a tiny spoon. This little bit of powder, no bigger than a hummingbird's meal, she set on her tongue and swallowed. She shut her eyes, sighed, and when the lid was in place set the jar on the shelf next to my mother's sarsaparilla root. Aunt Hazel held out a hand to my mother. "I'd like us to be friends, Cassie," she said.

Mother, elbow deep in suds, looked at the hand and nodded. "Don't need to be friends," she said. "We're family."

Since Hazel was to share the loft room with me, Papa had rigged a single oak crossbar to divide the loft and hung this with quilts. For the novelty of a guest in the household, I was more than willing to give up my bed and my window with the view of ruined, moonlit fields. That first night Aunt Hazel parted the blankets and stood before me in a white gown that hung loosely from her scarecrow limbs. "Asa," she called to me. "I'd like to make you the same offer." I'd been sitting up on my pallet and contemplating how to decorate my side of the room. She held out her hand. Unlike my mother, I took it. The hand that held mine had a surprising, bony strength. "Friends," she said, "but you have to promise me something."

Nobody had asked me anything important before this. I swallowed, nodded. She said, "Promise me you won't ever go into my belongings. They're all I have."

"Okay," I said. "I promise."

We shook on it and then she went back to her side of the room, turned down the wick, and lay on top of her sheets. A cooling breeze blew into the room and ruffled the blankets and the gown she wore. "Aunt Hazel?"

"Yes?"

"If we're friends it means I can ask you questions."

"Sure," she said. "But friends don't tell each other everything. If they did they wouldn't be friends very long. What is it you wish to know?"

"Were you afraid in the asylum?"

She didn't answer right away, thinking on the matter. Her voice seemed to come from far away when she did. "It isn't like you think," she said. "The St. Peter Hospital is like a city unto itself. There are farm fields and animals and even cabins where the patients on good behavior get to live. I wasn't really afraid inside there because everyday was the same. All the meals are set according to a weekly plan. Every part of the day is settled."

"But weren't there scary people?"

"Some," she said. "But most of them they locked away in their own section. You could hear them on quiet nights. A relentless kind of moaning came from their section, and maniacal sounds. But most of the crazy ones I knew were harmless. There was a man who thought he had a horse trapped inside his chest. He would go about the room, whinnying and pounding his breast." Aunt Hazel made the sound for me. We both laughed.

"Didn't you ever think to write any of us?"

"Ask me something else."

"What is it that makes you afraid?"

"You're kind of stuck on the same subject," she said. "Well, all right. I am afraid of forgetting things. I am afraid that sometimes it's too late for me to start my life over again." Then her voice hushed further. "I'm afraid I'll have to go back."

"I don't want that either," I told her. "Aunt Hazel, there's something you should know. I never really had a friend before. I might not be any good at it."

"It isn't all that difficult."

Then all at once I confessed to her about the Indian and what I had done. The words spilled out in a breathless rush. It might seem strange to you, for me to confess in this manner, but for whatever reason I'd made a decision right then and there to trust this woman. I was crying by the time I got to the end. I said, "That's why I don't know if I'll be a good friend. Look what I did to my own folks."

"Nonsense. I know somebody who would understand you."

"Who?"

"Your grandpa."

"Grandpa Jakob? Papa doesn't talk about him much."

I couldn't wait to hear more but from downstairs I heard the rumble of the loft's trapdoor. My mother knocked on the door three times. "You all go to sleep," she said. "We can hear every darn word downstairs. Your father needs his rest."

A quiet settled between my Aunt Hazel and me and it wasn't like all the other silences I had known in my lifetime. It was the kind of quiet that makes you feel content inside. I didn't worry that night about having any bad dreams.

We woke early the next morning to a crescendo of shattering glass. Still in her nightgown, Aunt Hazel rushed to the trapdoor, threw it open, and climbed down the ladder from the loft. I followed after, my mind still groggy with dream.

Downstairs, I woke up pretty quick. The mason jar of bromide lay in a million pieces on the floor and the powder sifted through the floorboards down into the root cellar below. Aunt Hazel knelt in the glass shards and tried to salvage what powder remained before it was all lost. Her face looked pale, stricken. Mother stood over her saying, "I didn't mean to. I was just reaching for my jar of sarsaparilla and I plum forgot what else was up there." Papa sat at the table with his head in his hands.

Aunt Hazel said nothing, but a shiver of grief traveled down her spine and she shuddered. Her hands trembled, spilling more powder. I knelt beside to help her.

"Don't cut yourself in the glass," Mother told me. Then she turned to Hazel. "We'll get you some more," she said. "We'll write that doctor friend of yours and he can send some more."

Like water the powder spilled down through her hands, speckled with spots of her blood. She stood with her remaining medicine in a bowl of bone china. Her hair jutted out in wiry curls. White-faced now, she was the very woman I had been expecting to show up at our door. Her lower jaw quivered. "There won't be any more," she said. "This is all they would allow me to take. You can't just order it in the mail, or get some from the apothecary. The only way to get more is for me to go back inside."

"I'll get a letter written to that doctor myself," Mother promised. "I can be very persuasive."

Aunt Hazel held the bowl close against her chest while she climbed the ladder into the loft where she would remain the rest of that day. She set the bowl in a corner where it was sheltered behind her carpet bag and then, still in her gown, lay down on the bed with her arms folded over her chest. An absolute stillness possessed her. Looking at her, I realized this was how she had survived all those years locked away. I watched her and tried to think up nice things to say, but nothing came to me.

Downstairs, Ma continued to carry on like she'd been wronged. "It was an accident. She acts like I meant to do it." Papa picked his hat from the door peg and walked out without speaking.

Papa had to leave us because of the crop situation. He was released from his duties as township constable, but the man in St. Peter didn't have farm work for him this summer. Instead, like many of the other men in Kingdom, he headed north to work in the pineries of the Big Woods. As he walked down the path to town, I trailed after him begging him to let me come along. "I'm big enough," I told him. "I can work like a mule. Look at these muscles." I flexed for him. I hoped he might forget how I'd let him down before.

He stopped and pinched my bicep with two fingers. "You're strong, all right," he said. "But I need someone to stay here and see to it that those two women don't kill each other." He flashed me a rare smile.

"You like having her home too, huh?" I said.

His smile faded some. "I think it was God's will that brought her here." I considered what he said. "Don't say it like that, Papa. People only

call it God's will when something bad has happened they can't control."
This was about the longest conversation he and I had ever shared. Aunt
Hazel being here had changed things. "A providence," I told him.
"You ought to call it a providence that she is here with us now."

A wistful smile curved the corners of his mouth. "You're awful
smart." He patted me on the head and continued on down the path that
would take him to New Ulm and beyond that to the shady dark of the
north woods.

The next day, while Mother took eggs into town to trade for salted
meat, Aunt Hazel opened the carpetbag and showed me some of her
treasures. I sat on the bed beside her while she took out a red leather
tome bound in rawhide. When she unwrapped the book it smelled of
dried spices and earth. The pages seemed as dry and breakable as leaves,
rustling gently as she turned them over. "Onionskin and vellum," she
told me. "It's all I could get hold of inside the asylum. One of the doctors allotted me a few pages each month." The handwriting was spidery,
each page cross-hatched to conserve paper. To read one you had to hold
it vertical and then horizontal.

"What is it?" I asked.

"My journal," she said. "Though there are many stories here. I suppose even yours."

"I can't read a single word," I said, squinting.

"My pa kept such a book and I thought the very same thing. Inside
it were formulas and spells concerning childbirth and water-witching
as well as dried specimens of flowers and herbs. He collected folklore
when we lived in Missouri."

"Grandpa Jakob? You mentioned him last night. Why did we ever
leave Missouri?"

"Oh, that was a long time ago," she said. "1859. Yes. I was even
younger than you then."

SALINE SPRINGS,
MISSOURI

1859

BOOK OF
WONDERS

THERE WERE THOSE who said Judas hanged himself from a redbud tree and ever after it grew stunted and strange. If you were to touch one of the flowers when the tree blossomed in April darkness you would see a vision of the devil. In the spring of 1859, the redbud that grew along the pasture fence put forth its blossoms a month early. Windstrewn, the red petals nestled against the cabin walls of the Senger family and lay like drops of blood in the dormant grass.

There were many things said and some were true and some were foolishness. Children of this age and place went about with muslin bags of live crickets strung around their throats to cure the whooping cough. They forbore from killing bullfrogs, fearful that such butchery would cause the cows to give bloody milk. When the moon waxed, they crept up on their reflections in still pond waters and waited for the image of their true love to rise to the surface. And they believed that in the center of a dogwood blossom, if you looked closely, lay the image of a crown of thorns and a brown stain like rusty nail.

All these things were said and many more, and they were written down on loose-leaf vellum pages that a Bohemian immigrant named

Jakob Senger cobbled together and called the *Book of Wonders*. A short bow-legged man with a dark, bristling beard, his one hobby was the collection of this folklore. In any weather he would hitch the brood mare to the swift phaeton buggy and set out to interview soothsayers, water-witches, and country healers. He never brought the book along, for his subjects would sink into sullen silence if they suspected he meant to write their secrets down, and in so doing destroy their magic.

Sometimes, he brought his *kinder*, especially his silent, black-haired daughter, Hazel. The presence of this quiet child seemed to quell the hill people's mistrust of strangers. Eleven years old, the girl had not spoken a single word since her mother, Jakob's first wife, Emma, had died of consumption four years earlier.

Both father and daughter understood that these journeys had much to do with Emma's death. To stand in a healer's cabin, where roots were draped from rafters, and inhale the redolence of earth and boiling sassafras, returned them both to the time when Emma was still alive. She had been such a country healer, but none of her potions, her bloodwort teas and salves of mullein leaves, could save her from the consumption that stole her voice and then her breath. Emma used up the last of her remaining strength to give birth to Daniel, Hazel's youngest brother, and then died a week later on a frigid day in January.

As dense as iron, the earth resisted Jakob's pickaxes and shovels. The ground would not be soft enough to bury Emma until March. He hauled ice up from the river, a great slab like a bed made of crystal, and laid her down in the stable with the horses. The girl went with her father and oldest brother Caleb each evening to kneel in the hay and pray for her mother's soul. The girl prayed with her eyes open. She watched the rising ghosts of their mingled breath. In her mind she tried to reconcile this blue-skinned vision of her mother—a figure in an indigo silk dress with her hands folded neatly over her chest, two silver coins for eyes, and a hollow purpling cavity where her cheeks sank in—with the one she had known in this life, a woman with chestnut hair who loved to sing.

Hazel had prayed that God would give her mother back her voice, and when it didn't work, she stopped speaking herself. Her father went a little mad that winter; they all did. Jakob kept that stall like a shrine and the girl could hear him go inside it and talk to her mother, and in the silences between his voice, guess the words Emma was answering. Only the thin, needling sound of newborn Daniel crying kept him sane.

Even on that bed of ice the corpse still had a slight odor of rot that made the horses nervous. Jakob rinsed the body with rosewater which froze to her skin, blue and pale in the poor light of the barn. The girl would dream of her mother at night, dream of her rising from the ice bed, breaking the thin lacing of frozen rosewater like a coffin of glass falling away, and grabbing hold of one of the terrified horses to ride through the snowbound hills and beyond. Every winter for the rest of her life she dreamed this dream when it turned cold.

And then in March, when the ground softened, the neighbors came with their shovels, and Jakob had to be physically restrained while they put Emma to rest under the ground and planted an ash tree over her grave.

Father and daughter rode together over hunched hills and through damp hollows. As they came through the woods he sang to the brood mare and described the shape of the world for the girl. He told her the world had been broken at the beginning of time and that we were all marked by Adam's fall. Plants and stones waited for the end of the Age, nursing poison and thorn, balm and flower. Such secret knowledge was like pollen on her tongue. The world was sown both with the seeds of God's love and thorns of man's age-old rebellion. And she thought she could keep her family safe if she knew enough, and could mark out a secure path through such a world. She thought her father possessed some kind of magic and when it turned out that he was only human, limited in knowledge and capable of failing his children and leaving them, as surely as Emma had, it nearly broke her. But for now he was the talespinner, the one who took them on journeys to visit places and characters long since passed from this place and time.

He would recite stories during these trips, especially *Der Marchen der Bruders Grimm*, a book of fairy tales he carried with him from the Old Country. Passed down from his own father, the stories were in part responsible for awakening his interest in local lore. He wanted to do for this new country what the Grimm brothers had done for his old one. Terrible things happened in these stories, but they were about knowledge as well. His favorites featured the night birds, *der nacht vogel*, birds that led humans out of sorrow. It was these birds that foretold Snow White's awakening from the coffin of crystal, these birds who guided the prince to Sleeping Beauty, who gave solace to poor *Aschen putel*, Cinderella. He liked to begin these stories with a question. "Have I told you the story of the three ravens?" he would say, while the mare trotted over the red-packed roads of Missouri clay. The girl would shake her head. He had told them that story many times, but she never tired of it. It began as they all did: "In the time of dwarves and mermaids, when plants and animals shared a common destiny with humans, and a common tongue, stones cried out, and the ravens spoke in prophecy."

In this time there lived a soldier in a far off land who was frugal and saved his coins for a time of need. His friends were not so prudent. They envied his small fortune and plotted how to steal it. One night they convinced him to abandon his post and come away with them in the woods. The owls and night birds saw this and followed after the men. The soldier heard their keening cries, but did not turn back. Deep in the woods the men fell upon him and stole all that he had. They were not content to take his gold only. They gouged out his eyes with dirty fingers and left him tied to a gallows to starve. When he awakened, the blinded soldier believed he was tied to a cross and prayed for mercy.

Her father liked to pause in mid-story. He would cluck to the mare and pull back on the reins, slowing her to a trot. He might look out at the thick woods around them—a place he called the *hexenwald* after the black forest, where the *seelenrauber*, the stealer of souls, was said to dwell in the shape of a wolf—as if searching for a missing thread of story. If Caleb was along, he would call out, "Go on Pa. Tell us the rest. How does it end?" But the girl only waited and watched the woods from her seat in the phaeton. "Are you sure I have not told you this story?" he asked her. She shook her head, smiling.

That night three ravens descended, talking amongst themselves. "Oh if only men knew what we know," each crow sang. They spoke of a dew that fell from heaven and allowed the blind to see again. Of a sick princess who could only be healed with the ashes of a toad from the pond. Of a village where the well had gone dry. The soldier listened and his face was upturned when the dew rained late in the dark. He was healed and broke his bonds to go abroad in the world, bringing ashes for healing and finding water for the village. The king rewarded him with his daughter's hand in marriage and the soldier settled into a life of ease. Later in his life, after all he had suffered, the very thieves who betrayed him found him once more. The soldier forgave them, telling them that what they meant for evil, heaven had turned to good. He told them of the prophesying birds. The thieves traveled to the gallows hoping to be enriched. There was a rush of wings, but when the ravens returned that night they descended in rage. The thieves were pecked to death and their bodies left to rot in the rain.

The stories fascinated the girl. In her own life, too, mothers died and fathers remarried. And sometimes the wicked were punished. She pictured that soldier beneath the gallows and filled in with her imagination details never meant for a children's tale: the soldier's gaping eye sockets, moonlight on the blue-black feathers of the descending birds, the harsh croaking they made in their throats while the thieves cowered below them in the falling rain. But the stories were also about knowledge, and justice, what this world reveals to us. She wanted that sense of order and looked for signs in her own life to show them to be true. She wanted to believe you could make good from evil, and be led, even while blind, out of sorrowful woods.

• • •

Spring followed winter and the head editor of the *Saline Springs Luminary*, Isaiah Thompkins, died in his sleep. Jakob, still grieving, sold his farm and bought the business and the 1854 acorn-shaped Franklin handpress wrought from iron that went with it. The family of four lived in a room above the office. A black stovepipe traveled up from the lower room and they laid their goosedown mattresses around it to keep warm. For a year they lived like this, feeding the baby Daniel on grits and goat's milk. (Once when the brother and father weren't around the girl tried to breast feed the child, but this effort satisfied neither party.) The oldest boy, Caleb, already taller than his father at thirteen, had wheat-gold hair and Emma's light brown eyes. He sold coal and firewood and his father's papers in the streets. People could read the news and then use the sections they didn't like for kindling, or more commonly, for wiping themselves in the outhouse. Hazel cared for her baby brother and went next door to Merton's Dry Goods to trade newspapers with Frau Volsmann, a fat mothering hen who gave them two loaves of fresh bread, blackberry preserves, and salted meat each morning. The girl didn't know what charity this was. But Frau Volsmann loved that baby with its pale white hair and quiet green eyes. She held it to her breasts, each as large as granary sacks, bulging out of either side of her apron, and made cooing sounds and said soft things to the baby in High German.

The town of Saline Springs became rich from settlers passing through from Independence, Missouri to Oregon and along the Santa Fe Trail. The streets were cobbled with limestone, even the gutters designed by slave artisans, and coursed with run-off in March and April. The buildings were all of a soft red sandstone that shone pink and flesh-hued in the first morning light. No one had ever occupied the old stone jail.

Daniel slept for hours and, once he was laid down, Hazel helped her father set type. She had clever hands even at the age of eleven. The type had to be set backward, akin to the way the ancient Hebrews wrote in their Bible. Her father did the muscle work, rolling up his sleeves to pull the rounce and coffin, the crank and bed of the iron handpress. Hazel liked the work and possessed an instinctive gift for composing the galleys in such a way not to make orphans, lone words at the bottoms of columns that took up space. She liked the smell of ink and wet paper which made her feel lightheaded and euphoric.

In return for two dollars a year, subscribers received a copy of *The Saline Springs Luminary* once a week. Jakob wrote stories down by hand for Hazel to set in type or gave her columns pilfered from *Harper's Weekly* or the *St. Louis Republican* to reprint. Along with the office they had inherited books by Poe and Walter Scott from which they filched stories and poems. They had a Webster's the girl used to search out words she didn't know, or alternatives, to make the galleys neater.

Making the galleys was all about space and order, whether she was printing recipes for winter hotch-potch or poetry. With her hands she brought meaning and harmony into a world where sometimes these things seemed not to exist. She saw that there were patterns in a person's life that were not discernible until the experience was over. She possessed clever hands, but she didn't always understand the articles she printed. When a slave was tied to a tree and burned alive in the woods after being accused of "touching" a white girl, her hands set the type for the story without pictures forming in her mind. All sorts of terrible things were told of during these years.

When the abolitionist John Brown and his sons used swords in Pottawatomie Creek, Kansas, to chop four pro-slavery men to pieces, her hands set the type without registering the import. Whether Kansas would become a free or slaveholding state would be decided by the incoming settlers according to the Missouri Compromise. Radicals from both sides flooded the state. Bands of border militia rode from Missouri to harass and burn out free-soil settlers. Senator Atchinson vowed to drive the abolitionists and "horse-thieves" into Hades and carry slavery to the Pacific Ocean. Abolitionists smuggled boxes of breech-loading Sharps Rifles for the war sure to come.

The girl's hand passed over all these stories, and didn't fathom how deeply their import would one day affect her family. Her father's paper remained neutral for now. The only stories the girl read with understanding were the ones Jakob invented along with fanciful woodcuts he drew late at night to accompany them: There was the cat-woman seen in St. Louis; the witch of Clove Tree Hollows; a naked man-child that ran with wolves in the hills bordering Boonville.

In the afternoon he hitched the brood mare to the phaeton and set out to find and interview soothsayers. The brood mare was a fine roan named Cinnamon. As soon as the horse felt the harness in place and Jakob half-seated in the phaeton, it took off like a pack of wolves were on its tail. They shot through the narrow limestone streets, the girl clinging tight to Daniel, her brother Caleb whooping with joy. Their iron-sheathed wheels bounced and clattered over the stones. All her pa could do was hold tight to the reins. Every day the horse took off like this and barreled straight out of town for a good mile, the phaeton tossing and bobbing behind like a child's forgotten bauble, before the roan became winded and slowed to a more respectable trot—high-stepping fully lathered through a roadway canopied by dark spreading oak trees. Pa said the roan was just spirited, but it frightened Hazel. It also frightened Frau Volsmann, who begged Jakob to leave the baby with her. Caleb took up with a group of town boys and began staying behind, so that Hazel often rode alone with her father through the *hexenwald*.

Only once did one of those country healers touch her: a midwife who lived near the ferryman in Boonville and who was said to stop the flow of blood with only her hands and a verse from Ezekiel. That night she greeted Jakob and the daughter wearing a light-blue dress of linsey-woolsey worn through to transparency and showing the pendulous swing of her breasts beneath the material. She had nut-brown hair, the bangs uneven, as though shorn with a knife. She had a child, but no husband.

On this still night the air was close and heated in her shanty. The girl smelled the melting tallow of the candles that burned along the edge of the wall, a sick, sweet odor of animal fat burning. The healer kept a hearth and a floor of packed dirt with a single handwoven strip of carpet. She had gray eyes and pale, elegant hands. When the child began to cry she pulled down the left corner of her dress and suckled it in front of them. The healer smiled when Jakob turned away. "Fetch me some of that yarrow that grows in the truck garden," she told him. "And then I'll show you what I know."

The father left without asking how she knew he would be able to tell yarrow from mustard flowers in the dusk. The walls of her dwelling were tissue-thin. Night air seeped in around them. Something in the woman's eyes bid the girl to stay and not follow her father outdoors. The baby made loud, sucking noises. Beyond the shanty the girl heard the sound of the wide dark river eating away the shore. Then the healer came toward her and she went stock still. The woman touched her under the chin and forced Hazel to look up into her eyes. Her hand was warm, close to the pulse in the girl's throat. She saw a pale mirror of herself reflected in the woman's gray eyes. She saw this and knew the woman would follow after her and haunt her in some way. The healer's voice was husky when she spoke again. "You walk in the dark," she said. "I see it. While kith and kin sleep, you walk abroad. Be careful you know the way home again, child."

The healer taught her something else before her father shouldered back into the room with yarrow clenched in his fist, something the girl would only dare try years later when a boy lay bleeding to death on a puncheon floor.

The schoolteacher, a widow named Kate Moriah, took an interest in Jakob's children. Kate was the daughter of Josiah Kelton, a slave-owner from Virginia who owned the salt mines, sawmill, and four hundred acres of good bottomland where he grew fat hemp forests to make rope and twine. Mainly Kate was concerned that Jakob's children were being allowed to run free instead of being kept captive in a hot, one-room schoolhouse—captivity being a natural state necessary for both children and "darkies."

Kate came into his office one summer afternoon, after the schoolbell had sounded and the limestone cobbles rang with clatter of bootheels and squealing children released for a few precious hours before they had to start evening chores. She frowned at the black-haired girl whose face was smudged with ink as she set type. The man before her was half a foot shorter than Kate, with hairy forearms and thick limbs. Dark locks of his hair fell in his eyes while he worked the press, the iron clacking down with a sound like an angry mouth. He was comely in a certain way, a small black bear.

Kate coughed politely. She wore a brown-checked gingham dress with leg of mutton sleeves. Her auburn hair was pinned up in an elegant coiffure. Her cheeks looked flushed or sunburned, but really this was just her temper rising, for after several coughs the man still kept his back to her. Finally, the girl went and tugged on his apron and only then did he take notice. In fact, he stepped back and caught his breath and the color rose in his own cheeks. He had only seen this woman from afar before this moment and admired her. "Ma'am?" he said. He bowed in an old-world fashion. His own grandpapa had been a serf in Bohemia. "How may I be of service?"

"I've come about your children," said Kate, fanning herself with one of the newspapers. She leaned against the hellbox table and the girl noted with satisfaction that one of the woman's leg of mutton sleeves was smudged by the slag type. "You are aware that county laws stipulate that these children should attend school?" Kate did not mention that the county laws also forbade a once-widowed woman with children of her own from teaching.

Jakob smiled and wiped his hands on his greased apron. "I did not know this," he said, exaggerating for her sake the Germanic lilt of his English. It was sometimes useful to play the dumb foreigner, though more often than not Jakob spoke in a precise, deliberate manner. He was known for his stories, in print or otherwise. "You see, these children are vital to my enterprises. They learn both reading and arithmetic through their everyday efforts. I provide all they need."

"Don't be insulted," said Kate, "but having perused this publication and seen the many grammatical offenses and wild flights of fancy it contains, I doubt their education is sufficient."

To Kate and the girl's surprise, Jakob's smile only broadened. He stepped closer to the woman and his nostrils flared. Kate's eyes shone in return. A look passed between the adults that disturbed the girl. In the woman's fine auburn hair and high cheekbones she was reminded of the brood mare. A handsome thing from afar, if it ever broke free from the traces it would keep running roughshod over everything beneath its hooves and never look back. Hazel had expected her father to put up a better fight than this. "Perhaps we can make some arrangement," he said.

"Yes," she said. "I . . . feel a bit faint just now. It is ever so hot in here. Might you have some refreshment?" The woman looked anything but faint to the girl. Her eyes were blue with flecks of gold in them, and right now they were fastened to her father.

"Certainly," Jakob said. "Allow me a moment to clean up and I will meet you next door at Burton's. Frau Volsmann makes the finest ginger soda. It will cure whatever ails you. Then we can discuss these arrangements in more detail."

"That will be acceptable," said Kate and she walked out of the shop, her whalebone hoopskirt and bustle so wide she barely fit through the door.

Jakob watched the vacant doorway a few moments after she went through it. "My," he said. "That's some woman." Maybe he figured a woman like that wouldn't get sick like his frail, willowy Emma had and leave him alone with children. For the first time ever Hazel regretted her vow of silence after her mother's death. Not that it would have mattered, for her father forgot she existed during the next three months as he courted Mrs. Kate Moriah and took her on long "sparking" rides in the phaeton and read her poetry, his own and others.

Hazel fought this in her own quiet way. As a new pupil in the schoolhouse, she wrote down charms on foolscap paper and sold them to her classmates for a penny a piece. The charms contained a rhyming ditty and instructions for making a potion with the fingernails of their intended. The girls need only get the poor fellow to drink this concoction, made with his own soiled clippings, and he would be theirs forever. When it didn't work and the boys continued to ignore them in favor of throwing dirt clods at one another and suchlike, the girls demanded their pennies back. Still without speaking, Hazel refused, even after one of the girls' mothers wrote a vehement letter to Mrs. Moriah.

When this failed to perturb the teacher, Hazel took to setting aside her *McGuffey Reader* and writing long, morbid stories about a woman with "russet hair" who seduced men to follow her out into the woods where she stole their soul like a *seelenrauber*. She wrote another story about a tall woman "built like a roan" who suffered a series of unfortunate accidents before meeting her untimely demise by falling into the churning scupper of a sawmill. She left the stories near her slate board for Mrs. Moriah to find.

The next day Mrs. Moriah asked her to stay after school. Hazel sat at her desk with her eyes downcast and waited for the woman to commit outrages upon her person which she could run to tell her father about. "I won't deny that you have a certain imagination and knack for description," Mrs. Moriah told her, "but these stories won't do at all. For one thing, I find them to be wholly predictable and ordinary in every circumstance. Like your father's newspaper, you misunderstand the nature of your reader. A good story defies the reader's expectations, and in doing so, brings them satisfaction. Do you hear how contrary that sounds? There isn't anything so contrary as the human heart." She gave Hazel a copy of Hawthorne's *The Blithedale Romance* and when she finished that she gave her Cooper's *Leatherstocking Tales*, and then a new book, Hazel's favorite, by a man named Melville.

If they didn't become friends exactly, through literature they reached a truce. Hazel saw what Kate meant about contrariness when the woman's father returned from overwintering in St. Louis. They journeyed out to his great stone manse through the bowered lane of elm trees and ate dinner that night and Jakob told Josiah Kelton that he wished to marry his daughter.

Over seventy years old, Josiah had a lean, bladed face and white Quaker-style beard. His skin was chapped and ruddy, the mark of years of fieldwork. One finger lightly traced the gold chain of a new watch tucked in his pocket. These fine clothes fit him well, the same dark suit he had worn to his wife's funeral this past winter, but he still seemed restless in them as though the wool chafed his skin. His left cheek swelled with a wad of tobacco, which he chewed with the determination of an old bull. His ruddy face reddened further at Jakob's request. "You really want this?" he asked his daughter and Kate only nodded, not trusting herself to speak. Her previous husband had been a carpenter who had drowned along with several other passengers when a ferry overturned in the flooding Missouri River. Without knowing the reason, she married beneath herself each time for the sake of angering her father.

Then Hazel saw two black children come in, twins around seven years old, with eyes the color of ice just like the old man. They helped a slave woman named Lula serve them a dinner of brisket and collard greens. Hazel saw how Kate pretended not to notice when Josiah's hand lingered on Lula's and saw how she pretended not to see the two children with haunting blue eyes. Kate's whole life was a study in contrariness. She despised her father and yet was beholden to him.

Jakob and Kate were married that spring and moved into the house that Kate's first husband had built, a two-room cabin with finely doweled joists and a neat overlay of walnut siding that just happened to be on Josiah Kelton's land, past his brick slave cabins on the north side of a cow pasture and tucked into the lee of a hill. Some nights, when Kate grew bored with Jakob, she reminded him that her first husband had possessed more practical skills.

Kate had two living children. Asa, twelve years old, had his mother's red hair and fine skin. On him the auburn hair looked like leaves on fire and because of his irrepressible cowlick and nasal voice, folks didn't take to him right away. Her other son Matthew, was six years old and had been blinded by the scarlet fever which also turned him innocent and simple-minded. The land held a graveyard where Kate's mother was buried along with three of Kate's other children who had died each summer when the bottomland air turned miasmal and florid with mosquitoes. Sometimes Hazel missed their old life above the printing shop. But here they had a salt spring where deer came, and wolves from the Ioway prairies, and once, a white albino bear with eyes like two drops of blood.

Two years passed and Jakob took his daughter out in the phaeton less and less, for his new wife didn't approve of superstition. Perhaps she intuited the reason behind these journeys, knowing Jakob had never fully let go of his first wife.

Seasons came and went until March of 1859, when on a warm day walking home from school Hazel held out her hand and caught a red petal curling past her in the wind and held it in the palm of her hand. *It is a false spring*, she thought, not knowing where the words came from. *The snows will return and what germinates in this season will perish. There will be little fruit for the harvest. It is false, false.* Then she realized she held a petal of the Judas flower within her palm. Chilled, she dropped it and listened for a time in the evening quiet. Nothing happened. No vision from the devil entered her brain. The breeze hushed over the hay meadow and stirred the dress at her ankles. A warm southern wind carried the smell of the spring thaw. She was looking north and wondering how far the wind had traveled. She imagined it lifting her from the grass and carrying her there. Maybe in this distant northern land there was an Indian boy with a feather in his hair, his pony's mane ruffling in this same breeze while the rider looked south and wondered what this wind was bringing toward him.

Hazel had arrived home from school ahead of her mother and brothers. On the way she passed the shop where Jakob published *The Saline Springs Luminary* and saw shattered window glass and a vacant dark spot where the press had once stood. Who would do such a thing? Of her Pa there was no sign. As she set about her evening chores, her mind filled with worry. First those red petals had unsettled her, now this. When she entered the barn to fill buckets with the milk she would churn into butter for tonight's supper, she was surprised to find her father there with the hand press, stabled like some living creature of iron and wood.

Her father wore a greased apron. Weak wintry light spilled over him through cracks in the slats. In the stalls the horses nickered, spooked by the strange smell of ink and oil. Her father took hold of the calfskin handle. The machine came down with a ringing clank while the horses perked up their ears and tensed their flanks. He was talking to himself while he worked. He released the lever and shook out a smeared sheet of paper and held it up in a shaft of light. A deep frown of concentration was etched between his eyes.

In Hazel's mind she was cast back to the winter when her first mother died and her father spent time alone in a stall talking to himself. From her place in the doorway, unnoticed as of yet, the girl made out the title at the top of the page: *Liberator*. She didn't know this was an anti-slavery pamphlet. She didn't know that he was publishing his paper from a barn because every window in his shop had been shattered the night before by the Blue Lodge Society and the spines of every book he owned lay broken and torn in puddles of ink. All she saw was their oldest draft horse, a gentle Morgan named Isaac, as he leaned over the stall and sniffed the new paper, nostrils wide and flaring. She thought the horse might snatch the paper right out of her father's hands and chomp it like an apple in his great yellow teeth, but then he snorted and turned his rump toward the publication.

Long after the candles were put out and the ashes banked in the stove the girl lay awake listening to her parents arguing over her father's newest publication. From her room below the loft where she shared a goosedown mattress and rope bed with her blind brother Matthew, the words were indistinguishable.

When she dreamed that night, she felt a familiar floating sensation. Night after night, she dreamed that she stepped out of her own body. She became a shadow girl made of air and darkness. As she drifted from her cage of skin and bone she looked down on her own sleeping form, fists tight, clutching the quilt.

Like vapor she drifted past her parents as they exchanged bitter words before the stove. Cold air seeped under the door and she traveled through that space and out into the night. Among the secret beds of the deer she came like a shadow and the does lifted their heads in the darkness, sniffing. Only the birds saw her. They trailed after her dream-form. She had the sense that if they caught her she would not wake again. Her parents would find her body, blue and cold, in the morning and know her soul had been carried off in the night. Crows cawed in the distance. The wind picked up and hurled her along like a leaf.

She closed her eyes while the air rushed past. When she opened them she no longer recognized where she was. She stood before a strange, mound-shaped house of earth and sod. The roof was green with grass and twisting vines of morning glory. The door made a squeaking sound as it swung open and shut on its iron hinges. Broken window glass lay upon the grass. A silent crow watched from atop a chimney of mud and wattles. The wind came across on quiet cat's feet and whispered *If only men knew what I know*. She felt a thrill run up her spine at these words. Something watched from inside the house.

She went past the broken door. Chairs were spilled and scattered on the floor. A pot squatted over the slackening flames in the hearth. The floor beneath her was packed dirt, not so different from that of the healer's cabin. A figure in a light-blue dress lay on a pallet. Only when Hazel came closer did she see the head was gone.

In the next moment she noticed the missing head upright in the center of the table. The hair was matted with blood, but she recognized the healer from the river. In dream fashion the facial features shifted and became her mother's. The girl was terrified now. Blood dripped through the table, ticking, as steady as a mantle clock. Hazel came closer, saying "Mama?" Her voice sounded strange in her ears. When she was right next to the table the eyes opened, white and empty. Her mother's jaws parted with a crackling sound and the carmine petals of the redbud tree spilled out and flooded the room. At last when the stream of petals stopped, the head spoke. "Hide," it said. "You must hide." There were footsteps outside the cabin. The thing that had done this was coming closer. Hide. She was up to her ankles in red petals, her feet fixed to the floor.

The door swung open.

THE RELUCTANT
ABOLITIONIST

Hazel wouldn't ever forget
seeing her pa as he was laid out on the kitchen table, his body splotched
with spots of viscous tar. Kate cast a shadow over him. Armed with a
boar-bristle brush she scrubbed the black spots on his thickly haired arms
and chest. His jaw clamped down as he strained to keep from crying out.
When Kate lifted the brush, flecks of his skin came away. The flesh
beneath was pink and raw. Light in the room wavered as Hazel—standing on a nearby chair and holding a tallow candle so Kate could see properly—nearly fainted at the sight. "Hold still," Kate said. Below the girl,
a sour-smelling bucket of well-water, lime, and lard soap sloshed around.
Oil and tar and blood scummed the surface.

How did it come to this? the girl thought. She could still hear the bad
men outside and she was terrified for Pa. *He will live, I know it. And if
he lives, what will become of us?*

In the shadowy corner, an old man leaned against the wall. He balanced on one mud-streaked boot, a broad-brimmed hat hooding his features. Sometimes, Kate glanced in his direction, anger rising in her
cheeks. Josiah, town squire. Josiah, slaveowner. Josiah, her father who

had done this. A vein surfaced in her temple, a danger sign that Hazel and her brothers had learned to recognize in the few years since they had lived with her.

Hazel clutched the melting tallow candle and strove not to swoon. Her pa wasn't much to look at now, stripped naked, only a damp wash-cloth covering his genitals like an Indian breechclout: a short, bow-legged man whose breathing was ragged and uncertain.

Outside in the yard, riders had dragged the press from the stable and worked with blacksmith tools to dismantle it. The tin box of letters lay scattered across the meadow. When nothing remained of the press but loose hinges of iron and wood, the men mounted their swaybacked horses and rode back to town.

The old man had to raise his voice to be heard above the rain spat-tering the shingled roof and coursing down, darkening the window frames. "I will not protect this man the next time they come for him." A white flash rippled and faded outside the window, followed by a close grumble of thunder. It was early in the year for such weather; a surge of warm air that came from the south and made men think and act in ways that went against nature.

Kate's expression was shrouded beneath the fall of her auburn hair, glistening in the candlelight. The skin of the hand working the brush was callused and chapped, not ladylike at all, too large, like the rest of her. Without looking at Josiah, she said, "You went too far." She didn't say any more, perhaps fearful that her husband would be con-scious enough to understand. When she spoke these words, she felt them inside her. She should not have shown her father the pamphlet before it was distributed. She should not have gone inside a room where angry men gathered. Her husband was on this table now because of her, and despite every argument, every moment of unhappiness she had felt in her life with him, she found that she still loved him.

"You need to understand how things will be if you are going to con-tinue living here on my land," Josiah said. He turned his attention to Hazel holding the dripping candle, a girl whose shivers cast uncertain shadows over her pa's body. Just then, candle wax dripped into one of the man's shining wounds. His eyes flashed open and his neck arched. A hiss of breath escaped through his clenched teeth. The legs of the kitchen table bowed outward while he twisted on the surface like a stuck hog.

Kate laid her hand on his chest. "We're almost done, Jakob," she said. "It won't help matters if you bring this table down." The touch of skin against skin, her palm against his clammy chest, gave her confidence. She might still be able to control this situation. "Hazel, you watch how you hold that candle now. Your father doesn't need any more burns." She settled the brush on the rise of Jakob's stomach and pulled her hair out of her eyes. "What is he to do now that your men have ruined his press?"

"He ain't much for field work, but he could keep the books for my sawmill and salt mines. Might do him some good to apply his mind to a more useful end."

"And if he refuses?" She couldn't hold his gaze any longer. Kate turned her attention back to the last dark spot on her husband's forearm where the tar was spread like a bruise. She had poured a tea of ground poppy leaves down his throat after he was carried in, a tea she used to soothe the children when the damp winters made them bronchial.

"I could not have foreseen what your husband was going to print in his paper. Had I done so, I might have been able to give him warning. If any speak against the border guard, they will be silenced. If a man among us questions our very institutions, his words must be trodden down. With all that's going on, Kansas turned to blood and Missouri on the verge, your husband picked a poor time to express contrary opinions." The words had a practiced ring in Kate's mind, like an orator working a crowd.

The girl didn't pay attention to either of them. She followed the shallow breathing of her pa and the blue rush of veins beneath his pale skin. His eyelashes fluttered and he seemed to be dreaming. She traced the curving bones of his ribcage to an outer dimple of a gleaming wound in his side. Lines of goosepimples rippled across his skin. The soft pine planks beneath him groaned in time with his breath. Where his breastplate joined his neck there was a hollow shadow, a gathering of darkness like blood spreading from a bullet wound. Her hand hovered over this spot and it came to her that her father would die one day, and there would be no one to defend her from her brothers, to bring her horehound candy when he walked back from town, candy that melted like molasses, something secret and sweet, while they rode together in the woods and he sang to her in the language of the Old Country. She couldn't stand to look at him any more, his skin already going blue and pale with the knowledge of what would come. Hazel set down the candle on the hewn bench and ran out into the rain. *How did it come to this?*

Once Hazel had walked with her father through a rare grove of mountain aspen and climbed the high hill that overlooked the Missouri River. The silver aspen leaves quaked and shuddered as the two passed under them. He did not sing to her, but walked slowly, holding her hand and allowing her to set the pace.

"Do you know why the leaves tremble like this?" he asked. The girl shook her head.

"The aspen trees did not recognize Christ when he came among us. They alone, in all creation, did not bow to the Son of Man, and so they are doomed to shudder until the end of time." The girl listened to the wind rustling in the leaves.

"You must be watchful," he told her. "This world brims with signs and portents. The leaves of a silver maple will turn upside down when rain approaches. A horned moon means snow. Trees, wind, birds, stones: They all have messages and we must listen and be ready when they appear amongst us."

Jakob's own sign had first come to him the Sunday afternoon he stayed and listened to the Reverend Benjamin Keene preach the Higher Law doctrine. But it was a hand-scrawled note that came the next day which changed things for good. Aside from yearly subscription income, the newspaper earned a tidy sum printing advertisements for escaped slaves and nearby slavery auctions. Like any other business in Little Dixie at that time—a region of the country that produced the hemp used to bind huge cotton bales and the hogs to feed the antebellum empire—Jakob's *Saline County Luminary* was dependent on the slave trade to put food in his children's mouths and he labored not to think too deeply about what this meant.

The hand-scrawled note and the dime that accompanied it arrived on Monday in the mail, along with a separate envelope from the north advertising the rich soil in Minnesota territory, which had just become a state. The note was written on blue butcher paper still stained with animal blood. It described an escaped slave named Ruth, a "mulato with skin the color of burnt chicori." The writer also mentioned, in passing, a distinguishing mark of a "circle brandid in the dark of her left thy." The last part said she came out of Callaway County and promised a reward of fifty dollars for her capture and return. Jakob set the advertisement for Minnesota aside and read and reread the note over again many times. Notices for escaped slaves sometimes described mutilations, lash marks, cut ears . . . but this marking stuck in his mind. He kept picturing the pink imprint of the wound in the soft skin of her inner thigh. For a reason he could not fathom he felt a connection with this slave. Even as he printed the information in that week's edition, he felt it somehow drawing her closer.

Two nights after he printed the ad, Jakob did Caleb's chores out in the cow barn since the boy had taken sick. A round harvest moon hovered low over the valley and its light pierced the slats of the barn. The milch cows and draft horses were dozing. A whale-oil lantern cast celestial shapes against the stalls. One side of the lamp was pricked out in stars and moons and these cosmic patterns flickered and danced while Jakob pitchforked piss-wet straw and manure into a rancid pile. He had just spread a fresh layer of hay in the stall when he heard a movement in the loft above him.

A rain of hay motes sprinkled down from the hayloft. The lantern hissed by his side. He held his breath, listening, and then heard a board creak again. The hairs rose along his spine. It was not a sound that belonged in his barn. The cats that usually trailed after him when he did morning milking were nowhere to be seen. Jakob lifted the lantern.

"Is that you up there, my shadow?" he called. Hazel often followed him about wherever he went and he hoped she might be playing such a trick now, but even as he said it he knew she was inside. Jakob looked at the slender ladder rising into the darkness of the haymow. It called to him, this shadowed place. He set down the lantern, but kept hold of the pitchfork as he climbed. His boots were heavy on the ladder rungs. He heard the sound of his own breathing in the quiet, the drum of his heart in his ears. The ladder creaked with each step. From out of the loft's edge far above him, he saw two pink palms take hold of the top rung. One shove and the ladder and Jakob would be spilled onto the hard ground below.

"Don't," he cried. "I don't mean you harm." Jakob let the pitchfork fall and it clattered against one of the stalls. When he looked down he saw the circle of lantern light on the floor and the constellations whirling and spinning around it. He closed his eyes to steady himself. When he looked back up, the hands had disappeared. He kept coming up the ladder, his hands slick with sweat, one greasy rung at a time, drawn like a fish with a hook through its gills. At the top rung he hefted himself into the loft and crouched there.

While his eyes adjusted in the shadows of the bales, Jakob listened. A dark shape breathed in the corner. The smell of hay, welcoming and warm with the memory of summer, pervaded the loft. A slat had been busted out in the side and through the gap Jakob saw his moonlit fields and the black woods beyond.

"Who are you?" he said, but the shape didn't answer. He could make out the white rims of two eyes looking back at him, eyes framed by a wild tangle of coarse, shorn hair. A girl, a runaway. He smelled the scent of her now, an acrid, fearful undercurrent in the hay. When he came closer she drew herself into a ball and hissed. Her ivory teeth flashed.

"I don't mean you harm," he said again. Her breathing had become hoarse. She trembled before him like something chased for so long that what was human in her had faded for a time. "You're Ruth, aren't you?" He thought by naming her he could bring her back. She didn't answer that night, but he knew it at once, had known it when he first printed the ad. It was as if his words had called her into being and summoned her to this place.

When she spoke her voice was parched, but the words formal. "Mister," she said. "I could've hurt you, but I didn't." Jakob had heard slaves talking among themselves before, though he hurried onward, pretending not to see them and putting them out of mind as soon as they were out of sight. This girl sounded nothing like them. She spoke in a careful, measured manner. She spoke like him, like some forgotten part of him he was just discovering. Once she said those words she began to cough violently.

He wanted to comfort her with a light touch, but didn't wish to frighten her any further. "I'm not going to turn you in," he said. "I've been thinking about you for days and now I understand why. Whoever did that to you, they don't deserve you. Not that I believe in it anyhow, the idea of owning another human being." He realized he was babbling and that he had not spoken his convictions aloud until this moment. She looked back at him, her eyes chalky in the shadows.

For the next few nights Jakob claimed to be carrying out food for the barn cats, but he climbed that ladder and brought the leftovers to her. He would sit and watch her eat, the way she licked her fingers clean, her habit of muttering a prayer in words so quiet he couldn't hear them. The second night after she finished eating, she stood and stretched, yawning. They had not discussed yet how to get her across the river and beyond that to Ioway country and freedom. Simply by hiding this fugitive he had dragged his own family into territory he didn't understand. She was taller and thinner than he expected her to be. The frayed calico dress she wore was pale against her skin and showed the bare flesh of her arms and legs, a pretty umber color. His eyes traced the smooth shape of her calves up to the ragged edge of pale cloth. She felt his eyes on her and turned away. Her hands smoothed down the low mound of her belly as she looked out the busted slat to the empty night beyond. "You're pregnant," he said, his breath low.

"It's why I ran away," she said. "I didn't want any baby. . . ." She didn't finish. She turned to him again. "Could I live here with you?"

"No," he said immediately. "It's not possible."

"I can be useful," she said. "I'm a hard worker. I know all sorts of things. I even know how to cipher; my childhood master had strange whims. I can cipher and recite the Psalms and Shakespeare." She paused as if hesitant to reveal more. So this was the reason she spoke so fluently. It was illegal to teach slaves to read and write. As she spoke her hands at her hips kneaded the dress and pulled it up to expose more dark umber skin. She looked at him, her lips parting. He felt breathless of a sudden. He longed to see the scar, to touch a wound he had no right to touch, to know the path he was setting upon was right.

He was going to tell her then of his plans for her: How he was going to approach the reverend who had spoken so ardently about abolition. Surely he would know people in Illinois where he was from. But then he heard the barn door creaking open. A voice called up to him. "Jakob?" His wife's voice. "What are you doing up there?"

A long pause: "I thought I heard rats. I climbed up to check." Ruth sat back down and huddled in her corner, her eyes wild once more.

"I heard voices, Jakob."

"You know how I am," he told her. "Always talking to myself."

"I used to know how you were," she said.

He pushed down a mound of hay for the milch cows. Then he climbed back down the ladder and smiled at his wife. Her eyes were still on the loft, where even now the boards creaked again. There was no point in further lying.

"A runaway," he told her. "The one I printed the ad for."

Kate inhaled sharply. "How long has she been up there?"

Jakob shrugged. "A couple of days," he said. He saw the suspicion in her eyes, the anger that he had kept this secret and he remembered his earlier resolve. "I am going to buy her passage out of here."

Kate's hands had curled into fists. She was a large, formidable woman, but Jakob kept his ground and looked up into her eyes. "Have you gone mad?" she said. "It's one thing for you to write your nonsense in a newspaper decent people don't read. But if you break the law. . . . Jakob, she belongs to somebody."

The next night he dreamed he was running from hounds. He plunged through a forest of thorn and felt branches rake his skin. He tried to catch his breath and stumbled over an exposed root. The sound of their barking closed in all around him.

His breathing came in short gasps when he sat up.

"What is it?" his wife said, taking hold of his arm.

He shushed her. He was awake now and there were dogs loose in his woods. The hill behind the cabin echoed with the sound of baying. The pack came closer. They crossed the haymeadow and he pictured their sleek forms bounding through the tallgrass. One gave a high, sheering bark of recognition. The hounds came past his cabin. Their claws skittered on his porch and for a moment he thought it was him they came for. But the hounds continued beyond his cabin until the sound of their barking faded in the far woods.

Beside him, his wife said. "You see. You see what you've done now."

Jakob heard male voices trailing behind the dogs. A gruff voice called out for them to come back. He thought of confronting the men for trespassing. It would take only a moment to prime the rifle hanging over the mantle, but Kate, sensing his thoughts, laid a hand on his chest. Whatever else came between them, they loved one another. They depended on their arguments to add some spark to their lives. Now this touch, even though he was angry with her, brought a stillness inside him. She loved him enough to be afraid for him.

Jakob lay back in the dark, but did not sleep, for it came to him that if his advertisement had in some way summoned the slave, it had also brought the hounds that now hunted her through the dark. He huddled deep in his layer of quilts, praying the girl had stayed hidden in the loft.

In the morning he climbed the ladder, knowing even before he reached the top that she would be gone.

That afternoon he ate lunch at Burton's. The door swung open, admitting the slave catchers he had heard in the dark. One was lean with a pointed chin and arrow-shaped beard, the other short and clean-shaven, even his scalp hairless and gleaming with perspiration. Both wore dirty fringed buckskin and coon caps and their eyes were red-rimmed from exhaustion. Jakob listened closely as they approached the barkeep, Timothy Burton, a genial, aproned host with his hair lying slick against his skull. They ordered pork chops, johnnycake, a bottle of rye whisky to split between them.

"Jumped right in the river," the lean one said. His voice had a twang to it. "Never did see the like, thought she was a bird and could fly clean to the other side." The bald one kept his silence. He breathed through his nostrils, the red-rimmed eyes taking Jakob in and then looking away again.

"I just hope we get something for the body," the lean man continued.

"You found her then?" Jakob asked.

"Had a time of it though," said the man. "She was tangled in some branches down the river. Not a mark on her, but her mouth hung open. Her belly was so full of gasses and water that when I lifted her out the damn thing groaned like she was complaining." He shook his head, grinning, his mouth jagged with yellow teeth. "Scared me so bad I dropped her back in the current and had to fish her out again." Jakob looked away from the man, left a silver coin on his table, a dime like he had been paid for the ad, and went out back.

The hounds were tied to a post and lay sleeping in the dust. They didn't even stir as he passed. Flies swirled around a mule and tormented its watering eyes. He could see the round mound of the tarp draped over the mule's back, and one hand with broken fingernails swinging below the canvas. Flecks of gray mud were caught beneath the milky nails. In his mind's eye he saw the muddy current pulling her under, the girl trying to claw her way back toward light and air. He looked at the hand of the slave woman named Ruth for a long time. The mule's flanks twitched and drops of mud shook loose from her fingers and spattered the ground below her.

• • •

Outside in the rain the voices followed after her, or maybe she would only imagine this, for memory cannot be trusted and her mind would often return to this scene and fill it in with new details. When her father spoke of the tarring, years later, she imagined herself back in that room with him and Kate and Josiah. The eaves dripped spooling waterfalls into barrels on either side of the cabin. She stood there for a minute before a flash of lightning lit up the ground around her and she noticed a rabbit shuddering before her feet. Tricked out of a long winter drowsing by a warming spell, the animal trembled in terror. Caught between the girl and the storm, its long ears flattened against its skull and it hunched down against the smooth surface of the pine porch. Hazel wanted both to run her hands through the soft fur and also to scare it away before her brothers returned. She nudged it gently with her toe, but it remained motionless as stone. Years later, in her moments of greatest terror, the girl would imagine herself like that rabbit. A thing as still as stone while the shadow of the owl passed over. A thing that could not be touched in its silence and stillness. Neither moved, both creatures listening to the spilling sound of water and the undertone of voices rising from the cabin.

"There's a way out of this and that's if your husband takes back his words. You don't want the entire county calling you abolitionists and nigger-stealers. You don't want what happened to that reverend."

Kate's voice came back, sharp and high-pitched. "You don't care about us. You care only for your own reputation."

Hazel heard the heavy tread of his boots coming toward the door. The rabbit shook itself out of its daze and vanished into the falling rain. Hazel ducked around the side of the cabin, not wishing to be seen. The door slammed behind him and the silence that followed his fading footsteps was marked only by the door's creaking hinges and the driving rain.

Her stepmother's voice called after her. "Hazel May," she said. "I still need your help. Come out of the rain, you foolish girl." Hazel was tempted to ignore her, to run away into the copse of hardwoods over the rise of the hill where her father often took her walking, but the wind blew the rain in horizontal sheets, and the thunder growled. She didn't want go back inside to see that spot on her father's throat, or acknowledge that one day he would pass into the valley of the shadow, but she was getting soaked standing there and had no choice but to return.

Before Hazel went back inside, she cast one last glance toward the grove of aspen trees where her father had told her about the signs. Lightning illuminated the ghostly white trunks and barren branches. The trees tossed in the wind, as if they might lift and move to new country. Then the low clouds closed in around them and the way was lost.

KINGDOM TOWNSHIP,
MINNESOTA

1876

ROOT OF
THE MATTER

T HE LONG SUMMER of 1876 spread
out before us in a vista of dry bristling buffalo grass and scabbed-over
fields. Our fathers were gone in the north, working for more prosperous
men. They would return after the harvest and beg relief from a state government that called them "mendicants and beggars" in the press, as
though they had brought the locusts on themselves through some weak-
ness of character. And if these men took to drink out of shame and helplessness and lashed out at those nearest, who could blame them? And
if these boys came to school wearing long-sleeved chambray in the full
heat of summer to hide their tattoos of bruises, it was understood. The
boys would in turn share their pain with smaller boys, and so on. I was
more fortunate than some, for my father turned his brooding anger on
himself. We missed our fathers, and yet we did not look forward to their
return. No, in this time I did not wish to draw attention to myself; they
had hanged me from that tree once before and I would not allow it again.

The children all knew who had come to live with us and so I endured
the sing-song rhymes which celebrated her supposed treachery: *Injun-
lover/you shall suffer/when you see/him on the tree.* Nothing inspires a child

like a cruel story. If Mr. Simons heard them, he would scold them into silence, but he could not be everywhere at once and so I learned to keep close to the schoolhouse. I was more alone than ever, and yet I did not blame her. It made me feel stronger to think of my grandfather, Jakob, and his convictions and search for signs. I wanted to believe that some of his courage was inside me.

Aunt Hazel walked to school with me every morning. In the dark we passed over an old Indian trail scarred by generations of ponies and dogs dragging lodgepoles through the tallgrass. Here the earth remembered them. Sometimes Aunt Hazel spoke and told me how it was when they first came here from Missouri. Words spilled out of her as if she'd been storing them up for a decade, hoarding them in her book. She talked of the past until her voice went husky. There was the shepherd's star before us, and the moon descending. Soon it would be sunrise, but for now the world was formed of gray shadows and the sound of her voice. I listened, half-asleep, a slate board and primer tucked under my arm and I will tell you this: her stories left tracks inside me and I was not the same after. I can't see her very well when I try to remember her in these moments. Her bare feet didn't stir the dust. She wore a homespun shawl and a slat bonnet that hid her face. One hand clutched a forked stick she dragged absently behind her, carving ornate patterns on the ground. The other held a bucket she would fill with ginseng dug from the loamy sediment along the Waraju River.

We crossed this mile of ground, the humpbacked spine of the town looming ever closer, her voice increasing in pace as the story rushed to its end. Her stories became more real to me than this place I knew. Later at school, I would finish my lessons early and set my head down on the desk and drowse in the hot classroom, children chattering all around me, and I would dream of the things she had said.

We parted at the town's edge where the road split the graveyard with its leaning crosses and names none of us knew anymore. There she might touch my shoulder lightly, a signal for me to continue on alone. The sun was up. If I looked within the shadows of her bonnet I might see her watching me with those dark, sea-green eyes. She never said anything, but I could see how she dreaded this moment of our daily separation and couldn't understand the reason. Other children passed and hushed when they saw her, some even crossing to the other side of the road. In turn they shrank from me as well in the schoolyard, as if she had carried some contagious madness with her from the asylum and passed it on to me. In a sense, she had. I was infected by her stories and filled with those contrary emotions her stepmother Kate had spoken about in Missouri. I was ashamed of this woman, and yet wanted to protect her.

At home we ran out of the laudanum Mother liked to layer into her sarsaparilla and terrible headaches began to afflict her. No money had arrived yet from Papa in the northern pineries and we also ran out of kerosene. Those July nights we passed by the light of tallow candles. Hazel said she was not sorry about the kerosene. She said she never liked the smell, or the way it stole all the shadows from the room.

"Witch," muttered my mother. "You have me under a spell."

Aunt Hazel was unperturbed. "The headaches and visions will pass," she told her, sighing. "How well I know it."

The only thing that soothed Ma's headaches was a silver comb I ran through her flaxen hair. She closed her eyes and let her head fall forward, still muttering things under her breath. I combed her hair until the gold shone through the dark roots, until my arms went stiff. Eventually, she fell asleep in the chair. All the while, Aunt Hazel drew pictures on my slate board. She drew hypnotic landscapes: pathways through labyrinths of sumac, pickets shaped like writhing serpents, a barn sinking into the earth. These images swirled when you looked at them. Storm-tossed trees crowded the edges and something always seemed on the verge of happening. A hawk's shadow passed over a rabbit. A crow flew over a wind-whipped sea in search of land. After some nights of this I began to recognize where I had seen the drawings before. "You taught Papa how to draw," I said. "Those are the same as the drawings in the book he made for me."

Aunt Hazel smudged the slate board, her brow furrowing. "Caleb made you a book? He was never one for writing."

"One winter we were trapped inside. He worked on it for three days and then gave it to me without a word."

"Can I see it?"

She was quiet for a long time as she studied the drawings. In the passage of six years some the drawings had smeared and the edges of the blue paper were yellow and water-marked. Still, Hazel's green eyes had turned cloudy with memory. "He didn't tell you what this was about? I think this is the story of Daniel's flight."

My mother picked her head up and loosed a rumbling groan. "A body can never rest," she said. She turned her bloodshot eyes on us. Aunt Hazel drew her fingertip along one of the drawings and said nothing. "You and your stories," my mother said. "There isn't anybody left alive who wants to hear any of it. Except maybe this boy, and he doesn't know what's best for him." She rubbed the back of her neck, her face scrunching into a grimace. There was a charged silence between the women, the sense of words traveling an invisible wire. I wanted to know what that silence had to do with me. A knot swelled in my throat.

"He's enough," Aunt Hazel said, "if he listens well."

"Listen to this," my mother said to me, affixing me with her eyes. Spots of color flared in her cheeks. "When the Indians came to our cabin, we knew something was wrong. They was only asking for water, but there was fires in the distance and we could hear shooting at the other farms. My mother told us to bring them the water and then she took our money jar, all our family money, and she fled for the woods. I was pregnant at the time. She just left us there like some kind of sacrifice, little Sallie and I. There were three Indians, maybe not more than boys. Skinny as devils with that smoke smell thick on them. The biggest one grabbed Sallie up by the ankles and me screaming the whole time, *Please! No!* He swung her around until her head smashed into the porch post, just like that. They held me down, the three of them, did the most vile things. I would have been dead if it wasn't for Caleb, if he hadn't come on them then. Such rage. He had the double-bladed ax from the woodshed and they didn't even see him coming and there was the roar of him; good Christ the sound of him, and their blood and my blood and the way he kept swinging long after they were dead." To Hazel she said, "Do you think I have forgotten? Do you think I want you here with your stories?" She went on, "Oh. It was a long flight into those same woods where my mother had run, but she was nowhere to be found; God curse her, we didn't see her again. Twelve miles to the fort and him carrying me half the time. . . . A lesser man wouldn't have had me afterwards." She drew in a deep breath, tried to steady herself even as the tears rushed down her ruddy cheeks. "There boy, that's your story." Her jaw was clenched tight. "Have you been listening well?" she finished before her voice broke.

Afterward nobody had anything to say for a long while. Aunt Hazel fetched some old rags which my mother used to blow her nose on. I sat down on the puncheon bench, exhausted by her story and the vision it had painted. When her sobbing had slowed, Aunt Hazel said, "Your mother went into the woods? And you didn't see her again?"

My mother ground her teeth. "Yes," she said and she grabbed hold of the sleeve of Hazel's dress and clutched it tightly. "And me pregnant."

Aunt Hazel stepped back. "When the war was done I used to walk in those same woods. I was looking for Daniel's hiding place. No one wanted me around then, either. I was beginning to show. Too painful. It reminded them too much of these things, stories like you have spoken. And so I walked, holding onto my belly, and the leaves coming down in a rain of red and gold, such beauty as you feel in your throat. I wondered how it was possible after all that had happened. I prayed so fiercely that whatever I carried, girl or boy, that it would know only beauty and not the hatred I had seen."

"Yes," said my mother, blowing her nose once more. "That's how it was."

An odd kind of magic was at work here, though it was made of only word and gesture. As Hazel spoke she stroked my mother's hair and I felt the hair on my arms begin to prickle. There was no more talk of spells or witchery. The two women had reached some kind of agreement. "There is one other thing, though, about those woods," Aunt Hazel said.

"What do you mean?" said Mother. "We no longer own the land. The Schillings, those bastards, they bought up entire parcels after the war. Those few that survived came back to find they owned nothing. It was all legal. A piece of paper. How Caleb talked his way back into this property is beyond me."

Aunt Hazel was lost in her own reverie. "It was beautiful in those woods, but there was a stump I stayed clear from. A terrible smell came from that place. The crows flocked there."

"What are you saying?" Mother said.

"I don't think your mother ever made it out of those woods alive," Hazel said.

We set out the next morning under a red sky that threatened rain. I had not known the place we walked to had once belonged to my mother's family. The Thompsons had tenanted the land for a time, dug out a soddie from the side of a hill and lived in it like moles for a winter before the wife got homesick and they went back to Virginia. It was strange to have my mother with us, but she said she would chew away her fingers waiting for us to return to the cabin. I carried the ax like a woodsman and walked between the two women. My mother spoke in a cheery voice, her terror of the night before forgotten. She showed us the place, a dark square in the gold grass, where her father had kept his still, brewing moonshine to sell to the Indians.

We didn't have to walk far before we came to the hill that sloped down to join the Waraju River, the banks steep here, a place that drew all those Old Germans who were lonely for the hills and dark forests of their childhood. Men like my grandfather Jakob. My mother quit speaking. Below us we could see the gleam of the winding river, sandbars glittering in the sluggish current. A few shrill-voiced crows harangued a horned owl on the other side of the river. There were immense cottonwood trees down along the bank, hoary-barked specimens that bore the wounds of the spring melt when the surging, snow-choked river battered them with ice. The locusts had left this place alone.

We moved single file behind Hazel, our guide. The air turned vivid with cottonwood fluff carried on the wind and my aunt caught a downy seed in the palm of her hand. "Waraju," she said, holding it out for us. "The cottonwood." She blew on it and the wind hurried it away once more. "The Dakota believed these trees were sacred." She looked off in the distance, a woman in a white apron. She had replaced the yellow dress with a sturdier one made of brown-checked gingham. Her nails were splintered and edged with black dirt from grubbing for ginseng. Her dark hair whipped in the wind, the bonnet slung behind her, held to her throat by a lute string. Aunt Hazel found a cottonwood branch, and kneeling, cracked it open for us. She passed it to me, asking what I saw.

"A perfect white star," I said, surprised, setting my ax down. I had passed these cottonwoods many times before and found them to be ugly, shag-barked trees, never suspecting that inside they held such a secret.

"The Dakota believed their ancestors went to the stars after they died, a journey across the Milky Way. There were perils along the path. But even here on earth there are reminders that their ancestors are never very far away."

"Enough about Indians," Mother interrupted. "It's them that have brought us here now." She looked back toward the rise of the hill. "Maybe this isn't such a good idea. I feel sick inside. My headaches are coming back."

"We don't have to go, Cassie," said Aunt Hazel. "But that stump is right over there."

It stood in the clearing, a lightning-struck oak tree split down the middle. A necklace of grape vines encircled the trunk. In the distance we heard the last of those crows as they harried the owl, an ancient killer, away from their nest. The light here was dappled. Aunt Hazel's eyes were the color of these dark leaves. We stood looking at the stump for a long time.

"Give me the ax, boy," said my mother. She took it and before she could doubt herself again, advanced on the stump. It stood about six feet off the ground, surrounded by grass and vines, the trunk stark and black. The first time she raised the ax, her pale calico dress billowing around her, she didn't have the strength to bring it back down. She lowered it once more, her shoulders heaving. Suddenly I wanted to be away from here. I didn't want to witness her in this most private of moments. But then she raised the ax again and attacked the rotted tree. It sprayed around her in black flecks, the spongy wood crackling with every blow of the ax. Aunt Hazel set her hand on top of my head. "Be brave," she said, quietly, "Be brave for her." And then with a sound like the tearing of some vast sheet of parchment the black oak tree split open.

It was there like she said it would be, and this too seemed a dark magic. The skeleton was yellowed by time. Grape vines coiled through the ribcage and pelvis like green serpentine veins. The woman wore only shreds of dark silk. Her jaw cracked open as though even now she wished to speak, as though even now she was crying out to anyone who passed her in these woods. "Look away, Asa," Aunt Hazel said, but I couldn't. *This was my grandmother,* I was thinking. My mother knelt before the skeleton, sobbing. In the center, curled in the woman's embrace like a child, lay the glass jar of tarnished coins.

"All these years," my mother said. "All these years I thought she had abandoned us and was living the good life." She picked up the ax again and raised it as though she might begin to hack away the skull.

"Cassie," Aunt Hazel called. The ax remained poised at the apex. "She suffered after her own fashion. A living death. She climbed inside there to hide from the Indians and got stuck."

My mother lowered the ax and then dropped it behind her. Her breathing came raggedly. "I always wondered what I would do if I saw you again," she said, addressing the skeleton. Then she laughed at the absurdity of it all. "I'm taking back these coins, Mother. I'm taking back every night I lost sleep thinking about you. You were a coward. Do you hear me? You were a coward and don't deserve the proper burial we will give you. Here in these trees, we will leave you to your rest."

Schilling later tried to claim part of this wealth, the 133 silver dollars my grandmother had carried into what were now his woods, but none gave his claim serious attention. If anything, the story, something tangible from the past, a real skeleton from the inside of a tree, served to increase the townspeople's fear and awe of Hazel. For if she could look inside the flesh of an oak tree, then what shield was ordinary human skin from those searching green eyes?

Thirty-three of those coins went to pay for the pine box the bones were stretched out in and for the Reverend Henrickson to speak a short homily over the woman's grave on a grassy overlook halfway between the stump and the remains of her husband's still. After we buried the body in the woods one rainy day, my mother told Aunt Hazel she wanted to know everything. What else was there in that book?

Most of the coins went to bring back Moses, the percheron draft horse we redeemed from the Schilling's livery. He was a year older since last we'd seen him, and hard used. His coal-black coat was lined with coarse gray hairs along the withers that the curry comb could not tame. His dark eyes were dulled, but he had new iron shoes on his hooves and seemed to recognize his home. We stabled him next to the ginseng that Aunt Hazel had been gathering. The ginseng brimmed over the stall beside him and Moses gave the odd, man-shaped root a sniff before snorting disdainfully.

"You'll have to go back and cut grass in the woods. We'll need enough hay to last until winter," Mother told me. In a normal year we would have cut the meadow hay from our own land, but in a locust year there was no grass to be had on our property.

The three of us stood in the barn, admiring our horse. "Bought with Judas money," said Mother. "What will your father say?"

It was late afternoon, the shadows lengthening within the barn. A few swallows skimmed through the murky light. Mother peered over the stall brimming with ginseng. "What do you intend to do with this?" she asked Aunt Hazel. "The man that used to buy the ginseng is long gone. People found out he was paying four cents a bushel and then selling it for ten times that to Chinamen and they run him out on a rail. Nobody has come since to buy our ginseng."

"I don't know," said Aunt Hazel. "I guess I've been gathering it out of habit. We would have starved some years without the money from ginseng."

Mother plucked one of the fist-sized tubers and held it up in the half-light. "What does that look like to you? Whatever did the Chinese see in such a root?"

Hazel coughed. "They believe it enhances their manly properties."

Mother quickly dropped the root back into the pile and then wiped her hand clean on the apron. "Oh dear," she said. "That's what it reminded me of."

Both women looked at each other and then burst out laughing. While I didn't see what was so funny, I joined in because such opportunities had been rare of late. My laugh had a tinny, forced sound at first and this seemed to bring the women to further heights of amusement. Mother even had to lean against the stall while tears sprang into her eyes. She wiped them away and then shook her head and drew herself up straight. "That's quite a load of ginseng," she said.

"A month's worth of grubbing," said Aunt Hazel.

"It would be a shame to let a root of such wondrous properties go to waste."

"It would be a sin," said Aunt Hazel, smiling.

"I have an idea," my mother said.

Mother's idea centered around a man she had heard about in St. Paul who sold things only by catalogue. She thought we could wash the root and seal it in amber mason jars along with a healthy dose of whiskey to give it kick. All we needed was the bottles and whiskey and for this she sent us back to Schilling's with a few of the silver coins.

Even in midday the shades were drawn in Schilling's and the light that trickled through the openings was pale and yellow as yolk. The shop-keeper claimed this helped keep the store cool and insulated. Mother said it was to hide the defects in calicoes and fabrics, and the sleight of hand he used to pinch away tobacco and coffee people purchased. The store smelled of sawdust and pipe smoke when I came inside with Aunt Hazel one Saturday morning. We blinked in the dim light and beheld the blacksmith, Julius Meighen, a broad-shouldered man with a walrus mustache, playing chess with my schoolteacher, Mr. Simons. The board perched atop a salt barrel, the two men so engrossed in their next maneuver they didn't look up.

This was Hazel's first trip into town. Outside, she had already been unsettled by a group of girls in the center of the town's dusty streets. While they skipped rope, they had been singing the Hangman's Ballad:

Slack your rope hangs-a-man,
O slack it for awhile
I think I see my father coming,
Riding many a mile.
O father have you brought my gold?
Or have you paid my fee?
Or have you come to see me hanging
On the gallows tree?

Hazel had paled; her mouth formed words, but nothing came out. The girls were all looking at her while they sang. There was Jenny Schilling with her rose-trimmed bonnet and the two Meyer twins who followed her every move. I took Aunt Hazel's hand and hurried her onward, until their jeering song faded behind us.

Now we stood in the store, and she drew in a breath, gathering courage. I could see that all these people—men sitting on the porch playing cards in the noon sun, people passing in the streets, riders from other towns—were part of a swirl of activity she had not accustomed herself to. She wore the brown-checked dress along with a lavender-lace shawl my mother had given to her. She peeled back the bonnet and gave August Schilling, busy pushing a corn-husk broom behind the counter, a hesitant smile. He glanced once at her, his thick black eyebrows arching above his spectacles, and then looked away again. He continued to sweep even after she said his name. "Excuse me," she said, much louder, "but the boy and I have come to purchase supplies. We want a case of amber mason jars and two jugs of whiskey. Your cheapest kind."

When it became clear that Aunt Hazel would not be ignored, he cast her a sidelong glance. "I don't sell hard spirits to womenfolk."

She swallowed, shrinking before the glare he sent her way.

Julius stood, pulled up his sagging denim britches, and said, "C'mon. We'll finish this game later."

Mr. Simons also stood. He had a long scholarly face with a down-turned mouth. He wore a white shirt with a pin to pinch closed the sleeve of his missing arm. His brown eyes were owlish behind his wire-rimmed glasses. "We're only three moves from checkmate," he said.

Julius knocked down his king to signal surrender. "Not my day again, I see," he said. "Let's go."

"You go on," Mr. Simons said. "I haven't been properly introduced to this lady."

"Suit yourself," said Julius, sagging toward the doorway. I wondered then what other stories had spread through town about Hazel. Maybe it was just the same old story, that she loved being with Indians better than her own kind.

Mr. Simons crossed the room and bowed slightly when he was close to her. His thin chestnut hair was parted to hide a balding place on top, but for a schoolteacher wounded in the War, he remained fairly athletic, and was the subject of a certain amount of gossip regarding his marital prospects. "Good morning, Mrs. . . . ?" he said, though he knew full well her name.

"Miss Hazel Senger," she said. "I thank you for your concern."

"It's early in the morning for whisky, don't you think?" he said, smiling.

"The boy and I are making a concoction. We are in the ginseng business."

"Ah," he said, including me now in the smile. "Young Asa, maker of elixirs. That's why you need the mason jars." He turned to the shop-keeper. "Well August, fetch forth those supplies." He raised his good hand and snapped his fingers.

Mr. Schilling remained steadfast, frowning sourly. "I won't do business with such as her," he said. "Have you not heard what happened to Custer and the Seventh at Little Bighorn? A terrible day for our nation. And now this woman comes in here. Escaped from an asylum no less."

As he spoke his voice increased in volume. His cheeks were splotched by his anger. "They should have hanged you along with *him* that day," he said. "You should never have come back here." His voice lowered to a menacing baritone. "I choose my customers. I won't do business with such as her."

I expected her to flinch before his anger, the way he spat those words at her. Her cheeks were plum-colored and her eyes glittered. "It was the Dakota that did this?" she said.

"It was Indians that did it, doesn't matter the tribe," said Mr. Schilling. "But there's some that say Inkpaduta was there." When he saw her mouth drop open, he added, "Yes, you know that name, don't you?"

"It can't be," she said. "He would be an old man by now."

"The old killers are the worst," he said.

Aunt Hazel had managed to hold her own, but now her face fell. Mr. Simons had turned on August and was berating him for speaking so to a lady. Hazel glanced once at me, her eyes brimming, and then gathered her long dress and rushed out of the store. She fled without looking back, past the gray-hairs playing cards, past the children singing their terrible rhymes, past the old graveyard filled with dead Germans.

I walked to school alone for a week, missing Aunt Hazel and her stories. When Mr. Simons saw my long face he gave me a book to read during lunch hour, *Journey to the Center of the Earth*, which took my mind off some of my troubles. At night Aunt Hazel stayed behind her curtain. I will tell you what bothered me worst. Her eyes had a flatness, a glazed-over expression that I'd seen on bullheads when I pulled them from the river and smashed them against a rock. All the light had gone out of her eyes as surely as a wick being turned down. What August Schilling had said in that store was terrible, but the mention of the name seemed to bother her worst. *Inkpaduta*. Her emotions seemed to surge between such heights and pure depths that I was afraid for her.

"Give me time," she told me one night.

"How long?"

"I don't know."

"Do you want me to brush your hair?"

She turned away from me.

The next Saturday it rained all day again and turned the barren fields into a hog wallow that sucked away my boots when I went to collect eggs from the hens. It was a cold rain for late July, beating like hail against the shingles, coursing down the eaves and overflowing the rain barrels where the women washed their hair and clothes. The root cellar filled with enough water that when I opened the heavy doors I heard the rats calling to one another as they climbed the shelves among the lard and onions for higher ground. It was the kind of rain that would have done us good a few months ago when we still hoped for a crop, but now just made a mess of things.

The only good thing it did was wake up Aunt Hazel from her daze. After I shucked off my muddy boots and jacket and climbed, wet and shivering, to the loft, I found her humming under her breath and rearranging things on the bed. She smoothed out her dress and smiled at me. "I've always loved the sound of rain," she said.

I nodded. There were lights in her green eyes again. Cat's eyes, that's what she had when she was happy. A feline, mysterious intelligence. On her bed, the scrapbook was open to a page of torn and yellowed newsprint. I thought it might be one of the newspapers she had somehow saved from Missouri, the ones grandpa Jakob wrote that caused everybody to hate him, but this was something different. PRAIRIE MASSACRE, read the headline. Closer, I saw that the article came from the *Saint Peter Tribune, 1869*. Studying it, I realized it was reprint commemorating something that happened a decade earlier on the prairies, 1859, the season the Senger family arrived in the valley. The subtitle read BLOODSHED FORETELLS GREATER WAR. I wondered why she had kept such a grim thing.

Aunt Hazel pointed at the illustration of Inkpaduta near the headline. The artist had rendered his face with a jack-o-lantern's crudeness, heavily pockmarked, with a long goblin's nose shadowing canine jaws. A necklace of wolf claws encircled the troll-man's squat throat, and below the drawing his translated name was printed: *The Red End*.

"A monster," I said.

"Yes," she said. "But we made him so."

Beside him there was an illustration of a young girl, her dark hair in a bun, showing her profile as she turned away from the artist. Her lips parted ever so slightly as though she were about to whisper something terrible and true. *Abbie Gardner*, it read below her drawing, *sole survivor of the massacre*.

"Don't you know," she was saying as she turned the page of her scrapbook, "that the children of darkness have always been more shrewd than the children of light? But how do you know which are which?"

Outside the rain continued to clatter on the shingles. The window was a blurred pane that reflected back the candle's pale flame and my own dark features. Somewhere the river was rising. Somewhere horsemen rode toward us on the narrow road, men in long dusters, oily with rain, riding hard to Northfield where they would do violence and once more bring the past into the present. I had a sense of them all out there, could feel the chill of the dark and wet on my own skin. "How do you know?" she said and I felt the pull of her voice drawing me away from this vision and into another place. "How do you know dark from light?"

WARAJU PRAIRIE,
MINNESOTA

1849–1859

"From the desperate city you go into the desperate country. . . ."
HENRY DAVID THOREAU

A BRIEF
HISTORY OF
THE OTHER

THE MORNING OF his birth the sun rose pale and rimmed with sun dogs, like a harried old man chased by wolves across the great emptiness. On the open span of prairie below, a scattering of a dozen teepees huddled near a wooded draw. Smoke rose in thin breathing streams from only four of those teepees. The rest shuddered in the north wind, the buffalo skin flaps opening and closing like slit mouths. On the outskirts of the village circle, one teepee had collapsed inward as though crushed by a giant foot.

A woman in fringed doeskin, her hair unbraided, passed this collapsed teepee carrying something close to her chest. Hungry half-wolf mongrels nipped at her ankles until she kicked them away. When she reached the edge of a winding creek, she broke through the skin of ice with the flat of one hand. A moment later she dunked the baby she carried headlong into the frigid water and then pulled it out again, holding it by the ankles. The village, silent until this moment, erupted with the sound of his squalling. She held him upside down for a moment longer, saying his name aloud: Wanikiya, *Savior*.

With his birth winter would return, and the strange speckling illness that flourished in the unnatural warm air, killing half of Seeing Stone's tribe, would release its hold.

The woman's name was Wichapewastwan, *Good Star Woman*, and after she dunked the child in the frigid water she carried him back to the teepee and coated his skin with bear grease and a fine layer of vermilion powder before binding him in the cradleboard. All that remained of her husband, Seeing Stone, was a lock of hair within a deerskin mourning bundle hanging from one of the cedar poles. This was where his second soul remained close to this earth, whispering inside her and telling her that this child, born to an old woman, would be proclaimed a "child beloved."

The baby had a fine head of dusky black hair and a single lock of silver. His mother would swear that sometimes the ghost of his father became visible in the child's dark eyes, like glimmers of fish seen in a river at night.

After the child's birth the medicine man, Hanyokeyah, *Flies in the Night*, led the remaining band back onto the reservation and the camp the white soldiers chose for them to live, a place they had fled from when Chief Seeing Stone's oldest son, Tatanyandowan, *Pretty Singer*, killed a cow that belonged to a settler.

The hair-faced soldiers had come to the camp to demand they turn the killer over, but Seeing Stone refused and instead took his band of Wahpekute, *The People Who Shoot Among the Leaves*, out onto the prairie during the moon when the wind shakes the leaves from the trees. Flies in the Night had advised against this journey, dreaming of the illness—which caused skin to peel away like layers of birchbark—coming down on them in a red rain of pollen as they passed through a maple forest on the way out to the grasslands.

Now, with the child's birth, they would go back and turn over Pretty Singer to the soldiers. Eager to escape this place of sickness, they would leave some of the teepees still standing. The train of dogs and travois poles and speckled ponies marched into the moaning north wind, and if the child Wanikiya's newborn vision had not been clouded, he might have turned his neck from the confines of the cradleboard and witnessed the grove of cottonwoods where bodies were draped from branches and leaning scaffolds, and seen his own father's corpse among them.

Like all Dakota, the Wahpekute marked time by winter. If this warm winter of illness made Wanikiya, it also made his brother, Tatanyandowan.

Sequestered in a windowless cell dug from the sod, Pretty Singer slept on a matting of urine-soaked hay on a hard-packed floor. He did not eat the food the hair-faced soldiers brought for him, fearing that it was poisoned. His brother, Touches-the-Treetops, went into one of these prisons after he was accused of stealing eggs from a settler and never came out again. Pretty Singer must live, if only to revenge himself on the medicine man, Hanyokeyah, who had given him over to these *wasicun*.

Already the soldiers had cut off his braids and scalp-lock, a source of his power. Pretty Singer was only twelve years old, but tall for his age. Thin and famished, he did not know enough English to tell the soldiers that he was only a boy and that he had killed the cow because he couldn't stand to hear the rasping, hungry cries of his youngest sister, Little Wheat, any longer.

If he lived this would be the summer the *Zuya-Wakan*, war shaman, led him through the ceremony of *inipi*, three days and nights of steam bathing during which he denied himself food and water. At the end of the ceremony he would be presented with his sacred armor and the vision of the animal who would be his spirit protector for life, an animal that he must never kill from that moment forward.

The starvation hurt worse than he imagined, coiling through his bones like the red sickness he had watched kill so many. His tongue felt heavy as a dark stone in his parched mouth. When his hands passed over his ribs they felt as hard and cold as knives beneath his fingertips. The wool blanket wrapped around him crawled with vermin. Every night he was haunted by the memory of his father, sores cratering and bleeding from pustules on his body, even his eyelids and tongue. The vermin crawling on him made Pretty Singer think the sickness had come to him too.

Pretty Singer's starvation had an unintended affect. His vision came that winter in the prison cell on the fourth day he was without food.

Outside it was snowing and as the soldiers passed his cell their boots crunched in the powder. He was too weak to turn his head toward the sound of their footsteps. Instead he watched the black ceiling above him, where sometimes dirt shook free in black clumps.

The fourth morning the ceiling changed shape before his eyes and became a canopy of leaves, wet and dripping with rain.

To his surprise he smelled braids of sweetgrass burning. He could smell the rain in the treetops. In his mind he saw an ancient cottonwood tree split down the middle like the opening of a teepee. Inside the tree there was an ugly dwarf-man only a foot tall with mottled skin and webbed fingers like a raccoon. When the dwarf spoke to him, Pretty Singer knew this was *Canotina*. The dwarf sat with his legs crossed, smoking a red pipe with a willow stem as long as his body. He beckoned Pretty Singer to sit beside him and share the pipe. While Pretty Singer smoked, the dwarf recited names of his living relatives: Little Wheat, and his mother Good Star Woman. Lastly he said the name of his new brother, Wanikiya. After each name the dwarf asked simply, "Will you give me this?" And even knowing what it meant, Pretty Singer nodded yes. The tree dweller then taught him a feast to prepare four times a year, and a song for days of hunting and battle, a song of power.

Pretty Singer opened his eyes from the vision. Around him was the musty-smelling darkness of the sod cell. He lay there in the dark knowing that each person he named for the Canotina, including the "child beloved," would be dead when he returned to camp. For the powers he would have now, he had traded their lives. He wondered why he did not mourn them, and if the Canotina also had taken a sliver of his soul.

He passed ten days in this cell, but when he emerged again the winter spell was over. When he emerged again he no longer thought and feared like a child.

His oldest cousin, Blue Sky Woman, secured his release. She loved one of the soldiers at the fort, a man named Eben Godfrey who had taught her English. When this soldier learned of Pretty Singer's age he convinced Lieutenant Jenkins to let the boy go.

All the way down the sloped ridge that led to the wide frozen river and beyond that to the camp of Seeing Stone's band, Pretty Singer leaned on his oldest cousin's shoulder. At the base of the hill he abandoned the striped trader's blanket the soldiers had given him as if to make up for his captivity. And he couldn't help noticing the swelling in Blue Sky Woman's belly and knowing that his cousin was pregnant with one of the *wasicun's* children. A quick moment of regret passed through him that he had not given her name to the Canotina instead of Little Wheat.

Back at camp he pretended surprise when he learned of Little Wheat and Good Star Woman's deaths when they broke through the ice crossing the river with firewood they had gathered on the far side. Good Star Woman had left the baby Wanikiya in a cradleboard she tied to an oak limb at the base of hill. Swinging by a branch, the baby witnessed his sister and mother crack through the ice. Bound against the flat board, trussed in blankets, the baby watched as the women floundered in the water and tried to free themselves from the heavy load of firewood they carried on their backs. He alone heard them scream, their hands trying to claw the ice edges while the swirling river pulled them down.

The two brothers lived for a while with their cousin Blue Sky Woman and her little girl, Winona. Pretty Singer figured it was an accident that the Canotina had not taken Wanikiya. Two beaded turtle charms hung from the boy's cradleboard, one with the baby's umbilical cord sewn inside, the other empty to fool the spirits trying to take the child's life. That winter, Pretty Singer cut away the charm that held the umbilical cord and cast it in the river where his sister and mother had drowned. But the child did not sicken or die.

Winters came and went, Wanikiya growing into a lean child with his father's high cheekbones. The single lock of silver shone in his black hair. As a "child beloved" he was set aside from the others in a teepee decorated with thunder beings and a new spirit Blue Sky Woman learned about from her soldier: Tunkashila, the Son of Man, whom she painted with yellow hair radiating out from him like spokes of light. With both his parents dead, Wanikiya should have lost his status as a child beloved because they were not there to donate gifts and food to the poor in his name. Pretty Singer fumed when the medicine man Hanyokeyah did this in their stead. He waited for the Canotina to kill the child and so complete Pretty Singer's power. As winter followed winter he grew impatient.

During the moon when the geese lay eggs he took his brother out fishing in the flooding river and while Wanikiya stood in the front of the canoe, watching the swift current with his spear poised, Pretty Singer caused them to overturn. Somehow Wanikiya dog-paddled to a floating cottonwood limb which he clung to like a drowning muskrat and so floated to shore.

The boy grew terrified of ice and rivers; his only concession was to wash himself with water from the skins his cousin carried up for him from the river.

By now Pretty Singer was part of the soldier's lodge, though he had not counted any coups in battle and earned the right to wear an eagle feather. One spring while hunting he cornered a small black bear in a wooded ravine. When he pulled the trigger of his single-action shotgun, the hammer came down with a rusty click and did not fire. The panicked bear attacked him, barreling into him in a blur of claws and black fur. One swipe tore open the flesh of his ribcage. A single bite of those jaws tore off his left ear. The bear would have mauled him to death had not another warrior, Good Thunder, heard Pretty Singer's screams and come to shoot it down while it was still crunching on the cartilage of his ear.

Pretty Singer survived and wore the white headband lower to hide his mutilated face. Slow to heal, he glowered all that summer during feasts and dances when Good Thunder reenacted his rescue, complete with a shrill imitation of the girlish screams Pretty Singer had loosed while being mauled. The maiden he had been courting, Jingling Dress, refused to come out of her teepee when he came to play for her on the red cedar flute, and turned away from him when he waited for her down by the river.

Meanwhile, as he watched his brother grow up before him, he began to doubt the vision he had seen so many winters ago.

The next summer he took his brother out riding across the prairie on the one skinny pinto pony he owned. The boy leaned against him while Pretty Singer taught him the names of birds and plants as they rode through bluestem grassland as high as the horse's belly. The boy had wide, dark eyes and his hair was scented with sweetgrass Winona had wound through the braids. A knot grew in Pretty Singer's throat when he thought of what he was about to do, but then he saw the boy's perfectly formed ears, now turned attentively to listen to his older brother's instruction, and he didn't feel as guilty.

They rode all day through wooded ravines, fording steep sloughs where mosquitoes lay in ambush from stagnant black puddles. They rode until they were far from any Dakota or whites, on a stretch of flat prairie spanned by an enormous blue sky where a white-hot sun burned like a cinder.

He bid Wanikiya lay down on a spine of red rock that rose from the grass. The boy did as he asked, his eyes curious. Pretty Singer drove stakes into the ground around the rock and then he laced leather cords through the stakes and bound his brother tight against the boulder. "You must not be afraid," he told his brother. "Every boy goes through this in order to become a warrior. This will be a second birth for you. If you are good and do not cry out, I will come back for you at the end of the day." The boy nodded quietly, not knowing that his brother intended to abandon him to die of thirst or starvation. Wanikiya was dressed only in breechclout, and his copper-colored arms and legs blended into the red stone. A stain of sweat spread like pooling blood around him while the white sun looked down on them both like a single glaring eye.

Then Pretty Singer rode to camp where he told a lie about a group of stray Pawnee warriors that he and the boy had come across while scouting for buffalo herds not seen in many summers on the prairie. He said the boy had been captured and shot when he tried to escape. Blue Sky Woman went into her teepee and cut her hair, weeping, after he told the story. The old medicine man Hanyokeyah studied him as though reading his soul in his eyes. Pretty Singer had to look away. He didn't feel any different. Not ashamed. Yet no wash of power came from the Canotina.

The sun dried the tears and sweat on his face, leaving white trails of salt lining his cheeks and chin until it looked as though his red skin had been painted for war. His throat was a torch. Wanikiya strained against the sinews, but was bound fast. When he shut his eyes he saw a wash of blue and reds and the sun, a darkly radiant ball of flame pressed close to his lids. He licked his lips, tasting shreds of peeling skin and his own blood. Pretty Singer was not coming back. There was only the hot wind in the tallgrass and the sun that would melt him like tallow before the fire.

His backbone went numb against the spine of stone and just when he thought the torture could not get any worse, the sun faded in the sea of grass. He could feel his own burned skin breathing in the dark. The wind, soothing now, was filled with voices. Good Star Woman. It was said his mother was a healer. If she had lived she might have taught him the ways of the medicine society. Already, like his father, he was a finder of lost things, once rescuing a lone burrowing owl that he'd kept alive through the winter. Who would find him out here? There were locusts in the bluestem, the vibrating song of them. Wanikiya prayed aloud for his mother's spirit and strength. He kept up the chant until his voice rasped down to a thread. The stars came and went. A sickle moon crossed the great span of dark on her pale horse.

Then the sun rose again and the boy no longer had a voice. His body was a husk. His arms struggled against the sinews to no avail. Every breath left his chest in a tongue of fire. He could turn his head and see the bluestem swaying, each stand of tallgrass tinged with a head of seeds. A swaying army of pale men come to see him die on this stone. Then the rain. First a few drops that speckled the ground, the boy straining toward them. Voices in the clouds. Riders on dark steeds, the thunder gods. Rain and more rain and the boy drinking it in. The sun descended through shredded clouds.

He slept and woke while it was still dark. Across the prairie a flight of dark birds, blackbirds the boy had been taught to fight to protect the corn. His enemy. All around him they descended like dark stones. One turned toward him with its bright yellow beak. It hopped onto the stone, only a few inches away from Wanikiya's eyes. I am dead and dreaming, he thought, and now they will steal my flesh. The bird turned instead and began to peck at the sinews that bound him to stone. The stars swirled; he had a sense of the earth turning and himself at the center. The birds came from this region of darkness, down and down from the stars. They pecked at pebbles, gnawed away at his ropes. He felt the tension release. Still he stayed on the stones, even as the birds rose again and disappeared in the dark. The wind came across the grass, the heads of seeds loosening and taking flight. He heard a voice in the breath of this wind. *You are like this grass*, the voice was saying, *that burns in the summer and comes again*. His mother's voice, *Child, the fire is coming and you are only a speck before it. How I wish I was there to guide you*. The wind faded and with it her voice. He called after it, his throat rasping Good Star Woman's name, but he was alone in the dark.

After three days Wanikiya came back, carrying the leather thongs his brother had bound him with. He said nothing while the joyous village embraced him and celebrated his return. His lips were coated with black blood, his skin peeling and blistered with sun sores. Finally, Wanikiya told of some blackbirds coming down at night and pecking away the cords that held him. He told of following the pony's hoofprints back across the prairie to find the camp again. He did not tell anyone that his own brother had tied him to the rock.

The village celebrated his return as proof of his status and power. They said he would grow into a warrior even greater than his father, Seeing Stone, had been. They said it was clear now that he would be their leader.

Pretty Singer listened and feigned happiness. In his younger brother's curious, dark eyes he read a caution now. Wanikiya jumped when he came across him alone at the creek or in the woods.

All the while the world changed around them. The buffalo disappeared. Leaders of other tribes signed away territories without consulting Seeing Stone's small band: Traverse Des Sioux, 1851. The years and names, meaningless to them. Every day more and more whites filled the valley, eating up all the fish from the creek, hunting out the lands, digging homes for themselves in the sod where they lived like rodents.

One such family moved directly across the river from where Seeing Stone's band lived. There was a tall, hair-faced man who carried a great toothlike gleaming thing he used to hew down a part of the hardwood forest that sheltered the people in winters of the past. He had a wife so hugely pregnant she waddled when she walked, a pale-skinned woman who wore a headpiece that made her nearly blind. Both had fine yellow hair and pink skin which they must have been ashamed of to cover up in so many layers of clothing. These *wasicun* squawked like prairie chickens and ran whenever any of the tribe came on their land. Worse, they had a huge, lumbering bear of a dog they would turn on the people who approached their side of the river.

One day a girl named Whispering Cloud went across this river to gather *teepsinna*—a juicy, delicious tuber that grew in the marshes over there—and was mauled by the bearlike dog. She ran screaming through the camp, blood soaking through her dress, one of her ears dangling by a single shred of skin. The injury, so close to his own mutilation, enraged Pretty Singer.

That very night Pretty Singer went over to the other side carrying with him some pemmican to feed to dog. Once the animal learned to trust him and grew greedy, Pretty Singer coaxed it to come forward and then plunged his knife into the animal's chest. He held onto the shuddering dog until the last low death rattle rumbled up out of its throat. Every single moment of fear and uselessness in his life felt purged by this dog's blood. This was what he could have done with the bear. This was the power that the Canotina's song should have given him.

Pretty Singer did not stop with their dog. He entered the sod stable where they kept the clumsy four-hoofed creatures they used to tear up the black earth. The smell of the sod around him returned him to the memory of his prison cell and his vision. The oxen inside shied at the strange smell of this man, the iron scent of dog's blood on his knife. But each was in its own pen and had nowhere to run. One of them began to bellow in fear. The lowing of this beast filled the small room. Pretty Singer opened the stall's door and stroked the ox's bristling fur, whispering soft things in the animal's ears. "I am Tatanyandowan," he told it. "Be still." Then he drew the knife across the wide throat and the great ox went down on its knees, spilling blood in a torrent through the sod barn. The other oxen began to panic and kick at the solid earthen walls. In the darkness their eyes glazed over with a terror that paralyzed them before the man with the knife.

Within his cabin, the settler heard the sound of the frightened oxen and his wife encouraged him to go out and check in case wolves were bothering the stock again, but he had been chopping wood all day and was too tired even to lift his arms.

One by one Pretty Singer killed the trapped cattle. Then he went into the grove of remaining woods and lay down in a spot of grass to watch for morning.

It was the wife who found them. She went down to water the stock before the sun's first rising. There was a silence in the barn, a smell that prickled the hair on the back of her neck. She held onto her huge belly and waddled through the door. In the slick warmth inside she slipped and fell, turning as she went down to avoid landing on her stomach. The black mud and straw kept her glued to the ground, but as the breath came back into her lungs she looked across the stall and saw the flat eyes of one the dead oxen looking back at her and knew then what she was lying in. She screamed and managed to scramble up out of the sod barn. She screamed as she ran all the way back to the cabin, her dress saturated with gore, her voice going hoarse.

All of this took place in 1857 by the reckoning of the white world. The Swedish family, the Gustavsons, who had lived in this place, abandoned the square-house they had made from the trees and returned back to where they came from.

Still drenched in blood, Pretty Singer returned to the camp, delighting in the fear he saw in his brother's eyes and those of the medicine man, Hanyokeyah. He had learned that he did not need to wait for the Canotina. That night in the sod barn, he had fashioned his own medicine from blood. When he returned again, he would complete the vision that he had seen so many winters before.

Fearing the soldiers would come for him again, he fled that winter out onto the prairies to live with another renegade, a Wahpekute named Inkpaduta, whose father was said to have killed a chief. He did not wait to see whether Hanyokeyah urged the council to exile him from his own people.

Wanikiya stood before the old man, his chin tilted up, while a charcoal stick coated his throat and chest with blackness. Hanyokeyah's hands were steady. He darkened even the boy's face, drawing careful ovals around the eyes. Both of them wore only breechclout and leggings even though their breath rose in white clouds around them on this chill spring day. Seeing the preparations for this fasting ceremony, a few of the camp's children danced around the boy with freshly cooked meat, taunting and tempting him.

When Hanyokeyah finished with the charcoal he stepped back and studied the boy before him. He looked in his eyes for that flicker of the father that Good Star Woman had said dwelled inside him. The boy watched him in return, not speaking, oblivious even to the children waving strips of meat under his nose.

A burrowing owl the boy had rescued from the prairie danced on his shoulder and squawked at this new creature his master had become. It fluttered up to perch on the boy's head, the talons fixing a hold near the single lock of silver in the boy's hair. The boy lifted it back down on his finger, speaking to it softly. Watching them together, the old man recognized that the boy loved this pet more than anything in the world. An orphan, like him. It would make a suitable sacrifice for the Great Mystery when the boy was ready.

A few flecks of icy drizzle spat from a low gray sky, but the old man made them leave the striped woolen trader blankets behind. Both he and the boy would wear only breechclout and leggings even as squalls of black clouds passed over the wintry sun and the north wind grew teeth and claws. They walked through the winter-dry prairie grasses and found a place to lie down on the opposite side of the still-frozen river.

Red Otter had reported that a new family had come to live in the place the whites abandoned after Pretty Singer killed their animals. The old man hoped to teach the boy lessons about watchfulness today, and also to discover just what sort of people this new family would prove to be.

He and the boy cut strands of waving bluestem and wove this through their headbands. Hanyokeyah left the two feathers he had earned in battle against the Ojibwe waving in his hair. Any who saw this from the distance would think him no more than a grouse or prairie chicken. Then he and the boy hunched down in the grass to get out of the wind.

They were not there long before some of the white family came down. The family followed a beaten path down to the river, past stumps of the trees the last white had cut out of the grove. Nearest the river, a dense matting of burr oak branches tossed above their heads like nests of dark serpents. The underbrush rustled with chickadees flitting about to stay warm.

They watched as the largest of the whites, a tall boy with gold hair and lean, hawklike features, chopped through the ice with a pickax to get at the water rushing beneath. Hanyokeyah felt Wanikiya shudder beside him at the sound of ice breaking. The taller boy leaned over the rim and dipped in a bucket he passed to another boy beside him. This boy was shorter, slightly bowlegged, with bright red hair and speckles on his skin. Neither child paid any attention to their surroundings except for a few nervous glances at the woods around them. An entire war party could have lain on this prairie and they would not have seen them. The old man told himself to make sure to point this out to Wanikiya later. Fasting taught watchfulness. The world never stopped being perilous and the leaf-dwellers were no more than kit foxes in a land of wolves and ravenous eagles.

A new figure emerged on the far bank, a girl with dark hair, her long dress thrashing in the wind. She came down the bank along with the boys and gazed out from the woods into the span of golden grassland that stretched around the watchers.

Her eyes quickly found the old man and Wanikiya. Hanyokeyah saw her jaw go slack with fear. *This is the moment she will yell and scream*, he thought. He lay low and placed a hand on the boy's back to make sure he didn't move. He imagined sending out his mind to the girl standing on the far shore. *I am only a bird in the grass*, he said. And later he wondered if it was only his imagination when a voice came back and answered his own, saying: *You are not. I see you.* Hanyokeyah sat all the way up in the grass, his head cresting above the waving tips. The two boys with this girl were still engrossed in their task. The older one laughed as he climbed back up the bank, water sloshing around him. But the girl stayed where she was, pale in her dress, her fists on her hips. Then he realized that she was doing what they had come here for. She was trying to understand how much of a threat they were to her family. She saw them because she had looked with the eyes of her heart and did not believe the disguise they had made. Finally, the girl scrambled up after her brothers and hid behind one of the trees.

In case she might run and tell the others and they had dogs or worse, Hanyokeyah took the boy away. There were enough lessons for him already in this encounter. They ran quickly through the tallgrass, keeping low. The old man cast one backward glance and saw the girl as she came out of hiding. Afterward he would wonder at her strange behavior and the gesture she made: the fingers spreading open and waving back and forth as though to clear the air around her.

After they were gone, the girl came down the slope and crossed the frozen river. The golden grass was pressed to the earth on this far side and she knelt and touched the ground and felt the remains of their bodies' warmth. She was not frightened even though the shopkeeper had shown them the article about Abbie Gardner seeing her entire family killed before her eyes. They had been hiding so close she could see the shine of the bear grease in the boy's braids and the glint of something silver. She thought if the Indians were going to kill them all they would not send one grizzled looking old man in dark paint and a boy. They had just been crouching there in the grass, black and glossy as crows. She hadn't sensed any menace in them.

A spotted white feather was nestled in the boy's place. Hazel knew when she took it in her hands that she would see him again.

STRANGERS
IN THE
TERRITORY

THE SENGER FAMILY had arrived on a bitter day in April of 1859. Snow whirled out of low clouds before the wind caught it and whipped it past their eyes, the flakes small and hard as fragments of broken glass. They could hear the ice breaking up like bones beneath the hull of their steamer, the *Independence*, the first boat to make it upriver to New Ulm that spring. The family hunched down behind rain barrels to keep out of the wind. In the tallgrass prairies along the shore the wind moved like a ghost army, bending down the stalks in a relentless march, flowing and moaning as they came, before dying with one final shriek. The sun was a white disk above them that vanished in clouds of mixed sleet and snow.

When the wind relented the children stood again near the rails as the steamer carried them into a heavily treed valley terraced by grassed knolls. Jakob called it a vision of the Old Country, the way his father had always spoken of it. If there had been stone castles on the highest hills, the vision would have been complete. They would have traveled from their old home, a family on the run, into a place out of a tale.

But instead of castles there were scaffolds: lean structures of lashed beams tied with fluttering red cloths where a man told them the Dakota laid their dead. They hadn't seen a single live Indian but their dead were all around the family, and when the great droves of blackbirds took flight from the leafless woods, the children were left with an uneasy sense of eyes watching from the trees. This was the false spring the girl had dreamed about when she touched the Judas flower. In a few days the river would grow a new skin of ice and trap the steamer upriver in New Ulm.

They came here, all the way to Minnesota, because of Jakob's paper. Back in Missouri, while recovering from his burns, Jakob had picked up the advertisement for the escaped slave, trying to remember her face. He saw this ad printed beneath it:

> Land out of the Bible! Rich virgin prairie soils are now open to homesteading after Dahcotah Indians sign peace treaty. Wooded draws and dark, alluvial soils capable of growing the crop of your dreams. Good wheat country and river transportation. Come to land where sickness is unknown and the summers cool and bounteous.

The advertisement included a man's name: Flandrau of New Ulm. With his printing press wrecked and an entire town incited against him, Jakob did not have to think long about taking his family to a new place only a month's travel out of St. Louis.

There were few difficulties but along the way they lost Kate, his wife of two years. One morning, soon after they set out, while traveling wet spring Missouri roads and camping out beneath the buckboard by night, they awoke to find her blankets empty, and Jakob reasoned she'd gone back to her father and the only home she knew. But she'd left her children with him, and for Jakob there was no going back to Saline Springs. A month's travel took him to meet Flandrau, the land agent, face to face, and from him he bought a section of land abandoned the previous winter and, with the last of his wife's money, supplies. He was told that there was a cabin already on the property.

It was also from Flandrau they first heard the name of Inkpaduta and of the massacre his tribe caused: forty settlers dead down near Spirit Lake in Ioway territory.

Hysteria had gripped New Ulm. The streets were empty and quiet. The newspapers the children read in the store while their father haggled over land and supplies, told only half the story. The children saw Inkpaduta, drawn to look like a monster, and the picture of Abbie Gardner. "She looks like you," Asa told Hazel. While snow dripped from their patchwork cloaks as they huddled around a cast-iron stove in the store, they read of Inkpaduta's rage. His brother, Sintonamaduta, was murdered by the horse trader, Henry Lott. Lott was a man of wicked inclinations and deserved punishment. When Inkpaduta took his complaint to Granville Berkley, the prosecuting attorney, the man responded by nailing Sinto's head to a post.

Then came a winter with snowdrifts as high as the cedar hills, a time when the settlers and a renegade band of Indians living outside the reservation boundaries were forced close together. Corn disappeared from cribs. In their hunger and fear, the whites took the Indians' guns and forced them to go alone out onto the prairies, unarmed and exiled, possibly to die in the snow. But Inkpaduta and his Wahpekutes, the leaf dwellers, had no intention of leaving.

As she read, the girl could see it. In her mind's eye she saw the severed head of Inkpaduta's brother leering eyeless from the post, a tongue swelling from the jaws. She saw grim, white-faced women rustling past in dark dresses, shielding their children's eyes when they walked by the head. Her awareness of her physical surroundings vanished. She couldn't feel her feet or hands. She was inside the vision and the severed head turned to watch her, as in her dream, and then turned past her to gaze at the horizon where darkness spread like spilled ink. Behind them a dark swarming cloud blotted out the sun, birds and more birds descending, and people turning toward this eclipse of the light, their faces pale with terror.

Forty dead when Inkpaduta's men were done, and the girl carried out onto the far prairies after seeing her family slaughtered. A troop from

Fort Ridgely sought to track down the outlaw band, but all they caught was frostbite, two of their own men vanishing in the treacherous pools of snow on the prairie. *Inkpaduta*. The name haunted those frightened people in New Ulm and would haunt the Senger family. *Don't stay out too late, they haven't yet caught Inkpaduta. Don't play with Indians or you'll end up like Abbie Gardner.*

The family didn't know what to expect when they came through the valley. Hazel rode in the buckboard beside her father while the boys ran alongside the wagon, anxious to arrive. Back in New Ulm they had purchased a new wagon, an iron stove, various pots and pans, one washboard, tin plates and cups, a barrel of buckwheat flour to grind in the coffee mill, salted pork, and the seed potatoes and corn they hoped to plant in May. They had four oxen to pull the wagon, a brindled milch cow tied to the back, and four laying hens in wire boxes. The cow moaned, pained or homesick, while they rode along. Of Kate's four hundred dollars, they had a smattering of silver remaining.

As they rode along, shafts of sunlight split the clouds hovering low over the prairie and touched the bluestem grasses with tawny light. The oxen came along, slow and relentless, following grooves in the ground marked by Indians' travois in their ceaseless migrations. Clouds of prairie chickens erupted in front of the wagon wheels. Colors sharpened in the unseasonable cold, ice glazing the gold grass, stark black trunks of trees bordering rigid creeks and steep sloughs. There were no people visible. Smoke spiraled from an occasional cabin set near the road. A few mangy dogs came out and barked at the entourage, but were too lazy to give chase.

Ashes drifted past them like flecks of dark snow. Jakob had to coax the oxen to get them over the top of the next rise. What spread out in the valley below them could not be possible: An entire field of dead blackbirds, acre upon acre, the cloud-light glossy on their still quivering wings. The dead birds made a sound in the girl's mind, a keening of betrayal at being called down to this place. Despite the stench, she held her hands over her ears to stop their cries. The boys scrambled back in the wagon. In her mind she kept seeing the vision from back in the store, the head nailed on the post and the blackbirds eclipsing the sun. It seemed as if they rode through the aftermath of a great battle between the creatures of the air. Hazel imagined clouds of them at war, beaks and talons speckled with blood, as they fell upon one another and dropped from the sky in a dark rain.

From the far fields smoke rose from tin barrels. They made out human forms moving through the carnage, children in gray sackcloth trousers, red kerchiefs tied around their mouths like masked outlaws, each carrying a wooden bucket stacked with dead, quivering blackbirds. A gaunt scarecrow of a woman in a faded calico dress, holding a pair of dead blackbirds in each of her hands, stopped her work to watch the Sengers ride past. Her face, lost in the deep shadows of her slat bonnet, had a forlorn cast, the mouth opening without words at this distance.

Ahead of them in the road, a sallow-faced man in a bowler hat stood before a dray cart where the birds were piled high as hay mound. He was red-eyed from the fumes, his skin and face the color of a shriveled pear. He scowled at the approaching caravan.

After Jakob drew the wagon to a halt, neither man spoke at first. Jakob caught his breath. "What is the meaning of this?" he said. "How could so many birds die?" His hands shook while he held the reins.

The man pointed to a silver canister beside him. "Strychnine," he said. "I laced the seeds with strychnine. Two years running these birds have stolen the seeds before they touched the earth. The birds got fat while my children starved. This year they are paying twenty cents a bushel for dead blackbirds in town. This year my harvest will come from the sky."

Jakob glanced behind him at the poisoned fields and the masked children plucking the poisoned birds from the ground. "You'll make them sick," he said. Softer, under his breath, but loud enough for the man to hear, he said, "Madness."

He geed the oxen into motion, whipping them with the reins. The man shouted after them. "Don't act like you're better than me. You don't know what it's like out here. You don't know." His cry followed them like a chant, this Hans Gormann and his fair-skinned wife, and his daughters, Cassie and Sallie. And then they rode over the next hill and saw, for the first time, the cabin they would call home for the next four years.

The wind came out of the west and they could no longer smell the field of dead blackbirds, but the clouds moved in squalls now, and there was the metallic taste of coming snow on the edge of their tongues. This was their first night in the new territory.

The new cabin squatted stump-like at the base of a hill. The first night they came here the girl was relieved it bore no resemblance to the sod-roofed house she'd seen in her nightmare. The shutters banged and flapped in the wind as though the house was stretching to take flight and vanish over the horizon. Only tatters of leather hinges hung where there once was a door. Jakob tacked a blanket over this opening so they would feel less exposed.

An untilled field encircled the cabin; a lone cedar tree stood at its center. There was a leaning structure of clapboards that yawned over an open pit. The sod barn proved to be a tight, cozy enclosure for the animals but Jakob had to manhandle the milch cow—shoving it by the rump while Caleb whipped it with a quirt—to get it inside. Something frightened the creature. That night as Hazel milked it the cow continued to make a mournful lowing sound with each tug of the teats. "Is she sick?" Caleb had asked, thinking maybe the calf she carried inside her was turned around the wrong way.

"Maybe she doesn't like this place," Asa said. "It's gloomy in here. Like being buried alive." None of them said anything about the coppery scent that burned inside their nostrils, a scent that had soaked into the walls and the packed soil.

By night the wolves came to serenade them. They slept fitfully, Hazel thinking of the two Indian watchers she had seen earlier on the prairie and wondering why they had come.

In the wake of their April arrival, the weather turned for the worse. That first morning they woke to knee-deep drifts beyond the cabin and a scouring wind that blew through gaps in the cabin's chinking. When the wind allowed the snow to settle, the children were awed by the spread of grassland and sky. Their old lives had been hemmed in by hills and hollows. Now there were endless seas of grass, broken only by small rises and groves of sheltering woods along the serpentine bends of the river. They stood at the edge of a raw country, a place of wind and storm, shifting and changing before their eyes.

By morning Hazel woke to the noise of wind howling as sunlight streaked through clanging shutters and gilded the sleeping children. They had kept the smaller animals they purchased inside with them. Four laying hens clucked from their wire cages. Freyja, a striped cat with tawny fur they had also bought from the shopkeeper, yawned and displayed rows of sharp teeth.

Hazel had been dreaming the ice dream again. In the dream her mother lay on the block of ice, her skin shining with blue light. A red sash coiled around her throat. Her fingers were gray, drained of blood, the fingernails as long as talons. *What happened to you?* Hazel said in the dream and her voice echoed through the cavernous barn: *What happened, happened to you.* Hazel awoke and felt icy drafts pooling on the floor below her. She woke thinking *she* was sleeping on a bed of ice. *I wish this winter would leave us,* she thought. *I am not my mother. What happened to her is not my story.*

She listened to her father splitting kindling. Only after she heard the flare of the lucifer match did she dare rise in the freezing room. Jakob's beard looked wild and tangled; locks of his dark hair fell in his eyes while he labored to get the fire going. But he seemed rested, content, even as the moisture of his breath formed ice beads in his mustache. All of them had been thinned down to an essence of lean muscle by the journey from Missouri. Thinned down and strengthened, Hazel hoped.

She helped Jakob get the bacon started, standing on a low stool, the heavy iron skillet popping with grease. This would be her job now with Kate gone. She would have to feed and clean for four boys and a man. None had marked the passage of her twelfth birthday in late March as their steamboat took them through Keokuk. She bit down on her lip, thinking what a petty concern this was when so much else was happening. While she forked over the bacon, Jakob ground beans in a mill and got the coffee started. When he looked at her his black eyes glittered under his heavy brows. *"Mein apfel,"* he said, his endearment for her. She loved to be spoken and sung to in the language of the Old Country. "We are a long ways from God's country now," he said.

What is hardest to believe is that for a short time they were happy. Without shingles to repair the roof, they ransacked the canvas from their Conestoga wagon and stretched it across. This kept out the snow, but at nights when the wind stirred and rustled the canvas it seemed their cabin was alive and adrift, rushing across the dark toward some unforeseen destination. They burrowed under their blankets and didn't get up at night since they didn't have chamber pots and none wanted to brave the icy trek to their tottering outhouse.

The cold relented and lamplit nights passed as Jakob read aloud to them from *The Book of Wonders* to remind them of home. *Always plant potatoes in the dark of the moon*, he'd read. *It's safe to plant beans when you hear whippoorwills in the rushes. When planting peach trees, bury old boots near the roots.* Hazel ground buckwheat in the coffee mill while Jakob chanted his litany. It sounded pretty read aloud, even if it wasn't true. What they heard in his voice was a spell to ward off ill-fortune. What they heard was a shared dream for a crop that would feed them through the next winter.

At night Hazel lay on the floor near her brothers with the cat, Freyja, nestled on her chest, purring like a small steam engine, a second heartbeat in time with her own. They listened, the cat and she, to the wolves down in the grove. The wolves didn't sound so lonesome after a time. *I amm heerre*, the wolves sang. *I am alive and a part of these stars, this April moon, this land dreaming under the snow.* The girl watched moonlight streaming through the canvas and listened. *I am here now*, they bayed, *I won't be forever, but tonight I am, under these April stars, in my warm fur coat and I am alive and glad of it. I am here, and this life is savage, and this life is good.* Once Hazel heard the joy in their singing she stopped thinking this was such a terrible place. She lay quietly with the fat tabby purring on her chest, warm in her burrow of blankets, and willed her thoughts to travel out to their voices resounding through the prairie darkness: *I am here, too. I don't know why or for what reason, but I am alive and all is well.*

She felt this even as she missed humid Missouri and thought about her stepmother Kate and wondered if the woman was lonesome for them. To her surprise she found that she missed her. There was too much work to be done and she was only a girl and not ready for it. She missed Kate bustling her into petticoats and bemoaning Hazel's slumping posture and glum frowns. For all her weaknesses and nitpicking, Kate brought a sense of order with her. *If only she had loved my father more*, Hazel thought. But the woman had seen an opportunity for escape and taken it.

Each morning Hazel rose and pulled on her night-chilled garments from a box by the stove where the ashes of the night before were banked. She rose and pulled on the one dress she owned and walked down the path to milk their cow, her footsteps crossing over places where paws had trod the night before.

After a week in the unseasonable cold, the cow went dry. She bawled at Hazel while the girl tugged on her teats and ducked the lashing tail. The girl's mittenless hands were freezing. She pressed her face against the warmth of the flank and listened for some clue to what was wrong. They brought the cow fresh grain, wrapped her in an old blanket, rubbing down the hide, but nothing worked. Jakob said the cow was homesick. He said it was a foolish and sentimental creature, but that it would get over it and not to worry.

The next morning the cow disappeared. They found the frayed rope in the barn and the splintered beams around the door as though she'd panicked in the night and smashed her way out. Flecks of blood speckled the beams of her stall. The wind had been up the night before and they hadn't heard a single thing. It howled around them now, a springtime wind out of the south to quicken the pulse of sap in sleeping trees and soften the ground. The wind seethed, melting snow, erasing all tracks of what had happened the night before. In the grove, the wind pruned winter-killed branches from the trees. They heard limbs crashing down in intervals while they paced around the sod barn and tried to make sense of the animal's disappearance.

It looked as though the milch cow had rolled across the damp ground, throwing up great drifts of snow and mud. Only one set of tracks led away from the barn and down toward the river.

"Do you think the wolves got to her?" Caleb asked.

Jakob shook his head. "I think she just run off. She's been raising a ruckus to beat the band, crying like she wanted to be back home. She'll be calving soon. Maybe there's something wrong. Either way she's acting crazy and I'm gonna have to track her. If I don't find her, I'll go to Fort Ridgely and file a report. They pay settlers out of the Indians' annuity funds for things that get stolen. Depredations, they call it."

"You ought to take me, Pa," Caleb said. "I'm good at finding things." It was true. Back in Missouri, if one of the milch cows wandered away, Caleb would find a daddy long legs and whisper a ditty: *Old Man Spider, so many eyes, tell us where milch cows hide*. He'd screw up his face tight as if listening for the spider's response, but this was just to impress his younger brothers, especially white-haired Daniel. Really, Caleb just read the tracks on the ground and knew the cows would head for the mud wallows when the flies got mean. Still there was something instinctive in how he hunted and found the lost.

Jakob studied him for a moment, this boy who had already grown taller than him. A boy with his first wife's gold-brown eyes and sharp features. "No, I'll need you to stay here," he said. "I'll be leaving the rifle with you. I don't want you to leave these premises, you understand? No matter how long it takes me, you are to stay here."

LOST

JAKOB WALKED ON water to find their lost milch cow. How the cow was lost and how he came to find it might have become the stock of Senger family legend had things turned out differently. He walked on water because the river froze once more and allowed him to pass over it.

The first time Jakob encountered snowshoe prints beside the cow's trail he thought of returning to his children. Snow dropped from trees in loud clumps and Jakob heard the subdued surge of the river as the ice plates crackled and separated along the shoreline. The milch cow had crossed and re-crossed the river three times, always coming back to these woods. At last she had barreled up out of them, through a grove of maples, and onto the wide, white prairie.

The sun came out and turned the landscape into a single translucent glare, a glittering terrain that looked like thousands of mirrors flickering in the light. A layer of sleet had come down in the night and further glazed the remaining snow. Wind had scraped the ground clean of snow in places; pockets of tall golden grass mixed with pockets of snow where Jakob sank to his waist. He had been walking for hours, he thought. It was more difficult to track her with the sun out. Green fires flared at the edge of his vision, and had he been raised out here like the Dakota, he would have known this was the first sign of impending snow blindness.

He was no tracker, but he knew he had to provide for his children. They needed this cow's milk to survive. It was here on the prairies that he first saw the snowshoe prints, faint impressions in the melting snow that appeared here and there around the cow's tracks as though someone were leading her on this crazed journey. He knelt and traced with his mittens the outline of the print, the lace of branches. He held his hand over his eyes and tried to peer into the distance, across the bleak sweep of snow. The cow was not going in the direction he'd expected. Jakob had assumed when he set out to find her that she was headed back for New Ulm, the home that she knew. He'd been sure this stubborn beast had been trying to get back to her old owner, but her trail circled back onto the prairie and there was the mystery of those strange prints beside her.

Ahead of him he could see a grove of cottonwoods lining a ridge, the limbs leafless and bare; surely the tree line marked the beginning of another river. Something fluttered within the trees, pale pink cloths the color of human skin. His throat was dry. He knelt and cupped some of the snow into his mouth and it chilled him straight down. The cloths beckoned him toward the woods like fingers. Everywhere the land was glazed and glaring with the sun's reflection.

He moved toward the woods, discovering as he came closer that the land dipped here into an ice-choked bowl of water surrounded by cattails and marsh reeds. The wind caused powdery snow to glide in serpentine patterns across the frozen pond. Farther out, past the pond's center, he saw the speckled hulk of the cow. Then he saw the wolves as they lurched to feed on the body, four or five skinny wolves with mottled fur and red snouts. Crows cawed from the edges of the marsh and flew in circles around the scene. His gut churned at the sight below. A fat wedge of blood trailed from the pond's edge. The wolves had torn her open from her hind end and strewn her intestines in a long red line.

There was blood in the snow and gleaming bits of hide and flesh. The cow lowed, a rumbling, forlorn moan. She was still alive.

The sight filled him with rage and before he knew what he was doing, he charged down the hill, bellowing, waving his arms, and he was among the wolves. He slipped once in the bloody snow and fought his way back to his feet, the briny, sweet smell of her blood and intestines clinging to his clothing. The wolves ran from him at first, a wild-eyed man hoarse with rage, and then circled back. The largest, a gray with shimmering fur and yellow eyes, trotted around Jakob in an easy circle, its black lips drawing back to expose long teeth.

Jakob charged them again and again they danced away. The gray snarled. Another began to growl as they reformed their circle. Jakob's breath wheezed in his chest. All the fury that had carried him into this fight drained from his arms and chest. He could not fight off five wolves with his bare hands. In his mind's eye he saw their circle tightening and tightening and him at the center. He shouted at them, called them *see-lenraubers* and other things in a language they had never heard, but still they came. And eventually, in panic, he charged once more to the other side of the pond and broke past them.

The wolves didn't follow him. He watched all the while: watched them renew their attack on the fallen cow, tearing out more and more ropes of intestines and then the terrible sac of skin that held the calf, breaking it open like a yolk on the snow, and the wolves drenched and radiant with placental blood, snarling and fighting after devouring the fetus, and then returning to tear out more organs from the still living cow until she loosed one last strangled scream, a sound almost human to Jakob's ears, one last wail before she lay her snout in the snow and ceased breathing.

The children, he thought, *I must get back to them.*

The sense came over him of being watched. Beyond the red-slick snow there were crows and the sun, always glaring. It had been glaring all along, a fact that only now he discerned as his vision shrank. He turned away from the carnage and looked toward that rise dotted with cottonwoods where he had seen the pink ribbons of cloth beckoning.

A man was there, the quick silhouette of him fading into the trees. The footprints. He remembered the snowshoe prints alongside the traipsing cow. He was sick with rage and helplessness, a red shroud in his brain. This must be the one who had led his cow out here to suffer and die. Jakob drew in a deep breath. Here was something he could fight. Not a spirit, not the relentless wolves, but flesh and blood. As he walked he plucked a sturdy limb from the melting snow and stalked after the figure he'd seen at the top of the hill. Why was his vision shrinking, a circle of darkness closing in on his eyes? Needles of searing pain spiked from his eyes and into his mind. Sight became agony. He slipped several times before he gained the snow-lit rise, felt the chill of his clothes wet against his legs and feet. One of the wolves in the valley below had begun to howl, an echoing celebration.

Jakob stood in the circle of barren cottonwoods. He was alone. He saw that the pink ribbons flew from scaffolds and that nearly all the color had bled out of the cloth. His breath came and went in white clouds before him. In the trees there were scaffolds and in the scaffolds there were bodies. On the other side of the ridge the hill dropped down toward a river where he saw the remains of a village, four teepees. The only things stirring were his breath and the wind among the fluttering cloths. Then, like a shadow, he saw the form of the man moving away from him, running easily back across the snow in the direction in which Jakob guessed his own cabin and children lay. The shadow-form moved fluidly in the glare of snowmelt. The tunnel of Jakob's vision shrank further. *I have been led here on purpose,* he thought. *My God.* All was radiant and glaring and then the tunnel of his vision closed and Jakob knelt, blinded, surrounded by the remains of a dead village.

The prairie night was immense and silent. The children huddled within their cabin and Caleb read to them from Pa's book to keep their minds off his absence. "He'll be back before dawn," he promised.

"How do you know?" Asa said. "How do you know he isn't gone forever, like my mother?" Daniel sobbed himself to sleep. Caleb drew Asa aside and voiced a threat only Asa heard. The youngest, Matthew, climbed beneath Hazel's blanket, his body icy to the touch.

That night, the girl dreamed of her father. In the dream Jakob walked through a field of bones. They were all around him, along the roadsides, in a yard where a woman hoed her garden—skulls and bones gleaming among the tomato vines. Her pa's head hung low as he stepped carefully to avoid treading on the dead. The skeletons were stripped of clothing and here or there a leather strap wound around an arm where someone had tried to staunch a gushing artery. He passed a skull with a stick clenched in its teeth, the jawbones sealed around the wood in a tight rictus of pain. Jakob was dressed in blue and carried a rifle mounted with a bayonet.

In the distance, lightning fissured in a blue-black sky. *Turn back, turn back*, she called to him in the dream. He was walking to a place at the edge of the world. The trees around him had been shredded into splinters and stumps by some earth-rending explosion. Fenceposts jutted from the road like javelins. He was alone in the dream.

Come back, she called to him, but the wind swallowed up her voice. He marched on.

Across the river from the children, the medicine man Hanyokeyah stayed late in the boy's teepee and fed slivers of cedar to the fire, smoke to guard against evil. "You are sure?" the old man said to Wanikiya. "You are sure he is back?" Wanikiya could only nod. The burrowing owl he kept for a pet flitted from his shoulder and circled about the room as if conscious of his owner's distress, his own thoughts in flight.

He had seen his brother when he went down to the river to bathe. Even after all these years, water terrified him and this morning ritual—breaking the ice, scattering droplets on his skin while he prayed to the Great Mystery as the old man had taught him—was fraught with devotion mixed with fear. He broke through the ice with his tomahawk and then dipped his fingers in the frigid water rushing beneath. He made the sign of the four directions and had just begun the old man's prayer when he heard the soft tread of moccasins in the snow. His own breath was a ghost; the sound of the water eating away the ice loud in his ears. Who was watching him?

He turned and there, after all these winters, was Tatanyandowan wrapped in a buffalo blanket with the hair turned out. He looked lean and healthy, his leggings and moccasins beaded and glistening. Wanikiya glanced down at his own clothes, the tattered wool pants favored by the *wasicun*, his soiled white shirt. No, there was something different about Tatanyandowan, beyond what had happened that day he'd returned to camp drenched in blood. Now he wore three eagle feathers in his headdress, each painted with a red dot to symbolize that the kill had belonged to him.

He told Hanyokeyah about the morning encounter while sweet burning cedar filled the teepee. His face shrouded by smoke, the old man asked Wanikiya, "Do you remember the story of Eya the Devourer?"

"Of course, the lost child of the woods. The one some say comes among the people like a sickness." Wanikiya kept quiet, waiting for Hanyokeyah to take up the tale. Though terrible, it had always been a story he liked.

Hanyokeyah began in the traditional way. "This happened when the people lived close to the big waters. One day a girl hunting berries heard a baby's cries echoing through the woodlands. Birds took wing. Squirrels and rabbits skittered past her as though fleeing a fire. Even a big shaggy bear crashed through brush and bramble until she was alone with the sound.

"The child's cries pierced the girl where she stood. It awoke something motherly within her and she went toward the sound. She found the baby lying naked beneath a cottonwood tree. Its skin looked touched with moonlight. Its eyes were as empty as the snow. So cold and helpless was this squalling baby that she took it in her arms and carried it back to camp.

"Inside her teepee, she studied the baby more closely. It did not look like any baby she had ever seen. Its belly was grotesque and swollen and it had long yellow fingernails like an owl. She fed it strips of pemmican, softening the meat in her own mouth first. She fed and fed the baby and still it hungered. Each the time its mouth opened wide she saw it had fully developed teeth, and once, looking deep down into the mouth, down into the baby's very stomach, she thought she saw human beings trapped there. She drew her hand back in fear. Still ravenous, the baby opened its mouth again and began to cry, 'Hoo, hoo, hoo.' The cries made the girl's skin crawl. It was not a baby she was hearing but the screams of those down in the stomach.

"She fled the sound and ran for her father. When she told him, he understood immediately. 'This is Eya the Devourer come to us in a new shape,' her father explained to her. 'And now you have taken it into our home and Eya will not be satisfied until it devours us all.' So saying he took his daughter's hand and gathered as many from the village as possible and they fled deep into the woods. And Eya came after them, lurching along with surprising quickness on its strange stumpy legs. There were elderly and small children with the people who were slow to escape. 'Hoo, hoo, hoo,' Eya cried as he came for them. When they could run no more, they hid themselves in the trees, shuddering as Eya approached."

Hanyokeyah paused and stared into the fire. He used a stick to prod at the embers and after a long moment of silence, Wanikiya urged him on. "Iktomi," he reminded the old man. "Iktomi, the spider, finds the people hiding and asks why they are afraid."

"Yes," the old man said. "That is how the story goes." He yawned. "I am tired tonight. You finish."

Thinking he was being tested, Wanikiya picked up where the old man had left off. "Iktomi made a great pile of mussel shells and when Eya appeared he called him 'Younger brother.' This infuriated Eya, who claimed to be among the first creations, older than the moon and stars. Iktomi shrugged and told Eya he knew what he searched for. 'They are very close now.' Hearing this, the people shuffled in the woods, thinking they were betrayed. Iktomi picked up one of the mussel shells and pretended to swallow it whole, smacking his lips. 'If you share your meal, then you I will let you have some of these shells.'

"Eya huffed. 'I will take what I want.' He grabbed handfuls of shells and inhaled them like berries. When he was stuffed, his empty eyes rolled back in his head and he swooned on his stumpy legs. His skin went green and then black. He had been tricked into eating poison. He collapsed and the villagers came forth from their hiding places and with bone knives sliced open the distended belly and released the trapped people inside. And they were singing in their joy, because the Devourer was dead, and they had been spared."

The boy shifted and watched the old man, wondering why he had chosen this story for this night. Did Hanyokeyah mean for him to trick his brother, the way Iktomi had in the story?

After a time, Hanyokeyah spoke. "There are some who say the *wasicun* are like Eya. They came to our villages helpless as children and we gave them what we had. But they only want more and more and soon there will be none of us left."

Wanikiya swallowed and looked away. He had not thought of the story in this fashion. The old man continued. "It is hard to know the way. Your brother believes such things, maybe even believes that the white people can be cut open and that afterwards things will be as they were before. The *wasicun* are not foolish like Eya. We may trick them for a time, but they will come back again. I do not think your brother's way is right. And now there is this new family living on the other side of the river. They are very strange to me, like all the *wasicun*. I knew them when I was a boy and lived among the black robes. It is true that they are greedy. But the Maker also gave them strange magic and I would like to understand them better."

The boy covered his mouth so the old man would not see him yawning. He shifted on the buffalo robes. When it came to the *wasicun* the old man's thinking became clouded. The boy sensed that he was both afraid and captivated by them. He sensed that Hanyokeyah would not want his older brother to kill them all.

Wanikiya watched the cedar smoke rise to the starlit opening above. In the distance a few wolves sang out to their brothers. He was thinking of the family on the other side, afraid of what Tatanyandowan had done.

• • •

Jakob wasn't sure how long he had been unconscious. The pain flaring behind his eyelids had grown to such an intensity that he had knelt in the cottonwoods and vomited until his throat burned and his mind went dark. When he came to, he was still blind. In the distance he heard the sound of the wolves feeding, the faint tick of the wind in the cottonwoods around him. Bodies, he had seen them, before the cloud came down over his eyes. There were still faint needles of pain prodding behind his eyes, but it had lessened. He could see enough to make out the rough bark of the trees and the scaffolds nearby. It was like looking on the world through smoked glass, and the strain of it caused the pain to come back. He could see enough to know he had woken while it was still dark.

It was not a pure blindness. The moon was out and Jakob knew only that he wanted to get away from this village and these trees freighted with ghosts. Jakob made a wide circle around the pond where the wolves continued their feast and headed in the direction he thought was home. He could not see to pick his way through the deeper drifts and he sank into these like a drowning man and had to pull himself along. *Keep moving*, a voice said inside him. *If you stay still you will die.* He was walking inside of a fever dream, the air moist and warm in his chest. He thought of the children and found the will to keep his muscles in motion. Somewhere out on the prairies he had the sense of the footsteps again, something walking behind him. "Who's there?" he called, but there was no answer.

He walked on through the night. Through the dark gauze of his vision he saw the sun rise. Jakob no longer knew the direction he was headed, but in the distance he smelled a wood fire and his stomach grumbled.

Ahead there must have been the bend of a river, a dark clutch of trees. Jakob moved toward this place, thinking, *I am home. Oh thank God, I have made it back to my children.*

He slipped while crossing the icy river, cried out as his sore hip crunched into the old ice with a splintering sound that at first he mistook for his own bones. But the sound spread in concentric ripples, a brittle crackling, and then the ice broke and Jakob fell through.

The shock of the frigid water revived him. He went under and windmilled his arms until he climbed back toward air and brightness. The current flowed quick beneath him, pulled at him like a hundred hands. He fought his way to the churning surface, choking out the bitter water. The surging river carried him into a shelf of ice and Jakob grabbed at it and held on to keep from being carried under, felt slick stones beneath his boots and the rip of the ice shredding his fingertips. And then within him he had a vision of the slave girl, Ruth, and saw her body draped over the mule, the mud beneath her shredded fingertips. This was the terror she had known when she jumped in the river to escape the slave catcher's hounds. This was how he had failed her. He was shouting, half-blinded and desperate, and the river had him in its grasp.

Wanikiya came to the sacred place as his father had come before him. This was part of knowing the Great Mystery. Hanyokeyah had told him he must make a sacrifice here if he was to become a warrior like his father.

Over centuries the stone had been hewn down from a pinnacle to an orb with channels and hewn features like the face of an old man. Now he saw that it was gone from its place in the center of the meadow. A circle of dead grass framed where it once stood. There was a sense of absence here, of violation.

All around the absent stone were the scattered gifts and offerings that Wanikiya's people had left here: a binding of tobacco, a grandmother's awl, an amber hunk of maple sugar. For generations they had passed the stone going from their winter camps out to hunt muskrat and turtles and ducks in spring, north to fight their enemies, the Ojibwe. Always, the warriors stopped here and prayed, for the stone was sacred, among the first things the Mystery created. And now the stone was gone.

Wanikiya's owl, Hinyan, perched on the boy's shoulder, made a chirping sound as if he shared his dismay. The old man had spoken of stones moving in the dark and carving furrows in the earth. Of stones that went among the stars and knew all things, and men like his father who learned their language. But this stone had not flown. Someone or something had taken it.

Wanikiya set the owl on his finger and huddled it against his chest, feeling the downy feathers close to his skin. This bird had been with him for three years, his lone companion with his brother gone. He had long preferred Hinyan's company to that of the other children, the boys racing through these woods, heedless, hunting squirrels and blackbirds with their small bows. He had never been the same as them, though he wanted to be. A quietness inhabited him. And the bird was his connection to the night he'd escaped, the night in which he heard his mother inside him.

Wanikiya took out the leather cord he had brought for this purpose. He felt Hinyan rustle against his chest, a muffled chirp, as the boy studied the place around him. The river was a subdued roar in the distance. Had a cottonwood tree not fallen along a narrow channel and formed a natural bridge, then he wouldn't be here. As it was, he had sat on the log and inched his way across, chill brown water and debris raging below him, the bird circling his head as if calling encouragement, shaking him out of his terror. He heard the river even from this distant high spot, the river loud with snowmelt as hunks of ice carried along the current battered trees on the tree line. He smelled a wood fire from the white family's cabin. Softer, he smelled the maple woods that surrounded the meadow and its stone god where the maidens did their dance in the summer.

Would there be any dance this year? Winona was of the age when she would dance and touch her palm to the stone, asking aloud to be crushed by it if she were not pure. Wanikiya looked at the blank spot in the grass. The stone would not be coming back. It had not gone among the stars. He glanced off toward the *wasicun's* cabin with its thin thread of smoke rising above the trees and hoped they had not been the ones who stole it.

Again Hinyan chirped close against his chest, asking to be let free. The bird shuddered and made a small squawking sound. Wanikiya knelt in the dead grass before the spot where the stone god had been. Now there was no chance to learn its language, to discover if he had his father's gift. Wanikiya was free to return to the village with his beloved bird still alive. He stood and prepared to head home, but in his mind's eye he saw the old man smoking his red stone pipe patiently waiting for him. He saw Hanyokeyah's eyes darken with disappointment that he had lacked courage and was not becoming like his father. They were in danger, all of them, and the boy had to learn to choose well.

He knelt again in the grass. Hinyan struggled as he tightened his embrace. Wanikiya began to sing as he wound the leather cord tightly around the bird's throat. Swift, he thought. Make it swift. This I bring before You, my offering. This that I hold beloved above all things, for You who made all things. Even the breath in my lungs. Such were his thoughts as he wound the cord tighter and tighter and felt the bird beat its wings, one talon hooking into the boy's bare chest. Hinyan did not go quietly to her death. She fought as every living thing did, and the boy whispering the whole time, pleading that its spirit would forgive him, dwell with him, until he wound the cord so tight that the bird's neck broke and Hinyan went still against his skin.

He laid the corpse before the place where once there had been a god. *It does not matter that You are not here*, he thought. *You are not in stones and men only.* His eyes brimmed. Why did he still feel nothing, only regret that what he loved was dead?

In his half-blindness he stood and movement from the trees drew his eyes. A quick flicker: The girl from the cabin who had seen Hanyokeyah and him watching that day at the river. She was breathing hard, as though she had witnessed something terrible. And then he knew that she had seen it all, had shared in this moment. His throat swelled. His cheeks were warm and bright with tears. The girl stepped closer to him, only a span of dark maples between them. She was coming his way and then he saw her brothers were behind her and that the blond one carried a rifle. Before he could raise it to his shoulder, Wanikiya was running back to the river and the fallen limb that would take him across.

THE CHILDREN
OF LEAVES

HE WOKE WITH a warm cloth over his eyes and the reedy voice of a man threading into his ears. The greasy smell of onions frying in lard saturated the air. He heard them hiss in the pan, felt the wind blow through the chinking of this cabin. The floor below him was packed dirt, well-tamped. After he removed the cloth, Jakob let his eyes adjust to the shadows. There were hewn stumps for chairs, a low pallet against the side of a wall. It was dark in the cabin, which had no windows to let in the light, but Jakob could see pelts of animals tacked against the wall—a mink, a fox, the matted silver-black fur of a wolf—along with the iron teeth and blunt chains of the traps used to capture them. The floor sloped downhill, as if the place was leaning sideways, or was that a trick of his mind? His eyes rose up from the floor and across the room he saw a man watching him, and the slash of a smile which framed brown-stained teeth.

"You're awake," the man said. He had the palest skin Jakob had ever seen, so pale he could make out the network of blue vessels beneath. The man had white hair, pinkish-bloodshot eyes, and just the stub of a nose. He was dressed in dark wool pants and a dark vest, but barefoot, his toenails yellow and curving, as long as claws. In his lap he cradled a raccoon that had rolled over on its belly and was purring like a cat. Beside him a rushlight burned on the table, a crude, oily light that consisted of a wick burning inside tallow. "Awake, just in time for dinner."

"Where am I?" Jakob asked. He was wrapped tightly in a striped wool blanket that itched his skin. Next to him there was an open hearth, a chimney of mud and wattles that blackened the walls around it with smoke. A Dutch oven squatted in the embers of the fire and it was from this that Jakob heard the onions sizzle and smelled the melting lard. The man set down the raccoon and let it hobble across the floor and Jakob saw that the creature only had three legs, but managed to move nimbly as it scurried past him.

"You don't know?" the man said. "You're just outside Milford. I found you in my river." Jakob struggled with the memory. The cow ripped open. Wolves. The bodies in the trees. The blindness and the pain that came with it. The shadow form. And then the river and the taste of the water.

"Who is Ruth?" the man asked.

"Ruth?" Jakob said, and then he remembered. The drowned slave. He had felt her terror as the river tugged him down. Then the voice calling to him from shore, a voice at first he had thought was only in his mind: *Stand up! You're in shallow water.* And Jakob had found a purchase in the sweeping river, wedged his boots between some rocks and felt his ankles twist. Standing, he was only waist-deep in the current, coughing and gagging out the water, and his vision dwindling down a single string of light. So weak. So much fire in his brain. "I never seen a man almost drown in three feet of water," the voice was saying now and Jakob remembered the hands grabbing him by the shirt, pulling back onto the creaking sheet of ice and toward the shore.

"You saved my life," Jakob said.

A thin, reedy laugh. "You were delirious, kept babbling about your blindness and someone named Ruth. Did you lose her?"

"She was a slave who drowned," Jakob said.

"A slave," the man said. "They don't keep slaves around here, and it's a pity they don't, if you ask me. Those Germans over in Milford, they hate it. Even just the talk of it makes them bilious."

"Can't say I'm fond of slavery either," Jakob said.

The man rose from the log stump where he had been seated and came over to crouch beside Jakob. "Do you feel strong enough to stand?" he asked and Jakob nodded. His bones creaked in the cold of the room, but it felt good to be up off the dirty floor. The man pointed over to a rafter where Jakob's clothes hung. Jakob turned away from him and let the blanket fall. He felt a tightness in his hip, remembered the shadow he'd seen and wondered at it. He could feel the other man's eyes on him while he dressed and suddenly only wanted to be away from this place. His clothes reeked of the smoke and the muskrat odors of this room. He dressed quickly and turned to see the man carrying over a loaf of bread on a slab of charred wood. Then he brought the Dutch-oven to the table and cut out ragged slices of dark bread and ladled the onions and lard over this, saying, "Aren't you hungry?"

Jakob shrugged and came over for a bite. The bread and grease slid down his throat and he felt his stomach turn over. He was famished and began to eat more quickly. "It's not much," the man said, "but I lived off this buckwheat bread and lard for many a winter."

Jakob wiped some of the grease from his chin and held out his hand. "Jakob Senger," he said. The man's grip was firm, his hands frigid. "I'm a newspaperman. Well, I was for a time. But now I'm going back to farming."

The man laughed. "Out here!" he said. He shook his head. "Well, Jakob Senger, my name is Silas Macaby. From the Maine shores. And pulling you from the river is the only good thing I've done in the three years I've been here." While he spoke, the raccoon swirled around his ankles and Silas passed down dribbles of bread and grease the creature took in its webbed paws. "In fact I was just waiting for the weather to break and then I was headed back for Maine. I've been lonely for the sound of the sea. For the taste of oysters. And sick, I've been. Sick of Indians, the flea-bitten beggars."

"Indians," Jakob said. "I think it was one of them who stole my cow."

"Likely," said Silas. "They'll steal anything not nailed down. Steal the shirt off your back and then taunt you with it. No, I won't miss them. Living near them for these three years has been a torment." The man seemed to eat very little of his own meal, passing much of it down to his fat hobgoblin of a raccoon.

"Why?"

"They might have been noble once. You can see flashes of that in them, a fierce pride. But now they are confined to the reservation to live like beasts, caught between the liquor traders on one hand and the government on the other. Now they drink their summers away and suffer through winter until another payment arrives." While Silas spoke, flecks of food dribbled from his mouth. A pulse came and went along his pale jaw line. Silas raged on, describing the degraded society he had witnessed, the raw fish–eating feasts and face-paintings and the way the German settlers in Milford had settled on illegal land that belonged to the Indians and made other plans, plotting to get their hands on land inside the reservation. "I don't blame the Indians for stealing. They've trapped this country clean out. Hardly enough game around to feed one man, much less the five thousand of them on the other side of the river."

Silas slapped his knee and laughed his reedy laugh. "But I got even. Wait until they see." A glint in the pink eyes.

"What do you mean?"

Silas nodded over to his bed where there was a skull-sized package wrapped in cloth and ropes. "Taku-skan-skan," he said. "Go look."

Jakob stood and wiped his hands on his pant legs. He looked back at Silas and saw the grin and the brown teeth. *Whatever he tells you, it can't be true,* he thought. *They said the same things about the slaves in Missouri. Degraded. Lesser men because of the darkness of their skin. I don't believe it. I remember the dogwood flower and how within each petal there is a cross, a rusty nail, the sign of Christ. If God inhabits a flower, so must he inhabit men. This man, this pale echo of my own search for good country, has not seen right. I will find the way to speak to them as Paul discovered the unknown god and learned to speak to the Greeks.* Jakob halted before the bundle. The sheets on the rope-spring bed stank of the pale man's musty skin. He didn't want to look inside. "Go on, now," Silas encouraged.

Jakob touched the bundle, felt the hard shape of it beneath. *A skull,* he kept thinking. *Has this man murdered someone, an Indian trespasser?* His fingers slowly unbound the ropes and the cloth fell away. Jakob didn't realize he had been holding his breath until he exhaled. He took another deep breath, steadied himself. It was only a stone, after all. A red stone carved with marks. "Do you know what it is?" Silas said. "I may not have made a living here, but I have this. It's their god, Taku-skan-skan. I mean to sell it back East. There's many a museum that will buy it."

"You stole their god?" Jakob backed away. "I'll leave you then," he said, thinking he owed the man at least this acknowledgment. The bread and grease he'd eaten churned in his stomach and made him feel queasy. "I should be getting back." *The children,* he thought once more. *They will be waiting.* A new question climbed up inside him. "How long," he said. "How long did I sleep?"

Silas showed his brown teeth. "You slept like the dead, my friend. Three whole feverish days after I pulled you out."

The second morning of his absence came with clouds liquid as quicksilver moving in the sky. All the world seemed to be on the move with spring here and the snows a memory. The children kept busy, cutting wood for the stove, leading the stock down to the river. Morning came with another dire discovery: a rime of green fungus scummed the surface of the salt pork. The entire root cellar smelled of rotting meat and they had to take the barrel and leave it out on the prairie, a month's worth of food left to the wolves. At least the hens had finally laid some eggs, which Hazel managed to fry without burning. Their bellies full, they felt hopeful and Caleb stood out on the porch side-by-side with Asa. "I'll tell you," the younger one was saying. "When I am dead I want to be buried like those Indians we saw along the river. Put me in a tree somewheres."

Caleb looked off toward the horizon where movement began to flicker. "Birds will get your eyes," he said.

Asa shuddered. "It's better than being put into the ground still alive.

If I was in a tree, I wouldn't feel as bad. You know I don't like root cellars or other dark places. You could all come visit me and leave me plates of food, the way the man on the boat said the Dakota do for their dead. Strange, huh? To believe that the dead hunger?" Asa peered over at his brother, who only grunted in response. "The man on the boat said that when they mourn their relatives they all cut their hair and charcoal their faces. He said the women wail like banshees and go down to the river and cut the backs of their legs until the water is pink with blood."

"You're about the grimmest boy I ever knew," Caleb said. "I might jest be glad not to have someone around talking about such things all the time. Can't say it will matter where you end up. Dead is dead."

Asa's thin lips pinched together and he frowned. "Well, anyhow, put me in a tree. A big oak with lots of shade. I don't want to go down under the ground."

"Hush," said Caleb. A rushing noise in the south had drawn his attention. Far off in the south they saw a squall line stretch out along the horizon and move toward them. Asa stepped from the porch and knelt to fan his hand over the still grass, one eye on the approaching clouds. The noise, though distant, was like a shriek combined with the rumbling of some great steam engine. And yet, if it was clouds, how did it move without any wind? The squall line splintered and fanned out in shapes like arrows and behind the initial line they saw more and more coming, some dropping lower to the ground, some rising high to blot out the sun. Lines coalesced into denser, darker spirals and one such thick flying ribbon came over their grove and circled back around.

They saw individual shapes in the circling clouds, birds with violet-colored bellies and flashing wings, bright and liquid. The birds cried out to one another, the lines swirling like milk in a blue bowl. It was a sound they had never heard before, thousands upon thousands of birds compressed into a single area of sky and land, flying so close together they became one voice and myriad voices simultaneously, a blur of motion and sound. The children could distinguish individual cries, a sharp *kee-kee* repeated countless times over as the birds focused on the lone grove of trees in the endless span of grasslands.

"Pigeons," Asa said when the sound had grown so loud they could hardly hear one another. "Passenger pigeons." As the roiling cloud of birds swept over them they felt the rush of their passing. The birds filled up the grove in a militant wave, row on row, landing in the branches and sweeping through the woods in search of mast and fallen acorns on the sodden ground. *Whump-whump-whump*, the sound of a thousand wings beating backward to halt the speed of their flight, a concussive sound that drummed in the minds of the children. The noise of the flock trilled, cooed, and *kee-kee-kee*-ed in a cacophony of birdsong. They landed in masses on clotheslines and the sod barn and in the trees as far as the eyes could see.

The children retreated into the cabin where the dense log walls blocked out enough of the sound for them to think again. "I wish that Pa was here," Daniel said. Their pa would be able to make sense of this wondrous gathering, whether it was a good or ill omen. This prairie with its violent tempers, sending snow in April, wind and wolves, now plagues of birds with equal fervor.

"Listen," said Asa. "I read about this in one of Jakob's papers. It happens along the flyways in Kentucky. We can gather them. They're supposed to be good eating."

"And how?" said Caleb.

"They're dumber than sand. You don't need any more than a stick."

"I don't want to go outside," Daniel said. "I don't like this place."

"You cut out the breasts," said Asa. "Then you smoke them over a fire. Listen to the sound of them out there. We could sell in town what we don't eat."

Hazel cinched her bonnet tight and followed her oldest brothers out into the coursing wall of noise. They left the two youngest seated on the porch where they could still see them and headed toward the grove where the birds were thickest. Branches crashed down from the weight of the many birds, often crushing entire congregations of pigeons below. The ground was slippery with white dung and dead birds. Caleb had carried along the rifle and fired once into a dense mass of swirling birds above his head and the resulting rain of blood and feathers drenched him. It was more efficient for him to swing with the butt of the stock and he moved into the woods and did this now. Asa and Hazel also swung staves of wood at the birds on the lowest branches, and true to what Asa said, the birds were stupefied by their own masses and easy to kill. They harvested them like apples from a brimming orchard.

The sound of the birds' wings and cries filled up their minds until it seemed like they killed them in a trance. They were hypnotized by the relentless flapping of wings, children moving like ghosts in a world where they made no sound. As many as they killed, more fluttered down from the vast ranks around them.

There was not a single thought in Hazel's mind while she killed them. Later this would trouble her, the absence of thought while she struck and struck them from the branches. Is this what the soldier felt in battle, this hollowness of being and thought, all the mind residing in the strength of the arm that swings, the unconscious pleasure of striking true?

Gradually they became aware that they were not alone in the woodland of pigeons. Creatures close to the ground: foxes bright as autumn leaves, bandit-faced raccoons, and hungry weasels fed next to feral dogs upon the carnage. Crows pecked at the corpses and stole away with gray hunks of flesh. Each animal was blind in its own feeding frenzy; they were joined together by this feast, all the ancient enmities of the animal kingdom forgotten in their common hunger.

When the Indians arrived, piling the carcasses on canvas sheets and buffalo robes, they didn't pay the children any mind. There were women and children mostly, and a few old men with white braided hair and leathery skin. They seemed to come from the trees themselves, emerging from the brown trunks to join the harvest.

The children weren't in any danger, but once Caleb noticed how surrounded they were, he shepherded them from the forest. They came back a little later with the wagon, dragging it by hand down to the grove, and piled as many of the dead birds on it as they could. Caleb wasn't sure how to hitch the oxen and it took considerable effort for them to push the wagon back up the small slope to the cabin.

Once back inside the cabin they smelled and heard themselves again. Matthew and Daniel huddled in a corner and watched them shuck off coats and jackets white with excrement and blood spatters.

The passenger pigeons stayed that entire morning, devouring every bit of scattered grain from the earth, every last acorn from the grove, and then as if by some inner signal, they lifted in more billowing lines, rank on rank, and streaked farther north.

The silence they left was a ringing sound in the children's ears and bodies. They moved about the yard as though they were the stunned survivors of some great battle. From the porch they watched the Indians gather the remaining birds from the woodland wreckage before they faded back to their side of the grove. One of them, an old man with copper armbands, stepped forward to wave at the children before rejoining his people.

In the echoing hum she heard within her mind, Hazel felt a great hollow space. The small mound of birds they had gathered had been only a fraction of the flock, a few blades of grass from a vast meadow. Individually, the passenger pigeons were beautiful. They had long sweeping tails and graceful azure-colored breasts. Their eyes were red jewels, the females dusky and elegant in their fine silver-brown plumage. She smoothed the soft down of them and didn't know she was crying until Caleb touched her shoulder, his brow furrowed. "No reason to be sad," he said. "You saw how many there were."

She wiped her eyes with the sleeve of her dress and then looked north where the flock had gone. Was there any name for such things? She thought of the woods and all creation humbled by this force that came and went. *Grace. We have been joined by this blood, made communal.* As she thought this she felt her throat thicken with emotion, a welling up inside her. *Yes, grace,* she thought, looking off toward the sky that had swallowed up the birds, *and you will never see such things again, here on earth or in heaven.*

A Dutch oven. Steaming buckets of water to keep Matthew away from. The cat Freyja gnawing on coils of intestine. Lift, dunk, plop.

Hazel's hands ruddy with steam. The boys with their sharp knives. Feathers coming loose in hot water with a slight touch to reveal a pale-saliva like film beneath that did little to stir their appetites. Slicing out the breast. Fingers slick with birds' blood. Lift, dunk, slice, plop. The weary routine of it. The smell of the death moist in their lungs. And then Asa singing for them, a hymnal, "How Great Thou Art," in a grown-up's voice. Buckets steaming. Scalding feathers. Down stuck to blood stuck to fingers and hands. Feathers in their hair and teeth. Spitting them out. The smell of the meat sizzling in the Dutch oven with sliced potatoes. All afternoon: lift, dunk, slice, plop, sizzle. And Asa, *Then sings my soul. . . .*

They took a short break to feast, not bothering with silverware. The pink-eye potatoes swollen with juice. Grease running down their mouths. "Like wolves," Caleb laughed. "Look at us." Their teeth tore into the meat that tasted of brine and leaves and blood and smoke. Meat they swallowed part raw and felt it run hot down their throats and fill their empty bellies. They ate the entire contents of the Dutch-oven and then, refreshed, turned back to the remaining mound of birds. Freyja slumbered, fat with offal, her belly swollen and Matthew, a sheen of grease around his lips, slept beside her. For the others there was more work. Caleb made a wickerwork of branches. Asa and Daniel fetched wet wood from the grove that smoked, black and oily, in the fire. Hazel's wrists went numb from the weary monotony of plucking the birds and laying them on the branches. Fifty, and then a hundred. A bonfire of wet wood.

The sun looked immense on the horizon as it faded into the far grasslands. They were sore and tired and stained with this world. "There," said Asa. "Do you see the fires on the other side of the river? How far do you reckon they are?"

"No more than a half-mile," said Caleb.

"Do you think they are as weary as us, or as joyful? Do you think they are over there saying, 'I hope to God never to see another pigeon in my lifetime?'"

The children laughed. Then it was dark and the children's fire burned down to a husk of flame. The fires of the Indian encampment flickered, spectral, and the night was warm and clear. A few stars swam close to earth. "Pa will come back and find we've gone wild," Caleb said and then regretted it. The invocation of his absence altered how they looked at the fires, the dark. "Let's go inside," he said, and they went to their beds.

In the morning the children woke to the reek of the guts piled outside. They'd lost count of the breasts they'd plucked after a hundred. Even the cat shied from the spoiling mound of gizzard and beak and the children began the process of carrying it away. Wind from the south brought with it the smell of rain. For three days their father had been gone. They tried to put it out of their minds, except Caleb. The oldest boy watched the tallgrass waving in the wind.

The gold grass was heated by the morning sun. Lower, the growth was green and new and itched against Wanikiya's belly as he lay upon it watching Tatanyandowan. This time he had followed his brother across the river, ducking behind the trees, keeping the shotgun close to his chest. With each branch or leaf that crackled beneath his moccasins, he expected his brother to whirl and confront him, but in his rage Tatanyandowan had not looked back.

When he heard of the missing stone, Tatanyandowan had painted his face and chest black and then drizzled white powder along his eyes and mouth. He wound gold grass through the same headband with three feathers and then, taking only his knife, went across the river. The white family was busy carrying away the corpses of the pigeons, their faces crinkling up from the sour smell. They did not see the warrior watching them in the grass, just as Tatanyandowan did not see his brother coming up behind him. Only once did the oldest, the gold-haired boy, turn in their direction, his nostrils flaring as if he smelled them out there in the grass.

I know what I must do, Wanikiya thought. *It is what the old man wants. This will save my people from future violence. When the time comes I will murder my brother, just as he once tried to murder me.* He felt a flut-

tering sensation in his chest, a feeling that had been there since he sacrificed his owl. Nights when he lay there striving for sleep, he had the
sense of his mind drifting across the prairies on white wings. A new sensation, this wandering while he slept. And he had the feeling too that
he was not alone out there as his spirit drifted. There were larger things
moving in the darkness of the trees, somewhere an old man's voice
singing out a spell of protection.

Caleb saw the grass that was not grass, the dark head that ducked
down. He remembered the boy they had seen throttling the owl. *They
are here*, he realized. His hands were slick with pigeon guts, the smell
brimming in his nostrils. *Why did they come?* In some sense he knew that
whatever lay out there was related to his missing father. *Don't panic. Stay
calm. The rifle is back in the cabin. This time I won't let him get away.* "Sing
for us," he told Asa. "Sing like you did before."

"Not in the mood just now," Asa said glumly.

"Do it," Caleb said, his voice lowering.

Yesterday's hymnal sounded sarcastic in the face of the grim task
before them, and Asa's voice warbled along. They trudged back to the
cabin and then Caleb ducked inside, his brother following after him.
"What's happening?" Asa said.

Caleb took down the rifle from the mantle and poured in gunpowder. He used the ramrod to tamp it down and then packed in one of the
lead balls. "The Indians," he said. "They're out there watching us. I've
felt them all morning. They might have something to do with Pa
going missing. I don't intend to scare easy."

Wanikiya inched his way close in the grass, keeping low, slithering.
When he was only a few feet away, at last his brother rolled over and
took notice of him. Tatanyandowan had the knife close to his chest. His
expression was lost in all the paint he wore, but his mouth opened and
closed.

"Forgive me, brother," Wanikiya said as he stood and pulled back the
hammer. His fingers were slick along the trigger. Beads of sweat began

to come down into his eyes. He looked down the barrel at the presence of his brother, prone before him, his face a mixture of black drizzled with ghostly white paint. The bow shape of his ribcage. The tongue darting out to touch his lips. The chance for this would never come again. He must pull this trigger. As soon as Tatanyandowan rose and tried to flee, he would shoot him. Wanikiya had been unable to pull the trigger with his brother's back turned and now looking down the barrel into his eyes, he still couldn't do it.

Tatanyandowan did not seem surprised or frightened. He smiled and then spread out his arms, letting his knife fall away. "Go ahead," he said. "I am not afraid to die."

An explosion of gunpowder and though he had sworn not to do it, his eyes were shut. The smell of blood and powder all around him in the grass. Shouting from the *wasicun* children. Tatanyandowan held his chest, touched along his skin. His brother had gone down. He was alive. Tatanyandowan stood and looked off toward the cabin where even now one of the white boys was beginning to reload, dropping the ramrod in his haste, the other boy beside him shouting, hopping up and down. Tatanyandowan went over and peered at his brother fallen in the grass, his blood staining the ground all around him. Wanikiya kicked and struggled, holding his stomach, his eyes glassy with shock. Tatanyandowan knelt and touched his hand to his brother's forehead, a farewell, and then he fled into the grass.

He'd left smears of his blood in the tall gold grass, a stained tunnel of bent, glistening stalks where he had dragged himself. She could hear him, but couldn't yet see him, the boy in panic or terror as he dragged himself along trying to escape her brother. He groaned; his breath came in short gasps. Everywhere, the striped trail of blood and crushed golden stalks. Then the grass opened she saw the boy, his eyes blurred by his sweat. She saw he how held the rusty shotgun, positioned against a red stone, and how he fought to steady his aim. "Sh!" she said, not quite a word, not able yet to talk. *If you don't say something at this moment, you will die. He can't see you, doesn't know that you've come to try to help him.* Hazel began to speak in low Germanic tones, the way her father had spoken to her as a child. The words felt strange in the unused muscles of her throat. She kept her voice low and lulling, held up her hands to show that she meant no harm. *You speak,* a voice said inside her. *Though you promised after your mother died, now you are speaking and there is no taking the words back.* The boy let the gun drop and it clattered against the stone.

Her brothers crashed through the prairie grass behind her, still calling her name. Hazel held up a hand, "Stop," she said. "You've done enough."

Her voice was a clear alto. All these years of silence and suddenly she spoke.

Caleb was shaking. He'd really done it, pulled the trigger. And he felt no exhilaration, only regret. Ahead of him he saw his sister kneel. There was the boy and the rusty shotgun lying beside him. There was his dark-haired sister cradling the boy's head in her lap and the boy's blood staining her apron. The boy was still alive. His skin was the freckled color of a fawn, his black eyes like mirrors, glazed with pain. Caleb saw the stark jut of the boy's ribs, each one like a curving blade. The boy was much younger than he'd imagined. His sister was studying him with her clear green eyes. Again she spoke, and her voice in all of this was the strangest thing in his ears, "Help me carry him inside," she said.

BLOOD
PRAYER

THEY MADE A space for him beside the stove, cleared the floor of blankets and laid him down. In the shadows of the cabin the blood pooling below him looked black, a ceaseless trickle from his abdomen. "The lantern," Hazel said. "Bring it here." She undid his medicine belt, felt the boy shudder when she pressed a hand to his chest. Lines of goosepimples rippled along his arms. When they fluttered open, his eyes were dark lakes, all pupil. Hazel was kneeling in a warm pool of his blood. She saw that the bullet had passed through the lower right abdomen at a downward angle. She heard her voice, a tinny sound in her own ears, so long unused, as she gave commands, sent Asa to gather wood for the stove, set Caleb to tearing strips of cloth and helping her pick up the grunting weight of this boy so she could study the exit wound. And the blood continued in a ceaseless stream, each breath a shudder. Hazel smelled the boy's fear and her own that matched it.

I am the daughter of a healer, she thought. She closed her eyes and tried to remember Emma, but the voice she heard in her mind was not her mother's but that of the blood healer she and her father had visited one night on the river, the only one of them that ever touched Hazel. That night her father had left Hazel alone with the woman. He had been a long time gathering yarrow flowers.

She saw the reflection of herself in the boy's black pupils and this image, herself within the eyes of another, cast her mind back to the close-smelling room of the healer. She shut her eyes, remembering how the woman's tallow candles smelled of the animal they once were.

That night the woman had withdrawn her hand from Hazel's throat and studied the girl before her. "I will tell your pa what he came to hear," she said. "But it is useless to him." The woman's baby continued to suckle at her breast while she spoke. Hazel heard the river all around them, ever-rushing like a heartbeat. The woman's gray eyes, the color of stone, held Hazel transfixed. "He is only a man and what do men know of the blood hours between birth and death? They go through this life as warring children. But you, child, will know both in this lifetime. Hold out your hand." Hazel's hand had shaken as she stretched it out. When the healer touched her palm, the skin felt fevered. Her fingers were long and fine. "You must understand that there is no magic. Do you hear me?" The girl nodded, mesmerized by her touch. "There is only belief, something far more powerful. Even demons believe in the Son of Man. They know his name and fear it. The yarrow flowers and the Bible verse are only a ritual. Power comes from your touch, skin against skin. Power comes when your belief joins with theirs. If belief is powerful enough to build and destroy nations, then surely it might command the blood in its narrow travels from heart to wound." She withdrew her hand from Hazel's and when she stepped away Hazel's reflection faded from her eyes.

The skin along her hands prickled now with the memory of the woman's touch. She had wanted to ask how it was possible for her to do such a thing if she had no voice. She was only a child and didn't understand all of what woman meant. If you cannot pray aloud, how can others share what you hope? Before she could find a way to communicate the door had creaked open as her pa shouldered back into the room with useless yarrow in his fist.

The memory lived within her as she knelt by the boy and saw her own reflection go dim in his eyes. Hazel felt her breath burn in her throat. It was that simple after all. The thing her mother would have wanted Hazel to do more than anything. She only needed to continue speaking.

The boy's eyes blinked open and his lips curled over gleaming teeth while his hands probed the wounds below and tried to brush away the cloths Caleb was pressing there. The blood ran black through his fingers. Hazel saw the small, coin-shaped hole and the burned tissue that puckered the edges of the wound. With each breath the boy took, a new stream slicked out to join the widening pool beneath him. All her life she had only been a witness for the things that happened, never someone with the power to shape events.

Hazel shut her eyes, imagining that she was that healer with the pale elegant hands. When she opened them again, she was certain what she must do. The boy had curled onto his side below her. Her thin fingers slid perfectly into holes of the boy's body as though made for the wound. Into either side of him she slid one index finger and felt the warm jelly of his tissue and the quick pulse of his blood. The boy shuddered but did not cry out. In the six years since her mother, Emma, had died Hazel had not spoken a single word before this afternoon, but now she began to pray aloud, imagining the healer's husky voice and her words, imagining the healer's touch moving down through her and into this boy. She spoke the verse from Ezekiel that the woman had taught her: *And when I past thee, and saw thee polluted in thine own blood, I said unto thee when thou wast in thy blood, Live: Yea, I said unto thee when thou wast in thy blood, Live!* Over and over she said these words like the men in revival tents who prophesied in spirit languages not heard since the beginning of time. The words were old King James and nonsense to the boy, and yet she felt him respond below her as though his blood recognized this language. She kept her eyes sealed shut and prayed that prayer into the room. Her head felt filled with light like a song, a chant of becoming. Hazel felt Caleb press his hand over the top of her own, applying more pressure, his touch cool while the blood between her fingers was thick as heated jelly. She forgot about the room and the boys gathered around her and felt the words travel like smoke through her own blood and down into her fingertips, until she could no longer feel the blood spilling. How long she prayed, she didn't know, but when at last she eased her fingers out of the hole in his body, the flow had slackened and congealed. Caleb pressed fresh cloth around it.

The Dakota boy's eyes were shut, his jaw clenched tight even in unconsciousness, but in the frail light of the cabin his chest yet rose and fell. Hazel held up her own fingers in wonder. Both she and the boy had been transmuted by this moment. He would continue on some underworld journey and come back no longer a boy, the gray in his lock burnished to silver. And what had she become, a girl long used to silence, yet capable of such utterances that blood spoke unto blood?

A humid night and the snow a distant memory. A half moon swelled over the far prairies and touched the grasslands with silver light. Within the cabin, a radiant slat of light coming through the shutter touched the boy asleep on the floor. He lay there, utterly still, as though the shock of his injuries had caused his spirit to retreat so deep inside him that there was only the shell of his body before her.

She left his side only for a few minutes to walk down to the river and fetch fresh cool water in a bucket. By his side again she dipped muslin cloths into the water and ran them over his heated skin. The moon made tall shadows in the room around them and dusted his body with silver. Through the muslin she dripped droplets of water into his open mouth and then let the cloth settle on his broad forehead. Everyone slept but Hazel and Caleb, surrounded by the whispery breathing of their brothers in the dark.

"Will he live?" Caleb asked. She saw his eyelashes flutter; the warm night was lulling him into sleep.

She nodded.

"Do you think they'll come for him?" The gun lay across his lap.

"Yes. You should put that away. If they see we have been trying to help him, they might not hurt us. You only have one shot with that."

Caleb grumbled, but did as she asked. It was true that if the entire tribe decided to come after them, they stood no chance. Asa had been for going to the fort, but what would they tell the soldiers? After all, now that the moment was done, Caleb could no longer recall in what direction the boy had been aiming his gun. "Hazel?" he said. "Hazel, is it a miracle that he's still alive?"

"I don't know," she said.

"There was so much blood, so much in the tallgrass, on the cabin floor. But you stopped it, and now he's breathing just fine. And I don't know what happened. In your hand there was this warmth. You didn't speak in English only. And now he's not bleeding anymore. How?"

"I don't know."

"Such terror in his eyes. If he hadn't lived I would have gone on seeing them. Do you think God would send me to hell for a thing like that?" This time she said nothing and to fill the silence, Caleb added. "Make sure he keeps on breathing. Make sure he lives." He'd shot without being certain. And now their father was still gone, somewhere out on the prairies and Caleb had only deepened the danger of their situation. Their one chance, he thought, was if the girl, his odd sister, could heal the boy. Such thoughts circled and circled inside him until eventually he grew drowsy with them and fell into a troubled sleep.

Hazel kept watch, listening for sounds out in the dark. She was surprised by her longing to have this boy stay here. Each time she took away the cloth that covered his wound she marveled at the knob of ruddy-colored flesh already beginning to web over the injury and she felt a tingling along the tips of her fingers. She was bound to this boy in a way she didn't understand yet. When she'd seen him before, even from a distance, there had been something in the way he carried himself, a quiet intensity that spoke to her. Tonight she had taken possession of him; now he belonged to her in a way that surpassed any spell her father had written down in his book.

She ran her fingers along her own throat. Her brothers seemed wary of her now that she spoke. Hazel had doubts about this. She'd long learned to watch the world in silence; people so often trusted her and told her their secrets. Would that trust continue now that she could answer back? The words she used still seemed like coinage, each one to be spent carefully for moments like this.

But for the boy she would speak at length. She whispered things to him while he slept his healing sleep. She told him about her mother's gift for healing and how the consumption killed her in the middle of winter, of riding through the *hexenwald* with her father and the conjurefolk they met there, of the escaped slave and the grove of aspen trees that had failed to recognize the Son of Man, and her own family's flight out of Missouri where they lost home, hearth, and their stepmother. And she told him of her fears for her father, his long absence, her sense of him out there somewhere fighting to get back. Still the boy slept and even had he been awake he would not have understood the words and stories she was telling him. But he had understood the prayer from the King James. He must have in order for the healing to take place.

She stayed awake wondering at what had happened in the grass. Had the boy been hunting something? Why had he carried the shotgun with him onto the Senger land?

The boy spoke back to her in a quiet sigh that sound almost like a word. "You will be whole again," she whispered to him. "I know it." He had a bow-shaped mouth which contrasted with his angular face, the high cheekbones, the broad nose, the arch of his dark brow. She had dared to undo the braids he had woven into his hair along with strips of soft fur. She brushed out the knots until his hair settled in an unbroken black sheen that fell past his shoulders. If he awakened would he have memory of the things she had told him? Would he remember the touch of her fingers inside him? She had dared to touch his hair and the supple skin that lined his boyish, slightly concave chest where each rib was clearly delineated. They had taken off his moccasins and leggings and medicine belt, a beaded doeskin bag that contained nothing but feathery down and stones etched with lightning bolts.

He wore only his breechclout, soured and rusty with blood. She had drawn her fingers along his narrow waist and paused here, uncertain. But this was only a boy after all. She had bathed with her own brothers since she was little. They bathed youngest to oldest, each climbing in the steaming tin tub of water, which became steadily grittier and cooler, until their father, last of all, a great shaggy bear, would plunge into the murky water with a wild shout, douse himself with a measure of soap, and then leap back out shaking himself like some half-drowned animal.

She undid the breechclout, feeling how it peeled away like a second skin. The boy's breathing seemed to quicken and suddenly she was afraid that he was awake. She had not meant to look at him, only wanted to clean away the blood, but the way his breathing changed frightened her. Her hands shook while she cleaned him with muslin cloth. He was beautiful, his waist narrow, the hipbones curving. The sour smell of urine and blood mixed together and she crinkled her nose. *You must do this*, she thought. In her mind she pictured generations of women in cabins just like this, cleaning the wounded, preparing bodies for burial beneath the ground, stripping men of their soiled clothes, bracing themselves. How many of them had paused at this moment just like her? Seen the coiled shape of him, the vulnerability, this boy who was not as young as she had thought. The healer's voice spoke inside her again, asking, *what are the generations of men who we see before us in birth and in death?* Hazel cleaned him with the cool muslin cloth and then dressed him once more. He had not looked like her brothers, not exactly. She rinsed her hands of his blood and smell.

Just before dawn, when the light in the room took on a translucent gray sheen and the shadows withdrew to the far corners, Hazel slept. She lay on the oaken floor beside the boy, one of the muslin cloths still in her hands. And while she dreamed the boy's hands reached under the cloth and traced the new geography of his scar and wondered over the lack of blood. He had been awake for hours now, dizzy with the sound of her whispering in his ears. Though it had made no sense he knew she had been telling him her life story and that it had just as much joy and sorrow as his own. He didn't know why he pretended to sleep except to see what she would do next. And then she had undone the breechclout and he had frozen, feeling a quick hot spread of shame that she should see him like this, feeling the cool cloth against him. Not knowing what else to do he remained still, wondering what sort of people these *wasicun* were. The moment spread out as if she had paused in her cleaning to study him. He was tempted to open his eyes, afraid of what she would do next, but then she had finished and put his stained breechclout back in place.

This girl must be *wakan*, he thought, a medicine healer. Only someone with strong medicine could keep him from succumbing to the wound. What had happened? He had been poised to shoot and then felt a bullet rip through him. The blond boy, he remembered catching sight of him out of the corner of his eye. The boy who slept so near him, no longer looking fierce. Why they had gone through all the trouble to heal him?

He looked at the girl asleep beside him, lying with her head pillowed by her hands, her hair so dark in the half-light that it had a blue gleam. Her skin was as pale as birch bark. Yet he had felt her touch upon him and in that touch a hidden strength. Watching her gave him something to fear for besides his own life. Looking at her he found he was frightened for her. Would Tatanyandowan really have stabbed one of them? His brother had been enraged at the council, spoke strongly of Inkpaduta's leadership on the prairies. Would they really become another band of renegades and flee out past the wide river where there were still buffalo but also the Pawnee and the Crow and so many other tribes much stronger than their own?

On the broad grasslands he heard what at first sounded like the prairie chickens calling to one another. A moment later he realized it was the warriors imitating the bird's song as they crept closer in the grass. There were only children here. Would his people react with rage because of what happened to him? Wanikiya carefully sat up on his elbows and felt the wound strain beneath the cloth, a raw tearing in his brain. In his mind's eyes he saw it opening like a third eye, a spout of blood shooting out. His mind flared with pain, but he bit down on his tongue and kept himself from crying out. The blanket doorway was tacked into the floor, a thin tissue through which the first light had begun to seep. Before they could enter and possibly harm one of this family, Wanikiya had to make it outside. He tugged at the tacks that held the blanket to the floor, freed enough that he could crawl beneath. One last glance at the girl showed she was awake and watching him, her lips parting slightly. She said something to him in her own language and he shook his head, nodded out toward the prairie where the calls continued. *I must go*, he told her with his eyes. Holding to his wound, he crawled out the door.

Hazel couldn't get his blood out of the puncheon floorboards where stripes of it remained behind like a permanent shadow. The morning he had left she'd seen him squeeze underneath the blanket-door and then heard, faintly, other voices greeting him as they carried him back across the river. The children kept near the cabin all the next day, driving the oxen down to the flooding river, fetching water and wood. They ate their pink-eyed potatoes and smoked pigeon breasts and longed for salt and seasoning. Fear came inside them like the stains of the boy's blood, something they couldn't wash out.

When Caleb spotted his father moving down the road, leading two shaggy creatures behind him, at first they didn't believe him. "Come quick," he said, "It's Pa." He knew this even though Jakob was distant, a man moving toward the setting sun and his own cabin poised at the edge of the grasslands.

On the fourth day, Jakob returned to them, leading two milking goats he'd purchased on credit in town. They ran to greet him, the youngest boys clinging to his legs, the oldest taking hold of his shirt and arms, only the girl hanging back. "Hello, Father," she said. She looked no different than before, thirteen years old and dressed in an apron drizzled with frightening rust and yellow stains. He had been waiting patiently all these years for her voice to come back, not wanting to press her, knowing eventually she would speak, and now it had returned. He could see that they were all changed, even in their joy. "Don't go away again," said Daniel. "Promise us that you're never going to leave."

"I won't," Jakob told his son, chucking him under the chin. "I give you my word." He looked across at his oldest boy and then again to his daughter. Her voice had sounded just like he'd expected. She spoke as her mother Emma had spoken, a husky voice that was not a girl's. He looked across at her in this moment of joy and wondered why her green eyes had clouded over at his own words.

This was their first spring. May was the planting moon for the Indians, too, a lean time of waiting when they subsisted on fish from the rivers and maple sugar. Only a narrow strip of hardwoods and one mud-swollen river separated Jakob's family from Hanyokeyah's band. Uneasy after the death of their cow and the shooting of the Indian boy, Jakob replaced the tacked blanket doorway with a sturdier construction of adzed-oak slats he discovered in the root cellar. He even rigged a leather latch that could be pulled inside at a moment's notice. He hung bells around the goats and oxen's throats so the children could track their movements through the tallgrass. The half-stock plains rifle was kept primed and hanging above the mantel and every night on the stove he melted down lead for bullets which he then cooled and kept in a leather sack like a child's collection of marbles. They settled down and prepared for a war that never seemed to come. Five thousand Indians, Silas had said, but all of them divided into separate tribes and bands and families. All of them independent, unpredictable, and one of the smaller bands lived just across from his family.

While Jakob traded for supplies in Milford he had been warned that the Indians were "ravenous as wolves." In addition to the two goats, Jakob had purchased a bull plow to break the ground. In town, he'd heard rumors about Inkpaduta; there had been cattle mutilations on the other side of Palmer's Ferry. Twice in the last month the entire town had retreated into the mill after a horseman passed through warning that the Dakota were on the warpath. "Just imagine them crammed inside that building," Jakob told his children. "The women indecent in their caps and gowns, men in long johns with scythes and pitchforks for weapons; all of them straining to hear every hoofbeat or creak in the dark, and then the women screaming fit to bring down the ceiling! Of course morning came and their scalps were still intact, but they were no less angry."

Jakob laughed and stroked his dark beard. In the lamplight, he'd been telling them stories of his long journey, lying about the cow, and the pale, sickly man with his stolen god. The children only knew for sure that he'd been gone so long because he'd fallen through the river ice. He was trying to build a different story around his journey, a tale to take away their fears. He had made friends on his way back from Silas's when he stopped in a town not far from New Ulm. Dark had been failing and he'd been afraid to continue on, afraid of a return to blindness. He never wanted to be lost again and so he stayed at Traveler's Home, where he met the shopkeeper Gustave Driebel. Milford, as it was called then, was primarily inhabited by '48ers, Germans who had taken part in the failed revolution to bring Democratic reforms to the Old Country. Many of the Germans he had met had spent time in prison because of their fierce belief in reform. They abhorred the practice of slavery and bent a sympathetic ear to Jakob's stories of his troubles in Missouri. All of them, it seemed, were on the run from previous failures in their old lives. Jakob had lingered there in the town, thinking that one more night away would not make any difference. Perhaps the children resented him for this.

Jakob hit it off with the portly shopkeeper and livery owner who talked him into buying the goats. "I spoke with Herr Driebel who runs the general store. He said to me, '*Mein Gott!* I won't be running to the mill ever again. Let those red devils murder me in my bed. Better to die there than crammed like a herring in a salt barrel. Better to die in my own bed than with sawdust up my heinie." Jakob laughed, but saw the children avert their eyes, glancing down at the stains on the floor. *I must earn back their trust*, he thought. But even as he thought this, he kept things to himself. He didn't tell them about what else Herr Driebel had said after Jakob showed him the smudged map of his homesteading. He didn't tell them what had happened to the people who had lived here before.

Why did I not rush back? he thought. The boys had done well; he would have acted the same, he assured them. And it was good that the girl was talking once more. Wonderful what they had done with those pigeons. "You got along better without me here," he told them. Tonight though, the conversation was decidedly one-sided. Even the candies he had brought back, horehound and licorice, seemed to cheer them little. "I tell you," he was saying, "the newspapers here are of a poor quality. One even carried an article about a headless Indian seen in the woods. A headless Indian!" he said, shaking his head. "If only I had my press, I would give them real news." Again the curious flatness in the eyes watching him, the unspoken recognition that Jakob's press was part of the reason for their present predicament.

"But Pa," the girl said, speaking for all of them, her green eyes flashing, "your newspaper carried exactly those kinds of stories!"

The dominating emotion that the local Germans felt for the Indians on the other side of the river was fear laced with a heavy dose of disdain. The Dakota, who sent their children to perform begging dances and trespassed across lands with little understanding of property boundaries, were a lesser race by Old World reasoning. These Indians were "gypsies" not worthy of the rich farming soil they occupied, land in the possession of "beggars and drunken thieves." While a few did business and maintained relations with their red-skinned neighbors, many chased Indians off their land with pitchforks and axes. It was only a matter of time, they thought, before the governor opened up lands on the reservation in the name of settlement and progress. All of this Jakob had gathered in his conversations with the shopkeeper and others at the store. There was talk of a militia, the men arming themselves to better deal with the Indians, and Jakob went quiet when this was mentioned, his thoughts turning back to Missouri and his own experience with violence.

"You shouldn't be afraid," he told the children gathered around him. "This is our adventure. One day you will be glad to have these stories to tell to children of your own. You will be able to speak of a world that no longer exists. And they won't believe the things you have seen.

Why do you look at me like that? Smile, Daniel. There, that's more like it. I'm not going away again. This place is good. Here a man can be free. Here a man can speak his mind and there are no slaves. . . . Only . . . an adventure, I tell you. Smile all of you. Be grateful. Why are you cry-ing, Hazel? Stop that at once. Come back here. *Mein Gott!* What is wrong with all of you?"

A

CROSSING

J AKOB'S PLOW TURNED up soil as dark as molasses; a network of roots as thick as a woman's hair spread beneath the sod. When the family held the chunks of earth in their hands, moist as leavening dough and brimming with earthworms, they didn't know it would make them sick.

Jakob felt it first, an itch that spread through his hands and arms like the pox. No sores appeared on his winter-pale skin, but he couldn't stop scratching. It spread from him to all of them, an invisible rash that burrowed into their veins. Hazel tried everything: a lotion of mullein leaves, tea made from willow bark, but the itch continued to burn beneath their skin like prickles of white-hot flame. The joints in their hands swelled. They felt it down to their marrow. The youngest boys scratched themselves until they bled and Hazel had to bandage Matthew's hands with socks to keep him from clawing open old scabs and raw tissue beneath. It near drove them mad. They wanted to tear the very skin from their flesh, to strip themselves down to sinew and ligament. At nights they lay awake and tried not to think about the burning sensation. They rinsed their hands with whisky, whale oil, goat's milk, and lye. They rubbed tree bark on inflamed skin, leaves, green plum juice, and buffalo grass. "It came from the ground," Jakob said after their third sleepless night. "How do you fight sickness that comes from the prairie itself?"

The next morning they huddled around him, red-eyed and trembling. This was his chance to earn back their trust, prove his worth and strength as their father. "There isn't any doctor in Milford and it's a long ride to New Ulm."

The girl's voice startled him. His first wife's voice, smoky, assured of its knowledge. "They won't know anything, Pa. What do they know about such things in Germany? What do any of us know about this place?"

"We have to do something," Asa said. "Or I'll throw myself in the river to stop this itching."

"The Indians," Hazel said. "They'll know."

"Hazel, we can't," said Caleb. "What if they hurt of us because of . . . because the boy was shot?"

"It's not safe," Jakob agreed. "We don't know anything about them." The image of the cow lowing as the wolves tore her apart was imprinted on his memory.

Hazel went and plucked Matthew from the corner where he was hunched and trembling. The boy had red scratches running from his eyes. "Look," she said. "Look at him!"

They crossed at the lowest place that very evening, along a fallen cottonwood that bridged the rain-swollen river. Hazel's bridge, Asa named it. In the west the sun descended like a stone cast into the grassland seas and left a slow fire burning in the clouds overhead. A line of gashes marked the ground, the travois marks of Indians who had used this path for generations, traveling with their dogs and belongings. They followed the path to the threads of smoke from the camp's fires, a mere half mile. The children were quiet in their misery and listened to the sound of the wind coming through the darkening valley, a gentle hush as it touched the tips of the tallgrass waving around them, sighing against their clothing.

They came to the outskirts of the village where a collection of a dozen teepees were arrayed in a loose circle. Spotted ponies cropped grass along the sides of a winding creek while dark birds rode on their haunches and pecked insects from their hides. A group of boys spotted the family first. Though evening fell with a touch of chill in the wind, they wore nothing but breechclouts and carried toy-sized bows and arrows. The girl didn't see the boy she'd helped among them. There were six boys, and at the sight of the Sengers they scattered and raced ahead of the white family into the camp, raising the alarm in high-pitched voices.

"Keep walking," Jakob said to the children arranged behind him. "If there's trouble, run back home." Against his better instincts, he'd left the rifle there. His hands were too swollen to fit inside the trigger guard. Besides, there was this knowledge: each time the gun had been taken up in a moment of need it had been fired, almost as if the weapon had a will of its own to do harm. They carried one sack of potatoes to trade for medicine. In short, they were at this tribe's mercy. Jakob was not afraid for his own skin, but his children were another matter. He must protect them from harm; he could not fail them again.

Campfires burned in the dusk and iron pots shaped like large spiders squatted over the flames. Dakota women in loose dark-colored skirts and billowing calico blouses hunched over the fires while a few old men sat outside the teepees and smoked in the gathering dark. They stood as the family passed, a few with brows furrowed, but none of them looked violent. In the gaunt faces that watched the family, the girl saw an emptiness. It was as if these people had been stolen out of a land and time they understood and dropped down into this one, hungry and desperate. In that sense, she felt, they were kindred.

Her other senses sharpened as light faded. She smelled the strange odor of the meat in the pots, the sweet sage smell of *kinnikinnick* in the men's pipes. Lean, mongrel dogs barked and snarled and began to follow in the family's wake. The boys' shouting echoed around them. First the old men rose, still carrying their pipes, and then the women joined them, so that as they moved toward the camp's center they became a procession, dogs and old women and men, and the noise and shouting gathered strength. They were drawn especially by Hazel and some of the older women reached out and touched the girl's dark hair as she passed, saying *wah-kun* in low, reverent voices as they ran a hand across her hair or let a finger graze against her frayed dress, a cry the smaller boys picked up and repeated in a chant, *wahkun, wahkun*. The smell of so many Indians so close, like smoke and singed grass and human sweat, the circle tightening, was overwhelming. Daniel clung tightly to Hazel's skirts, his eyes rolling back in fear. It was impossible for them to go further: They were surrounded.

Jakob had his bandaged hands raised and was speaking, but the words were lost in all the noise. Then the crowd parted, and the old man Hazel had seen on the prairie and that day after the flight of the passenger pigeons came forward. He was a lean, tall old man with a string of crow's beaks for a necklace and copper bracelets encircling his arms. His chest was bare and there was an aura of quiet competence about him, as if he'd been expecting the family all along.

Jakob continued to hold up his bandaged hands as he made signs to indicate their need. The Indians closed around them in a curious circle, pointing and talking in their own language. One of the mongrels whined and growled before someone kicked it away. "Hold out your hands," Jakob said. "Let them see the marks."

Still the old man moved toward them without speaking. He came close to Jakob and pulled one of the upheld arms down and unwound the bandage. He said a word in Dakota when he saw the red streaks marking the skin. A younger woman had come to his side, her eyes lowered. The two of them conversed in Dakota and then she looked up at Jakob with her dark eyes, appraising him. "Itches?" she said in clear English.

"Most terribly," Jakob said.

"You come," she said and they followed her into a teepee, ducking under a skin doorway over which two deer hooves hung. It was dim within the interior, but roomier than it looked from the outside. The children seated themselves on buffalo robes and mats of woven grass, grateful to be sheltered from the crowds outside. They watched the smoke of the woman's fire rise up the cedar lodge poles into the indigo sky and tried to not to scratch themselves. The inner side of the teepee was painted with scenes of battles: painted men on horseback carrying feathered lances while the sky above them rained arrows. There were figures in the clouds, black riders gripping thunderbolts in their fists. Great lakes and turtle-shaped islands. Children coming down from the stars. The skin of the teepee moved in the wind and the figures shimmered in the firelight. It was the closest the children had been to a church in some time. "A tapestry," Hazel said. On the other side of her, a man hung from a tree, nails visible in his palms. In the next scene he was taken up into the clouds along a ray of light. The Indian woman saw her watching. "Tunkashila," she said to Hazel. Then she turned back to her work, taking the bag of potatoes they had brought and burying them one-by-one within the embers of her fire. After she did that she stood and dusted the ashes from her hands.

A girl entered the teepee and stood alongside her, her daughter apparently. They each wore a skirt of red broadcloth, tied around their waists, and beaded shirts. The girl had tin earrings that tinkled when she moved her head from side-to-side, and she had gray eyes. The older one touched her daughter's shoulder, "Winona," she said. Then she touched her own chest, "Blue Sky Woman," she said and then the two ducked out of the teepee and re-entered the swirl of noise outside. A moment later, the flap opened again and the old man came inside, now dressed in his finery, soft leggings of doeskin, a beaded war shirt with long fringes, his hair braided with mink-fur strips. He carried a pipe and seated himself across from Jakob. The children shifted uncomfortably, Matthew pawing at his bandages. This old man had glittering black eyes, a strong nose. He lit the long red stone pipe, held it up in four directions and to the earth and sky, and then passed it to Jakob. Not knowing what else to do Jakob did the same, coughing out the odd, sweet smoke. After a long moment of silence, the old man spoke. "I am Hanyokeyah," he said. "Flies in the Night in your tongue."

"You speak English too?"

"We live long time near the *wasicun*, many winters." He nodded toward the section of the teepee where the Christ figure had been painted. "I live with missionaries one winter. Away from my people. I am only this tall." The old man held his hand a few feet off the ground. "They give me new name, Elijah. I do not know what this name means, but they say is great white man."

"A prophet," said Jakob. "It is a good name." He sensed there was something else to the story, asked, "What happened?"

"Our men grow tired of the missionaries speaking against the dances, the face painting. The women . . . they miss children. They come, take boys back." Hazel noticed that Hanyokeyah could only speak English in the present, and sometimes it was hard to tell from his speech what happened in the past and what was happening in the now. There were long silences before the woman and her girl returned with a collection of roots. She took out a trader's knife and shaved the outer bark before setting the pale root to heat beside the fire.

With every ounce of their will they strained not to scratch, not to leap forward and seize this healing root. Blue Sky Woman took her time. She fetched out another of the pipes and smoked it over the root, chanting some prayer, clicking her tongue against her teeth. After this ceremony she turned back to the root. Once the tubers were warmed, she ground them into a poultice and rubbed it into their hands and then took the rest of the shavings outside to scatter in the wind.

"It's gone," said Asa. "My Lord, the itching stopped just like that."

The old man seemed to smile with his dark eyes, though his face did not alter its expression. When Jakob saw that the woman was busy digging the potatoes out of the fire, he resolved to stay longer. This Hanyokeyah might know who killed his cow. They might be able to reach some bargain that benefited both of them. That night they ate the potatoes Indian style, brushing off the embers and peeling back the flesh to eat the steaming, crumbling nuggets. Another woman carried in boiled water turtles the size of small melons which she cracked open on a sharp rock. The flesh tasted muddy and chewy, but the children were hungry and glad to share in it. From time to time, the skin of the teepee behind the children was lifted up and curious faces peered inside. When they were spotted, the curious howled and scurried away.

The teepee flap opened again and the boy whom Caleb had shot came inside and sat beside Hanyokeyah. He was dressed in a soiled shirt and kept his eyes low. Hanyokeyah patted his head and said nothing about what had happened. Only once did the boy glance in Hazel's direction, quickly looking away again. His cheeks were red in the fire-light and he looked to be healed and whole.

The whole time Jakob and Hanyokeyah talked. It appeared all the young warriors in the tribe had gone off on a raid against the Ojibwe in the north now that winter was over and they were done hunting the muskrats. The Ojibwe had staged a surprise attack several moons ear-lier that had killed two warriors from Little Six's tribe and now the young soldier's lodge of the tribe had joined other bands seeking revenge. The Dakota were at a big disadvantage in these battles, for while the Ojibwe could drift downriver in their birch bark canoes with little effort and then flee after setting ambushes, the Dakota used up all their energy just making the long journey north.

Jakob went on to tell about his cow's disappearance, the strange foot-prints he had seen alongside her, the abandoned village he encountered in the snow. He worded the story carefully, afraid the children would catch him in a lie.

The old man could only shrug, in turn describing for Jakob a stone where the people came to dance in the summers, that had disappeared. Jakob's face darkened and he shook his head, but he was thinking about Silas.

They talked for a while longer. "Is it true that the cities by the big waters have so many white men they build on top of one another, like ants? Wamiditanka see them and say there as many whites as blades of grass on the prairie and they build thunder wagons that roar on tracks across the land."

It was Jakob's turn to be silent, thinking of the ancient cities of the Old World and those new ones along the East Coast and of how the cholera and fevers spread through the masses of people, all of them longing for a better life, for land of their own. He was thinking of the Germans in Milford who couldn't wait to get more land on the reservation opened up for settlement.

"I like to see these great villages," the old man confided. "But I do not wish for all the white people to come here. I do not wish for my people to become like the whites and cut up the earth, their grandmother, and live like women."

It was getting late by then, the novelty of the visit already exhausted for the youngest boys who had curled up to sleep on the buffalo robes. They bid each other goodnight and took their leave.

A full moon rose in the east, a pale mirror of their world. Jakob tried to imagine a day when the earth had so many people they ran out of space and had to find a way to cross the great starry darkness to inhabit such a place. Windblown clouds darkened the face of the moon and hid the path before them. Then the clouds passed and the grass appeared once more, silvered with milky light.

Later they would learn that the affliction that had troubled them was called "prairie dig" and that settlers in that county often experienced it the first time they cut the sod. Then the girl's only thought was how beautiful it was to be out walking on such a night and not feel the terrible itching anymore. For the first time she began to hope they might find peace here. The lull of the moonlight that came and went, and her long tiredness took its toll. She fell asleep on her feet, though she kept moving. She had no memory of walking home, no memory of crossing back over the river at night to sleep in their cabin, as if a part of her dreaming self had never made the journey, but stayed there at the Indian camp beside the boy and the old man.

KINGDOM TOWNSHIP

1876

SUMMER
STORM

THEY CAME WITH the rain. Hadn't I foreseen them as I stood by the window and Hazel began her story of light and dark? I felt the way Jakob must have felt finding Ruth, the runaway, in his haymow, as though words had a summoning power. The more Aunt Hazel spoke, the more it seemed the past was quickening under the surface of the present. I thought of the old medicine man's tale: all those bodies trapped inside the stomach of Eya the Devourer, quaking to get out. Something was about to break through, something was reaching for me, and I both feared and longed for it. Hazel was just finishing her story now, saying, "A year before Jakob left for the War, Kate came back into our lives."

The rain swept over the ravaged countryside and turned the Waraju River into a torrent. The wind shrieked through thin spaces in our cabin's chinking. Here in the loft I felt that Aunt Hazel and I were closer to the storm; we only had to step through the high window into a landscape of cloud and lightning. Occasional spats of hail clattered on the shingles. We passed the long dark night as she told me her story. A candle on the nightstand cast flickering lights and shadows through the room. My hands shook.

"Came back?" I said, "How? She left you in Missouri. She wouldn't know where any of you were. And the War . . . you're moving too fast. What happened the rest of that summer? Did the boy tell the others you had healed him? The girl with the kerchief, the one in the field of dead blackbirds, was that my mother? And what about Tatanyandowan? Did he come for you again? Did he kill his brother for what he'd done?"

Hazel sat beside me on the bed. "It's late," she said. "Aren't you the least bit tired?"

I was about to open my mouth and answer when we heard a new sound in the storm, the shrill whinnying of horses and the cries of men shouting to be heard above the thunder. We looked at one another; a shadow passed over her face. I knew then she was thinking of Jakob, tarred and feathered on the table, and the sound of the riders outside as they rent his printing press to pieces. Who would be out riding on such a night? Our place was set back a ways from the road leading to Kingdom, so we didn't often see strangers. Downstairs we heard voices, the rasp of spurs on the porch, a low gravelly voice and my mother's nasal response. Hazel threw on a lavender shawl before leading the way down the loft ladder.

Two men stood just inside our doorway, their long oilskin slickers dripping with rain. One held his hat to his chest as he addressed my mother. He had a lean, boyish face and a spidery beard. He glanced once in our direction and I saw his eyes were a wintry gray. His mouth twitched and he gave just the faintest nod to acknowledge Hazel before turning back toward my mother. His partner was a larger man, his features obscured by a bushy goatee and long sideburns. Under the shadow of his hat his eyes scanned the room, passing over us with a dismissive glance.

The one thing in the room that held his attention hung above the mantel: my papa's half-stock plains rifle, his constant companion during the Devil's Lake campaigns. It was a .45 caliber flintlock that had been converted to percussion caps. My papa oiled that stock until it shone like an ebony skin. He never let me shoot it but sometimes, while my mother took her laudanum naps, I fetched it from its place and looked down the barrel and out the window. It was a heavy thing, cold and yet somehow alive against my shoulder. I imagined Indians charging my position before falling at the gun's roar. Here was a thing that could end a person in a glimmer. Here was knowledge my papa did not share with me, though I did not know why.

The other man felt my eyes on him and gave me a quick half smile. His coat steamed in the room's warmth. Behind him the door remained open; more men milled outside. "There's a hotel just down the road," I heard my mother saying. "It's not more than a mile." She had to raise her voice to be heard above the storm.

The younger one smiled and parted his coat. Two revolvers hung from a belt looped around his waist. He had long fine fingers and his gestures were smooth and practiced. One of his hands slid into a shirt pocket and plucked out an Indian head gold dollar that glistened in the pinkness of his palm. I didn't realize I was holding my breath until after the coin emerged like some magic trick. "It's worth more than what they would charge us in town," he told her. He had a slow, easy way of speaking, his voice drawling over the words. His pale gray eyes and gold coin had my mother entranced.

Hazel spoke up then, looking directly at the one holding the coin. "Let them keep riding, Cassie. Caleb will be back soon and he's not overfond of strangers." This was a lie. My papa would not be back for at least a month. Despite the lateness of the hour, I felt exhilarated, almost punch drunk. Aunt Hazel flickered as she moved between candlelight and shadow. She wore her hair in two dark braids that twisted down her back. I saw her as a woman in a deep purple shawl and a long sweeping dress: a sad, quiet woman. But with her braids like that I also saw the girl from the story, the daughter of a healer.

For the briefest moment the man's face hardened into a wolfish glare and his fist closed around the gold coin. But then he smiled again. "Only a mile, you say?"

My mother narrowed her eyes after the fist swallowed the coin back up. "If you was to stay here you'd have to sleep in the haymow," she said. "I wouldn't want you to go back out in the storm. You'd catch your death."

The fist opened again to reveal the gold. "I knew there was hospitality yet in the world," he said. "It's a cold rain this far north. I'm very certain death rides in just such weather."

My mother took the coin and slid it into an apron pocket. She swallowed before speaking again. "Are you lawmen?"

He laughed, showing gleaming white teeth. His hair was slicked back so cleanly it was difficult to believe he'd been out in a storm. "We're cattlemen," he said. "Up from Iowa. We're searching for stock to buy and bring back to our steading." He bowed slightly. "My name's Jordan Jackson. This here's my brother, Fred. But some call him 'Stonewall.'"

My mother appraised him. "Stonewall? Like that Secesh general who got killed?"

At the word "Secesh," Fred's faint smile went dead and he walked out the door to join the men on the porch.

Jordan frowned briefly, before taking out another coin, this one silver. "He didn't get his name for his sociability," he said, handing my mother the coin. "That's for any hot vittles you could sling in our direction. We got six more men outside."

"Vittles?" Mother said, taking the coin quickly. "All we have is beans and bread."

Jordan nodded. "Our needs are small." He, too, looked at the rifle hanging above the mantel. "Your husband, Caleb, was it? Was he in the War Between the States?"

Mother shook her head. "I wouldn't let him go fight over niggers," she said. She smiled, proud of herself. "He stayed on account of me. The only ones he ever killed were red devils, not really men at all." She walked over and pulled me by the arm. "Asa, you go help these men get their mounts stabled and brushed down." She nodded at Jordan. "This boy's good with horses."

Jordan muttered a brief "Appreciated," buttoned his slicker, and set his hat back on before rejoining the men on the porch. Out of the corner of my eye I saw my mother and aunt exchange hostile glares. But I was too excited to worry over them. I shrugged on a heavy wool coat over my nightshirt and followed Jordan into the storm. Most of the men had already headed toward the barn and I had to run through the wet muck of the yard to catch up with Jordan, the mud gumming up the sides of my legs. His collar was up and he had his hat pulled low. His horse was a big beautiful bay and her nostrils steamed in the dark. These men had been riding hard.

Inside the barn, the men were already tending to their own mounts. Swallows kept up a steady high chatter in the eaves. Our draft horse whinnied in greeting to the other horses. I had crossed the yard in my bare feet and the mud was chilly against my skin. I hugged my arms close to myself while I watched them, looking for an opportunity to help. All eight of the men I counted were dressed in identical oilskin slickers. Beneath the slickers they wore fine vests and wool pants and most had beards and mustaches and kept their hair clipped short. All of them were armed, revolvers mostly, like something out of one of my dime novels. Only strangers carried guns wherever they went. Or Pinkertons. Or outlaws. But they had been generous with my mother, so it was hard for me to imagine them doing evil. All ignored me, except for Jordan. "Fetch me a currycomb, boy," he said. "And show me where we get grain for our horses."

At the grain bin, one of our old barn cats, Esther, kept vigil for rats. The cat had been part of our land for as long my memory and was said to have descended from Freyja, the cat my family got right after they came here from Missouri. She was the only one who let me hold her, purring steadily. But tonight she limped away, her back leg dragging. After I filled a bag with grain, I helped Jordan brush down his bay. She had a glistening coat and had worked herself into a lather. We brushed in silence though I could hear the others calling coarse things to one another, glad to be out of the rain and the cold. The horse crunched happily on the grain and then seemed to go still and droop her heavy head; again I wondered why they had driven her so hard. I brushed the knots from her mane. It smelled of wet moldering hay in here, as if all the world were washing away in the storm. Jordan came around the other side and handed me a coin when I was done.

"No, sir," I told him. "You don't need to pay me."

Jordan closed a cold hand over mine. "Keep it," he said. He had the palest gray eyes I had ever seen, shining like clouds carrying snow. "I'm glad to hear your pa isn't a Yankee."

"We're from Missouri," I said.

"Is that a fact?" Jordan said. "Good country, Missouri."

The other men were done caring for the mounts and gathered around. I felt all their eyes on me and wanted to say something important. "My grandpapa was run out of Missouri on account of counter-rary views. They put tar and feathers on him."

Jordan smiled and other men guffawed. My cheeks and neck reddened. I didn't see anything funny in the matter. To stop their laughing I said, "My papa killed ten men." I had tried to make my voice sound low, but it rose and crackled.

It stopped their laughter, but Jordan still smiled. "Ten?" he said. "That's a powerful lot of killing. I guess he didn't like Indians."

"If you don't believe me you can go see the scalps hanging in his jail."

Jordan took off his hat and drew a hand across his brow. "Your papa's a lawman?" he asked.

I was about to launch into a story about the horse thieves he had tracked and captured five summers before, when Hazel spoke behind me. "Asa, come help me carry the food." She had her hands on her hips. "I hope you boys are hungry," she said, before leaving the barn.

I followed her back across the yard into the mud and rain again, grateful to be released from the men's scrutiny. When I came up to her, she whirled and clutched me by the arm. "Don't you talk to those men anymore," she said. Her grip tightened, but I yanked my arm free. I was tired of people telling me what to do, how to act.

"I'll do as I see fitting," I said. The thunder and downpour had moved on while I had been in the barn. Now it was just a chilly penetrating rain that went to my core.

Her voice was gentler when she spoke next. "Trust me," she said. "I need you to believe me."

I heard the imploring tone in her voice and didn't say anything more. My mother was waiting for us on the porch. She carried out two loaves of bread while Hazel and I used iron tongs to balance a heavy pot of steaming beans between us. We had to go slow over the slick mud and patchwork puddles and my teeth were chattering in my skull by the time we reached the barn. The men received their food gratefully and didn't ask any more questions.

We left them to eat and crossed the yard. Back inside the house, my mother went to her room without speaking any further about our strange visitors. I yawned, feeling at that moment how truly late it must be. Dawn was maybe four hours away. When I tried to make for the loft ladder, Hazel stopped me. "Just a minute," she said. "You have mud caked straight up to your knees."

"Leave it," I said, suddenly petulant. "I don't mind."

"Please," she said. "I don't want you to catch chill."

Though I longed for the warmth of my bed, I obeyed. I waited for her while she filled a washbasin with steaming water on the stove. She had a cloth slung over her shoulder and knelt before me and began to rub the mud from my skin in soothing circular motions. For some reason then I thought of Wanikiya, the wounded Indian, and how she had cleaned him after my papa shot him. There was nothing of such shame in what she did now. Hazel knelt on the hard floorboards so that I could see the top of her head. Even in the light of a sputtering candle I could count the gray hairs mixed in with her braids. The sour cakes of mud fell away from my skin. I knew she must have been every bit as tired as I was and I felt a sudden longing to protect her. My throat got knotted with emotion and I had to wipe my eyes. I hoped she wouldn't ever go away again.

"Sleepy?" she asked.

I nodded, not trusting myself to speak.

Back in the loft, we crawled beneath our separate blankets. I wanted to ask her about the men, about why she was afraid of me talking to them. I rolled over to speak, felt my head against the sweet coolness of the pillow. I was asleep before the question ever left my mouth.

It was noon by the time I woke up and Jordan Jackson and his men were long gone. They left no note and no trace that they had ever been in the barn.

With so much of our grain gone, for the next few days, I walked to a small wood-encircled lot the locusts had left alone to cut hay for our draft horse, Moses. Swinging the heavy scythe in the sun allowed me to forget about those men, how I had embarrassed myself before them. Haying in the heat took muscle and endurance. It made me feel strong. That rare summer storm having passed, puddles evaporated and a July sun turned the earth tawny and boneyard brittle once more. Nights I drifted off and dreamed of the men. Their horses were black with eyes of fire. We were pounding over a wet road at full speed and I had to cling to the man in front of me. Hail sliced into my skin. I shouted at them, *Where have you taken me? Why did you choose me?* The wind swallowed up my voice. I only knew in the dream that we were running away and that we'd done something terrible and I was just as guilty as they.

One night as we got ready for bed I got up the courage to ask Aunt Hazel about her story again. "My father," I said. "You don't talk about him much." When she didn't say anything, I rushed on. "I wish I could see *The Book of Wonders*," I told her. "I could teach myself the country spells inside there and then I wouldn't be ordinary anymore."

"You're far from ordinary," Hazel said, laughing. Then she paused. "Is it true that Caleb keeps scalps in his jail?"

I wondered how long she'd been listening while I talked to the men. I nodded. Though I had been bragging to those men about it, in truth the scalps made my skin prickle.

"Will you show me them?" She didn't look into my eyes. Her hand smoothed over the quilt on her bed. I wondered why she would want to see something so terrible. But I agreed to show her what she wanted to see.

She patted the bed and I sat down. "I could tell you about all of us as we were then, if I only had those journals my pa made us keep our first summer. He was worried about us turning wild, you see. But those journals and Pa's book were lost in the fire."

MILFORD PRAIRIE

1859

THE
PARABLE OF
THE SOWER

JAKOB   MAY 12, 1859

SPRING RAINS ARRIVE nearly every night and wash down through the holes in the shingles to pelt the children while they sleep. The rain pings in the copper pots we set on the floor and soaks into our blankets. Rain and sun and wind: I feel this country stripping away what we once were. In the sunlit mornings we stretch the blankets out on the prairie grass to dry.

Along with the iron plow I bought in Milford, I have carried back these blank journals and a book by a man named Thoreau for myself and the children. What we will become frightens me. As the boys cut wood for the worm fence they are building to keep the stock out of our fields, they catch glimpses of the Indian boys running in the woods. Leaf children, Hazel calls them. I can see the bitterness in Asa and Caleb's face as they hack at the forest and drag up heavy limbs. How they long for such freedom yet there is so much work to be done. I tell them those boys are like the grasshopper of Aesop's fable. They play now and will not be ready for winter. I tell them whatever I can to keep them working, even as I wonder. Who is wiser after all? We who plant more than our family needs for the sake of commerce? Or they who take what nature provides? Who has greater faith?

This is what we've lost: two mothers. One printing press. One milch cow. Clean summer clothing. Ordinary life, predictability. I am afraid the children have lost faith in me.

This is what we've gained: a daughter who speaks, two milking goats, four laying hens, four oxen, friends beyond the river.

Hazel neatly folded away her winter petticoats and the bonnet that should keep her skin like milk. She braids her hair Indian-style down either side. Her skin turns coppery in the sun. The boys strip off their shirts. Asa burns and freckles. Caleb's skin is a deep golden brown and there is golden hair on his mouth and chin and his eyebrows have darkened. Darkening. They are turning wild, my children, after only a season in this territory.

And so the journals. The days before I sent my children to Kate's school seem a long time ago. Then the only lessons they had were practiced in my printing shop. I taught all three of my own children to read, taught them what mathematics they needed to sell the papers in the streets. I can teach them all they need to know once again. We have the Grimm brother's fairy tales from which they can learn German. We have the book by Thoreau and a Bible.

I read them a section of Thoreau each night and ask them to respond in kind. Tonight I read to them this passage: "I see young men, my townsmen, whose misfortune it is to have inherited farms, houses, barns, cattle, and farming tools; for these are more easily acquired than got rid of. Better if they had been born in the open pasture and suckled by a wolf, that they might have seen with clearer eyes what field they were called to labor in. Who made them serfs of the soil? Why should they eat their sixty acres, when man is condemned to eat only his peck of dirt?"

Their response was immediate. "I don't like wolves," said Daniel.

"No, not me either," I told the boy.

"Pa, that man wouldn't build a worm fence. He wouldn't have any oxen to break up the fields." Caleb, never much for academics, had seized upon a key point. In fact, I regretted somewhat reading this Thoreau, since he would disapprove of much of our present enterprise. Lacking a suitable response, I bid Caleb to set down his thoughts in his journal, which he did with a sour expression marring his facial features.

Each night, when we come home weary from the fields, after the table is cleared and the dishes washed, we write. A lantern smokes with whale oil. The heat in the cabin is stifling. I pick passages out of the books we have left and order them to copy down the words, hoping the wisdom will sink in. Five goosequill pens dip dripping into the inkwell and stain the pages. Daniel often draws instead. Caleb yawns, writes slowly. Against the ocean of grass and the span of sky, we have these journals. If we stop writing and reading, stop planning for the winter, strip off our pasts the way we have stripped off clothing, what will we become then?

JAKOB   *MAY 19, 1859*

My furrows are the most crooked in the county. They wind through the rich black fields like twisting rivers. The prairies grasses have roots that reach deep beneath the earth. Despite the great force of the two oxen it is hitched to, my iron plow comes to a stop. I strike stones and skip to the side; the soil opens in a furrow like a dark skin, underneath this network of root and earthworm. I had to seat Daniel on the hatch to get the blade to bite deeper. His skin burned away in layers until I gave him one of my hats. Now he rides the plow, eating dust the oxen kick up, bumping over stones and thick roots until his teeth chatter in his skull.

It took an entire week just to break four acres. This is what we sowed: King Phillip corn, four kernels per hole in the ground. Durham wheat. Potatoes cut into eyes. Garden squash and pumpkins to keep out weeds. We sowed when the moon was waning, which is how *The Book of Wonders* promises we will get a good crop.

"So, we are told," I read them from *Walden*, "the New Hollander goes naked with impunity, while the European shivers in his clothes. Is it impossible to combine the hardiness of these savages with the intellectualness of the civilized man?"

Such questions ring through me. Our farm is at a point where shallow sandbars gleam now that the spring melt has receded. Every morning the Indians come down to the river to bathe. Women stoop to fill skin bags which they carry on their backs, the weight balanced by a buffalo strap around their foreheads.

Twice an old woman with a spotted white dog has herded a group of children across to dance for us. They stamped their feet slowly in the dirt, one boy singing in a high pretty tone. When they finished they waited with outstretched hands and we were made to understand that we should pay them for the entertainment. One night the men came back from their war party in the north. The flames of their bonfires leapt higher. All night the beating of the drums throbbed in the dark and made sleep difficult. My mind was filled with the images of fiends dancing around a fire.

For the most part, I do not fear them. There is one who wears cobalt face paint and three feathers in his hair. The right side of his face is deformed by some injury, the ear shredded. If I see him at the river or in our woods, he pauses to study me, making low sounds in his throat. I feel that I know him from some previous encounter and the thought chills me. When our eyes meet, I stand my ground. This act does not grow out of courage, however. I stand my ground, because my blood has gone cold and I can't move.

The old man with the copper armbands comes some nights with the young boy and a half-breed girl who is the daughter of the medicine woman that healed us, Blue Sky Woman. I sit and smoke with him out on the porch, a smudge fire burning nearby to keep off the mosquitoes. He has asked me to teach this boy and girl to read "the tracks in books" and so I assigned Hazel, thinking she would enjoy the task. In return the boy teaches us sign language and words in his own tongue. I have been across the river to see the gardens their women plant, simple circular gardens of beans and squash that are raised above the ground. They build slender scaffolds of lashed willows nearby where the boys keep watch for blackbirds. Such economy, I am certain, would meet Thoreau's approval, and yet I am told in town these people are dying out.

When I asked him if he was chief, the old man nodded. "I lead the people until one greater than me comes along. We are a small band. It is not how you think, the missionaries not understand. Sometimes the people listen to me. Sometimes not." I could only nod at the answer. Cryptic as it was, he seemed unwilling to say anything further. I surmised that his people are less like a kingdom, more like a large, bickering family presided over by an uncertain patriarch. Though he does not speak of the past I gather that the Wahpekutes were once greater than they are now.

The girl's mother, Blue Sky Woman, sometimes accompanies the old man too. She sewed me a set of moccasins which fit my feet like a second soft skin. Turtles were beaded into the upper lip and when I asked her what the animals meant, she lowered her eyes. I like the look of her, in truth. She is not so stoop-backed as some of the hags you see about their camp. She has a strong nose, black, shining eyes, and a sense of fierceness behind her quiet manners.

HAZEL   MAY 20, 1859

Papa told us to keep these journals so we wouldn't forget our learning. After dinner each night he reads us short passage from *Walden*, which I find I like very much. Afterwards he bids us to write. We are told to set down whatever comes into our brains. Tonight he read: "I say, beware of all enterprises that require new clothes, and not rather a new wearer of clothes. . . . Our moulting season, like that of the fowls, must be a crisis in our lives. The loon retires to solitary ponds to spend it. Thus also the snake casts its slough, and the caterpillar its wormy coat, by an internal industry and expansion; for clothes are but our outmost cuticle and mortal coil."

I am positive Kate would shriek if she could see me now. I tend the goats, named Pifpaf and Clever Elsie by Daniel, and milking takes talent. I have to stand over the top of them and pinion their bony ribs between my legs while I reach down from behind, my face pressed close to the flickering tail, and squeeze the udders. Any other method and the goats shoot forward and overturn the bucket. I am sure there is a better way no one has taught me. Each goat can fill a bucket by itself. By the time I am done I reek of goat hair and souring milk and the excrement-laced mud I step in while holding onto the beasts. The goats have lively, intelligent eyes. Pifpaf stalks after Daniel in the yard waiting for an opportune moment to skewer the wary boy with her horns. Once Papa took after her with a board she gave up that particular pastime, but sometimes she lifts her head while munching the grass and you can see a glint in her eyes, a wicked squinting, while she plots against her blond enemy. Pifpaf will also get into the wild onions if I don't watch her, and turn her milk into sour vinegar.

Papa is not very good about his own journal. Raw sores opened up in his hands from clinging to the plow all day. I soaked his hands in liniment and bound them in gauze. I was afraid to pray out loud over them. I was afraid the prayer wouldn't work. Each day he goes out and reopens the wounds in his hands. All at once he looks old to me. There is gray hair in his temples, crow's feet around his eyes. I don't remember seeing those before.

Each night I sit between Winona and Wanikiya while Papa smokes out on the porch with Hanyokeyah. For an hour each night we work on the alphabet and I show them words. The boy has such serious eyes. The lantern catches the russet color of his skin, the lock of silver in his hair. Thoreau says we are like birds in our season of crisis, shedding feathers to grow into something else. For this boy I would gladly shed my apron and grow new clothing that would capture his attention. Is that so terrible? When he teaches me the sign language, sometimes he touches my hand and my fingers tingle along the places where our skin is joined. It seems a long time since that night he lay bleeding on our floor. *Boy run fast*, I can say in sign. *Why not here?*

So far, their education goes slowly due to the exasperating presence of my brothers. I taught them the 23rd Psalm. Caleb teaches them dirty words in English in case "their honor is insulted." I taught them both the Lord's Prayer. Caleb taught them a boast that begins with the words: "You yellow-bellied, lily-livered, clod-pated, son of Jehosophat . . ." Asa loves to play on his fiddle and sing for Winona. A captive audience. She has learned some of the words and sings along with him.

Afterwards, when they have recrossed the river, Asa will go on about the thinness of her shirt, how the girl is not even aware of what she reveals when she leans over and her blouse falls open. "A pretty sight," he says, "for a prairie nigger." I hate such talk and told him so, but he only sneered and said I was jealous because I didn't have any.

The next day I let Pifpaf into the onions. After milking her and letting the milk sit a good long while in the sun, I gave Asa the first taste of it when he came in thirsty from the fields. He drank down the entire mug full in that greedy way of his. Oh, how green his gills turned when he realized the milk was sour; he rushed outside and vomited in the grass. He was down on his knees, gripping the bluestem by the roots. I stood over him. "Those sounds are prettier than the things you said last night," I said when he was done with his misery.

DANIEL   *JUNE 4, 1859*

A boy has many enemies. Pa gave me and Matthew copper pots to bang to chase blackbirds out of the corn and wheat. Matthew is no fun. I tried to show him how to clap the pots together and yell like a injun. He just stands there. I had to do all the work by my lonesome. I ran. I howled and made noise to scare them out of the fields. But there were birds and more birds. They went over and landed by Matthew and ate the wheat right next to him. I told him we wouldn't get any bread on account of the birds ate it all. But he just smiled and let out some drool.

Pifpaf did something funny. I showed her the pan and said I would knock her to Missouri if she hooked me with her horns, but she wasn't interested. Her and Clever Elsie went into the tallgrass where I couldn't see them. I was nervous because that is where the wolves are, but Hazel told me to watch them good, so I followed. Pifpaf was making grunting noises like something was hurting her. Something big was coming out of her rear end. A big green blob. It looked like the biggest poop ever. It was quivering. She kept on moaning and bleating like she was gonna die. There was blood too. Then it come to me that it was stuck inside her, that she wasn't making a poop but having babies. I did not know what to do. The noises she was making hurt my ears. I thought the wolves were going to hear her and come for us. Nobody else was around. So I went up to her and put my hands into her opening. It was squishy and it did not smell just like poop. But I could also feel something moving so I pulled on it. Pifpaf bleated and made gnashing sounds with her teeth. Then it all come it out with a sucking sound and I fell over and the whole mess come down on top of me. Next I knew it was squirming and there was not one but two of them and Pifpaf was licking off the blood. They were all wet from being inside her. They could hardly walk. She lay down with them. But I was afraid that wolves would come so I tried to make her get up. Then I took her babies and she came after me in the grass making angry sounds. But I made it to the cabin. Now me and Pifpaf are friends. Everybody agrees that I am a hero but I don't feel no different.

CALEB   *JUNE 15, 1859*

There is both terror and beauty here. Papa reads to us from the book and sometimes my mind can't wrap all the way around the passage and sometimes it makes a load of sense. "It would be well, perhaps, if we were to spend more of our days and nights without any obstruction between us and the celestial bodies, if the poet did not speak so much from under a roof, or the saint dwell there so long. Birds do not sing in caves, nor do doves cherish their innocence in dovecots." What I thought when Papa read this was: mosquitoes. They must not have skeeters at Walden Pond like they do here. I too would like to sleep out under the stars but only so long as a good smudge fire burned near to keep off the bugs.

Hans Gormann came onto our land to cross the river. I could tell right off that Papa didn't like him. Hans was wearing a slouch hat and had lean, spindly arms and small eyes. He had a swaybacked mule that was pulling a dray cart filled with puppies and a barrel of what he called "spirit medicine" for the Indians.

There were two blonde girls following behind wearing come-kiss-me bonnets and lemon-colored linsey-woolsey dresses. The material had been washed so many times you could see their pale white chemises and skin beneath. They each had dark blue eyes, dark as lake water, and were fetching to look at. It was strange to be around white folks again after a month seeing just Indians. All at once I felt embarrassed not to be wearing any shirt and the oldest girl looked at me with a kind of scorn, but I didn't see any reason for her to be uppity since her Papa had sunk so low as to sell moonshine to Indians.

I recognized them from the first day in the country. These were the ones who'd poisoned the blackbirds and what a load of good that did; we have more birds now than ever . . . as if they've come for revenge. The man introduced himself and his daughters, Cassie, the oldest, and Sallie. Cassie did a curtsy and the little girl mimicked her, but the hem of her dress was so frayed with grow-stripes the gesture looked pathetic. I used my deep voice to say my own name and I could see they were impressed and all at once I wished to have a shirt on so I could impress them more. That man Thoreau says we are to beware of enterprises that require new clothes, but just between you and me I think he is a jackass.

Hans had yellow skin like a pear. He offered to sell Papa some of the puppies which he said were well-bred and when Pa said no he offered to sell him some of the liquor. Pa told him he didn't think it was right to sell moonshine to Indians because in town he had heard it made them crazy. Hans sighed. "You're a stubborn man," he said. "I been told me about the wolves getting your cow and I come here with good intentions to help your family."

Papa swallowed and his face turned red. "My cow drowned," he insisted. I noticed his lower lip quivered when he said it and then I looked over at my sister Hazel who sees things straight and we both realized that Papa had told us lies that night.

Then Hans lifted out one of the mewling creatures from the cart and held it by the hackles. They were pretty dogs with brindled fur and long ears and snouts. "Drowned or not," he said. "It's a shame all these puppies are going to end up in the red man's stew pots when you might use 'em for protection." The puppy loosed a high whiny bark to let the man know it didn't like being held in such a way.

Daniel went into a frenzy. "You mean they eat them? Pa we can't allow them to get ate up." He tugged on Pa's pant legs and Pa's face went from red to a darker shade of purple and then back to white again. No, he didn't like this man at all.

"What breed are they?" he asked.

Hans set the puppy back in the cart. "Half wolf, half Newfoundland. They won't stay scrawny for long."

"So be it," Papa said. "I'll buy two of them." Then Daniel stepped forward and plucked out one that kept getting stepped on by its littermates and another that nipped his fingers. He said he was going to teach them to keep the blackbirds out of the corn, but only Hans laughed at that. They were done doing business and I could tell Papa was waiting for the man to leave but Hans only shifted his feet in the dirt and nodded over to his girls. "You wouldn't mind if they stayed here, would you? They could help out around the property."

"Why?" Papa said.

"They don't like Indians. Terrified, in fact. I let them to see a scalp dance one time. And well, it frightened them."

"I reckon," Papa said, though I could tell he was still perturbed. And with that, Hans drove his mule across the river shallows, the cart of doomed puppies mewling and whining for their mates, as they squirmed to avoid the jug of spirit medicine that rolled in the cart along with them. Papa looked over at us and told us to get back to work laying fence.

The girls stayed behind with Hazel to help her with the wash, but it didn't seem that Hazel liked them much. Women are particular. They get their feathers all in a huff for no reason, so pretty soon I noticed the girls weren't helping Hazel but just sitting on the porch, with that older one watching me. So I made sure to carry extra-heavy limbs and heft them over my head like they were mere twigs. Cassie came over and said, "My you're strong," while I was laying fence. I could only grunt in response because that was clearly God's truth. "I feel safer here with you," she continued.

Then Asa came beside us dragging a skinny log through the tallgrass. He grunted as he lifted the branch up onto the fence and then sagged beside me trying to catch his breath. "It's mighty hot out," he said. Both girls nodded. I was afraid he was going to make them uneasy by starting to talk about how he didn't want to be buried beneath the ground or Indian torture practices or some of the other gruesome things he likes to speculate on. Cassie twisted the hem of her dress in her hands and you could see that she had firm, pretty legs. She told us about her pa and how he liked to dress up and play Indian sometimes and how he could be gone for weeks. She wanted to know if our pa was part of the militia in town to protect the white people. "Protect," Asa said. "From who?"

"Why, Indians," she said. "They steal and trespass and . . ." She lowered her voice and leaned closer to us. "They kill livestock to frighten people away."

Asa ignored that last part, and said, "But you just said your Pa dresses up like them."

"Only to keep an eye on them," Cassie insisted. "To keep us safe."

I wanted to hear more from her perspective, but Asa tugged at my arm and we went down to finish our afternoon's work.

Evening came and the girls were still here with no sign of their father. "I suppose it's too dark for you to walk back, what with your place being a whole half mile away," Hazel said. I still am not used to the sound of her voice. She's only been talking again for a month and I am not sure I like it. Her tongue is a getting an edge to it, too smart for her own good. But the girls only nodded and ate some of our supper.

They were still here later when old man Hanyokeyah came with Winona and Wanikiya for their evening lessons.

Right away, Cassie got upset when she saw that Hazel was giving them book learning and I realized they must have argued about Indians earlier in the day. Still, I was willing to listen to her when Cassie drew me aside and said that the boy had a look about him that she didn't care for. I was starting to like her less and less, the more she talked. Asa was also nearby, peering at her with his squinty pale eyes. "I see," he said. "You don't know how to read, do you?" I don't know how he came to that conclusion, but that did it. She flew into a rage and said that we were the most ignorant folks that had ever moved into this country, aside from the Indians. She took her sister by the arm and stormed off the porch past the old man and my Papa and across the prairie to her home. I went over and sat down next to Daniel and played with his puppies, lifting them up by the scruff until their eyes rolled back in their heads and Daniel got angry. "What a hussy," Asa said and I nodded, though in truth there was a part of me that was sorry to see her go.

ASA   JUNE 30, 1859

I am tired of all of them. Tired of Caleb bossing me around during chores. Tired of sleeping on a mattress tick stuffed with marsh grass and waking in the blue-gray of dawn. This is not the life for me, not what my mother wanted. She always told me that my fiddle was for hicks and that I would cast it aside and learn finer things—the viola, or pianoforte. And then she had to go and marry this printer and look where that has brought us. Mother. She is alive out there and there is no one who cares but me. The rest of them are happy to grub in the dirt. Every day that passes I am less and less able to tell us from *them*. Now that there is not as much work in the fields we have more time to spend with *them* and Caleb has made up stupid games to play in the woods along the river. It bothers me that no one grieves for my mother's absence. How can people be so quick to forget? She wouldn't have left Matthew and me on purpose. I am going to run away and then what will Jakob think when he opens this stupid journal he bought me and beholds my thoughts? Then it will be me who is laughing.

Always that old man is here with that boy and the half-breed girl with her great big eyes like a cow. I can see her watching during Hazel's boring lessons, waiting to see if I will take down the fiddle or sing. She butchers the words when she sings along. Her little laugh rings through the room. And that way she has of putting her hands over her mouth and lowering her eyes. But I have seen the blush that spreads along her throat and chest when she knows I am watching. And she always wears that same shirt, white doeskin sewn with conch shells. When she sits beside me the fringes of the doeskin brush against me. She leans forward and I can see the swinging curve of her breasts, the dark, cherry-colored nipples pressed up against the white cloth. It makes my own blood surge and boil and I forget what I was thinking or singing the moment before.

Mother said the slaves were like that, breeding like animals in the fields. So what if her skin is not as dark; she is the same as all of *them*. Mother said to be careful around the slave girls because they could lure you away from a life that is pure and right with God. She said that is what happened to Josiah. He sold his soul for African ebony and then turned away from his own wife to go down into the quarters after dark. I was not sure what she meant until we came here. Oh, but I know now. Winona with the pretty cow eyes. I know what this girl is up to and I will not fall for her tricks.

CALEB   *JULY 1, 1859*

I didn't mean to, but there was so much blood, I lost control of my senses. The half-wolf puppies got into the chicken pen while we were eating breakfast. In a few minutes the two puppies tore the henhouse to shreds, blood and feathers everywhere. All the hens that provide us with breakfast eggs were dead. I think I blacked out I was so angry.

Those puppies with their lean snouts drenched in blood. I just started swinging, pounding them into the wet mud with my fists. They were yowling, cringing. It felt good to hit them like that, my knuckles cracking against their skulls. I picked one up by a leg and twisted it around and threw it through air.

He shouldn't have tried to stop me; it wouldn't have happened then. But they were his and he was fond of them. Turnip and Tadpole, he'd named them. Like I said, I couldn't see, there was this dark curtain before my eyes. When Daniel grabbed hold of my leg, begging and crying, I swung for him too. But the noise he made was different and he lay there afterwards for a long time among the chicken carcasses. Then everybody was all around me, pulling me away and Hazel was inside the pen rocking Daniel back and forth. When she helped him to his feet, I almost cried with relief I was so glad to see I didn't hurt him too bad. But Daniel ran behind her, hiding in her skirts, and she was red-faced and using words I hadn't ever imagined she'd use before.

The old man came here again that night and I stayed out on the porch because my brothers and sisters inside were all still afraid of me. I don't know how, but it was like the old man knew what happened with the puppies and the chickens and me. He told Papa a story about a witch that put a spell on this place after the last white people wouldn't let her come across anymore to visit the burying ground. He said that the woman is dead now, but that her spell and her spirit are still hovering around us. Papa asked how to take it away and the old man promised to do a dance.

The next night he came back with his body drenched in black paint. He was naked except for a breechclout and there were scarlet streaks along his chest and face like some great creature had scraped him bloody with claws. It frightened Daniel considerable. He made a fire of cedar brush and danced around it. The sounds he made were even more frightening than the paint. The surviving puppies whined and pressed their snouts close against the porch and put their paws over their ears. I thought it was working but then Asa started laughing. Asa looks like a fox with his red hair, and even his laugh, a yipping bark, sounds like a fox. Papa glared at him and told him to hush so the old man could finish but once Asa started he couldn't stop. Eventually even the old man noticed and must have thought we were treating him with disrespect. He stamped out the fire with his bare feet and took the children back across the river and was gone.

I believe in the curse, especially now that we are stuck with it. This land made us sick the first time we touched it. This land killed our cow and made our Papa blind and almost killed him too. And yet it sent passenger pigeons after our pork went bad. It sent us to the old man to get healed when we were sick. I hope we come to know this place well before it hurts us too badly.

Eventually, Daniel allowed me to come close. He showed me the bruise my fist made on his chest. I apologized and swore I would do anything in my power to make up for it. I even knelt down on the ground in front of him, but that seemed to bother him too. When I looked up there were tears in his eyes. "Caleb," he said. "If something bad was to happen, you wouldn't let it hurt me, would you?"

I saw he wasn't afraid of me anymore and felt relieved. "I swear by everything I know to be true."

"You ain't supposed to swear."

"Well, I promise then."

"Good," he said, and then went off without telling me what it was that made him afraid.

The old man came back after a few days. And to my surprise, Cassie and her sister Sallie have also begun to visit again, arriving in the nights at the same time as the Indians. Cassie with the dark blue eyes. Cassie who touched the gold letters of Kate's family Bible and said, "I would like to know what is inside this book. I don't know any of the stories. I haven't ever been to school." Cassie with her dark blue eyes who brought a tarnished silver cross and gave it to Hazel, and insisted she take it, saying: "A trade. If you can teach Indians, you can teach me and Sallie to read. But I am not a beggar and this is all I have to give."

HAZEL   *JULY 8, 1859*

Wakan. There are many meanings for this word. Holiness, sacred, won-der. Wanikiya says that the prayer I taught him is wakan. He touches the four points of the cross Cassie gave me and says this same word. He touches my hand, the fingers that once touched his wound. Then he looks up past the cabin ceiling and says *Wakan Tanka,* which I take to mean their name for God. Less than two months have passed and we know nothing for certain of one another. He and Winona know our curses and boasts thanks to my brothers. They know our names for what is holy. How strange it is than when two races first meet they trade in both the sacred and the profane.

We do commerce in the words for food as well. Winona's mother, Blue Sky Woman, speaks the best English of the lot. She taught me how to find strawberries among the tall bluestem grasses and pointed out the new growth of plum bushes that border the river. This is what I have learned: Blackberry juice cures a sour stomach. Mullein leaves are best for wiping. Boiled willow bark soothes aching teeth and heads. Sumac branches can be woven into a garden fence to keep out rabbits. Sap from milkweed takes the sting out of poison ivy. Songs in Dakota keep the blackbirds out of the corn. Blue Sky Woman worked a salve of comfrey into my Papa's bleeding hands. He shut his eyes while she did this, his lips falling open as he loosed a long breath of relief.

Papa and Blue Sky Woman. Caleb and Cassie. Asa and Winona. Me. Wanikiya. We wake each morning to the sound of the prairie chickens, the roosters drumming the ground and calling to their mates with throaty, vibrating songs that resound even within the cabin. In the hot humid nights our corn swells and ripens as thoughts and feelings swell inside of us. There are fevers in this land, a miasma that clouds our rea-soning. The air is already sultry when we wake in the morning, think-ing we are not ourselves, thinking what once was not permissible is now possible. We wake thinking of the other.

My mother, Emma, was a child bride. One of the possessions Kate threw away after she married my pa was a daguerreotype taken just after

Emma ran away with my father to Missouri. Emma was only fourteen. In the picture she tilted her chin, like she was looking back at the camera with challenge, her eyes narrowing. Papa, six years older than her, boyish without his beard, looked the more innocent, his eyes blank and uncertain. I miss that picture, but I know this: I am my mother's child. I am thirteen but if you could take a daguerrotype of me wearing my fraying summer muslin dress, I swear I would look back at the camera with just such an expression of challenge.

I am a child but I am not a child. There are secrets I keep from the men, secrets that have do with blood. I was not afraid when I felt the quickening cramps and found the spots on my chemise. This stain that did not wash out no matter how much I scrubbed, as if to say there is no going back; what you were you cannot be again. The healer with the pale, elegant hands had told me as much. It is one of the ways a woman learns to speak with blood. So much depends on me now. Winona and Wanikiya have begun to arrive earlier in the afternoon and I am teaching Cassie and Sallie as well. Our cabin has become a regular schoolhouse. If there is a breeze we sit outside on the porch and work with the slate boards and reading materials.

There were fireflies in June and in July cicadas churring in the hot tallgrass. Thoreau writes, "I was suddenly sensible of such sweet and beneficent society in Nature, in the very pattering of the drops, and in every sound and sight around my house, an infinite and unaccountable friendliness all at once like an atmosphere sustaining me, as made the fancied advantages of human neighborhood insignificant, and I have never thought of them since."

And if I could write back I would tell him first of Daniel marching out on onto the prairie in the mornings, his barrel-shaped dogs bounding ahead of him through the tallgrass. I would tell Thoreau of the speckled prairie chicken eggs the boy and his puppies find in the nests and bring home and how sweetly they fry in our pan. And I would tell him of how one of the dogs limps, its back leg useless, for their are darker things that move in these woods and sky that do not love human company and darker things still that move in human hearts. I would tell him the Dakota have names for this darkness, that there are tree-dwellers with webbed feet like raccoons who lead children into the woods to be lost. That Unktahe the water monster waits in the rivers and ponds and is jealous when the proper sacrifices are not made. That in the clouds there are thunder beings who ride through the lightning on dark steeds and great shrieking birds who make the thunder. Yes, I would tell him, there is a beneficent society in nature, but loving it can also kill you.

CALEB   *JULY 12, 1859*

I didn't realize when we first played the game how popular it would become. It started as a lark really, I just wanted to play-act the massacres the winter before down in Ioway. Inkpaduta and the Soldiers. Wanikiya brought over some of his cousins, Hissing Turtle and a slant-eyed boy called Otter. The game works like this. All the girls, red or white, play settlers and sit in the long grass, their skirts cushioned beneath them. They pass time weaving shuck dolls from goldenrod stems and doing girl things while the Indians sneak through the bluestem coming for them.

How real it felt that first time! The girls squinted in the harsh afternoon glare, Cassie and Sallie blind in their bonnets. When the Indians rose from their hiding places and wailed battle cries, I felt a tightening in my throat. What they sing is a death song, the words simple and soft. *I am here*, they sing as they come through the tallgrass, *I am here*.

Each Indian carries a loop made from basswood to represent his tomahawk. If he touches the girl with any part of it, she has to fall down as if dead and spend the rest of the game napping in the swishing tallgrass. If he touches the girl with his hands, then she becomes a prisoner and is taken back into the shadowy groves down by the river to await her fate. Here in the gullies, where streams trickle down steep slopes, the girl remains with her captor while the soldiers come searching. The Dakota boys have eaglebone whistles and the high shrill sounds echo through the woods to confuse the searchers.

We play in all weather. Rain drips through leaves. Clouds of gnats spiral in the shafts of light that penetrate the canopy of the deep oak woods. The soldiers come searching carrying sticks and clods of clay. The clay can be hurled from the stick with grim, inaccurate force. Many times we end up hitting the girls alongside their captors. If the soldier misses, the Dakota can spring forth and tap his enemy with the basswood loop. We play until everyone is dead or captured.

The first time there were only a few of us and Sallie got so frightened she started screaming like they were really coming to kill her and she peed in her pantalets. But she got over it. Now more and more Indians are coming to play this game, so many of them I don't know all the names. Some of them smear their faces with white chalk and join up with the soldiers. I've noticed the Indians like playing whites best, while the whites like being Indian. Sometimes my brothers and I put some of the dusky red mud on our faces and play Indians. It doesn't matter who is who. Most of these Indians don't even know English and I have to say all things considered they play the game pretty fairly. If I am an Indian I always try to capture Cassie and kill off my sister before Wanikiya can get to her.

I even dream about the game at nights, but there is a question that has begun to trouble me. Had those children in Ioway ever played such games? Did they know the ones who were coming to kill them?

JAKOB   *JULY 13, 1859*

Thoreau says we should not fear if our castles are in the air. "There is where they should be," he writes. "Now put foundations under them." I have made a lifetime of building just such fantastic structures. Today, as I scanned the pretty acre of wheat, shimmering in the sundown, I wondered at my own foundations. Against circumstance, the children prosper and the crops that have survived incursions of ravenous geese, ducks, and blackbirds, glistened healthy and green in the last light. As I set these words down, I can still smell the kinnikinnick in Hanyokeyah's pipe, a sweet, peppery herb. I have not seen the blue-faced Indian with the damaged ear for some time now and when I asked Hanyokeyah about him, he told me that the soldier's lodge of the tribe was preparing to leave along with Little Crow and leaders of other bands to hunt for Inkpaduta. He said he would have to join them.

"But he is from your tribe, am I right?" I asked. "And the army is sending your people to hunt their own down? The army is making brother fight brother?"

"They withhold the moneys and food and the children go hungry," the old man said. "For what one does, all are held guilty."

I agreed that such thinking wasn't right and asked if he had known Inkpaduta and if he was always such a monster as the newspapers make him out to be. Dark was coming on and the whippoorwills had begun to sing in the lower marshlands. A shadow passed over the old man's face as he turned away and breathed out a tendril of smoke. Within the cabin we could hear the chittering voices of the children. When he spoke the old man did not answer my question directly. "The army no be afraid of Inkpaduta."

"Oh, but they are," I said. "It's all anyone can talk about. They want to ferret him out before other young bucks get the same idea."

He was quiet for some time before adding, "The army make more Inkpadutas."

"What do you mean? You mean like Blue-face?"

"Him, others."

I stood up and began to pace along the porch. "Have you heard anything in your camp? Do you know of some plan? We are friends, right? *Ho Coda* as you say in your tongue. 'Yes, friend.'"

"*Ho Coda,*" he said. "I hear many things. I dream many things. I dream of your daughter. She stand beneath a tree and all around her there is black. The leaves are orange and black and come to life. They fly around her, so many, dark as birds."

I was quiet again, thinking on this. It was a strange vision, but I had learned not to make fun of this proud old medicine man. We talked further and I told him the parable of the sower and how Jesus speaks of an enemy who sows weeds among the wheat. I told him how the farmer stays his workers' hands, because if they try and root out the weeds, they will destroy the good crop as well. "That is what I think of the army's campaign," I said.

"Ho," the old man said. "But why does this Jesus let the enemy be in the grass?"

"I don't know if he lets this enemy enter," I said. "It seems like the enemy has been there all along."

Blue Sky Woman came to lead her daughter back across the river. She glanced once in my direction and I said, "Winona grows tall," and watched as a flush of pride spread along her cheeks, visible even in the dark. A fine-looking woman.

"She marry," Blue Sky Woman said.

"Your daughter?" I said. "Who?"

"His name is Lean . . . Elk. She promise to him."

"And you?" I said. "Are you promised?"

Asa had come out on the porch and seemed to frown at this question and conversation. I watched her walk into the gloaming and down the bank to the river, Asa forgotten by my side. I kept thinking how with each passing day even the nearest town seems so distant, how what I long for is not the white society but for things to be as they are now. Then I looked over and saw Asa watching me through half-lidded eyes. I tried to think of something to say to him, something cheering, something fatherly, but nothing came, and if I had expressed some sentiment, it would have been false.

ASA   JULY 15, 1859

Jakob did not come home last night after going to visit with Blue Sky Woman. He has fallen under their spells. He has forgotten my mother and does not hold true to his eternal vows. There is not one of them who understands. As we prepared for bed I told Caleb, "Dirty, to be taking up with Indians."

"You should get your own mind clean," he said. "You don't know why he isn't back."

"So he can tell us more lies? You're too lovelorn to see straight. You just want to sleep and think of Cassie lifting up her dress back in the woods."

Caleb's face darkened. I waited for him to strike me, steeled myself so that I would not flinch when the blow came from that stupid ox, but he only swallowed, saying, "Keep your dirty thoughts to yourself," and walked off.

It's not inside me, like he thinks. That night as I struggled with sleep, I turned over in the dark. And I was thinking of Jakob in the teepee with its dream figures etched into walls made of skin. The cloth rose and fell with each passing wind and the figures danced in the firelight. "Dirty," Caleb says. He does not know adults, even though he is older. His imagination is too dim to reckon what is happening in that room. I saw how Jakob watched her walk away, his eyes following the curve of her hips. No, they are not talking in that teepee made of hides. I began to sink into dream and it was not Jakob that was there but myself, not Blue Sky Woman but Winona, and she was sleeping under a trader's blanket, her cheeks plum-colored, her pretty lashes flickering. I shook the image away. No. I won't let Jakob dishonor my mother in this fashion. I will bring this to an end in my own fashion.

DANIEL *JULY 18, 1859*

I am the best Indian when we play Caleb's game even if I cannot run fast. But I do not like to bother with girls. Girls slow a boy down. I can run faster and hide better without them. Caleb says I miss the point. But if I was a real Indian I would not take a white girl because they talk too much. Nobody can find me because I have a secret place with my dogs within the hollow of an old cottonwood tree. My dogs do not like the eaglebone whistles. They are good hiders too but the whistles make them perk up their long ears and whine like they are afraid of birds which I know they are not. Caleb says if I was a real Indian I would be kicked out of the tribe because I miss the point and do not like killing or girls. But if I was a real Indian I would kick him out of the tribe because he is mean to dogs and has hair growing in funny places.

One time I followed Asa. But I will not follow him again after what he did. When I am a soldier I am good at finding the other hiders because nobody knows about my secret place and my dogs can smell and hear far. I like to sneak up so that the Indians do not know that I am there and my dogs will lay down when I tell them to. One time Asa was an Indian. But he is a terrible Indian on account of his hair is red as a crabapple and he is no good at hiding. I was not surprised that he captured Winona because he is always staring at her. They are both terrible Indians even if she is halfway a real one because they were giggling as they went to hide. I was not sure who captured who since she was leading him by the hand. They were giggling so much they did not know that me and my dogs were on their trail.

She took him to a spot where the grove opens to a grassy meadow. Right away I saw that it was a poor hiding spot. But they did not seem to care for following the rules. They just stood there right out in the clear sunlight and all of a sudden got real quiet so that I had to make my dogs lie down. They were not giggling anymore but looking at each other in a way that I did not like. Winona brushed back her hair and called him Tatanyandowan.

Who? he said. Asa tugged on his ear to show if she meant the same one we called by that name. He frowned when she laughed at him. Yes, she said, it mean one who is singing good. Then he did not seem to mind so bad to have the name of an Indian who is ugly.

They were quiet and Winona showed him an empty place in the grass. Wakan, she said. But there is nothing there, he said. She did a little dance around the place and said some words in Dakota. I don't understand, he said. Why are you showing me this? She was not laughing anymore and her eyes were very serious. Far away I heard the eagle-bone whistles that signaled the battle had begun and I was afraid my dogs would whine. But they did not.

God, she said. Here. She touched the empty place. Then she touched the place above her heart. Here, she said. Asa seemed to get very angry about this. No, he said. There is nobody here but us. Winona cast down her eyes and then she looked over to the spot where I was hiding but she did not see me and while she was looking away Asa stepped close and put his arms around her. She looked surprised. Then he put his mouth over hers and they both sank into the grass. She started to push him away and he got mad and pushed her down. I had seen enough so I went away because my dogs did not like this business either and were getting upset. I went quickly but I could still hear them. No, no, no, she was saying. Sh! He was saying, Quiet! Tatanyandowan, I am Tatanyandowan and you are my squaw. She was making hurt sounds and I heard the ripping of cloth. I thought of Pifpaf and the time I was a hero and thought about going back. But I was afraid. Even though I had my dogs I did not want to see. When the game was over Asa came back by himself.

As soon as I can I will tell Caleb about this because this is not part of the rules and Asa is wrecking the game.

HAZEL   *JULY 19, 1859*

Even as we played the game there was a sense that this was the last time. That Winona was not here troubled me, but Wanikiya only shrugged. It was a humid day, sluggish with low clouds and that heavy feeling that the air takes on just before a storm breaks. When the game began, the boys running low through the tallgrasses, I knew it was done with. All the terror we had once felt was gone. There was only the mystery of whether we would die or be taken captive. The battles had begun to degenerate into massive wrestling matches, all the rules forgotten. Still, on that humid morning it was Wanikiya who came to find me and led me past a wide calm pool in the river, around a bend, to place I had never seen before.

We were far from the others now. Embankments of rose-colored stone rose up on either side of brown river. Teal-winged cliff swallows hunted insects from the cliffs and skimmed over the surface of the water, their wings brushing past us. A great burr oak towered over the bank, and beneath its roots a small waterfall trickled down and blackened the stone with moss. Wanikiya cupped his hands to the waterfall and then brought the water to my mouth. It was cooler and sweeter than the brown murk from the river. Far away we heard the tinny shrills of the eaglebone whistles.

It began to rain. We saw it dimple the surface of the water and heard it in the leaves of the woods on either side. Then a clap of thunder resounded and in the wake of the sound the rain increased and began to drum on the water and pelt us where we stood in the middle of the river with the sluggish current coiling around our legs, my dress wet to my knees.

"Come," Wanikiya said. He showed me a place where a natural stone staircase climbed the rose-colored cliffs. The swallows chittered around us as we began to climb, Wanikiya pushing me from below so that I would not lose my balance. The cliffs were only twenty feet tall, but the stones were slick with moss and I scraped the skin of my fingers pulling myself up. We climbed to small shelf that overlooked where the river fell away into another valley and we could see a great forest and the slow-moving dark clouds that coasted over the treetops like a flotilla of black ships. The clouds ate away what blue remained in the sky, a boiling orange light at their edges, and then turned the air vivid with lightning. The wind picked up. For a moment it felt wild and wonderful to be standing on the edge of that shelf while the clouds whisked around us. It seemed we were inside the clouds themselves and I thought about the thunder beings Winona said lived inside them and how sometimes they kidnapped humans and took them away with them into their cloud citadels. I thought, wouldn't it be wonderful to be taken out of this world and into another where the ways we were different no longer mattered?

My dress was soaked through to the skin. I tasted the rain in my mouth, but then it began to hail, little ice beads that battered us on the promontory. I could no longer hear the sounds of the distant eaglebone whistles and figured the other children had long ago fled for shelter. The clouds above us began to swirl and rotate and the hail increased. Solid pellets of ice dropped from the dark clouds and pitted the trees and water around us. The swallows had retreated inside their caves. A large hailstone struck me in the shoulder with enough force to bring me to my knees.

When I struggled up I saw an ugly, yellow-green light pulsing in the belly of the clouds and the wind ripped leaves and branches from the bur oaks and whirled debris around us. "Here," Wanikiya said. "Hide." He showed me a small cave the falling water had hollowed into the side of the cliff. We had to squeeze ourselves into the tight enclosure to be sheltered from the hail. The small dwelling place was shot through with sticky spiderwebs. Brittle animal bones or branches crackled beneath us in the musty darkness. We could only fit by lying close together. I smelled the dry leavings of some creature that had taken shelter here just like us. It should have been terrible. A storm raged outside and thunder echoed through the enclosure. A sharp rock jutted in my back. My shoulder ached where the hail had struck me.

But I was lying next to a boy in the wet darkness. I could feel his heartbeat close against my own. He smelled of sweetgrass and cedar smoke and the rain. He was so close that his mouth pressed against my cheek, the heat of his breath washing over me. The only place for me to put my hands was around his slender waist. Outside the hail drummed into the stone promontory as the storm tore through the valley. I lay against him, wet and filled with wonder, an unfamiliar lightness in my belly. The boy's body, his ribs and elbows sharp, felt rigid and coiled so close, as if I had him paralyzed. Lower I pressed against him and felt his response and remembered the shape of him the night I undid his breechclout. His breathing quickened.

I prayed then that this storm wouldn't stop. That we could stay here like this, laying together in the warm dark, his mouth against my skin. That we would disappear and people would say the thunder spirits had carried us away, one white girl, one red boy, riding black steeds among lightning and villages made of cloud. Did Indians kiss? The boys said not.

I kissed him on the mouth and felt a quick pulse of light and warmth spread through my blood. And he kissed me back. Later, when I returned to this memory it seemed that the kiss lasted only five or ten seconds. In that short time I felt my spirit lift straight out of my skin and fly among those cloud citadels on a black mare with a mane of thunder, the blood hot in my face and ears. I drew back from the pulse of power, from that opening I felt coursing all through me. Outside the hail dissipated and the storm cities sailed into the distance and the sharp stone pressing against me woke me back to reality.

Wanikiya pushed away from me and I wondered if I had gone too far and frightened him somehow. I squirmed my way outside onto the dripping promontory, a throbbing pain in my back from the stone, and looked on the surging river and the dripping forest.

The forest was emptied of sound as we walked. Small willow trees had been uprooted by the wind's passage. A shredding of green leaves carpeted the forest floor and floated in the sweeping brown river. Pellets of hail lay thick as snow on the ground. It was so silent in the storm's wake that it seemed we were the last boy and girl on earth.

Then we came back to our place. As the wind abated ranks of mosquitoes hummed through the moist, gray air. A moment later we saw the ruined fields below, and I heard Papa calling my name. I started to run to him and turned back to look at Wanikiya. He stayed where he was. "Come on," I called, but he only shook his head and nodded in the direction of his own people. I shrugged and ran to my father.

The hailstorm had shredded every living crop in the furrows, the pretty green rows of wheat and corn. Only the potatoes and pumpkins survived. All the rest of that day Papa wandered the rows searching for one undamaged line of crop. Inside the cabin our blankets were soaked and the storm had ripped shingles from the roof and exposed gaps of sky. I swept water out of the cabin while the boys helped Papa out in the fields.

I didn't think things could get any worse, but I was wrong. While I write this Papa sits before the open maw of the stove and he is tearing out Thoreau's book page by page and feeding it to the fire.

ASA   *JULY 23, 1859*

I knew she would be here and so, after the hailstorm, I came searching. The river was up and the crazy-looking medicine man has been across to tell us they fear Winona was swept away in the rising water because none could find her. Only I could guess where she was hiding and so I went alone to the meadow.

On the edge of the meadow a towering tree she calls Waraju grows. Waraju just means cottonwood, as I understand it. She showed me the perfect five-sided star that lives within that hoary branch. It was she who told me that the tree was sacred.

An emptiness here. A group of crows flew cawing away as I came to the meadow. In the wake of the storm there was no wind. All I heard in the distance was the faint surge of the river and on the other side the sounds of her people calling her name as they walked the shore. At first I thought she wasn't here, but then I heard the creaking sound in the cottonwood as I came around to the meadow.

She had hanged herself with that buffalo strap that they use to carry water up from the river. Her face was dark with blood and her tongue was pinched between her teeth. She was looking down; I won't forget that. Those cow-brown eyes bulged in their sockets and stared right at me so that at first I called her name thinking she was still alive. From the cottonwood tree white fluff drifted down around us like snow. I kept hearing her kin across the river calling her name. At first I was sorry, but the longer I looked at her ripe body twisting by the leather strap, the more angry I became. My stomach turned over and there was hot bile in my throat. Why? I might have even said this aloud. Why would you do this to me? I heard water splashing in the distance and turned to move away. Suddenly I didn't want to be found here with the body; they might blame me for it. But I was thinking too slowly and the crunch of footsteps crossing through the tallgrass came behind me. Wanikiya. He saw me first and then the body behind me and his mouth fell open and a high plaintive cry came from his throat. He dropped to his knees. I was running before I knew it, running back through the woods.

There is only a thin stretch of trees along this riverbank. I kept reminding myself that soon I would be out of this oppressive gloom. Creaking sounds followed me as though every tree held a hanging body. The crows cawed and cawed. I ran and the branches reached out to scrape through my shirt and claw my face. I tripped, got turned around. Overhead, a dense canopy of leaves. Mosquitoes swarmed to feed on the blood that dripped from my skin. And this was strangest of all: There was a little man in the forest, no bigger than a raccoon. He was laughing and his mouth was filled with razor teeth. I knew then that this was the tree-dweller, the one Winona taught me leads children into the woods until they are lost forever. Tatanyandowan's spirit brother. I knelt and prayed that God would take the vision away but there was only the tree-dweller's laughter and rank clouds of bloodsuckers. Thick bile rose hot in my throat until I couldn't breathe right and I knelt in the woods and purged myself and when I was done the little man was gone. I knew that it was not God's doing but my own willpower and I walked out of those woods resolved. Let someone find this journal and see me for what I am, a strong boy who is not a fool. A boy innocent of blood who will put all of these stupid people behind him.

JAKOB   *AUGUST 1, 1859*

A disaster in every way. I can't imagine what drove that girl to hang herself, but her death changed things for good. For whatever reason the Indians blame us, as if she might have acquired the idea from the words and letters that Hazel was teaching her. She was going to be married according to Dakota custom. I do not blame the girl, but in town I have heard it is fairly common among her people because the women have no other way out of sick relationships. When we let our passions rule our thoughts, such tragedies are bound to result.

Every night Blue Sky Woman comes down to the river to cut the backs of her legs and the soft inner flesh of her arms. Her hair is sheared down to ragged edges. Like a widow, I am told, she has given away all of her belongings. Our cabin stands secure behind this knoll, a few hundred feet from the river. But all night long we go on hearing her, the pathetic, trilling wails, a sound ripped from her throat. Her wailing haunts our dreams.

The first time we heard it Daniel ran away into the tallgrass and Caleb had to go find him. The boy was red-eyed from crying, snot running from his nostrils, and he had shorn his blond hair in Indian fashion using a buck knife. What an ugly thing is true grief, the way it crumples a human being. Asa was enraged when he saw what Daniel had done, but when he tried to say something Caleb took him by the hair and threw him against the wall. I jumped in to stop the fight, but not before Caleb whispered something angry into Asa's ears that made Asa clench his teeth and go pale.

JAKOB   AUGUST 15, 1859

Asa ran away, but didn't get far. Farmers from the militia brought the boy back a week later after they found him hiding within the hayloft of a settler's barn. The boy caused a rash of reported thefts—eggs gone, corn missing from cribs—to spread through the county and be blamed on the Indians. One farmer told me it's lucky the boy had such fire-red hair, otherwise he might have been taken for Indian and shot. I have never seen the boy look so ravaged. The skin along his cheeks was sunken, cadaverous. His eyes seemed to be receding into his skull. He looked as if he had been pursued the whole time he was away. After the militia rode away, he hung his head. "Does she still wail every night?" he wanted to know when I asked if he was going to run away again.

"No," I told him. "I haven't seen Blue Sky Woman in three days." I tried to put my hand on his shoulder and he shrank from me.

"Will you send Hazel out to talk to me?" he asked.

"Hazel? Why?" The other children had not come out to greet him. The boy averted his eyes and said nothing. His clothes were filled with needles of straw, his pale cheeks speckled with acne.

The girl came out and they went away into the ruined wheatfield where an ancient cedar tree stands. I watched them the whole time. Asa was telling her something, but the wind stole his words. Once she glanced in my direction as if she wanted to run away. Then he knelt on the ground before her and grabbed hold of one of her legs. His chest and back heaved up and down while he wept. She looked frozen there, unable to move, but at last she knelt beside him, touched his hair, and held him.

This is how Asa came back into our family. All the hostility is gone from his eyes. He keeps quiet and seems resigned, waiting for something to happen.

JAKOB   *AUGUST 30, 1859*

We began early one morning when the Shepherd's Star watched from an ash-colored sky. I'd seen catfish and large-mouthed bass all summer long and hunted them without success. In this dry spell the river thinned down and exposed wide sandbars on either bank. With the boys beside me, I used the oxen to drag heavy logs across the shallowest crossing place, where the river formed a natural bow. For each log we dug post holes on either side and buried them firmly in the ground. Into the slow-moving current we embedded a series of wood stakes in the sandy soil. Between the stakes the boys packed in stones and clumps of wet clay. The river began to back up behind this dam and deepen to fill a broad pool. We could not fully contain the river even in its wasted condition and water ebbed and dribbled around the posts.

The leaf dwellers, as I still think of them, came down to observe at different stages of our project. The warriors, Blue Face among them, watched from a high bank. I have not seen a friendly face in a long time. I tried to cross once before and speak with the old man, but the younger ones turned me away from the camp with their cries of "Puck-a-chee," which means *go away*. A few even menaced me with the glinting tips of their bone knives.

Using the oxen we were able to complete the project in a day. The boys still didn't know what was happening until I showed them the final feat of engineering, just as I'd seen it down in the country around Saline Springs. I had been weaving a network of willows into a large basket. I took away one of the stones to allow the water to flood through and then bound the basket into a kind of sluiceway. Most of the fish came through this opening. Basket after basket were filled, the fish flopping on the shore. We took more than we could possible eat, more than we could dry over a fire for our winter stores. "Now we will be able to eat in winter, children," I told them. "We don't need any crop."

I thought the Indians would be happy and would share in our feasts, but they came in the night and reduced the entire day's labor to debris. The young warriors of the soldier's lodge watched us from that same high bank. They'd taken all the fish rotting on the shore. In the early morning light, they looked glossy as crows. A menacing presence.

I did not try to rebuild the dam.

How will I feed my children? The only things that survived the hailstorm were the pumpkins and gourds I planted to keep down weeds. Hazel says we should not worry. This land that kills our milch cow and pillages our crop with hailstorms is also rich. She has gathered the plums along the river and works every day boiling the fruit into jam. Daniel wades into the marshlands to gather teepsinna, the Indians' potatoes. And the Indians themselves, they are still here, though now it is not the children we see, or old men like Hanyokeyah. The ones who come on our land are younger, like Blue-Face, and they do not ask for what they take. They love to eat the pumpkins sprouting in our fields. There is one called Cut-Nose who will seat himself in a furrow and eat a pumpkin raw, slice by slice, tonguing the orange flesh from his knife.

I've begun to think of the militia, of answering strength with strength. I am convinced there are few families out here as exposed as we are.

In the meantime there is haying to be done in the bottomlands. On these hot dry days we work to cut the long-stemmed bluegrasses. Caleb and I cut down the stalks with scythes while Asa and Hazel follow behind with the hay cradles and the youngest, Daniel, keeps watched over Matthew. Hazel carries cool water up from a secret spring and we drink it by the bucketful in this heat.

What relentless work is haying. The hay needles into our clothing and skin until we go home a mass of welts and wheals. It sticks to our faces and pokes through shirts and hair and soft tender places. We breathe the dust and heat and grass yet forget our troubles in the intensity of this labor. Rain is a sweet dream in our minds. There is nothing in these days but sun and swinging scythes, a summer stillness before what is to come.

This new feat of engineering holds me in thrall. Each stack must be laid up just right so that when the rain and cold comes the hay does not mildew and rot. In three days of cutting we made two house-sized stacks, Caleb climbing to the top of each one and tamping it down. "You ought to see the view from up here," he said. "I can see clear to Tatanyandowan's camp." That name seemed to chill Asa and made him drop his cradle and leave us for a time. Tatanyandowan's camp. So it is true that the old man and his medicine society do not run things anymore. In place of fellowship we have the sound of their drums in the night like some great throbbing heartbeat of the prairie itself.

The scythes flashed silver and the grass lay golden in the sun. Silver and gold and the hot wind in the grass, a gold river of light that flows into our tired muscles and out through us.

After a week of backbreaking work, we had made five high bundles, neat mounds of hay impervious to sleet and rain, enough to feed our stock through winter.

The next morning we woke to find Dakota children playing in the stacks. As they jumped from stack to stack, shouting with glee, a golden rain sprayed downward. My precise mountains were tumbling apart. They were mostly small children with the mischievous Hissing Turtle for their leader. Dressed in their breechclouts, they leaped from mountain to mountain, wild with joy as the gold grass cushioned each landing. A few slid all the way down, dragging clots of hay in their fingers, before scurrying back up to leap to another mountain.

I was not aware even of picking up the pitchfork. I only wanted to make an example, to frighten them. When they saw me coming—red-faced, the tine of the blade sun-tinted, a hoarse shouting in my throat—they ran for the woods. All except that Hissing Turtle, who tried one last leap. My shout at the moment of his jump must have distracted him just enough because the boy slipped and tumbled downward, heedless, with nothing to stop his momentum, hay whirling around him. He fell from the highest point in the stack, down and down to the hard ground where he landed at an awkward angle. I don't think I even heard the break. My own momentum carried me toward him. It was only when I saw the awful glistening shine of the bone in his dusky skin and the blood around it that I stopped and let the pitchfork drop. A shout came from Caleb and I saw Cut-Nose coming on with Tatanyandowan and retreated back to my children. They bundled the boy in their arms and were gone.

That night we smelled burning. I woke from a deep sleep to see a glowing orange light dancing along the sides of the inner cabin wall, illuminating the puncheon shelves, our meager belongings, glaring against the copper pots. My sleep-fuddled mind took a few moments to register what was happening and then I was shouting for the children, rousing them from their beds.

The Indians had set fire to all five stacks and each blazed in the dark, a mountain of surging flame. The fire spread down into our grove of hardwoods, down into the marshlands where the cattails exploded like firecrackers, hissing *pft!pft!pft!* as they blazed like torches. Only the dead fields and the river stopped it. The stars above us were lost in the falling ashes. Daniel's dogs circled on the porch whining and growling. The night was filled with the sounds of the prairie chickens as they sang out in terror before the fire. Long-eared jackrabbits flashed from the tallgrass, a few red-eyed wolves, eyes rolling back in terror, and one great stag with a fine rack that bounded away, whitetail twitching, ahead of the flames. The fire swept through the bottomlands and rose up at the edge of the black waters before seeming to doubt itself, run out of rage or breath, and gradually hiss into smoke and steam and nothingness.

In the morning we saw how close we had come to destruction. In the morning I started over again, moving to the field on the far side of the bottomlands, where the tallgrass had been untouched. The smell of smoke saturates our cabin and clothes and hair. We breathe ashes each night we strive for sleep. But I will not leave this place. If there had been no hailstorm to destroy our fields, I don't think I would be writing this now. I've been running since Missouri and I am determined to stand steadfast here. Whatever I build, this land tears down or destroys. What is not destroyed, the Indians ruin. Wild. It's still too wild. All I have are my children and I am weary of life.

ASA *SEPTEMBER 20, 1859*

Since I told Hazel the whole story about the girl and how I was the one who found her I've been able to sleep at nights again. Jakob went to the fort to report our losses and I went alongside him. We never were able to lay up enough to match our previous efforts and it will be thin eating for the oxen come winter. If it gets too hard for us, we may have to slaughter one of them. I drive them through the burned lands and into the tallgrass to water in the bottomlands and they have stupid cow eyes, glazed over, and do not know what is coming.

HAZEL *SEPTEMBER 21, 1859*

I can scarcely believe that only two months have passed since we ran as children in the woods. I hate nights in the fall. That crispness in the air that means winter will arrive and turn the ground to a sheet of black metal ice.

I have taken to going down to the river to watch for him, but he has not come. A section of burr oaks and sugar maples escaped the fire and in the early cold the leaves are beginning to turn. I stood on the frontier between the black swath of burned land and this place that is untouched. What random destruction a fire brings. There are trees that are crisped and torched beside trees still green with sap. I stood beside one burned tree by the river bend that leads to our secret place and when I looked up he was there, appearing as if from nowhere. They always come so quietly, a habit they have learned, I suppose.

He paused about ten feet away from me and didn't come any closer. My throat felt thick and I couldn't find any words. Then he pointed to a burned burr oak beside me and I turned to see that while I was day-dreaming a thousand monarch butterflies had filled the barren branches. Once they sensed me moving they took flight and swirled around me, a vortex of black and orange, wings of light, wings of pollen, myself in the center, and I held my hand against my lips, aching to speak to him but not finding any words sufficient, and Wanikiya, watching me, mimicked my gesture. The butterflies swirled around me and then lifted up and I shut my eyes wanting to go on seeing them, keeping my arms folded and when I looked again he was gone as if he had never been there.

I will remember. Fall is coming and then the long winter. A range of mountains may as well stand between us, a river with torrents. I know I will not see him again for a long while and that he is gone with his brother, Tatanyandowan, to learn what it means to be a warrior. And if I see him again how will he be changed and will he remember the night of the healing and the cave where I breathed his breath? Or will we both be so changed that there will be no language to bridge our differences?

ASA OCTOBER 28, 1859

She is coming and nothing will be the same. When we rode into town, Jakob got the letter at Herr Driebel's store. They talked for awhile and then Jakob bargained for a barrel of flour, trading smoked prairie chicken that Caleb had snared and the jams that Hazel prepared. Just when we were getting ready to leave, Herr Driebel stopped us, squint-ing behind his spectacles. "Say," he said. "I have some happy news I almost forgot. A letter came for you the other day. It was addressed to New Ulm and they sent it on to my shop out here, must have remembered you coming through in the winter. I gather it's from your sister."

"I don't understand," Jakob said. "I don't have any sister." I saw how his dark face whitened with this news. He must have feared being found out.

"It's from someone named Kate Senger," Herr Driebel said and I shouted for joy. My mother, after all this time. "I thought you told me your wife was dead."

Jakob looked so stunned he didn't know what to tell the shopkeeper. He still hadn't figured out how his wife had found him here. I sprang forward and seized the letter and tore it open. Jakob came and stood beside me, silently reading.

My dearest Jakob,

I have found you at last if you are reading this now. Not a moment has passed since we were separated in Missouri that I have not thought of you or the children. I can only imagine how betrayed you felt to wake and find me gone. The decision cost me dearly. You know how terrified I am of wolves and Indians. I couldn't bear to leave a land I'd known all my life, this land where some of my children are buried. I tried to picture myself living in a wild place with you, tried to imagine bearing more children and each one tearing away a piece of me as they came into this world and then had their lives snuffed out. As much I love you, I knew that I could not follow.

What I didn't know was that my father wanted nothing to do with me when I came back to his house. My rightful place is with you and my children, he told me. He said he had washed his hands of me, as well as you. He agreed to give me enough money to journey after you to the place where I belonged. I had no say in the matter.

I don't know if you will have me still. I don't know if you love me any more or can bear the sight of me. But I am coming, Jakob, and I will do all in my power to try and make things right between us.

Kate

KINGDOM TOWNSHIP

1876

INDIAN
SUMMER

"**H**O CHUNK," HAZEL said when she was among the scalps in my papa's one-room jailhouse. I strained to hear the word again, wondering if it was Dakota for violence or revenge. The world outside fell away. Just behind me wagons still creaked along the rutted main road. Squealing children chased one another while frowning women in dark dresses looked on, but I no longer heard any of it. I stayed near the doorway, all my attention fixed on Aunt Hazel standing in a thicket of human hair taken from dead men. Her lips continued to move, but now no sound emerged and it seemed she had forgotten me entirely. Her breath came shallow. She had peeled back her bonnet to see better in the gloom of the jailhouse. My attention was so absolute I could hear a host of bluebottle flies droning angrily in the sallow light of the room's only window. Somehow the drone of these trapped insects came inside me and it seemed not the flies that were speaking, but the things twisting from the ceiling.

All at once I remembered a nightmare I had last summer when my papa was gone to St. Peter. I dreamed I was in the woods near the river, fishing for bullheads, when I looked up to see my papa coming toward me. Blood saturated his hair and clothing and shrouded even his eyes and at first I thought he had been scalped himself but then I knew that the blood was not his own. Dry leaves crunched under his boot soles as he lurched down the slope toward my spot on the shore. I screamed when I saw the glistening knife he held. "Papa! Papa! It's only me, Asa. It's me, Papa!" But he couldn't see for all the blood and I knew he mistook me for an Indian and was going to kill me like he had done the others. When he was only a few feet away my legs came unfroze and I threw away my fishing prong and ran into the woods. The trees closed in around me; branches raked my arms. I ran until I could no longer see him, but as I fast as I went I always heard him coming on behind me, crashing through undergrowth and snapping branches like old bones. Eventually, I found a hiding place within a mossy log and I scrunched up inside and in the absolute darkness I heard the thudding of the blood in my ears. When my heart quieted, I also heard his husky breathing outside. Occasionally he would let loose a choking sob, a wounded animal sound. I wanted to run out and tell him again that it was only me, to wake him from his killing rage. It's only me, Papa, not an Indian.

I always awoke screaming from that dream, the pulse hot in my chest, until my mother rushed up the loft ladder to hold me. She could quiet me, but I never slept afterward. These nightmares only came when he was far away. They didn't make me any more afraid of my papa. Strangely they made me afraid for him, for what he had done and still might do.

These memories coursed through me while I watched Hazel reach up and touch one of the scalps with a finger. Her eyes found me. "*Ho Chunk*," she said again. "Oh, Asa, that your father should keep such things."

I felt sick to my stomach, the dream memory still vivid in my mind.

"*Ho Chunk*," she repeated. "Do you understand me? These are not Dakota. The Dakota never wore roaches in their forelocks. These are Winnebago, '*Ho Chunk*' as they call themselves. He is not keeping these for trophies. It's to remind him of his sin."

I nearly jumped out of my boots when I felt a rough hand on my shoulder. "Step aside, boy," a voice said behind me. The sounds of the outside world came back to me. I looked up to see that the large hand was attached to a hairy forearm that belonged to the blacksmith, Julius Meighen. The storekeeper, August Schilling, stood beside him. I stepped out of their way reluctantly, sensing they didn't mean my aunt any good. Herr Schilling's ruddy cheeks were a splotched pink color. He huffed and sputtered at Hazel, still inside the room. "You have no business here," he said. "This is private property."

Hazel's voice echoed in the small room. "You," she said. "You were there too, weren't you?"

"Out!" Schilling said. "You are not wanted here."

"Do as he says," the blacksmith advised. "I'd hate to have to carry you out of there like a sack of cornmeal, ma'am."

Hazel came slowly, drawing the bonnet back up to shadow her face. In the streets beyond people had turned to look at us, the men outside the store forgetting their game of checkers, a few gaggles of women huddling together in gossipy circles. The whole scene reminded me of the day my papa dragged the Indian into town on a leash. Only now all that unfriendly attention was fixed on me and Hazel. On her way out, the blacksmith gripped her by the arm and he leaned in close to whisper something to her that I could not hear.

We didn't speak until we were away from the town and heading back home across the prairie. "I don't understand," I told her. "I thought those scalps were from the Devil's Lake campaign. Has Papa been lying all this time?"

It was the middle of the afternoon and a dry summer heat baked the barren landscape. Locusts, my teacher once told me, came from the Latin *locus ustus*, meaning *burned place*. I can't imagine a better description for a summer landscape after the locusts are gone. It's as though as every living thing has been purely scorched. "It's best you ask him yourself, Asa. I don't know what happened. After the war, there was a group of men calling themselves 'The Kingdom of Jones,' that organized for protection. People were still so very terrified of Indians. They hadn't yet caught Little Crow."

She took my hand and squeezed it and looked at me with those serene, sea-green eyes. "Let's not talk about this anymore, huh? I need to think this over. I only know that Caleb has been carrying far too great a burden." Away from town she peeled back the bonnet to feel the sun on her freckled face. Squinting in the hard light, she looked both willowy and frail. I was afraid to let her be alone. "The first settlers here thought these prairies were a desert. They always settled the wooded valleys first, thinking that the absence of trees meant poor soil. But there was such good black ground under the grasslands. It was a living skin. You could see why the Indians called it 'Grandmother,' why God shaped us from dirt."

She led me toward the river where a copse of oak trees had been left untouched by the locusts, the leaves coated in a film of August dust. In the stubbled gold grasses she found an empty carapace of a locust, a dry thing like a withered leaf or the abandoned skin of snake. It quavered in the palm of her hand. "Their time is done," she said.

"Oh no," I told her. "They've been coming back for years. If you were to dig your fingernails under this ground you'd find a river of their eggs. They'll hatch again come spring."

She was looking toward the river. "They thought that about the passenger pigeons in my time. And the storms of blackbirds. Wolves. But these locusts are things that take and take and never give anything back." She made a fist and crumpled the carapace. When she opened her hand what remained blew away like chaff. "They will spend themselves with their appetite."

With the toe of my boot, I was drawing a pattern in the dust. I didn't care much to contradict her, wrong as she might be. We walked until we came to a marsh that had once been surrounded by cattails. A thick carpet of dead locusts clustered on the surface. Aunt Hazel sat on the shore, untied the laces of her shoes, and took them off. Barefoot, she pulled up the hem of her dress and waded into the murky water. "There might be leeches," I called to her. I was frightened that someone might see her like this, unashamed as a child. If they did, it would be all the confirmation they needed to prove her madness and send her back to St. Peter.

"No," she said. "Not here. This is spring-fed. I know this place. Join me. The water feels nice."

I hesitated. This wasn't how a woman was supposed to behave. They didn't go wading into black water, exposing the wintry skin of their thighs. But I didn't have to think long. A line of sweat snailed down my back. The hot sun stole all the shadows from this bare country. I kicked off my boots and followed her into the pond.

She had the bonnet slung behind her, her black hair woven into two braids that swung rhythmically as she moved. This is how I like to remember her: water lapping at her knees, her dress fanning out to almost touch the surface, and sunlight blazing on the small pond and turning the water to gold. Her eyes were shut while she moved her feet through the cool mud. A moment later she let her dress hem fall into the water and brought up something between her toes. She plucked it out triumphantly. It looked like a gray human fist, knotted with roots. "Teepsinna," she said. "Swamp tubers. They taste better than any potato. C'mon, there's plenty more." The mud felt wonderful between my toes as I felt along the silken ground for the lumplike root. I completely forgot the dead locusts floating on the surface. My patched pants were soaked by the time I found my first one.

We gathered these marsh tubers along with water lilies. She taught me where to find wild grapevines that the locusts left alone. We gathered all these things into a wooden bucket she had brought along for this purpose. This was my last good day with her. I learned to see a living layer beneath what appeared to be a wasteland. I think she foresaw what was coming. On the way back home I asked her what the blacksmith had whispered into her ear, not expecting an answer.

"No crows," she told me. "There will be no crows in the Kingdom."

"That doesn't make any sense."

"He meant Little Crow," she said. "He meant Indians, or those who like them."

Hearing this made me angry enough at the town to wish it all burned to the ground once more. If only they knew her as I did. They didn't have any reason to fear one small woman. And I didn't think she had any reason to be ashamed of her past. Hazel continued talking as we found the path. "Crows are often misunderstood," she said. "The Dakota also have a story of a great flood that drowns the entire earth. The Creator sends it because he is angry at mankind. But no humans survive and nothing is spared save a single, solitary crow flying over a wilderness of water. It is this crow that begs the Creator to have mercy, to restore humanity. Only the crow is there to see the earth destroyed and then made again."

After the jailhouse incident, things got worse for my family. My mother had already used a good portion of her remaining coins to restock her laudanum supply. She didn't care that Aunt Hazel called it a demon potion. She said it was the only thing that made her feel right inside. In town Herr Schilling stopped buying my mother's eggs. He raised prices on any calicos or salted meats she requested. I was glad not to be there to witness the confrontation between those two. Mother threatened to ride to Sleepy Eye, but that was just talk. We only had one draft horse, good mostly for field work. She might as well have threatened to ride to the moon for what our family needed. Herr Schilling had us where he wanted.

Two days later, I spotted Orlen Meighen and Franz Schilling watching me from outside the schoolyard's white picket fence. Both boys had dropped out of school earlier that summer. I had long been invisible to such rough-and-tumble older children unless they needed a sacrificial victim to swing from a rope. They lazed now, smoking cigarettes in the spare shade of a crabapple tree. Wherever I turned in the schoolyard during our lunch break, I felt their hot eyes boring into me.

After lunch, Mr. Simons delivered an interminable lecture on the Sioux Uprising, his voice a droning monotone of dates, numbers, and facts, while the students fanned themselves and hunched under the oppressive summer heat in the small room. Mr. Simons paced the rows, his eyes dreamy, as students sank lower and lower in their desks, their spines turning to butter in the humidity, their eyelids drooping. Then, he must have caught sight of Orlen and Franz outside the window.

Those boys, sons of important town citizens, had tormented Mr. Simons with their constant misbehavior. The sight of them kindled something inside our teacher. "Most people," he said, his voice suddenly sharp, "died like cattle in a slaughterhouse."

He was no longer lost in dreamy abstractions. The students straightened. "What a fine fever swept this country in 1862. There were parades, marching bands, brave speeches. Like any patriotic young man, I went to war against Johnny Reb that year, not knowing the home I was leaving behind would be washed away in a river of blood."

His good hand stroked the sleeve of his missing arm. He didn't sound like he was addressing children anymore. "A body doesn't know what it will do until the moment arrives. That's how it was all around this country when the Indians rose up with their shotguns and scalping knives. In terror, some men ran and left their wives and daughters behind to be killed. Some sank to their knees in the red grass, their eyes glazing over, too stunned even to beg for mercy. They went to their deaths thinking, *this can't be happening. This can't be happening to me.*"

Mr. Simons continued to look out the window, lost in his recollection. My throat felt dry. "What does it mean to have courage in such a time? Far away in Virginia, when boys your own age occupy a stone wall at the top of a hill, their guns trained on your advancing line of infantry, do you walk into that withering fire because you are brave, or because you do not want to be trampled by those marching behind you? And when the minié ball shatters your forearm and you feel the hot metal burrow inside, are you secretly relieved? Do you huddle against the scarred ground while your friends fall around you, praying only that you will live and your war will be done?"

No one was drowsing in that room now. Every one of us had turned toward Mr. Simons, our breaths hushed. Watching the other students, I knew I was not the only one who had grown up with silence. What he told us was forbidden knowledge. "Some of your friends get sick. Dysentery. They die of scratches, infections. Some, you suspect, die out of plain homesickness. But not you. Later that evening when the doctor saws at your ruined arm, you're awake to feel every terrible second. And the angry sound of that saw is branded into your brain. You pray for death then, but your prayer isn't answered.

"No, you get to go home. And that vision of home and hearth is what keeps you ticking. It's something that will make you whole again. But your home doesn't exist any longer. Your entire town was destroyed one fiery August day while you lay in the hospital on the other side of the country. The mother and younger brother who stopped returning your letters occupy unmarked graves. Killed by Indians who thought they could take back what once was theirs."

Mr. Simons swallowed, was quiet for a solid minute. The others began to shuffle, one boy's cough echoed through the room. "The survivors left behind are so very afraid. You think it should kill you, the loneliness. But deep inside you feel a small red flame of hatred awakening in the emptiness. It keeps you warm. You fall in with men who are as hateful as you, as haunted as you. You don't call each other by name. Everyone is Jones. You are men of the kingdom, the Kingdom of Jones. And you wait for the Dakota Sioux to come back, because you're ready this time, armed and vigilant. Wanting death, ready to kill. Days pass, weeks, soon a whole year of waiting. Then one day they come, a small band passing through. . . ."

Mr. Simons turned and scanned the room. Then he scratched his jaw, his train of thought lost. "I'm sorry," he said quietly. "I didn't mean to tell you all that." He shook his head slowly and then waved us away with his good hand. "Class dismissed."

We filed out silently into the schoolyard, some of the students forming into groups gossiping in low tones. I went out alone, and Franz and Orlen fell in close behind me as I walked out of town. I didn't know where to go. Papa, my main protection, would likely be away for another month. These boys meant to fall on me when we were alone in the woods. They meant to punish me because Aunt Hazel had come to live with us. She had unsettled our household, unsettled the town. She even unsettled quiet Mr. Simons, who must have heard through gossip what Hazel had said about the scalps in the jailhouse. Scratch the skin of this ground and you'd uncover locust eggs. Scratch the skin of these people and you'd uncover feelings they thought were buried far deeper. I mulled over Mr. Simons's words while I walked, trying not to act afraid when the older boys closed the distance between us, until I swore I could feel their breath on the back of my neck. What had the men of the Kingdom of Jones done? That was the second time in a week I had heard that term. What did it mean to have courage?

I didn't have much time to think on these matters because at the base of the hill Aunt Hazel waited for me near the old German graveyard. She was carrying her customary grubbing stick and bucket, squinting up into the hard afternoon light. I saw her take stock of the boys behind me, Orlen with his long troll-like arms, Franz with his thin boyish beard. She peeled back her bonnet and gave them a narrow-eyed glare. I felt the boys hitch to a stop. How had she known that I might be in danger?

"How was school?" she asked when I was close.

"Different," I said. "Frightening." She didn't ask what I meant. We fell in side by side and headed for the old Indian trail along the river that would take us home. Orlen and Franz shadowed us through the woods. Aunt Hazel stopped walking and turned to face them. They stopped too. They didn't speak a word.

"What do you want?" Aunt Hazel called. Thirty feet separated us, and the boys' faces were splotched by tree shadows. "You leave us alone, hear? We aren't frightened of you." They watched her, empty-eyed and silent. As soon we turned around they started walking too, always keeping a careful distance. Aunt Hazel stopped to tie the laces of her boots. Then she plucked her stick from the ground and whirled around to advance on the boys. They held their ground at first. She was a little woman, whittled down by her lost years, but she held that stick before her like a sword and I could imagine the grim expression on her face. When she was ten feet away, they broke and ran away, laughing. They mocked us from a distance, following us the whole way home. They called her a whore. Injun-lover. Witch. No expression showed on her face.

When we were close to home, she took my hand. Her palm was cool and dry. "Shameful," she said. "To send boys to do a man's work."

Yes, I thought. *But no one will punish these boys. They can say what they wish and likely do far worse*. I felt a simultaneous pride in Aunt Hazel along with a sense of helplessness. What could one boy do to defy an entire town? We walked the rest of the way home, hand in hand.

Later that night, Aunt Hazel left the house after dinner to go wandering. I didn't think she should be out by her lonesome, in case those boys were waiting, but she wasn't afraid. Alone in the loft, I decided to break my promise and look through Aunt Hazel's private things. I noticed that the bowl that had held her medicine was empty before I fetched out the book from her carpetbag. Seated on the edge of her bed, I turned the wrinkled pages. The book was a heavy, warm weight against my legs. I don't know what I was looking for. I was angry at myself for not doing more in the woods. I could bear up under any abuse; this was my own private battle with cowardice, the way I let people hurt me without retaliating.

The cross-hatched page was difficult to read. What had she been writing here? Had she been hoping to recapture her pa's *Book of Wonders*? That book had been supposed to keep her family safe, to mark out a path in a perilous world. It was a dark, cloudy night and I had to squint to decipher my aunt's printing. From downstairs, my mother called up and asked what I was doing. I shifted and set the book on the nightstand and went over to call down my answer.

I don't know how it happened exactly. The book was heavier than I thought. Its presence on the nightstand must have disturbed the wooden candle-holder, which made no sound as it turned over and touched the edge of the book. The flame caught one of the brittle pages and a brightness filled the room while I called down my answer. There was a smell like burning applewood, or sugar maple, overpowering and pungent. Even from downstairs my mother smelled it, and called my name again in a questioning manner. The scent came to my nostrils at the same time my head turned and I saw the book engulfed in flames.

I leapt for it and tried to beat out the fire with my bare hands, but the flame coiled through those pages like a prairie fire in a quick, hot wind.

I threw the burning book down on the floor and stamped on it with my feet. Dimly, I smelled my own skin burning along with those pages and then my mother was in the room with a washbasin of sudsy water that she threw on the flaming mess. The water splashed up and soaked my nightshirt and bare legs as it put out the fire.

I remember standing there over the blackened remains of the book and looking across the room at my mother and the O shape of her mouth. Moments later her shock turned to anger and her cheeks flamed with color. I don't know what called for such fury. Earlier that summer, I had saved a letter she meant to burn and in doing so brought a woman she never wanted to see again. Now, I had burned up something she wanted to save, a book that she might have hoped would bring us coin in a hard season. A few senseless words sputtered from her mouth and hung there, suspended like spittle. She began to hit me with the flat of her palms, striking me in the face and along the top of my head. She grabbed hold of my hair, shrieking, and tossed me against the back of the wall, knocking the breath from my chest. Too much was happening too quickly. I began to feel the searing ache along my palms and feet and knew that I was already hurt. I curled into a ball and tried to protect myself as best I could while she swung for me. How much time passed I am no longer sure. Neither of us heard Hazel hurrying up the loft ladder to pull my mother off me.

My next memory is of Aunt Hazel later that night, bent over my bed, wrapping a cool cloth around my burned hands. Even in the dark I could see pouches under her eyes. She had been crying. I opened my mouth and tried to tell her just how sorry I was, but my tongue was thick and no words came out. I wanted to tell her how much I longed to be like Peter from the Gospels, fierce and brave, and sometimes stupid. Someone who would draw his sword when the Roman soldiers came for what he loved. Instead, I was Judas. I had proved a poor friend to the one who trusted me; my own hot tears shamed me. She touched a finger to my lips and shushed me before I could speak.

Then she rose again and went over to her side of the room and stood by the window so that the wind caused her nightgown to billow around her. I could still smell the sweet applewood char of the lost book. The aroma swam in my nostrils, filling me up like breath. Along with the scent, I heard the voices of my grandfathers and uncles. I saw the ghosts of their journeys and trials. Hazel was looking out the open window and seemed to be listening too, as though she had summoned the voices here to take the place of the book. I had the sense of them all around us, here in the room for only a moment before they rose like smoke and out the window into the pure darkness of a country night. She started singing so quietly then. I strained to catch the words.

What though my joy and comforts die? The Lord my Savior liveth.
What though the darkness gather round? Songs in the night He giveth.
No storm can shake my inmost calm while to that rock I'm clinging
Since Christ is Lord of heaven and earth, how can I keep from singing?

Aunt Hazel had a habit of grinding her teeth at night, like a rabbit worrying a branch to keeps its molars short. The sound grated on my ears as I tried to sleep. I lay awake in the dark, thinking about those boys shadowing us in the woods and wondering what they would try next. Sometime past midnight, Hazel stopped grinding her teeth. A moment later she rolled all the way out of bed and clumped down to the floor.

"Aunt Hazel?" I asked.

There was no response. I could hear her feet kicking against the bed-post. I called her name once more and then came around the side of the bed. What I saw in the moonlight flooding through the window I will never forget. Her eyes had rolled back in her head and there was pink, blood-flecked foam on her lips. Her torso jerked like a hook had been pulled through her spine and her arms bent at odd, insectlike angles, a locust. She was not breathing. Gurgling sounds frothed in her throat while she threshed in spasms on the floor. There was a terrible sense of absence here, of violation. I screamed for my mother and knelt beside her on the floorboards.

Mother came rushing up the ladder with a lit lantern. She sucked in her breath when she saw Hazel and then set the lantern down on the floor. Minutes had passed without Hazel inhaling. She continued to twist on her spine as she struggled to draw a single breath. All at once, I saw what my life would look like with her gone, the space she would leave within me. There would be no stories, no laughter in the household. She could die before I ever had the chance to tell her what she meant to me. I was petrified by the thought. Mother came and knelt beside me. I thought of all the stories Aunt Hazel had told me. Now she lay before me like the Indian boy Caleb had shot so long ago. I put my hand on her stomach then and began to pray. "Breathe," I commanded. "Breathe in God's name." That's the only part of the prayer I can remember, for I was chanting you see, half addressing her, half addressing God. It was less a prayer than a command, my own fierce desire to call her back into this world. One of them, Hazel or God, must have heard, for her stomach rose to meet my hand. Mother joined my prayer and we continued to encourage her. Hazel's breath returned in short, ragged gasps. Her eyes were huge, the pupils coin-sized. She didn't seem to recognize us and at first kicked as if she wanted us to go. Mother stroked her hair, saying, "It's okay, dear. You're safe now."

We helped her back up into the bed and I turned away while Mother stripped off Hazel's gown, which she had soiled during the seizure, and then wrapped her in the blanket. Waves of shuddering passed through her. Mother and I took turns keeping watch, but Hazel didn't seize again that night and sometime in the early gray hours her breathing deepened into true sleep.

In the morning Hazel could hardly speak because her mouth was filled with raw sores. She had chewed up her tongue and the insides of her cheek during the seizure. Her voice came thick. "I scared you," she said.

I felt a warm rush of tears and blinked them away. She reached out to touch me with a cool hand. "You see," she said in a thick whisper, "I'm all out of medicine. I can't stay here much longer."

I squeezed her fingers. "You can't go away."

Mother came up beside her with water drawn from the springhouse. "You shouldn't be talking," she told Hazel.

"Asa," Hazel said. "Open up my bag."

I did as she asked. Within there was only the yellow-print dress she had come with and a small doeskin bag. I took out the bag and brought it over. Hazel did her best to smile. "I have to tell you about the one who carried this," she said.

"It can wait," said Mother.

"No," said Hazel. "The story's not done yet. And I'm afraid I don't have very much longer. Before the seizures come, I see this radiance spreading through all the world. There are wings behind it. Angels, I think. Or birds made of light. It sweeps over me and takes me away with it." She spoke slowly, the words coming out slurred. Her eyes watered with the effort.

"To someplace terrible," I said.

"No," she said. "But not someplace for mortal flesh." Her hands wrapped tightly around the beaded doeskin bag and she looked over at me. "I need to tell you something, but the story won't come easy."

"You need to just rest," my mother said in a low voice.

"In a few days, when my mouth heals right," Aunt Hazel said. "It begins one summer, a hot summer much like this one. Even the wind in the tallgrass seemed to whisper: *If only men knew what I know.* The adults went about their business, hearing nothing. But I was sixteen, half child, half woman. I listened close."

MILFORD PRAIRIE

1862

THE
NIGHT BIRDS

IN THE MONTH of the harvest moon, a Dakota youth named Otter told the Senger family that Indians were coming to kill all the white people in the valley. After three years of living just on the other side of the silt-laden Waraju River, a shallow boundary that separated them from the Dakota bands, the children were used to such warnings and paid this one little heed. Other matters weighed on them. They had been banished from the cabin where their stepmother tended their youngest brother, Matthew, sick with a fever that speckled his face and throat with white pinprick sores.

Caleb cut a swath through wavering bluestem grasses and made a bed for the four of them. They spread quilts over the fallen grass, knowing that Caleb would leave them as soon as Asa returned from the creek bearing buckets of water. Caleb was sweet on Cassie, who lived with her sister at a nearby farm. One night the previous winter, her father, Hans, had poisoned himself with his own liquor. He had been ladling small doses of strychnine into the rotgut he sold the Indians, just enough to give it kick. His own distillation he kept pure. How Hans confused the two still troubled Caleb. He remembered digging the grave during a January thaw, a shallow grave they layered with stones to keep the wolves from unearthing it. Once he'd looked up to catch Cassie's mother, her hair streaming in the keening wind, looking off toward Milford, pale eyes shining. Caleb had the sense that this woman wouldn't stay in the territory much longer. He'd gone ahead and bought a ring for Cassie, a used silver ring he wasn't sure would fit, as well as a crate of table wine from New Ulm, now hidden away in the root cellar for the wedding.

Near the children a smudge fire burned to keep off hovering mosquitoes. A hot summer wind fanned clouds across a moon that hung like a glimmering talon in the dark. Clouds drifted, low-bellied and pregnant with rain, over the fields of waiting corn. The corn raised leaves like green arms that sought to stroke the rain from the passing clouds. Around them a few drops spattered the dust.

"Will it rain?" Daniel asked in his quiet voice. His white-blond hair caught what light there was from the smudge fire.

"Not tonight," Caleb said. "Not yet."

Caleb knelt to be closer to his siblings. Here he was, eighteen years old, about to be married, but he wasn't ready to leave them yet. Not with his father Jakob away in Virginia fighting the rebels. He thought of that wine down in the cellar and how in church it represented God's forgiveness and he wondered if there was enough of it to take away the sin of the things he knew and had done. Cassie had reached the stage where her swelling belly was difficult to disguise.

His younger sister, Hazel, glanced at him once, her dark green eyes unreadable. She lay between Daniel and six-month-old Ruth and she was looking at him as though trying to divine his thoughts. The look disquieted him. There were things she shouldn't know.

The slow-moving clouds parted to reveal a scattering of stars. Caleb pointed out *Mato*, the Bear Star, to his siblings. He told them how the Bear Star died each autumn and painted the leaves red with blood. Or so the old medicine man Hanyokeyah had told him. Red leaves from a bear dying to prepare the way.

Across from him Hazel was lost in thoughts of her own. She turned from Caleb and looked at her sister Ruth, barely breathing in her bundle of blankets, and remembered the day of the girl's birth. She had been born during the same three-day snowstorm during which Hans Gormann had died. There had been no way to fetch a doctor. Hazel was the one who cut the cord and felt the infant life quicken in her hands. In that moment when Ruth first began to howl, she had hesitated before handing her to the waiting arms of her stepmother. "Hazel, give her over," Kate had commanded, sweat-soaked hair pasted to her skull. Hazel had paused because something in her said if she handed the girl over she wouldn't live. But she did. Ruth had Kate's copper hair and green eyes like Hazel. Did she know who had nudged the air into her lungs? Now the baby slept while the boys watched for what stars the clouds might reveal.

Hazel tried to imagine what was happening back in the cabin where her stepmother tended Matthew, a boy already blind from scarlet fever. This new fever that held him didn't have any name. Around the edges of his lips the sores looked hot and angry and bled with pus. Matthew muttered in a heated dream language that was not English or Dakota, but sounded like prophecy. Once he said the word *fire* and Hazel had dripped water down his throat to quiet him. When his skin took on a smell like side meat cooking in the sun, she felt sure he wouldn't live past the night. Kate's bloodwort teas, the cloths soaked with liniment she lay across his chest, could not stop his breath from becoming more labored. On this humid summer night the cabin reeked with the smell of his dying. Kate had known it, too; that was why she sent them outside. When Hazel tried to stay, thinking she could be of some use, Kate slapped her so hard her ears rang. Hazel knew she didn't mean it, but hated her just the same. Matthew needed her; her touch could soothe him. Blinded by her own tears, she had felt Kate press little Ruth into her arms and thrust her out the door with her brothers.

After Caleb led them to this cool spot by the river where they could no longer hear Matthew crying, Daniel fetched some plums from a nearby bush. Hazel was sixteen years old, too old to cry. The sour juice spilled down her cheek and made her feel still and calm on the inside. The imprint of Kate's hand burned on her skin, the bruise ripening and swelling in the dark.

Across the Waraju River lay the Dakota reservation and even this late the cookfires of their camps shone. Drums began to throb in the west, low tomtoms that sounded like the beating of a great heart, before they went still again.

Asa returned with water from the creek. He set the yoked buckets down and stood in the smudge smoke swatting away troublesome mosquitoes. At sixteen he was the second oldest boy, old enough to join Jakob in the war against the Secesh. Asa carried Jakob's last letter in his shirt pocket. His sweat had stained and smudged the ink, but he had the words memorized by now and he often spoke of joining Jakob with the Minnesota 1st volunteers; he hoped Johnny Reb wouldn't be licked before the year was out.

The two oldest stepbrothers stood together, one short and red-headed, the other tall and broad-shouldered, and looked out toward the aurora hovering over the reservation.

"Something's stirring," said Caleb.

"That's what took me so long," Asa said. "I ran into Otter down by the creek." Though they were alone in the dark, Asa whispered the last.

"What mischief is he up to now?"

"He was excited," Asa said. "His whole body was smeared with black paint and all I could make out was the whites of his eyes. When he called my name I would have jumped out of my boots, had I been wearing any. He was on the other side of the river. He told me the soldier's lodge had met and decided to kill the white people in the valley the next day."

"Not that again," said Caleb. "Every year they get riled when the annuity payment's late."

"That's what I told him," said Asa. "But then his voice got low and he asked in Dakota: *Kinnesagas? Are you afraid?* Before I could answer he ran off into the dark."

From her spot on the quilt, Hazel perched on her elbows and listened closely. Would Otter have come if the threat was real? Wouldn't Wanikiya, their closest friend, have been the one to warn them? Her cheeks flushed to think of him out there before a fire, his face painted.

And did he think of her, too, and would he remember the promise he had made?

Caleb didn't say anything. This last year he had grown moody and quiet as he approached eighteen. He looked back toward the cabin where one window guttered with candlelight like a single blinking eye. "Your ma won't run," he said. "She won't let us hitch the wagon."

"On account of Matthew?"

"Even if he was well, she wouldn't go."

"Maybe I could swim acrost the river, and tell the soldiers at the fort?" Asa said.

"Water's too high. It's been storming upriver. Besides you don't swim so good."

"Do so," Asa said, but neither had the energy to argue as usual.

A whippoorwill started up in the rushes. In the stillness the song of that night bird magnified in their imaginations. Instead of whip-poor-will it sounded like the bird's song was oh-you're-kilt. Oh-you're-killed, oh-you're-killed, echoed through the dark and they didn't know if the bird sang for Matthew, or their father far away in Virginia headed toward Miller's cornfield and Antietam, or for them now, in this flimsy shelter of grass. Asa threw a plum stone in the direction of the bird and chased it away. "That wasn't any natural bird," he said. "Pa told me the whippoorwills turn to nighthawks past twilight."

"Hush," said Caleb. "That's just a story."

After some time, Asa turned to his brother and asked, "Will you go to her tonight?"

"Yes," Caleb said.

Asa took a deep breath, said, "It's not fitting. You aren't married yet."

Caleb's face darkened. "Don't tell me what's right and what's not."

"It's a sin," Asa said.

Caleb hand's curled into fists. With his moodiness there had come inside him a sense of restrained violence. He didn't know what he was capable of anymore. Cassie had kept him out of the war this far, saying the fight was really just over niggers. His stepmother Kate also grew angry when the subject came up and talked about herself and the children as though Jakob had abandoned them. In this, the two were unlike most women in the territory. Out of pride and patriotism, most women begged their men to go. "You're only jealous is all," Caleb said bitterly.

"Not of her," Asa said. He saw something brewing in his stepbrother's lean hawklike features.

Caleb exhaled deeply then and let his fists drop. He turned and walked away from all of them, not caring what happened anymore. He had a life to live separate from theirs.

"Not of her!" Asa cried again, his voice high and petulant, as Caleb disappeared into the tallgrass prairie that would take him to Cassie's farm.

Asa paced in the dark and threw the remaining pile of plums, one by one, out onto the prairie where they landed without a sound. "You're wasting them," said Daniel.

"I don't much care."

When the drums started again in the distance, Daniel, disquieted by his oldest brothers' inability to get along, asked about Jakob's letter.

"Too dark to read," said Asa.

"You know it by heart," Daniel said. "My dearest children" he began. "I write you now beneath the shelter of my overcoat, warmed by the fire of a split-rail fence. I have not slept since Chicohema."

"Stop," said Asa. "That's not how it goes."

"Then tell us," said Daniel.

Asa began to recite, lowering his voice to sound more like Jakob's. As he spoke the other children forgot the beat of the war drums and heard only him:

My dearest family,

I write from the shelter of a rubber overcoat by the dim glow of a rail-fence fire. After a year of inactivity, slogging through mud fields, we fought the Secesh at Chickahominy River. Twice since the fight I have been caught walking in my sleep, Sharps rifle slung around my shoulder, and I fear that I will be shot by one of the pickets if I don't learn

to sleep better. In my memory the fight is only a fever-dream. With the
falling rain came artillery and through the wet leaves minié balls whistled and searched for soft flesh. I don't remember the charge up the field.
I can only recall that there was so much rain our guns stopped firing:
the powder was too damp. The fighting turned close up, men grappling
in mud and rain. The Rebs screamed their battle yell and I screamed
back, holding my bayonet like a spear. . . .

It does me no good to remember now except that something came
inside me during that night of rain that I have not been able to shake
loose. I cannot believe months earlier we met the Rebs at Edward's
Ferry and even shared dinner with them. I cannot reconcile myself to
the idea that even now across the miles of rain-soaked fields some
Rebel soldier sits writing to children of his own. But then I find the newspapers that advertise escaped slaves. Then I remember why I am here,
all that violence that chased us so many years ago from Missouri. Our
cause is just.

What I wouldn't give now for some of Kate's fried doughnuts.
What I wouldn't give to see Daniel running through the fields, towhead
flashing, as he chases the hated blackbirds from our corn. How is the
crop this year? Has Caleb broken ground on the south pasture, put in
potatoes like I said? This war will not last forever. I will return soon.
Look for me in the East where the sun rises. Look for me at the dawn
and one day you will see my weary silhouette as I walk the trail that at
last brings me home.

Your loving father,
Jakob

"Pa sure can write pretty," Daniel said. "Do you think you will write
like that one day?"

"No," said Asa. "There's no future in writing. Besides, only Hazel can
write like him. I'd like to live in such a way that others put down on
paper the things I do. First I'm gonna take my fiddle and join Pa with
the First Minnesota."

"I hope I can recall words like you when I'm grown up," said Daniel.

Asa's teeth flashed in the firelight. "Always did have a good memory. Jakob says a man with fine recall will be good at speechifying. An orator. Maybe when the war is done I can come back and be mayor of Milford."

"Or the governor," said Daniel. "Now that we're a state."

Silence fell over the children as again they heard the distant drums. Unlike the boys, Hazel was bothered by her father's letter. What was this thing that came inside him during the rain? She remembered him in Missouri, spread out on a kitchen table, his arms bruised by tar, and her just a girl, passing her hand over a shadow spot she saw on his throat, and knowing one day he would die. Four years had passed since they'd fled here to Minnesota. And if something came inside him, it could only be rage, and she feared what that would do to her father.

Asa lay down on the other side of Daniel. The children's ears were pressed close to the earth so they could hear the wailing of the Dakota dancers moving around their fires. They knew the words of their death song. *I am here*, the warriors sang as they danced, *I am here*.

They all sat up when they heard a rustling in the grass and a moment later the lean wolfish snout of their dog, Turnip, emerged. This half Newfoundland, half-wolf puppy they had purchased from Cassie's father three summers before had grown into a huge, lumbering bear of a dog. Her playmate, a brindled male with a distinct limp, had disappeared the previous winter. "Did Ma exile you as well? said Asa when he recognized the familiar, shaggy form. Turnip loped forward and stuck her moist black muzzle into the baby's blankets. Hazel swatted her away before the dog woke Ruth up. Turnip seemed continually mystified by the presence of a baby in the household and never missed a chance to sniff or lick the child, who did not enjoy this attention. After circling their nest of blankets three times, Turnip lay down, but kept her long wolfish ears perked and listening to the drums. She whined uneasily.

"Asa," Daniel said after they had lain back down. "Don't go away just yet."

"Go to sleep," Asa told him. The web of speech the boys had made, a netting of words, spread out over the children and dispelled their fears:

the wailing dancers, their missing father, the dying brother. Through it all Ruth slept, a quiet baby who woke only for occasional feedings before retreating back to her dreams.

Wind stirred in the tallgrass and the sliver of moon came and went, the talon of a dark bird descending. Soon, the children slept too.

Ruth woke crying sometime before dawn. The smudge fire had burned down and mosquitoes descended on the children. Ruth's tiny hands clawed at her face and eyes where the buzzing insects clustered. The sun had not yet risen, but the morning was already hot and sticky. They walked through a cloud of mosquitoes—Ruth hungry, inconsolable—back to the cabin from which Kate had banished them. No sound came from within the thick log walls. Kate had left the latch on the outside.

Within, they found the woman leaning on a wall near Matthew's pallet. Her jaw hung slack and there were deep shadows beneath her shut eyes, the haggard look of a woman who has bargained with angels and paid some price in return. She woke when she heard Ruth crying and signaled Hazel to hand the baby over. As Hazel passed the child to her Kate must have seen the imprint of her hand on Hazel's face, for she inhaled sharply. It was like that sometimes. Kate was fierce in her love and hate. She possessed the strength to stay up all night with a sick boy, but lacked the restraint to stay her hand when one of them crossed her. And her stepdaughter, Hazel, seemed always to be working at some cross-purpose to hers.

Of the children, only Ruth belonged to both Kate and Jakob. Jakob's children never forgot it and were wary of their stepmother. They never quite forgave her for leaving them for a time when things went wrong in Missouri.

Asa and Daniel hung back near the stove, uncertain, not wanting to see Matthew if he was dead.

He wasn't. Whatever Kate had done after she sent them out had worked. The angry ring of sores around Matthew's mouth had dimmed. His breathing yet had a raspy quality, but his skin no longer smelled so sour.

"Don't touch him," Kate cautioned Hazel. "I don't want any of you to get like him." Any new sickness that came through the valley, Matthew caught first. Years of sickness had left the child with one foot in this world and one in the next.

Kate stood and undid her dark dress of green silk, exposing pale skin and the aureole of a nipple to which she guided Ruth. Sometime in the night her auburn hair had sprung free from its tresses and now hung in listless curls about her brow. In the children's happiness to see their brother still among the living they briefly forgot the strange night and Otter's warning. Kate took inventory and prepared them for their chores. "Caleb?" she asked, looking around. Asa shrugged and said nothing. It was the morning of August 18, wash day for the Sengers. The goats needed milking, the stock had to be watered and loosed on the prairie, eggs gathered, the garden weeded.

Outside the night clouds had dissipated, but there was a heaviness to the air. After milking the goats, Hazel busied herself at the churn and watched Asa return from the grove carrying a bundle of ash branches. He kept looking behind him. A moment later the girl's sleepy eyes registered the pall of smoke that darkened the western horizon. Three years had passed since a prairie fire had nearly taken the farm. This smoke seemed far off, just a distant threat, but like Asa, she remembered the warning of the night before. Asa set his bundle of wood on the porch and went inside to speak with his mother. A moment later she came out of the cabin, Ruth balanced on her hip, one hand held over her eyes as she scanned the horizon.

"I don't believe it," she said, "but that smoke is right where the agency stands." As she spoke Asa lay down on the ground and pressed his ear to the earth. "Sounds like gunfire," he reported.

"That's ten miles away," she said. "You couldn't possibly hear anything."

Daniel lay beside his brother and pressed himself to the ground. "I hear a popping like fireworks," he said.

"You get up out of that dirt," she said. "I've got enough to do today." But she kept looking toward the horizon, chewing on her lower lip. "Asa," Kate said as the boys stood and dusted off their homespun, "why don't you hitch the oxen and take the others into town. See if anyone there has heard something. You take that ginseng and sell it to Herr Driebel. Don't take less than four cents a bushel, no matter how he gripes."

"Won't you come?" Asa said.

"Your brother wouldn't survive the trip," she said. "I need to stay here." She turned and went to finish making their breakfast: fried prairie chicken eggs and biscuits greased with lard.

Asa was neither strong nor good with livestock, so it took some time to get the wagon hitched. His freckled face was sweaty and mottled with purple splotches from straining to make the uncooperative oxen, who didn't seem to hear his high-voiced commands, move. Asa cursed Caleb under his breath for not being there to help, while Daniel and Hazel loaded ginseng root into the wagon box.

Dug from the loamy river soils, the ginseng they sold to Herr Driebel had helped them through the lean years, which had been every year save this one summer of plenty. After the hailstorm the first year, they had a summer of rain that rotted the crops in their furrows and the next year an infestation of cut worms blighted their wheat. Now with their father gone to fight in the war, the corn grew eight feet tall, a vast green forest tipped with bright tassels, and at last it looked like they would prosper.

As they loaded the ginseng, Hazel thought of her pa's last day here, the autumn of the previous year. It was not his promise she remembered, how he told Kate he was going to take her out of this territory when he returned, a mistake to come here before it was settled. When she thought about his last day she remembered the sound of him cutting wood for the coming winter, the heavy ax splitting good oak, and Kate too pained to watch, listening within the cabin, her face pressed to the coolness of the wall, one hand on her belly where Ruth was yet a seed. Kate knowing, surely, he would not come back.

By the time they had the wagon ready it was midmorning. Hazel sat in the buckboard with Asa and Daniel and was surprised when Kate again thrust Ruth into her arms. "She likes to be out in the sun," Kate said. "The fresh air will do her good." Swaddled in a blanket, with a woman's slat bonnet to shade her head and torso, Ruth sucked her thumb and stared at Hazel sleepily. Lastly, Kate gave them the rifle. "I primed it," she said. "In case you see a rabbit for the pot."

She stood watching them while they rode toward Milford, the oxen slow and stately. Turnip trotted by the side of the wagon, keeping a steady pace, but eventually the heat of the day took a toll on the bear-like dog and she fell behind, her tongue lolling out. She followed them into town every time, never stopping to chase rabbits or investigate strange smells, always keeping the wagon in her sight. Once she got into town she would find herself a shady spot and then fall back behind them again on the way home, singleminded and determined not to let them out of her sight.

Asa, entrusted with a man's work, held his spine straight and gee'd and haw'd the oxen in an unnaturally deep voice. Soon Daniel got bored of being jostled in the buckboard and climbed out to jog along beside them. They had only covered a mile through green fields fattening in the August sun when they saw smoke up ahead in the direction of Milford's sawmill.

Wind from the east carried the smell of fire and hurried burning ashes aloft like flickering fireflies. There was so much smoke in the sky that the sun shone through the pall like an ugly, rotten orange. Asa halted the wagon and stood up in the buckboard. He caught one of the ashes in his palm and watched it whiten like a melting snowflake. More and more ashes flared and faded in ditches and green fields. "Let's turn back," Hazel said to him. Her stomach had knotted into a cold fist. There was something wrong.

The road followed a curve of forest that sloped down to the curving Minnesota River. From the woods came three warriors, greased with war paint. They wore only breechclouts and a few feathers in their head-dresses. Their hair was glossy-black and parted in twin braids twined with animal fur. Each carried a shotgun at his side. Asa sat down in the buckboard, unsure of what to do. The road narrowed here and the oxen could not turn around easily. Up ahead the warriors fanned out, blocking the road. "Get back in the wagon," Asa told Daniel.

Behind them two more Indians appeared moving in a quick trot. Their dog Turnip lumbered along, desperate to catch up. Not knowing what else to do, Asa continued to drive them forward while Hazel took up the rifle and prepared to hand it to her brother. "There's the Stoltens' cornfield up ahead," Asa told them. "If trouble happens we'll abandon the wagon and run for it."

As they came closer the individual shapes resolved. In the middle of the trio of warriors stood one they knew as Cut-Nose, his face painted half in bright green, half in vivid yellow. This warrior often came to their farm and ate the pumpkins while they were still green and raw, carving them up slice by slice with his knife. He never asked their permission or spoke to them. Cut-Nose held up a hand to signal for them to stop, so Asa drew the wagon to a halt. Ashes came down around them like falling snow.

Hazel handed her brother the rifle. She saw how his arms shook as he received it. He stood in the buckboard and hailed the Indians in their own language. The men on either side of Cut-Nose were greased with black paint and streaks of white. They came around the wagon and one of them took up the reins, his eyes dark and unreadable. After listening to Asa's salutation, Cut-Nose told the children not to be afraid. In Dakota, he told them there was a bad bunch of Ojibwe here in the woods that had attacked the sawmill. He asked Asa to set down the rifle.

"He's lying," Hazel told Asa under her breath, in case Cut-Nose's English was better than they thought.

"How do you know?" Asa said through his teeth.

"It doesn't make sense," she said.

At that moment, Turnip, barreling down the roadway, caught up with the wagon. The children had been unsure of their danger, thinking Asa could talk their way out of it, but for the dog this roadside encounter, the smell of things burning, the rust-colored bloodstains along the men's torsos, had little ambiguity. The Indian holding the reins scarcely had time to turn before the great shaggy form slammed into him and bore him to the ground.

"Run now!" Asa shouted.

He leapt down from the buckboard and made for the cornfield, Daniel and Hazel racing behind him. Cut-Nose was busy slashing at the snarling dog with the butt of his shotgun to keep his companions from getting mauled. Turnip lunged at him, while the oxen lowed in panic and surged forward, dragging the wagon behind them.

The children were running blindly through the corn when the blast that silenced the dog reached them. They ran on with their blood hot in their ears. The leaves of the corn tore at their clothing and scraped their skin. Heavy as stone, Ruth began to slip from Hazel's arms as she stumbled along, her lungs burning. She would see this cornfield in her dreams the rest of her life, Daniel running ahead of her, Asa, white-faced, urging them to move quicker.

Before them, a gathering of blackbirds feeding on the tassels stormed out of the corn, their many wings making a locomotive roar. Birds and more birds, singing around her a nightmare song. Halfway into the field, Hazel tripped in one of the furrows and Ruth's screams turned to shrieks as she was crushed to the ground. When Hazel tried to stand again, a white-hot pain shot up from her ankle and sang in her skull. She thrust the shrieking baby into Daniel's arms and pushed him ahead of her.

"Keep running," Asa shouted. Behind them, one of the Indians ran crouched, low and quick, parting the corn as he came. Asa knelt in a furrow, the rifle at his shoulder. He fired and the resulting acrid cloud of gunpowder stole their sight. When the cloud cleared, the Indian was gone.

Asa dropped the half-stock rifle and grabbed Hazel's hand. She could recall the feel of his fingertips—warm, slick with sweat as he tried to pull her along—and then the terrible shudder as a shot from behind tore away the back of his skull, and twisting, he fell on top of her, his legs folding beneath him.

She was blinded by his blood and had to wipe her eyes to try to see around her. Daniel was gone and she could no longer hear Ruth crying. She sat in the corn and held her stepbrother's ruined skull in her lap and waited for his killer to find her. Asa's blood soaked through the linsey-woolsey dress she wore, gluing them both to the black earth. His legs lay twisted beneath him. The front of his face was unmarred, his jaw clenched tight. She shut his eyes and placed his bloodied hands over the shirt pocket that held her father's letter. Ashes fell around them, dropping down through the corn leaves, and streaking Asa's hair with gray. She hoped they would be quick when they found her.

She heard stalks of corn being crushed in the chase. Someone shouted something in Dakota. The smell of blood and gunpowder burned in her nostrils. Where were the Indians who had been behind them, cutting off their hope of escape?

Then the corn parted and revealed one of the Indians, bright and terrible in his war paint, face charcoaled, owlish circles of white around his eyes. She looked up to meet her death. He was only a boy, his ribcage prominent. In her terror she failed to recognize him at first. He was breathing hard from the long chase. Smoke streamed from the barrel of the rifle he carried.

She held her brother's head in her lap and looked up into the face of Wanikiya and saw that his eyes were dark with what he had to do next. Her lips parted to say his name, but no sound came out. Behind him there was more shouting and he turned once in that direction. When he turned back toward her, his jaw was set, his nostrils flaring. He swung the barrel of the rifle around and hit her square in the forehead with the stock of the gun. Hazel heard the crack of the impact at the same time her mind flooded with shadows. She was unconscious before the back of her head struck the harrowed ground.

THE
CAPTIVE

SHE LAY DIRECTLY across the withers of a skinny pinto pony, its spine against her ribs, the smell of sweat and fear that rose from its hide filling her nostrils. The ride jostled Hazel and worsened the pain behind her eyes where it felt as though a nail had split her flesh and bone. Beyond the animal's fear she smelled a world on fire. The boy's voice, speaking in Dakota, drifted to her at times. It was not to Hazel passing in and out of consciousness that he spoke, but to encourage his pony as they rode past burning cabins and dead settlers by the roadside. *Waditanka sunghuna*, he said: *My brave pony, their ghosts will not hurt you.*

When she came to next, she found herself alone in the teepee of Blue Sky Woman. She had dreamed of birds again, twin ravens that led her through a dark wood. In the dream a dense canopy of leaves above them occluded the sunlight, the birds before her little more than liquid shadows flitting from branch to branch, urging her on. And then the woods opened unto a cornfield, green-gold in the sun, and somehow it was snowing in the dream though there were no clouds. There were children playing in the corn, a boy singing to a child, his voice high and sweet. Hazel would wake with his song in her mind, not knowing at first where she was. She woke in the gray time before first light. The pain in her skull receded to a dull ringing as the song of the boy faded. Below her she felt the itch of wool trader blankets. Someone had wound a light cloth around the wound on her forehead. Smoke spiraled and twisted up the cedar lodgepole and rose out the smoke flaps. Her dream rose with the smoke until it vanished. Outside, rain pattered against the lodging.

She knew where she was only by the constellation of markings painted on the inner skin of the room. Unlike the newer canvas teepees, Blue Sky Woman's dwelling was made of brain-tanned buffalo. Most Dakota marked their teepees on the outside for all to see. This was a private display. Here, in Blue Sky Woman's dwelling, tradition and the new religion intermingled. Though Hazel's head faintly ached, she watched the figures on the tapestry, a strange mixing of Christian and Dakota spirits now animate in the firelight. Then she swallowed, fully aware of her surroundings, as she remembered all that had happened the day before. No angels had come for Asa in the cornfield.

The memory stopped the breath in her chest. She touched the light-blue dress where her stepbrother's blood had soaked through the material. She remembered the sensation of his fingertips. Why had he waited for her? She recalled Daniel's face, white with terror, the baby howling in his arms as he turned to run deeper into the corn. What had happened to them? The last thing she remembered was the corn parting to reveal Wanikiya, and then later, waking tied to his pinto pony.

When she shut her eyes briefly she saw Asa reaching down for her once more, and then her mind blurred. Her memory let her step near the horror of his end and then reeled back. Her eyes flashed open again, her gorge rising. A knot began to swell in her chest as though she had swallowed a seed of ice and now it spread tendrils through her blood. *Don't recall him that way*, she thought as the numbness spread. Instead, she tried to remember his words of the night before as he sat near the smudge fire and recited Jakob's letter, a proud boy, full of himself and his plans. Only when she thought of him this way did she realize that she herself couldn't recall what words the letter contained.

My *dearest family*, he'd recited, and then there was a blank space in her memory. And the realization of this small loss amidst so many great ones burned through her and allowed her to cry. Hot and quick, the tears washed Asa's blood and her own from her face. Once she started, she couldn't stop. She cried until the ice tendrils in her chest cracked open, until her sides ached and her head throbbed. Tearful gasps shook her whole body. She was alone in a room of painted angels, grieving for her stepbrother.

She didn't know how long she cried but eventually, through the blur of tears, she saw a small goblin kneeling before her, a child-sized creature with black hair and glimmering eyes. The thing talked but the words made no sense. The world seemed to rotate around him, and Hazel shut her eyes and let her other senses spread out. The fire that burned nearby smelled of cedar, smoke to chase away evil spirits. Her body was slick with sweat and tears. When she opened her eyes again, the goblin resolved into Otter, the boy who had brought the warning to Asa. The boy whom none of them had believed. Otter's skinny body was mottled with paint the rain had blurred. He held a hand to his mouth, signaling quiet. "You must not cry," he said to her in Dakota. "Some of the warriors want to kill all the white captives. The women they took cry too much."

He kept his voice at a whisper. Smoke from the cedar fire billowed around him before rising past the lodgepoles. Where was Blue Sky Woman or Wanikiya? Sheets of rain came and went against the outer skin of the teepee, but here she was warm and safe. Caleb had said the rain would come. The last time she saw him he had stalked away into the tallgrass, furious with Asa. Had the Indians killed Caleb as well? If he was alive, her brother would come for her. Caleb was the hunter, the finder of lost things. Is that what she was now, a lost girl? She was beginning to think more clearly and realized she had cried her throat raw. She signaled this to Otter by touching her neck. He nodded and ducked past the teepee flap out into the rain.

While he was gone the heat in her throat spread through her like fever. A name rose up from memory, a name she had learned when they first entered this valley: Abbie Gardner, who had seen her entire family clubbed to death before her eyes by Inkpaduta's tribe in the Spirit Lake Massacre. A woman who became a warning for the children. *Be good or you'll end up like Abbie. Don't play with Indians; remember what happened to Abbie. Inkpaduta is still out there so you best come home before dark.* But the more they talked about her the more it became a tale, not something that happened to a real person.

An image of Abbie floated through Hazel's mind, the girl with her hair in a bun turning away from the artist, her lips barely opening as though she were seeing what happened again in her mind's eye and crying for help. *Only I have returned to tell these things,* she was about to say. The Senger family had seen this portrait their first day in the valley, more than four years before, on a wintry afternoon standing near a stove, a clutch of frightened children who could not fathom the new place they would call home. It had been Asa who said then, "Why Hazel, she looks just like you."

Again the breath stilled in Hazel's chest. She went on hearing her stepbrother's voice and the loss of him struck her once more, a fresh wave of sorrow sweeping through her.

By the time Otter returned with water she had been crying until her chest burned. The boy knelt beside her and tried to put his hand over her mouth. She tasted the salt of his palm through her tears. And suddenly she was angry with him, this boy who had tried to warn them of what was coming, who had done all he could to keep her safe. She bit down on the hand held over her mouth hard enough to draw blood. Otter shrieked and withdrew his hand. The anger which brought color to her cheeks, a pulse threading through tired flesh, made her feel strong. If he came near her again she would bite him like a wolf girl. Otter held his wounded hand against his chest and said, "Please, they will hear you and come." She let out a cry that was part animal and Otter ran out of the room still holding his wounded hand. When Hazel's throat was too raw to cry, she slept.

Blue Sky Woman came at last, carrying the childhood garments of her dead daughter. A short woman with a round face, she had been a captive herself long ago when the Dakota took her from the Ojibwe. She had black, lustrous hair and a pretty, heart-shaped face. Three summers had passed since Winona hanged herself with the buffalo strap used to carry water from the creeks. Asa had been the one to find her body. Winona had loved Asa. After the day he found her swinging from the branch he ran away. A week later he came back and confessed to Hazel what he'd done to the girl in the quiet of the meadow. He told her this and then never spoke of Winona again. At the time Hazel had wondered how men and boys grieved, if it was possible to cut someone out of you so you never thought of them when you turned over in the dark.

Blue Sky Woman was rough with her. She shushed her cries and pulled her up from the grass mats and trader's blankets where she lay by the fire. Too numbed to fight her, Hazel did as she was asked. She undressed Hazel, pouring water on the places where the linsey-woolsey dress had gummed to her skin, the dried blood like a second flesh she peeled away. The layers of her white self, her memory, Hazel thought. Blue Sky Woman had to use a knife on the blood-soaked petticoats that wrapped her so tightly. Naked in the firelight, Hazel held her hands over her breasts. Then she pulled on the beaded doeskin dress that had belonged to Winona, a costume that most Dakota didn't wear anymore, so common was the cotton and calico they purchased by trade or with their government annuity. The garment smelled faintly of earth and was cool against her skin.

Only when Hazel had sat again and Blue Sky Woman began to braid her hair did she at last understand what was happening. "Winona," Blue Sky Woman told her, "How long will you punish me with your silence? The white boy does not love you." Blue Sky Woman drew a vermilion streak down the center of her forehead and touched a red dot to either cheek. When she was done she sat back and studied her handiwork. This is how Hazel came to change places with a dead girl, even though she was no longer certain she wanted to live herself. "Oh my daughter," Blue Sky Woman said, her eyes glazed in the firelight, "my heart fills with happiness to have you here."

. . .

After Blue Sky Woman sent her out with a buffalo strap to gather water, Hazel discovered the other captives, none of whom she'd seen before. They numbered a quarter of the village, in fact—white women in frayed dresses, here or there a few surviving children, and one Bohemian man called Pieter the Indians kept alive because he was good with the many oxen they had taken. Hazel came down through a circle of teepees arranged around the brick house where Little Crow kept his wives. And though she was dressed like an Indian, her pale skin, previously hidden from the summer sun by a slat bonnet, showed her for what she was. The buffalo strap wrapped around her skull like a headband and behind it she felt the slight weight of the empty skin container she was to fill with water. The headache from her wound throbbed, but Winona's beaded doeskin dress felt soft and cool against her skin.

When she first encountered the other captives they were seated in a circle of wet grass shucking corn for the soldier's lodge. They would soon be sent out into the agency fields to gather more. Faces smudged by smoke, the women looked haggard and dirty. One of them had a long shawl beneath which she nursed a child. Most didn't notice Hazel or bother to look up as she approached them. A cadaverous woman cowered when she heard Hazel's footsteps and dropped her shucking pin. The others looked at the clothes she wore, brilliant with beads and rain, and scowled.

Hazel wanted one of them to be her mother, for one of them to rise and hold her, saying: *It will be all right. We've come through something terrible, but you're with me now and things will be fine.* Hazel wanted to speak them, to ask them: *Have any of you seen my brother Daniel? Were any other babies spared?* She begged them with her eyes. *Oh please, oh God. Tell me they are still alive.* But the women looked away, except for the nearest one, a large woman in a ruined black silk dress who spit on the ground before Hazel's feet. "Look at you," she said. "A little Indian princess. Folks not even in the ground and already you've forgotten them. Disgraceful."

Her words cut into Hazel like a rusty saw. Hazel turned away from her, tears spilling down her cheek and blurring the vermilion dots Blue Sky Woman had painted there.

"Leave her be," said the woman with a baby sheltered beneath her shawl.

"For shame," the big woman repeated, her voice low and hissing.

It seemed then that she might rise and strike Hazel, for she shifted her heavy rump on the grass and grunted like she was going to get up. Hazel stayed where she was, ready to receive the blow, a part of her wanting the pain even as the buffalo strap tightened around her forehead. But at that moment a group of young warriors returned from the prairie bearing scalps. The young men glistened in the rain and shouted for a crier to carry news of their deeds through the camp, of the whites they had killed like dogs. The array of scalps they carried were tied to their medicine belts and sashes and they had painted themselves with the blood of those they killed. Four of them danced around the circle and let the blood drip down from the scalps and shook stained tomahawks in the frightened women's faces. The emaciated woman fainted dead away while the other women held each other, eyes shut tight. But the fat woman set her jaw and looked only at Hazel as if the girl was to blame for what was happening now, as if this display confirmed every word she had spoken. The warriors ignored Hazel, catching sight of her dress only out the corners of their eyes and not recognizing her for the captive she was. An old man with iron-gray braids shouted for them to leave the women alone. He was hungry and the women could not shuck corn if mistreated. They should not have taken scalps. Were any of those killed warriors? There was no honor in the taking of *these* scalps, he told them. The warriors grumbled at the old man, but did as he asked and stalked away. Soon a crowd of young boys with toy bows surrounded them and filled the air with high trills.

Only then did Hazel see one of the scalps they carried was white-blonde, a boy's scalp, pink with skin and brain matter. Daniel!

She turned away from the woman's hateful glance and ran into the tallgrass where she vomited and heaved until her throat felt scorched and inside she was as empty as a field stripped by fire. How far had she run? She turned back toward the camp and saw the many cookfires glowing against the underside of the clouds. No one had seen her. Thunder groaned in the sky and the rain came harder now, thrashing through the tallgrass. In that moment, she smelled Winona's skin against her own.

Below her lay a creek and a steep ravine and across that the Lower Sioux Agency, charred stone buildings still smoking in the rain. How long ago had Asa seen the smudge of smoke against the sky and begun to reckon the danger coming their way? All around the agency were fields of corn ready for the harvest and across the grassy lawns Hazel saw a gathering of crows picking at the dead left out in the open and carrying hunks of flesh away to the woods.

Why had the Indians stayed here after the slaughter? Weren't they afraid the federal soldiers would come? She didn't care anymore. The sight of the scalp resolved her for what she had to do next. She didn't want to be alone in this world. Hadn't she been given this strap for a reason? Now she was sure she smelled Winona's skin, her hair and sweetgrass fragrance. She was no longer herself in this moment. Winona was inside her, but not the girl she knew once, a gentle girl who had broken open a cottonwood branch and shown her the pale white star inside the pulp and explained why the tree was sacred: a tree that sheltered her ancestors close to earth, where she might tie a prayer. It was from such a tree that Winona hanged herself. Now her voice came inside Hazel, stripped of its quiet cadence. *They all hate you*, it said. *It's your fault they died.* The words rolled out, heavy with malice. *If you hadn't fallen, Asa would still be alive.* And that was true. The voice kept on and then it took up a tone like the fat woman's, saying, *Look at you* over and over. *Look at you.*

Hazel walked past another corpse, a headless body riddled with arrows. She stumbled over the head and saw how the jaws were cracked open and stuffed with grass. In place of eyes, gold coins shone in the sockets. She kept going directly into the rain, keeping her head lowered to avoid seeing any more of the dead, until she found a cottonwood tree.

It was easy enough to make the buffalo strap into a noose and find a stump where she could balance herself. She could have run away then, but where to, when all was ashes and corpses, a prairie littered with bodies? Where, when all the world had turned to blood and hate and fire?

She slipped the knot around her throat. Her skin felt hot and fevered, all thoughts dwindling down to just one. Even in the shadow of the tree the rain found her and she felt it down inside her bones. Then she realized it was not thunder she heard in the clouds, but distant cannon fire. Fort Ridgely must be under attack, surrounded by warriors who would overwhelm the defenses in minutes. No hope even for them.

She kicked away the stump and felt the cord cinch tight around her throat. The branch crackled but held. She was choking now and as her legs swung out what she saw before her was the body of Winona, her face blotched, tongue distended. Winona stood directly in front of Hazel, beckoning. Hazel heard a screaming void in her ears as though a hole had opened in the ground below her. She remembered only then that suicides were said to go to Hell. In death, Winona's hair and fingernails had continued to grow, or maybe it was only her skin that had shrunk. Winona's hair whipped around her as she reached one long, horny fingernail toward Hazel. Even as she choked, Hazel was swept with terror and tried to twist away. Her face purpled as it filled with blood and spots burst before her eyes. Her mind was full of blue fire. And then the cord snapped and she fell.

Wet tallgrass cushioned her fall. She lay in the rain and mud, gasping as the air burned down her injured throat. When she felt a hand on her shoulder she shrieked, remembering her vision of Winona. The rain thrummed in the cottonwood leaves. Wind bent the grass around her. She kept her eyes shut and waited for the ghost to leave. But when she opened her eyes, the figure was still there, holding a bone knife she had used to cut the cord, a knife to give second birth. It was Blue Sky Woman and she had followed Hazel out of the camp.

The woman set the knife down and reached for the girl and Hazel did not find Blue Sky Woman's delusions terrible any longer. Hadn't she longed for one of the other captives to touch her, to take her into her arms like a daughter? Blue Sky Woman held her, rocking back and forth, a low rattling wail in her throat, the same sound she must have made when she had seen Winona dead in the tree three summers before.

Hazel's mind filled with the sound of her sorrow and the distant can-nonfire from the fort, miles downriver. Briefly, she tried to imagine the outer buildings, squat structures of stone in the wind and rain, crammed with refugees and soldiers shouting orders, but her mind couldn't form the images. There was the distant thunder, an unstoppable storm that had only now started to touch red and white alike. And Hazel was a sur-vivor, now twice borne from the wreckage. As was Blue Sky Woman, left behind by a husband and daughter.

Soaked with rain, her throat raw and bruised, Hazel shivered in the arms of a madwoman and for the first time didn't feel so lost and alone. She reached up a hand to touch the woman's face and felt hot tears against her palm. Blue Sky Woman stopped wailing. She held the hand pressed to her face and drew deep breaths. Then, as though Hazel were no more than a child, she carried her back down the hill to her teepee painted with thunder beings and angels, a place where the two might heal together.

To walk down to the river, the captives passed the agency whose charred stones stood like ancient ruins. Like the rest of the captives, Hazel learned to mark the places in the grass where the dead lay. Crows rose before them. A few Indian riders watched to make sure none of them tried to run. Hazel was the same as the others and yet not the same. The fat woman, she learned, was named Henrietta Grolsheim, and she reigned over the other captives like a petty tyrant. Very few of the other captives spoke to Hazel, following Henrietta's lead. Dressed in white doeskin, a quiet girl fluent in the Dakota tongue, she was sep-arate from them, but like them she did chores and walked past the killing ground to carry water up from the river.

In the river itself there were bodies. Once a soldier in a brass-but-toned uniform floated past, his face eaten away by bullheads and sun-fish. Hopeless. The captives had heard by then about the ambush on the other side of the river and how the soldiers had been lured down into a roadway surrounded by tallgrass and slaughtered there. But they had also heard that the first attempt to take the fort had failed, rain arriving in wind-driven gusts just as Little Crow's warriors shot their fire arrows at the buildings' shingled roofs. They would attack again soon, in greater numbers, sweeping away Fort Ridgely and New Ulm and driving the last of the whites from their valley. The captives did not think much about this as they walked past bodies blackening in the August sun. They thought, mostly, of themselves.

The woman who had kept the baby under her shawl disappeared before Hazel could learn her name. Killed, some said. Escaped, said others. Rumors came and went: All the hostages would be killed. They would be traded to the Lakota on the far plains or sold to other horseback tribes. Each was to be given a new husband. Some said there was a low building of green boughs into which women were brought and all that was later seen of them were their empty dresses, folded and laid in the sun. Hazel listened to them all, hoping for news of her family, hoping that she was not the only one left alive. As her skin began to darken she learned to respond to the name of Winona.

Hazel admired Henrietta's courage even as she feared her. When the captives came down through the corn fields and the killing ground, Henrietta intoned the twenty-third Psalm, her voice calm and assured. Henrietta did not deal in rumors like the others. The women's fine silk dresses and whalebone hoopskirts were taken from them and they were dressed in broadcloth skirts and loose, billowing sacques. Even in this crude costume, Henrietta carried herself like a woman in charge. *Yea though I walk through the valley of the shadow.* Some of the captives rubbed dirt into their pale skin to darken themselves and blend in. *I shall fear no evil.* A few went mad. The thin, frightened woman took off her saque dress one morning at the river and crouched there naked, the sunlight harsh on her bony body.

Henrietta stopped intoning her Psalm and called, "Clarissa, honey, you come here," as though speaking to a child, but the woman bared her teeth and a shudder possessed her entire body. When Henrietta approached her slowly, wading into the water, Clarissa turned and ran, kicking up water behind her until she found the center of the broad river and sank. There she flailed out with her scrawny arms, cackling the whole time, before she swallowed a great gulp of water and began to choke. The current took hold of her while they watched and as she rounded the bend only her pale, mouse-brown hair was visible and then, not even that. Henrietta turned, glancing once at Hazel before she spit in the water and went back to the other captives.

The third morning of Hazel's captivity, Wanikiya came to visit. Blue Sky Woman cooked him pork from one of the many slaughtered hogs—the meat speared on branches and dripping with grease—along with mashed corn. Hazel had not seen him since he'd brought her here on his pony. The last vision she had of him was when he parted the corn leaves and hesitated before striking her with the stock of his shotgun. He brought with him the memory of that pain and those deaths she had been trying to forget. Asa. Daniel. Ruth. He had promised three years ago when they lay together as children in the grass that he would care for her. He was the one who had brought her out of silence. What had that promise meant?

Blue Sky Woman left them alone after the food was cooked. Even though he was seated, Hazel could tell that he had grown taller in the three years that had passed. His skin shone a burnished copper color. He had the same narrow boyish waist, but his shoulders were broader, the muscles thicker along his arms and chest. He had the same black eyes and lock of silver in his hair, but his face had changed. His nose was long and straight, his mouth and chin more aggressive. From time to time he glanced up from his meal, as if he, too, were measuring the changes in her. He was not painted for battle, but there were dark circles under his eyes. She remembered Blue Sky Woman had once braided sweetgrass into his hair and the scent had mixed with his boyish smell. His body now reeked of sweat and a faint acrid smell that reminded her of gunpowder.

This odor brought her back again to Asa's last moment. When Wanikiya parted the corn, smoke had raveled from the mouth of his gun. Any words she meant to offer him were snared in her throat. A mixture of emotions surged through her now and the one that surfaced, bright and hard, was hatred. Before she knew what she was doing, she sprang across the room and started swinging for him with the flats of her hands. She knocked the bowl of mashed corn from his grasp and tore at his hair. In the back of her mind she heard her own high shrieking. Her hands were curled into claws and she scratched at his face and throat.

He absorbed these blows for only a moment, then caught each of her swinging hands in his own and hurled her to the other side of the teepee. Before Hazel could spring up again, he was on top of her, pinning her to the grass mat. She tried to struggle and felt the lean, corded strength of him holding her down. Along the hollow of his throat she saw how she had laid the skin bare, a long ribbon clawed open. She could smell his blood. "Murderer," she hissed. "Murderer." Beneath the sweat she could smell his odor, a sweet fragrance like fry bread. He looked bewildered, his mouth opening and closing. All this time he said nothing, and then he let her hands go. She could strike him again now if she wanted. He stayed on top of her, his hipbones joined with hers. A fleck of blood dropped from his throat and speckled her cheek. She wiped it away.

Another wave of emotion swept through her and this time she wept, a convulsive sound that ripped through her. Her entire body shook. And still he did not release her. She felt his hands touch her hair. He touched the warm tears along her face and then touched his finger to his own lips. How long they stayed like this she didn't know, but eventually he rose again and stood over her. She wanted to go on weeping, curled into a fetal circle, but all the weltering feelings had drained away. She found, as well, to her dismay, that she missed the gentle press of him against her.

A day later he came again when she was alone grinding dried strips of pork to make pemmican the warriors could carry on their journeys. He sat across from her. With the large stone she used to grind the dried meat she could have hurt him, but all the rage had gone out of her. Wanikiya watched her work in silence. She glanced once at him and saw wounds she had laid open along his throat and chest. She saw too that he wore two feathers in his headdress, one for each coup he'd counted in battle, and did not know if these feathers were for dead Ojibwe, or dead whites.

"I don't know you anymore," she said at last. She waited. Did he still remember his English? Three years had passed and he'd had only one summer of learning. One brief summer that she had not stopped thinking about ever since the fire. Ever since he'd beheld her under the blackened tree that had filled with monarch butterflies, a tree the old man had seen in a dream. Hanyokeyah. They hadn't heard what happened to him. After Winona died, he'd just stopped coming across the river.

When Wanikiya spoke it was in Dakota. "You should be careful about going too far," he said. "The bullet the red-haired one fired . . ."

"Asa," she said in English. "His name was Asa."

". . . struck Tatanyandowan in the leg and went out the other side. He wanted to kill us both when he returned, but I brought you here knowing what would happen. Blue Sky Woman is under the protection of Tamaha. As long you are here and Tamaha decides you are helping Blue Sky Woman, he will let you live. In a way you belong to him, just as Winona once did." He paused at the name and looked away. "But be careful. Don't go alone for water. Don't go alone into the corn. Tatanyandowan knows you are here. His wound has kept him from the fighting and he is very angry. If he finds you alone, he will not care about Tamaha."

Hazel set down the heavy stone. She felt a renewed headache coming on. Wanikiya rose and headed for the blanket doorway. She held out a hand and touched his leg, saying in Dakota, "Please. Stay."

He paused. "I have to prepare," he said. "Taoyeteduta and the other leaders will soon attack the big house."

She searched in her mind for the words in Dakota. "Did you kill Asa?" she asked at last.

He was a silent. Outside in the village, they heard a crier moving from teepee to teepee announcing the preparation for the battle to be joined the next day. A boy's voice full of promise and excitement. The fort would fall, his voice promised. The *wasicun* soldiers would surely die like mice in the jaws of wolves. It was there in the background, this child's voice singing of destruction.

"Yes," he said, speaking English for the first time. His head turned as he listened to the crier outside. Hazel waited for him to say more in Dakota. *I had to kill him, so that the other warriors would let me carry you from the field. He died so that you might live. He died so that I could revenge Winona, so that her spirit would no longer be restless.* Wanikiya was silent and turned back toward her, his eyes shining. Did he think she would strike him again? Was he sorry for her, or for what he had done?

At first, she didn't see anything like pity in Wanikiya's expression. As a boy his voice had been soft, but now he spoke in hard monosyllables. She saw a quick flash in his eyes, a glittering darkness. His adam's apple fluttered within his throat. For just one moment the mask he had been wearing fell away and he was a boy again. It was there in the dark bruiselike circles shadowing his eyes. And she knew then that he had done and seen terrible things in these past few days. Hadn't she seen that same haunted look on Asa's face so long ago? She saw as well that he needed her as much as she needed him. It lasted for only a moment and then he swallowed hard and his nostrils flared. The mask of the adult remade itself. Before he could leave, she asked, "Daniel? And Ruth?"

"They did not find the children," he said, and then pushed out the doorway into the gathering dark.

BURIED
ALIVE

HAZEL DID NOT sleep the rest of that night. Alongside Blue Sky Woman she poured lead for bullets that would be used against her own people. She pounded plum stones into grit and mixed it with sun-dried pork for the men to carry in their parfleches, meat so that they would not go hungry while they tried to kill those inside the barricades.

Bonfires speared the dark while men dipped their bare hands into steaming dog stew to lift out hunks of meat. And they told stories of what they'd done and how easily the whites had died while Hazel kept her eyes on the ground and tried not to hear.

She made the bullets well, felt their cool weight in the palm of her hands. Bullets made to pierce flesh, to burrow into bones and vital organs. She contemplated tossing them into the darkness where they would never be found again. But then she would be seen, then she would have shown herself to be of little worth. It was better to do what was asked of her. In this way she hoped to be spared so that, in turn, she might save others. Daniel and Ruth were still out there. The young blond boy and his russet-haired half sister. Daniel had always been good at hiding. She closed her eyes and tried to picture where he was now. Maybe he had made it across the river to the fort. But if that was true, if somehow he'd found his way to Palmer's Ferry, then one of these bullets might find him.

When she stopped working, the song of the wailing dancers came to her. She heard the death songs and the telling of the deeds and her hope faded. Hazel did not see Wanikiya among the dancers. She sought to lose herself in her tasks, to pour the lead into molds and hear the metal hiss and cool into casings, to keep pounding the meat until her shoulders and arms were raw and sore from lifting the heavy stone. Not to think of her dead stepbrother. Her mind swam with the songs around her, with the memory of Wanikiya close to her, the way he had taken one of her tears into his mouth, as though he had wanted to taste her sorrow. As though in the years that passed he too had not stopped thinking about her.

In the morning, captives joined the long train to Fort Ridgely. Arrayed on horseback and on foot, the warriors were painted in many shades, charcoal to vermilion, a glorious sight in the morning sun. Hazel could not count their numbers, lost in the dust their ponies and wagons kicked up. The warriors sang as they came through the valley toward the fort, certain of victory. She moved as part of that train, knowing that her hands had made some of the bullets in their guns; her hands had tied the ribbons to their festive ponies bearing the bells that now jingled and glinted.

In all that long train, Henrietta found her and limped by her side. Hazel saw that the woman had bound her swollen feet in white linen. She gritted her teeth with each step she took across the razor grass. Hazel's own soles had been toughened from summers running barefoot to spare her worn leather shoes and now she wore moccasins to complement Winona's doeskin leggings. She moved with ease beside the crippled woman dressed in broadcloth and fraying calico. When Henrietta was side-by-side with her, she hissed, "Squaw." The word had an ugly sound in her mouth. "You are not the only one who has friends."

Henrietta squared her broad shoulders and looked around to make sure no one was listening. Wherever captives gathered there were also half-breeds who could report their words and plans back to their captors. The woman stepped on a shard of rock and snarled. She stopped and Hazel stopped by her side, instinctively reaching out to a person in pain. Henrietta's face, glazed with sweat, glistened like a ham hock in the sun. The skin along her cheeks and arms had pinked and burned away in layers. Her bandages were soiled with dirt and yellow ooze. Henrietta gritted her teeth and told Hazel that she had bribed some of the half-breeds to protect her by promising them there was buried treasure on her land and only she could show them the place. Hazel thought at first she was being accepted into the woman's confidence, but then she saw how the woman looked at her with blazing eyes, her fat chin quivering. "I saw you making those bullets," she said. "One day the soldiers will rescue us. You don't really think a tribe of savages can humble the United States military? And I will be alive to tell what you did. I will live to see you punished for your treachery."

Hazel left Henrietta to hobble behind her and caught up with Blue Sky Woman, who was walking beside a lumbering ox that dragged along travois poles loaded down with her teepee and sinew-bound belongings. They trundled up a steep ridge through dark oak forests until they rose to a flat prairie tableland. Below her Hazel saw the spread of the river valley and the brown curve of the river. A half-mile wide, the valley rose up in heavily-treed ridges on either side until it met prairie. To the west, thunderheads percolated on the horizon. East of her, where the tableland fell away into steep ravines, she thought she saw thin ribbons of smoke that marked where the fort stood. Hazel tried to imagine the refugees and soldiers crouched within the low stone buildings.

Here on the prairie, only a mile from the fort, the Indians began to establish their camp under a hazy mid-afternoon sun. Hazel helped Blue Sky Woman set up the teepee. A cool breeze graced the bluestem grasslands. She saw beads of moisture quivering on the strands of grass, the remnant of the previous day's storms. If the rains came again, the Dakota would not be able to use their fire arrows. Their earlier jubilation would soon be replaced by the low keening of death songs as the men prepared themselves for battle. Hazel held the teepee poles while Blue Sky Woman drove in stakes, and she glanced up from her work to watch the men weaving gold grass in their headbands so the soldiers would not see them coming. It was so quiet during these preparations that she could hear a meadowlark singing in the grass. Even the dogs had ceased their barking. Her own breathing was still and measured.

How many? Hundreds and hundreds of warriors with shotguns and bows, all gleaming now in shades of ochre and yellow-green. When the men moved into the tallgrass only their feathers and grassy headbands were visible. A sea of dark-haired warriors, moving across the prairie so that it looked like the land itself had come to life and was boiling down in an unstoppable wave to smother the fort. Who could stand against so many? Then there was only the dust following after them in low brown clouds and Hazel waited for the shooting to begin.

Caleb stood next to man a named Noles or Noel, he couldn't be sure which. In the first battle, two days previous, Noles had been shot through the mouth, the bullet passing through each cheek, grazing a few teeth along the way, but leaving the gums untouched. The wound had not stopped him from talking. Noles had a flowing black beard and wore a blue kepi he had taken from a wounded soldier. "Seventy-one thousand in gold coin, did you see it?" (Except it sounded like "Ssseveny-one ousan in ole oin, d' ya sssee eh?" because of his injury.)

Caleb said nothing. The annuity payment that had arrived by stagecoach the day before was a favorite subject of Noles. He had seen the glittering coins after one of the soldiers lifted the lid of a keg to show boyish Lieutenant Gere. Sick with mumps, the Lieutenant had blanched at the sight. Captain Marsh and twenty men had been annihilated in an ambush down at the ferry, and if the Indians chose to attack there were only a smattering of soldiers and civilians armed with muskets to defend more than two hundred women and children fled from prairie massacres. "Seveny-one ousan," he said again, loosing a choked whistle. "All for lousy savages." Noles loaded a pipe with a dark plug of tobacco and then squatted in the grass trench to light it with a lucifer match. The bitter smell of English tobacco drifted up to Caleb a moment later. Noles rose again and breathed out a cloud of smoke from his nostrils. Thin streams of smoke also spiraled from the hole in either side of his cheek. Noles swore the tobacco was keeping him from infection.

Caleb judged him to be about forty by the gray hairs woven in his beard. A forty-year-old Welsh bachelor farmer who for some reason had taken to Caleb and followed him everywhere he went about the fort. Unlike the other shocked settlers, Noles had been preparing for this war all along. His cabin had been carved from the side of a hill, the windows mere slits, just large enough for a man to steady his rifle. But the Indians had set fire to his grass roof and left him to burn to death. Noles, hidden in the root cellar, had dug his way out with a cracked plate.

Caleb didn't believe what the others said about the gold. If this was all about the $71,000, he would fight to deliver it to Little Crow himself. But no amount of gold could stop what had started now. He tuned out Noles's chattering. Around them soldiers and civilians scurried up from the ravines carrying all the water they could in tubs and buckets and basins. There were women in aprons working side by side with men to whittle down slugs that would fit the rifles. Caleb's hands were blistered from helping dig trenches in the parade yard. "Will rain 'gain," Noles was saying, his teeth gritted around the pipe stem. "Look at them thunderheads buildin'." Caleb nodded. Swift dark clouds had already eaten away fringes from the blue sky and obscured the sun.

Their situation no longer seemed so dire. Reinforcements had arrived the previous day, the Renville Rangers from St. Peter, and Lieutenant Sheehan and his men from Glencoe, who had force-marched all forty-two miles in a day's time. Sheehan inspired more confidence than the mump-faced Gere. He had a bladed, angular face with prominent cheekbones, slate-gray eyes and a well-groomed beard. This was no boy in uniform. Still, if Little Crow attacked again, he was sure to bring overwhelming numbers and the last time the hostiles had only been stopped by the rain and the skill of McGrew and Sergeant Jones working the mountain howitzer. Joined by Jones and O'Shea tossing brimstone from their six-pound hellfire fieldpieces in the southwest corner, the artillerists bombarded the Indians with howling shrapnel.

Caleb was weary from digging the trench, but he didn't want to go back inside and see Cassie again. Their flight from the woods still haunted him. Caleb had been in the trees cutting wood with the double-bladed ax when the Indians came to the farm. He stopped to study them, small figures from this distance, two of them little more than boys. Otter's warning played at the back of his mind. A moment later he saw Cassie's mother fleeing across the prairie, arms wrapped around a jingling jar.

Caleb had huddled in the mosquito-loud shadows, where he saw it all happen. The Indians carried shotguns; his ax would be nothing before them. One of the warriors took Cassie's little sister by her heels and swung her around in a tight circle until her head dashed against the porch post. Caleb heard the splatter even from the woods. And still, he'd remained hidden. His gorge rose and choked off breath. His arms and legs felt heavy and wooden. He saw them chase Cassie into the garden and grab her by the hem of her dress, hauling her down. She gave one desperate hoarse cry, then called his name. "Caleb! Oh, Caleb." Two of the Indians had held her against the ground while the other slit open her dress straight down the middle, until it opened to expose her pale naked skin and the mound of her pregnant belly. They had to lay their guns to the side to do this. The one with the knife had looked once in Caleb's direction and scanned the area around him before undoing his breechclout.

His betrothed. His baby. The thought of what they were doing loosed Caleb from his terror. He came on through the woods, mosquitoes humming around him in rank clouds. He was running by the time he crossed the prairie, keeping low in the swishing grass. If they looked up, at any moment he would be a dead man. He heard Cassie retch and sob, heard the Indians' low muttering. His momentum carried him directly into their midst, and then he was among them, swinging. His terror turned to rage. He felt the heft of the heavy blade, heard the thunk of it as it burrowed into ribcages and split clavicles and sundered heads like rotten wet lumps of wood. Blood spattered him and he kept swinging, a roaring in his brain and throat, a red haze shrouding his vision.

When his sight cleared, he saw the blood-streaked grass and for a moment feared that he had killed Cassie along with the Indians. Then he saw her, holding the split dress, her face pale with horror. Caleb let the ax drop. He cleaned the blood from his face and wrapped her in a blanket from the cabin. He wanted to leave her hidden in the woods and go for his family, but she wouldn't hear of it.

"Oh, please," she said. "If you leave, it will be my death. I know." And so he had carried her, keeping to the woods, as they made for Palmer's Ferry, smelling the ashes and burning cabins all around them. At a cabin by the river's edge, he'd found an abandoned birchbark canoe and ferried her across.

She'd been laid up in the hospital ever since. He couldn't stand to look at her, even as he was sure more than ever of his love for her. The sight of her reminded him too much of how slow he'd been to react.

Around her in the hospital there were dozens of wounded. A woman stabbed with a pitchfork. A hysterical German lady who kept crying out *"Mein kinder! Mein kinder!"* her arms upthrust, as though she expected them to swim out of the air and join her again. Cassie lay among them, terrified of the cramping she felt ribbon through her womb and abdomen. It was not time for the baby to come. She must will it still inside her. Last night—before the reinforcements had arrived, when all felt sure the Indians would come to kill them before the sun's rising— she had clung to his shirt sleeve, saying, "Caleb, do you think God is punishing us?"

When Caleb had approached Lieutenant Sheehan and asked for permission to leave and search for his brothers and sisters, the man didn't even bother to meet his eyes. "Absolutely out of the question," he told him. "We'll need every man that can still shoot straight." So he stayed outside here with Noles and chatted about the weather and all the things a man could buy with $71,000.

Caleb looked out over the waving gold-tipped grasslands. There was nothing to stop Little Crow if he came with enough warriors, just a few scattered buildings: a barracks of sturdy granite, officer's quarters made of flimsy clapboard, low log houses for the hospital and laundry. All sited on a grassy plain surrounded by ravines and deep woods that provided an enemy with perfect cover. Couldn't he pretend to head down to the well and just keep walking? He could swim the river and then search for his family. But a whole day had passed without any more refugees trickling in. If they were not here, Noles had said, then they were dead.

Caleb saw a flicker of movement in the grasses at the same time as he heard one of the scouts cry, "Indians. Oh my God!"

Scattered gunshots strafed the prairie, men firing at phantoms in the grass. Here and there Indians rose from the tallgrass and loosed flaming arrows that thunked into the shingled rooftops of the fort. Caleb paused then, entranced by the slow arc of the burning missiles which hissed like fire serpents as they came. The arrows dropped in the grass, struck rooftops, met rain-damp surfaces, and went out. A moment after the fiery barrage, the grasslands parted to reveal more and more braves, screaming high and shrill, as they charged the fort. Some of the Indians crouched to fire their shotguns and the air whistled with shredded lead. Caleb opened fire alongside Noles, whose answering explosion instantly deafened him.

He heard that same oceanic roaring in his ears and for a moment entertained the wild thought of charging out among the Indians alone, swinging his rifle butt. He knew in those moments what his father Jakob had written about, the thing that had come inside him at faraway Chickahominy River. His blood throbbed in his chest and head and each thing he saw out there in the grassy plain imprinted onto his brain, so that he would remember ever afterward the sound of his heartbeat in his eardrums and the way the grass seemed to grow limbs and arms and painted faces distended in howls, as though the prairie itself were come for them now. Caleb was made for this violence, but he was no fool. It was safe here with his face in the black mud. Noles, somehow, still had his pipe gritted in his teeth, and he hooted when McGrew and Jones opened up with the mountain howitzers and the shells howled among the Indians. The artillery broke their charge and the Indians retreated back into the woods

"Like a gold wave," said Noles. "Pretty to see 'em comin' on. Even prettier to see 'em fall."

Beside Noles and Caleb, there was a farm boy in honey-colored homespun. The boy looked even younger than Caleb, his face grimed, eyes a cool German blue. This boy propped up his rifle and spat out the gunpowder that blacked his teeth and tongue. "Will they come again?" he asked. "Too many of them to shoot."

His answer arrived when a group of Indians charged the stable and took cover there. Rifle fire failed to bring them down, but McGrew had also seen them go inside and the resounding blast of the howitzer split the barn in a great ball of flame, scattering fragments of burning wood and torn limbs. Twice more this happened. As the Indians gained an outer building, artillery demolished it.

Then it was raining again: thunder in the sky, thunder on the ground. The Dakota boiled up out of a ravine at the southern edge, shrieking like catamounts, faces smeared with wet and colored paints. Caleb tore open the gunpowder papers with his teeth and poured in the powder and rammed home the cut slug. Again and again, he did this, not bothering to aim, discharging his rifle at the oncoming wave. The artillerists found them, too, and when the explosions fell among them, the Dakota broke and fled for the woods.

After an hour of this, it grew still and the roaring in their ears was replaced by the pattering of rain. An aproned woman climbed out among the boys, distributing new cartridges she and the blacksmith had whittled down, promising coffee if they stayed steady. Caleb swallowed and felt his stomach turn over from the gritty taste of the gunpowder. He leaned his head back and drank in the rain. It had seemed that every Indian in the entire valley had come against them, and they were still alive.

He thought again of his brothers and sisters, shut his eyes, as he used to be able to do when he was a boy. Then he had a sight, a way of finding people and things that were lost. But now he saw nothing, only felt the rain chilling his skin, the gunpowder raw in his throat.

. . .

If Blue Sky Woman suffered from a delusion, it was elusive and inconstant. After the second attack at the fort failed, the warriors, so radiant that morning, returned wet and grumbling, the echo of artillery shrill in their eardrums. Hazel's heart rose at this news and then fell with the next words of the crier. One of the chiefs demanded payment in blood, and would take it from the captives. Many of the captives who were being protected by sympathetic Dakota were sent out to hide in rainchilled ravines. It was said only two warriors had been killed by the "rotten balls," but there were many injured and soon some of these would come to Blue Sky Woman's teepee for healing. Hazel could not be there when they came. She found herself wondering about Wanikiya, if he was among the wounded.

Blue Sky Woman ducked under the teopa, rattling the elk hooves hung above the entrance. She said all the captives were to be "*Pa Baska*," heads chopped off. Her face was glazed with rain. Hazel wondered how she could still call her Winona if she recognized at heart who she was. "My daughter," the woman said. "You must hide. Come, I know a place for you."

She took Hazel to the teepee of Spider Woman, an old widow the girl had sometimes seen at the Episcopalian Church near the agency. Spider Woman had a Bible, though she could not read, and spoke fondly of the Holy Spirit, calling him Taku-skan-skan, the same name the Dakota had for the god of motion. Her English was limited to three words. Her teepee, like Blue Sky Woman's, was made of buffalo skin, tattooed with blurred symbols of Dakota and Christian belief. Hunched like her namesake, Spider Woman pulled aside a long strip of carpet laid under a ratty buffalo fur. She had been busy digging the hole that Blue Sky Woman had asked her to make.

As bidden, Hazel crawled into the hollowed-out hiding place. Fibrous roots spread out below her. The smell of wet earth tickled the insides of her nostrils. Blue Sky Woman handed down a skin of water, some pemmican they had pounded together earlier while listening to the thundering artillery, and, more ominous, the bone knife. "Sleep, daughter," she said. "It won't be long." Then she went away to tend the wounded. Hazel stared up at the buckskin dress and wrinkled moon-face of Spider Woman. When the old woman smiled her black eyes disappeared into a nest of wrinkles. "I pray thee," she said, and then pulled the covering over the hiding place.

Time blurs when you are under the earth. She thought of a Poe story her Pa had reprinted in the days when he had his press, "The Tell-Tale Heart," and the great beating heart the murderer went on hearing in his sleep. Questions swirled inside her. Did the warriors' defeat mean they would have to leave this valley soon? How could Blue Sky Woman know that Hazel was not her daughter and yet continue to act as though she was Winona? Above her, Hazel heard low muttering, a gruff male voice addressing Spider Woman. She tightened her grip on the bone knife. Dirt sprinkled down in clumps from the low ceiling.

No light could penetrate the covering. It was so dark she could not see her hand before her face. When the voices stopped, she nibbled some of the pemmican and swallowed a sip of water. She waited. Gradually, she became aware of other sounds down in the ground with her. Through the holes made by snakes or some large rodent, a cooling wind blew that chilled her to the marrow. She felt goosepimples rippling along her arms and thighs. In the blackness the fibrous roots fanned out beneath her like long-nailed fingertips. Hazel squeezed her eyes shut. She could hear her heart beating in her ears. Her breath came short. *Calm yourself*, she thought. *You can't panic down here.*

Faces swam out of the pitch before her. She saw Winona with curving yellow nails and long, streaming hair. Asa with his staring eyes and slack jaw. The soldier who floated past her in the river, his face gnawed by fish. Something seemed to be crawling out of the hole and she rolled and felt the roots scrape her like claws, like the corn leaves that had torn her dress as she ran blindly behind her stepbrother. She began to panic, her lungs constricting in her chest.

One. Two. She kept counting until the images went away. She whispered The Lord's Prayer and heard the dim echo around her. The sound of her own voice soothed her and so she continued to recite things in the dark, stories her Pa had spoken to her while they rode in the *hexenwald*. Words became fluid, shifting from English to Dakota and the stories changed too. There were princes who hid from their own brothers coming to kill them, a man who could change himself into a crow, a Dakota girl kept captive in a low square soddie by a blond ogre. As long as she murmured these things she was not swept up in the fear of being buried alive. She told the stories, picturing imagined worlds shaped by her voice, a lulling that eventually allowed her to sleep.

In the morning the old woman lifted the lid from the hiding place. Even the muted morning light within Spider Woman's teepee blinded Hazel. She smelled sunshine and dew evaporating outside. Blue Sky Woman reached down a hand and helped her out of the hole. Hazel's limbs were stiff and swollen; minutes passed before she could stand straight.

Things had quieted throughout the camp. Blue Sky Woman told her the warriors had left to raid New Ulm a second time now that they had failed to take the fort. There were no big guns at New Ulm. If this attack did not succeed, soon they would leave for Yellow Medicine country. Blue Sky Woman took her back to her dwelling and fed her a stew of stringy meat and bitter roots. Hazel was afraid to ask her about Wanikiya. When the two were done eating, she handed Hazel Winona's awl, a curved elk antler used for sewing.

Notches ridged the edge. Just as the warriors gained eagle feathers each time they counted coup in battle, the women kept measure of their accomplishments on the awl. Each notch stood for a thing made. Hazel let her finger run along the grooved bone and remembered the moccasins Winona had made for Asa. A girl that gives such a gift means for the boy to become her protector. Had Asa known this? After she hanged herself, he threw them away in the river. There were three notches in Winona's awl. What else had she made?

Blue Sky Woman passed her an old red stone pipe with a two-foot-long willow stem, a pipe just like hers, so they could both smoke kinnikinnick while they sewed, holding the stem gently between their teeth and exhaling the sweet herb while their free hands stitched together the garments and clothing their loved ones would need most. Blue Sky Woman had brought Hazel a few long strips of white doeskin and some colored beads. She spread buckskin containers of earthy pigments and a scattering of porcupine quills before her. Hazel was practiced with a needle and thread, but the awl felt clumsy in her hands, more like a weapon. She looked over at Blue Sky Woman, who smiled back, eyes crinkling, smoke curling around her. The sunshine coming through the teepee skin was a liquid amber. It was easy to believe that there was no war. She was content for it to be just like this, no difficult choices, no hiding in dark holes, no blood or terror. How often had Blue Sky Woman and Winona sewed, mother and daughter, in a comfortable silence? She gave Hazel a nod of encouragement and the girl began to make a set of moccasins for Wanikiya, unsure if he would even accept them.

She did not possess Winona's skill with an awl. The holes she punctured in the doeskin were jagged and uneven. She didn't punch through the material so much as stab at it, as if it was still alive, and she was afraid of it. After a half hour of mangling the leather she threw the deformed fragments down in disgust.

Blue Sky Woman didn't seem to notice. "I will tell you," she said, "how I came to belong to the leaf-dwellers." She took up the damaged pieces of leather and rubbed tallow into the skin to stretch and reshape it. "It was summer near the big waters, a day of sun after rain like this one. I was only this tall." She held her hand about two feet above the grass mats where the two sat working and she went on to tell of her childhood with the Ojibwe, her mother warning her not to cry out as she hid Blue Sky Woman under a buffalo blanket during a nighttime raid by Dakota warriors. This is how she came to live among the leaf-dwellers, after all her family were killed. This is how she came to love her enemy.

Her hands moved in time with the story, the awl punching neat holes through the skin. She was finished with preparing the soles of the shoes. Her heart-shaped face was downcast and Hazel wondered what other stories the woman held inside her. The story of the man she loved, a soldier at the fort her people had just attacked. Of Winona.

Blue Sky Woman nodded at the porcupine quills, as if this were any other day. Hazel looked at her, thinking, *will I be like her one day, having forgotten the people I was born among?* Would her English fall away along with her white skin and clothing until she too became inseparable from the leaf-dwellers? It was not a terrible thought. She would do whatever it took to survive.

SONGS
IN THE
TALLGRASS

HAZEL CONTINUED TO muse over these things as she walked down to the river. Where was she now in the valley? How far away from home? In the heat of midafternoon the entire camp seemed to be drowsing. Despite losing two battles at the fort, the Dakota evidenced no fear of soldiers. Sunlight glared from stolen mirrors, copper pots, and silver tureens carried as booty from the traders' stores and settlers' cabins and strewn about the camp. The half-wolf curs the Indians kept lay sleeping in the hot grass.

The only thing stirring was a group of girls playing with toy teepees who did not look up at Hazel. The teepees were exact canvas replicas and they played with dolls of twined grass with intricate beadwork dresses and dolls of cornshuck dressed in shreds of calico. When Hazel came past them the girls were holding a pretend council with the grass dolls debating what to do with the ugly shuck dolls. She hurried on before they looked up and noticed her. No other captives were around and she wondered if they were all still in hiding. Her mind reeled from the kinnikinnick smoke and the story Blue Sky Woman had told.

Past grazing speckled ponies, Hazel went down a long sloping hill that took her a quarter mile to the Minnesota River. A light wind touched the oak treetops into motion and dappled the light. The river was gilded by the afternoon sun. In the wind Hazel heard a woman singing a hymn and caught her breath. The woman was singing "What Wondrous Love is This?" a sweet sad hymn that Hazel's mother Emma used to sing to the children in the cradle, willing them to grow with her voice. The song came to her now, rising up from the golden river, and filled her with a longing to see her family again:

And when from death I'm free, I'll sing on, I'll sing on;
And when from death I'm free I'll sing on; And when from death
I'm free I'll sing His love for me, And through eternity I'll sing on,
I'll sing on, And through eternity I'll sing on.

The woman's voice held the last note before fading off. Around Hazel the shadows of the trees flickered in the wind. On either side of the river, banks rose up toward plateaus of swaying tallgrass. Where had the woman's voice come from? It came and went, leaving a hollow space within Hazel. And what she thought she heard was the ghost of her mother. This filled her with hope. *My mother lives inside of me. There is yet beauty in the world. There is no place I can go where she will not find me.* It could not have been an actual woman she heard singing. Who among the captives would sing in these circumstances?

The brown river below glimmered in the sun, curling around a bend that would eventually lead to Palmer's Ferry and the bluff high above where the children came to watch the steamboats wind toward the agency in early summer. She thought she could keep walking now, follow the bend of the river toward home, searching after that lost voice again. If home still remained. If any were alive. Wanikiya had said that she was safest here. Abroad on the prairies roamed warriors who had been turned back twice from the fort and now still searched for vulnerable settlers.

Hazel waded in the warm tea-brown water and dipped in her container. The reflection of the sun blinded her. Her stomach felt full, content, and she was at peace kneeling in the water. She felt the ridged shape of Winona's awl, which she had tucked into her sash, poking her in the side. All she noticed in that moment was the faint pressure of the awl, the curious silence along the river now that the woman's voice had come and gone, and the sun on her skin.

When she turned back to shore, she saw Tatanyandowan there, watching her. She mistook him at first for Wanikiya and her heart skipped a beat. The two brothers had the same facial features, but Pretty Singer's headband rode lower to hide his torn earlobe. Besides his war shirt he wore only breechclout and leggings. His eyes, pulled into slanting angles by the tightness of his braids, narrowed to slits as he watched her in the water.

The river sloshed against the shore. Hazel looked back toward camp and saw that they were alone. The man who watched her had vacant, empty eyes. Every fiber of her being strained to run, but her feet were planted in the deep river mud, her muscles rigid. Pretty Singer came toward her holding out his hands to show that he didn't mean harm. Hazel's stomach lurched at the sight of him and the blood flooded back through her locked muscles and allowed her to move at the same time as he sprang for her. Even injured, he was too quick. An arc of water trailed after him; his outstretched hands hooked like talons and one caught her by the hem of her dress. She pulled away, wild to get back up the hill and take shelter in Blue Sky Woman's teepee. The dress tore open and his hand slipped free.

She was running, the water spraying around her, a shout for help rising in her throat. Then the next moment his arms were around her waist and she was lifted and carried from the water. She struck along his abdomen with the flats of her hand but this just made him squeeze her tighter until she couldn't breathe anymore.

He hurled her down on the silty shoreline and the breath was jolted from her. Out of the corner of her eyes she saw the skin container floating off down the river, in the same direction she had contemplated escaping moments before. Pretty Singer took off his war shirt and breechclout. His body was scarlet in the sun, his muscles taut, but her eyes were drawn to the side of his leg where the blood crusted around a recent wound. The wound her stepbrother had made just before he died. She turned away from his nakedness. His breathing came in hoarse gasps. He reached down and pulled up Winona's one-piece beaded doeskin dress, the cloth ripping as he yanked and tugged.

And the thought came to her: this cloth had been torn in such a way before, and Blue Sky Woman had mended it. The sash fell away with the dress. Hazel's throat felt charred, her breath weak and light inside her chest. Even as she felt the warmth of the sun on her exposed skin, her blood was chilled. Pretty Singer knotted his fist in her hair and forced her to look at him. She shut her eyes. His breathing continued to rasp. She felt the warm grains of sand along the backs of her thighs and arms.

Pretty Singer began to talk to her in a hushed voice, as though she were a child. "Be still," he said to her. "I am Tatanyandowan." He continued to repeat his name as he pried apart her legs and took away the hands she was using to hide herself. She lay supine on the ground. He ran his hands along her stomach, saying, "Sh . . . sh." His voice thickened. And then her name, as she was known now, "Winona."

This had happened before. The thought filled with her renewed horror. This was why Winona had hanged herself. Asa.

Then Pretty Singer touched her at her very center, the core of her most intimate self, and her stomach clenched. Like that day below the tree, when she had wound the cord around her throat and kicked away the stump, Hazel stepped outside of herself, a shrieking in her ears. It was Winona whom she carried inside her now. Was not this her dress, had Hazel not taken her place? Her scream filled her veins and gave her a strength she did not possess. Beside her, in the undone sash, lay the horned bone of Winona's awl. She felt her hands wrap around the handle. Then she swung the awl with all her strength.

Like a falcon's beak the awl found the cords of muscle within Pretty Singer's throat. It punctured skin and artery as easily as it had the dressed hides. The hook snared in his windpipe. Pretty Singer pulled away from her, but Hazel hung onto the awl. A warm jet of blood drenched her arm. Hazel pulled the awl toward her and Pretty Singer fell over backward into the water.

His legs thrashed. An oily slick of blood blossomed around him. He wrapped his hands tightly around his throat, desperate to staunch the pumping fluid. *This should not happen*, the slanted, staring eyes said. *My power comes from the tree-dweller. My own death should come in battle.* He sank down on his knees, the river swirling around him. His face was the color of ashes, his arms red to the elbows. He tried to stagger out of the river, to come toward her, but the effort made more blood spurt. His head drooped low; his mink-fur-entwined braids touched the water. Then he sank face down in the shallows. Rosettes of blood continued to flower around him.

When Hazel's breathing had calmed she wrapped the torn dress about her and stood shivering in the warmth of the sunlight. One hand still gripped the awl. The sunlight glittered on the water and she saw herself reflected, the spots of vermilion painted on her cheek, the twin plaited braids, her skin dark skin. Winona. The Dakota sometimes left offerings of food outside their teepees to entice ghosts of the recently departed to return to dwell inside their own children. It was forbidden to speak the names of the dead aloud. It had seemed a strange practice to Hazel before now, but this afternoon she wanted more than anything for Winona to go on living inside her.

If the other warriors discovered what she had done, she would be killed. She didn't know how much time had passed since she had first come down to the river. Far above her in the camp, she heard a dog barking and knew other women would be headed down here soon to gather firewood and water. The men coming back from their raids would have to be fed. She let the awl drop the ground and waded into the shallows where Tatanyandowan floated face down. She smelled the iron sweet odor of his blood. Along with river water it dripped from the fringes of her dress.

She pulled him by his shoulders into the swirling current of the deeper water. As she tugged, the long jagged tear in his throat was exposed, a wide mouth drinking in the river. She remembered the heaviness of him pressing her down against the silty shoreline. Now he was light, a ghost weight in the water. The current took hold of her and she released him to the river.

On shore again, she watched him for awhile longer, the marionette jerk of his arms and legs as the current tried to pull him further down-river, but a tree branch had hooked him. Then the current caught him and he was floating once more. She watched until he drifted around the bend, his body sinking into the river.

Her other senses sharpened while she listened for anyone coming her direction. Now, she was filled with the horror of what she had done. She looked down at her thin, birdlike arms, saw what a small, insignificant thing she was against the backdrop of the looming trees and the wide brown river. Yet she was still alive. The sunlight felt good on her skin. She felt the spreading necklace of bruises Pretty Singer had left on her throat and she enjoyed even that. All these contrary things blazed inside her. Terror at discovery. Joy to be alive. Her power to kill or to heal.

Even in the summer heat, she was shivering so badly that her teeth chattered. She took off the torn white doeskin dress, crouched naked by the shoreline and rubbed sand along the bloody fringes, rinsing it in the river until the stains were pink.

Then she put the dress back on and rounded the bend, where other Indians crouched filling their skin bags, a few old women who frowned at her. Hazel held the frayed doeskin against herself. She was so weary that her eyelashes were fluttering but she knelt to retrieve the awl and staggered back up the hill. Later she would wonder why she had not chosen to escape. She could have drifted with the river; the fort was not far. Her feet did not take back to her own kind, but to Blue Sky Woman's teepee.

Her new mother found her there as dusk was falling. Hazel had curled up on one of the grass mats and let sleep take her. Her dream-self hovered over her and watched the pretty woman with the heart-shaped face bend and take the awl from Hazel's fist, watched the woman hold the awl and study the serrated skin still clinging to the edge, saw her take this piece of skin and cast it into the fire. Blue Sky Woman undressed her and studied the stains on the torn dress in the firelight, then wrapped the shivering girl like a swaddled child in a thin blanket. She was singing a song to herself, something low and barely audible, a song for protection as she folded up the dress and put it away for good.

Hazel slept far into the afternoon of the next day to be awakened by Blue Sky Woman gently shaking her. The skin of the teepee shimmered in the afternoon brightness, the painted figures indistinct. Everything that had happened the day before seemed unreal, until Hazel again felt the bruises encircling her throat and remembered the pressure of his fingers. She looked down and saw that she was naked beneath a blanket. Blue Sky Woman nodded toward a ruddy-red broadcloth skirt and a calico shirt fringed with courie shells. How much did she know? Hazel remembered half waking once to hear Blue Sky Woman singing, watching her clean the blood from the awl.

This morning Blue Sky Woman fed her a bowl of mashed corn and then helped Hazel into her new dress and cloth leggings. She put her cool hands to Hazel's cheeks. Her round dark eyes brimmed with moisture. In English she said, "You no safe here," and then bent to pass under the teopa.

Hazel followed her across the camp. That Blue Sky Woman had spoken English to her seemed a kind of death. She knew that Hazel was not her daughter. They walked the circle of teepees where the akicita, the soldier's lodge, set their dwellings, at the camp's center. Blue Sky Woman paused before one of the dwellings, a greasy, traditional buffalo-skin teepee painted on the outside with the colors of the four directions.

Hazel ducked inside and waited for her eyes to adjust. The teepee, shadowed and dim, reeked of cedar smoke, rotting wounds, and urine. On the other side of the room, reclining against a woven backrest, was the oldest Indian Hazel had ever seen. Her first impression was of a grotesque. The old man had iron-gray braids and the folds of his skin were so deep it looked as though his face had been carved by an ax. His umber throat flesh swung like turkey wattles when he turned to observe her. His black eyes were small and glittering, partly hooded by puffy eyelids. He wore a headpiece of buffalo horns and around his throat a shining gold medal with an eagle on it. His breechclout was fringed and beaded, and other than a dirty blanket twisted around his waist, it was the only thing he wore.

She was sweating in the smoky teepee, the memory of yesterday still swirling within her. The old man inspected her, his eyes surveying the dark necklace of bruises on her throat before he looked away. He raised one hand, the fingernails so long and yellow they curved like claws, and pointed to another backrest. Blue Sky Woman lit a tomahawk pipe, one edge a blade, the head a bowl for kinnikinnick, and smoked from it ceremonially before passing it to him.

No expression darkened his features as Blue Sky Woman knelt at his side and peeled away the blanket, yellowed by the man's pus and blood. Hazel smelled the festering wound. She watched while Blue Sky Woman knelt, chanting under her breath, and pressed her mouth to his leg, making a sucking sound as she drew out things with her teeth and spit them into a wooden bowl: a shred of shrapnel, a fragment of sapwood, human skin. The old man shut his eyes, his breathing measured and calm while he smoked the pipe. Blue Sky Woman swirled around the things she had drawn out of his leg wound, chanting once more, her lips dark with fluid, before casting it into the smoky fire.

The old man continued to smoke silently. His eyes closed as he exhaled through his nostrils, his breath occasionally wheezing. Minutes passed while he drowsed and Hazel waited, not knowing who this was or why she had been brought here. He did not seem to be in any hurry to punish her for her crimes. She waited for him to question her, for sentence to be pronounced. Her palms felt clammy and she could smell her own sweat.

From the lodge poles hung the scalps of his enemies, the scalplocks decorated with feathers, roached forelocks, and designs Hazel had never seen: Pottawatomie she guessed, Winnebago, Chippewa, Sac. His bow and accouterments of war were suspended from another pole.

The old man set the pipe aside and began to weep, but Blue Sky Woman did not seem concerned. The old man wept until his voice went hoarse, an old Dakota custom to show that he had a true heart, and then he wiped his long nose on his arm and began to speak. "Daughter of Blue Sky Woman," he said. "I am called Tamaha. My heart is weary from this war I did not ask for. I have fought on the side of the long knives ever since I was a boy, in the battle by the big waters when we fought the red-dressed ones from Grandmother's country."

He paused. Now his eyes were dry. Was he speaking about the war of 1812? She looked with new respect on this wizened man before her. She was sure he meant the British; it was said many Dakota had fought on their side. Hazel looked at the gold medal on his chest. She realized that Blue Sky Woman had brought her to a friend.

"But now my people's hearts have hardened against the Ameri-cans," he continued. "The traders and agents they send speak with forked tongues. They are not like Taliaferro or Clark, who spoke with true hearts. And so the young ones have gone to war and made much suffering in the valleys even though there are those who spoke against it. I have seen the great villages of the Ameri-cans. The young braves are not making a war, but their own death song. Like wolves who fight the grizzly for a scrap of meat, they will make a few scratches before they are ended. So I have spoken."

"*Ukana*," said Blue Sky Woman. *Grandfather.* "This girl has nothing to do with these things."

"Yes," he said, waving her away with his long yellow fingernails. "I know who she is."

While Tamaha was speaking a man shuffled past outside, throwing his shadow against the teepee. He was dragging a wounded leg and Hazel was filled with the sudden fear that he was Pretty Singer, risen from the river. But she'd seen the torn flesh along his throat. Tamaha was smoking his tomahawk pipe in the dimness. "I have heard what you did for the boy. Would you do the same for me?"

A healing. That was what she had been brought for. After the summer she had healed Wanikiya, other Dakota had come to their cabin, men with abscessed teeth, squaws unable to conceive. Hazel had prayed over all of them in her own tongue and they went away again. But each passing month fewer and fewer had come. "No," she told Tamaha. "It will not work for you."

The old man coughed. "You are afraid of yourself," he said. "That is what Hanyokeyah told me." Hanyokeyah, their first friend, who had disappeared in the summertime after relations went bad between her family and the Indians. They had never heard what happened to him. "Come here," Tamaha bid. "The eyes of my head no longer see as far as the eyes of my heart."

Hazel did as he asked. He smelled of the sweet herb he smoked and his rotting wound. Her knees sank into the mounds of buffalo robes. Tamaha reached out one palsied, umber hand and felt along her face and throat and Hazel steeled herself to keep from flinching when he touched her bruises. "Who hurt you?" he asked.

"Nobody," she lied.

"You speak Dakota well," he said, his hands to falling away.

"Yes."

"You know how we do *wowinape*?"

Tamaha turned to Blue Sky Woman. "She is old enough, yes?"

"Yes, she is of the age."

The glittering dark eyes turned back on her. His hands were trembling. Hazel was stricken with revulsion, thinking the old man meant that she should marry him. He must be a hundred years old, she thought. She shivered to think of those callused hands touching her again. "I will not marry you," she said.

This made him laugh. "It is not for myself I ask. My days beneath the blanket are done. I see clearly what has happened to you, woman. Do you understand that captivity is bad both for captor and captive?" These words were so similar in Dakota that only later at night was Hazel able to realize what he had said. "The other braves will not harm you if you belong to one. Is there not one of us who your heart speaks for?"

Hazel mumbled a word.

"Who?" Tamaha asked again.

And she said his name once more, her throat thick, her mind turning back to the press of him as he held her in the teepee, as he had held her so long ago in the cave where they'd sheltered from the storm. Wanikiya, brother of the man she had killed at the river. Blue Sky Woman's kin. The killer of her stepbrother.

The old man laughed again. "It is fitting," he said. "The child beloved and an Ameri-can."

Blue Sky Woman took Hazel back to the teepee and undid her braids. "Will you run away?" the woman asked. "Are you hurt in any other way?"

Hazel shook her head. "You do not look well, daughter," the woman said. Hazel wanted only to sleep and put this day behind her. And yet there was a nervous fluttering in her stomach, fingers of excitement tapping up and down her spine. Wasn't this what she had wanted all along? To be free to love the boy whom she had healed so long ago. Her mind spun. Something else struck her, too. The other captives would learn of the marriage ceremony. They would despise her and call her a traitor. What would happen when was reunited with her own father and stepmother? If they were still among the living. And then there was Wanikiya. Did he still want her? Would he, if he knew what she had done?

In her dream that night Tatanyandowan pressed her against the shore. He traced his fingertips along her abdomen, speaking her name, Winona. He called her "wife," promising not to harm her. He promised to be a good husband, to care for the children they would make together. *Lies*, she told him. *All lies*. She brought the awl from the sash, watching its slow swing. As it traveled through the air, Tatanyandowan's face shifted to become Wanikiya's. *No*, he cried as he saw the hook coming for his throat. *Stop*. But it was too late. The awl struck his throat and he stumbled backward.

Why? his eyes asked. He was slipping away from her, the river rising all around them. *Why have you done this to me?*

KINGDOM TOWNSHIP

1876

THE NEW
COUNTRY

I DIDN'T SLEEP well for the week because sometimes Aunt Hazel moaned softly in her sleep and the pain in her cry went right through me. Somehow I thought if I stayed awake, keeping vigil, I could make sure that another fit didn't come on and steal her away from me. I wondered if in her visions she ever traveled back in time to that summer of terror. After the sores on her tongue went away, she had started into her story once more. The words spilled out of her, as though she were afraid something might happen to her before she could finish. The more I heard the more I understood my parent's reluctance to speak on these matters.

Past midnight my mother carried up a cup of tea that she bid Hazel drink. Hazel blinked sleep out of her eyes, sat up in bed, and let my mother tip some of it down her throat. Hazel's reaction was both instant and violent. She swatted the cup away, spilling dark fluid across the floorboards. Then she spat out the liquid to the floor, making horrible retching sounds. Mother backed away. I went to Hazel and stood by her bedside. When she was done spitting out the last of it, she leaned back against her pillow. "No laudanum, Cassie," she said. "I can't abide opiates."

Mother held the cup against her. "I thought it would help," she said. "I thought you'd be grateful."

Hazel's voice was so soft I had to lean close to hear her. "To dream the dreams of Lethe. The dark river of forgetting."

Mother drank down what remained of her own tea. "Suit yourself," she said. "I'm going back to bed. Asa, maybe you should keep your distance. Leave her to rest."

"Why?" I said. "She doesn't have consumption. I can't catch anything from being near."

Mother chewed on her lower lip. "I'm not so sure. They have reasons for keeping people apart from those who get sick like her. Leastaways, put out that tallow before you start more fires." Mother shook her head and climbed down the loft ladder, muttering darkly about betrayals. I heard the creak of her bedroom door swinging shut a moment later.

Hazel lay in the half dark, her eyelashes fluttering. "Asa," she said, shutting her eyes, "You need to sleep too."

"Sure," I said, as I released a big yawn. Hazel's breathing deepened as she descended into sleep. I didn't go back to bed like I'd promised, however. Instead, I gathered up my things in a pillowcase, including a rusty pocketknife I'd found once in an abandoned cabin, my canteen, and some Lucifer matches. I made for the loft trapdoor, creeping on my tiptoes.

Hazel's quiet voice stopped me in my tracks. It was as if she knew all along what I was intending. "Asa," she said, calling me over. She held up the embroidered doeskin bag. "I want to give this to you," she said. "It's yours rightfully." She managed a wan smile. I bent my head and she slipped the leather cord around my neck so that the doeskin pouch touched my chest. I wondered if Hazel thought there might still be some magic in it. I tried to take it off, but she shook her head. "You don't give back a gift. Anyhow, I said it was yours."

I hadn't known what I intended until I was next to her. I leaned in and kissed her in the center of her forehead. A shiver passed over her. She grabbed hold of my hand and squeezed and then held it close to her cheek which was warm and damp with tears. "*Tachunkwashta*," she said. "That means 'I hope you find the good road.'"

With my mother fast under the spell of the laudanum, I didn't have any trouble finding the last of the thirteen silver coins under her jar of sarsaparilla, coins meant originally for our long-forgotten ginseng enterprise. I took them, hoping that I could buy bromide with what remained. Aunt Hazel had said you couldn't get any from a catalogue, but I knew Mankato was a big river town. It was fifty miles from here. A hundred miles there and back. Mankato, where they hanged the thirty-eight Dakota warriors four months before I was born. Mankato, where surely they would have the healing medicine for Hazel. If not there, then I could go across the river to St. Peter and beg more medicine from that doctor who had been fond of Hazel. I only had to follow the Waraju River down to New Ulm and the Minnesota River. Maybe from there I could catch a boat or a steamer.

Dawn came with red clouds that meant rain and I was glad I had swiped my pa's old oilskin slicker as I passed through the barn. The only other thing I had grabbed was my three-headed prong to fish for bullheads in the shallows. I had enough bread to last me through a day.

The world was soaked with gray light, mist rising from the pale brown river. I moved through it half asleep on my feet. From the marshlands I heard whippoorwills calling and thought of a huddle of children driven out in the dark, listening. *Oh-you're-kilt, Oh-you're-kilt.* I knew hearing it that the past was no longer the past. I had crossed over as I walked through this mist-hung morning and I was moving into a new country, a place of bad men and violence, a place my parents had hidden from me but that had been there all along. I had to keep walking, tired as I was, much as I wanted to curl up beneath one of those trees and sleep until the sun burned away the mist and gray and chill. I was afraid that something terrible might happen to Hazel if I tarried in my journey. I had resolved to stay away from the main road that crossed the flat prairie and instead stick to the bends and twists of the old Indian trail beside the river. It would take longer, but I was less likely to get caught.

The Waraju River had carved a shallow canyon through the prairie and I walked on the upper ridge, floating above the trees, miles of shapeless prairie surrounding me. My mother would find the coins missing soon after waking. She could smell a theft and would know her own future laudanum supply was in danger. But she would also wake with a headache that only her opiates could soothe and I knew she wouldn't search for me for long. I walked past the stump where my grandmother had trapped herself in a living tomb, past the town rising on its humpbacked hill, past what was once a cornfield that my namesake and my aunts and uncles had fled through to escape men seeking to kill them.

Such thoughts whirled inside me when I heard the husky cough of a man moving toward me on the trail. I felt all sorts of illogical fears. My mother had somehow sent out men after me. Or this man might be a warrior from the past, painted in ghoulish colors. I made for the trees, wanting to get out of his way. Even if he was just an ordinary man, he might report what he saw in town and maybe my mother would hear of it and convince men to search for me.

I lay down in the dew-wet grass and watched the man pass. He wore a chambray shirt and carried a haversack. His hat was pulled low to hide his features and he lurched down the path as though sleepwalking. Then he seemed to smell something in the mist and raised his head and I saw his features clear for the first time, that familiar hawklike nose, those dark searching eyes. My heart began to thump in my chest. Caleb, my papa. I almost cried his name aloud I was so happy to see him. Papa would know what to do about Hazel. Papa would have money earned in the North. But for some reason, maybe the memory of the scalp dream, or perhaps because of my own tiredness, I just lay there. His eyes passed over me and then he pulled his hat low and continued on into the morning.

I waited for my cowardly rabbit-heart to slow and then climbed out of my hiding place. Why had I not greeted him? As I walked following the river to New Ulm, I understood the real reason: I hadn't done anything good in my lifetime. In one summer I had released an Indian from prison, robbed my mother, burned a treasured book, and allowed hatred to be directed at Hazel while doing and saying nothing. If I had greeted my Papa he would have made me return home with him. He might not have agreed about the bromide. He might decide to send Hazel back to St. Peter. No, this was something I had to do alone. As I walked I was conscious of the faint pressure of the doeskin bag against my chest. It belonged to a man who was a stranger to me. Within lay owl's down and stones said to find the lost and to prophesy. I didn't feel like a boy who had been awake all night with a fifty mile journey ahead of him. I felt as though I carried a lodestone close to my heart and it was pulling me north.

Midafternoon I came to a place where the trail dipped down into a hollow to reveal a small tallgrass meadow left alone by the locusts. Such spared places were charmed, the way a survivor was charmed. I lay down in the wet grass and as the wind came through the bluestem I thought of Hazel's nightmare in Missouri: *If only men knew what I knew*, wasn't that what the wind in the grass had whispered? I ate some of the salt rising bread, chewing slowly to stretch the meal out.

Then, I shut my eyes, meaning only to rest for a few minutes with my head pillowed by the grass. As my mind drifted, I thought of the Indian belief that everything was alive. From dust to the stars, it was all connected. Locusts, crows, thorns, and hemlock. Butterflies, meadowlarks, strawberries, and sweet grass. I held up the things of night and the things of sunlight, weaving together words in a whispery incantation. Why had God made the world knowing all the time it would fall? And even as I thought of all that was poison and peril, my head growing heavier as sleep descended on me, I also wondered why God allowed such sweetness into a world we were called to leave behind.

I woke disoriented, sometime near sunset, my head throbbing. Moments later I realized part of that throbbing was the drumming approach of a fast-moving horse. A rider came pounding down the trail on a skinny dun, raising a cloud of dust behind him. Other than my papa he was the only one I had seen the entire day. He saw me out of the corner of his eye and swung around and brought his old mare trotting back. I thought of running, but knew that would make me look suspicious. I was a stranger here but I could pretend I was just over from the next farm. His mare foamed at the mouth and its great black eyes bulged in its sockets. The man's hat was behind him as he leaned forward in his saddle to address me. "You boy," he called, half out of breath. "Is this the old road to Kingdom?"

"I think so," I said, "Just keep heading south a ways."

He caught his breath. "You heard the news? I don't think a boy like you should be abroad on the prairies by his lonesome."

"What do you mean?"

"It's in all the papers by now. Happened two days ago, the whole damn countryside is afire with the story. The James-Younger gang tried to rob a bank in Northfield. There were eight of them, must have figured us Yankees had gone soft. But nobody in town turned tail. Some of the men knocked out windows from hotel rooms to shoot at the gang with Henry repeaters and shotguns. Bloodiest firefight we seen since the Indian Uprising." He paused again for breath. "Would you have any water?"

I gave him my canteen, the whole time thinking: *Eight men, my Lord those must be the very ones who we put up in our stable that night. No wonder they had laughed at my Missouri stories. That was Jesse James who asked about my papa being a lawman. I had been face to face with killers.*

The man took a good long swig and didn't notice how pale I'd gone when he handed back the canteen. "What carnage," he continued. "Inside the bank, a teller refused to open the vault and one of the gang blasted out his brains across the desk. Outside it was blood and bullets. Two of the outlaws were shot so many times they hardly looked human. But the rest of the gang got away on their horses. They're running scared back toward Missouri. Word is a few of them are wounded bad."

The man's horse sagged beneath him and tried to crop some grass. He pulled her up by the reins. "I've stayed long enough. Say boy, you should be heading home. There's no telling where those men are now. The only thing we know for sure is they were headed in our direction." He tipped his hat and without a goodbye spurred his horse on down the road.

As twilight descended I kept close to the river. I managed to spear two large crawdads in the shallows. Dusk came and I stood in a woodland stripped by the locusts. I gathered dead wood, but hesitated before making a fire. Anyone might be out here in the woods with me. But my stomach grumbled and I wanted something with my bread. I used the pronged spear for a post and lashed the other end of the oilskin slicker to a tree to make a small tent. A soft rain fell after dark and I huddled near my smoking fire and strained my ears, listening. A night hawk keened and swept out over the river and then it was quiet again. I should have been tired after the sleepless night before, but my long nap had done some good. There was too much going on in the world for a boy to sleep. When the hawk keened once more farther off I realized how alone I was and how vulnerable. To keep my mind from fear, I crouched near the fire and mulled over Hazel's story. It had taken her days to get it out and I still puzzled over the meaning of it all. I watched the dancing fire and thought of the end of things, letting my imagination settle back into the stream of her story. I figured that escaped outlaws would make a thunderous amount of noise moving through woodlands at great speed. I escaped such fears by letting my mind settle back into a story I had longed all my life to hear.

MILFORD PRAIRIE

1862–1876

YELLOW
MEDICINE
COUNTRY

Otter brought news of the failed second attack at New Ulm the day before. The warriors had returned with a single captive: a boy with sunlit hair. Otter watched Hazel warily, his hands behind his back, as though she might attack him at any moment. "Soon we will leave for the Yellow Medicine country where the Sisseton live," he told her. "They will most likely kill you, especially since you bite like a dog."

He had a mouth harp given to him by some warrior, what Hazel's father would call a Jew's harp. He plucked at the twanging metal and danced a mocking jig around the teepee, overturning a pot of quills in the process.

Blue Sky Woman set down her pipe, crying "Puck-A-Chee!" as she chased him out of the teepee. Otter grinned openly, backing away. He glanced once toward Hazel. "Wanikiya looks for his brother," he said to her. "He is not in his teepee." With these words, he ducked under the teopa and was gone.

Hazel went outside in search of the new captive. A blond boy, Otter had said. Maybe her Daniel had come? Cicadas churred in the hot tree-shadows. There was no wind this afternoon, only a glaring white heat as Hazel moved toward voices on the other side of a hill. She paused near a grove of red sumac and looked down into the gathering below.

The Indians had taken the captive child to a meadow of short razor grass. At first Hazel was disappointed the boy was not Daniel; his hair was too dark and he was older. The captive had been stripped of his clothing and stood pale as a gosling in the sun, his hands sheltering his privates. Like many other farm children, his neck and arms were a dark red color from repeated sunburning, and the rest of him moon-pale. His skin looked striped in the glaring light. His eyes searched the crowd for help as he tread carefully on the razor grass under his feet.

The Indians had surrounded him with children of their own. While the adults, both men and women, stood in an outer circle, boys and girls picked up sharp rocks. Then the boys began to hurl their stones. Hazel cried aloud and covered her mouth with her hands. Otter was with the others, his mouth harp swinging by the cord from his neck. One stone struck the boy in the head and dropped him to his knees. He knelt there and touched the wound on his forehead and when he took the hand away a squib of blood leaked down his cheek.

Blood changed the game. The children quit laughing. They found larger stones and hefted them. Boys shouted their war cries as they rushed toward the child and hurled the rocks as hard as they could. Welts and wounds opened on the boy's shining skin. Each time a rock dropped him to his knees, he climbed back to his feet. And though the adults had to urge them on at the beginning, once blood was spilled, the children didn't hesitate. Otter picked up a stone like all the rest.

Hazel's stomach churned. When she tried to back away she ran straight up against a solid wall of flesh. Henrietta had come up behind her. The woman clamped her hands onto Hazel's shoulders. "Why aren't you down there with the other savages?" she said. Hazel tried to pull away, but Henrietta dug her nails in harder. "Stay," she said. "This is what your kind does."

Hazel stopped resisting. Henrietta wouldn't allow her to leave. The blond boy climbed to his feet more slowly. His entire skin was slick with blood. At this distance, the stones didn't make a sound. There were only the cries of the shouting children, an almost tangible hum spreading through the air.

Once the boy looked in their direction. His eyes lingered on the two of them, a woman and a girl, both obviously white. Behind her, Hazel heard Henrietta's voice catch. "Oh child," she said. His mouth made a small O shape; Hazel could guess the word he cried. *Mother.* And though he was not Henrietta's child, Hazel knew the woman behind her was reliving the death of her own. Henrietta dropped to her knees, weeping. Hazel was free to leave now, but couldn't. Transfixed, she watched until the end, when one of the children picked up a large, melon-sized rock and heaved it at the captive. The rock struck with an audible crack, a sickening sound she heard all the way up on the hill. The blond boy fell to the ground, dead. The adults melted away. For a while, children continued to pelt his shattered body.

Hazel left Henrietta sobbing in the grass, her face glazed with tears and snot. She went down the hill. She didn't know why, but she felt bidden. The boy had looked into her eyes and she had not raised a hand to stop what was happening. She had looked on, helpless, while he was killed.

The boy was surrounded by stones and pebbles, his legs splayed out. His face no longer looked human. One cheek had been crushed; his nose clung to his skull by a single shred of glistening cartilage. His eyes continued to stare back at Hazel, their color already fading, while sunlight beat down on his blood-splotched skin. Out of the corner of her eyes she saw crows descending to watch from the red sumac. The birds looked glossy and fat, so heavy that thin branches of the sumac bent under their weight, and Hazel wondered how they had arrived so soon.

A moment later Henrietta stood beside her, looking down on the fallen child. She was red-eyed from crying. "First the birds and then the wolves. I had to leave my own out in the sun like this. Oh God. Nothing to cover them."

"We can't bury him," Hazel said, thinking of her own dead, guilty that she had felt relieved the boy was not Daniel. She remembered Asa and wondered when he would be found and if the ashes, falling like snow, had hidden his body. "But we could put him up in those trees," she said, recalling Asa's strange request their first winter here.

With fragments of their own clothes and spit from their mouths they tried to clean his torso. Mostly the blood smeared and pinked on his skin. It was matted in his hair. Henrietta shut his eyes and then, grunting, lifted the child in her arms. They left him in the boughs of a low burr oak and chased off the crows with stones. They paused below the tree. Henrietta tried to pray but the words got stuck in her throat. "Lord, we ask . . ." And finally. "I can't anymore."

Hazel spoke for both of them, remembering a prayer her mother had taught her. "Our Father, who art . . ." She paused. She couldn't say the word father without choking up. She didn't know if she was crying for the boy or the things the prayer reminded her of. When had she last remembered to pray?

Henrietta picked up where she left off and they finished the prayer together

"Thank you for that," Henrietta said.

Dark was falling. They walked back to camp side-by-side, Hazel dwarfed by the large German woman. The dogs milled at the outskirts of the camp and a few of them slouched out to sniff them. Henrietta smacked them away with her large meaty hands. At the edge of camp they parted ways. "I will remember this day," Henrietta said. "I will see every one of them burn for it."

"Not all of them," Hazel said. Only a small group from the camp had been involved in the stoning.

Henrietta took her by the arm. "All of them," she said. From the hill above, Blue Sky Woman called for Winona. Hazel flinched. There was quavering note of fear in the woman's voice. She must have heard what had happened to the captive child. Hazel twisted away from Henrietta. "All of them," Henrietta called after her. "Even you, if you get in the way."

That night her thoughts turned toward her brother Daniel and her baby sister Ruth. Daniel's features blurred into those of the boy she had seen killed. Ruth appeared newborn, still bloody with afterbirth. The images scared her and to stop them she began to weave a story around the children. For some reason it seemed to her that they would live as long as they lived inside her mind. The moment she stopped imagining the story, they would die.

That evening she imagined her brother and the baby as she lay across from Blue Sky Woman. The night wind moving through the camp smelled of cinnamon and cloves, an impossible aroma in this valley. It gathered strength as it channeled down the open river, passing the charred hulls of the agency buildings, the dead in their half-mown fields. A ghost wind that smelled of baking cinnamon. Some heard voices in it. Hazel heard Asa reciting the letter her Pa had written from Chickahominy River. Wanikiya, turning over in his sleep, heard his brother Tatanyandowan singing of the tree-dweller. Blue Sky Woman heard Winona bidding her keep this girl safe. Across the encampment the wind picked up intensity and tore down teepee after teepee as though the voices of all of the dead were contained within it and bent on vengeance. Then the wind rose to the starry darkness and the great open mouth of heaven.

Hazel woke that morning with her throat parched. She felt the buffalo skin flapping against her; the teepee poles had blown down in the dark. Their fire was already ashes. The two women had snuggled together during the windstorm in the early dawn hours.

Hazel felt tired and stiff as she surveyed the wreckage. All across the camp, teepees had been blown over and captives and Indians had taken shelter under wagons and trees. The wind was still sibilant in the grasses, passing over in gusts that Hazel felt swish through the broadcloth of her skirt. She stretched and yawned and then helped Blue Sky Woman collect their belongings. Today was the day of the journey. They were going to Yellow Medicine Country and, despite Otter's dire predictions, Hazel found she looked forward to it. She couldn't wait to leave this valley where she'd seen and done terrible things.

Despite the two defeats at Fort Ridgely and two at New Ulm, despite the strange night wind and their morning stiffness, the air rippled with excitement. Barking dogs ran among the fallen teepees. Everywhere people moved in the tallgrass and prepared for their journey.

Blue Sky Woman sent Hazel down to the river to gather water. On the way back, the strap tight around her head, she was surrounded by boys with stones. A tall, lean boy flung one that struck her in the shoulder and dropped her to her knees. Others raised their arms. As a few pebbles skittered past her, Hazel threw off the headstrap and splashed the contents of the skin container on the boy who had hurled the rock. "Shame on you!" she shouted at the others in Dakota. "I am *tiyospaye*. I am the wife of Wanikiya. When he returns he will punish you. He will tear your braids out by the roots!"

It was an empty threat, but the children shrank from her. Hazel picked up the handful of pebbles they had thrown and hurled them back, all the time shouting and calling them dogs and mice. The children scattered before her anger. She was breathing hard, her face hot and red. Another shadow appeared on the hill above and she looked up into the sun, her arm cocked back and ready to throw.

"Wife?" said the voice in Dakota. Wanikiya's voice. Hazel let the stone drop. He must not have heard yet. This was not the way she envisioned him finding out what Tamaha had said. With what dignity she could muster, she gathered the spilled container and headstrap and walked past him.

Wanikiya stepped aside to let her pass, watching her with curious eyes.

Many images troubled Hazel during the Dakota's long flight into Yellow Medicine Country. The first was of a white-spotted dog that lay in the crushed grass near Pretty Singer's fallen teepee. Long ago, when they had first come among the Dakota, Hazel had seen this old hound nuzzling Tatanyandowan's hand. The dog's ears were lowered; it showed no signs of joining the train. The rest of the encampment had been bundled up, ready for the journey. The canvas fluttered white and ghostly in the morning wind, the cedar teepee poles sheared off in some places by the night storm. It was as if the wind had carried him off. Not a trace of Pretty Singer anywhere. None remembered where he had last been seen. He was a headstrong warrior, known to ride off alone, obeying only his own impulses. But his accouterments of battle, his tree-dweller totem—a hag figure sewn with raccoon skin, hoary cottonwood bark and Ojibwe scalps—and other belongings had been left behind.

Blue Sky Woman whispered something to Wanikiya. The boy glanced at Hazel and then back at the remains of the teepee. She waited for the Indians to decide to search the river, to find the body. But it was time for them to go. Pretty Singer had left them once before without explanation and perhaps he had done so again. Only Blue Sky Woman, and now perhaps Wanikiya, guessed at the truth. Only that white-spotted dog, which remained behind while the rest of the camp rode on, seemed to care.

Hazel rode in the back of an ox-cart beside Tamaha, who was somber, fully dressed in his regalia topped off by the cap of buffalo horns that made him look fierce and devilish.

It was rumored that the Long Trader, Colonel Sibley, was coming for them with wagon guns, but the Indians did not hurry. Again the ponies were decked with festive ribbons, the spotted horses neighing with excitement, tails and manes tied with bells that jingled as they pranced among the dust-clouds raised by the bawling oxen. Even some captives couldn't help smiling at the sight unfolding before them: warriors dressed in their captured booty, wearing women's bonnets and silken pantaloons tied around their shoulders, streaming behind them like nobleman's capes. One warrior wore a necklace of gold pocket watches strung around his throat. The cases of the watches had been emptied out, stripped of the innards that once gave them purpose. Boys blew on tin horns and clapped copper pans together and there was a constant ululation, the women trilling victory songs, the sounds rising and falling in waves along the mile-long line of ox-carts, livestock, and riders. Men wore American flags sewn into war shirts, fancied themselves in white-crepe shawls wound like turbans around their heads. They raised such a cloud of dust in the bright morning stillness Hazel was sure they would be seen from miles away. Around them clouds of blackbirds erupted from the burr oak forests and Hazel's mind was cast back to their first sight of the valley, that snowy day they rode on the steamer to New Ulm, to see only the birds, alive and moving like so many dark leaves.

Throughout the journey elders from the Wahpetons and Sissetons rode up on their ponies and visited with Tamaha. One of the warriors greeted Hazel in English, a short black-skinned Indian in white man's trousers, topped with a beaver hat like a gentleman. "I am called Paul," he said. "You have not been hurt?"

Hazel shook her head. Indeed she had been lucky, protected. Paul turned back and continued to talk with Tamaha in Dakota. Little Crow and the Lower Sioux had not consulted before attacking the settlements. The majority of the Upper Sioux had no intention of taking part in the war. They were angry. When they made camp the Sisseton and Wahpetons separated themselves and went to the other side of the river. They declared themselves the "peace party." With them the captives could find safe treatment. With each passing day Little Crow's hold on his own people diminished.

In the Yellow Medicine country they camped in a valley. The teepees were set up near a set of undulating hills of grass where it was said the ancients had buried their dead in elaborate mounds. The Dakota claimed the ancients lived in the time of giants, *Unkteri*, and hunted great beasts, twice the size of buffalo. In time the ancients acquired such powerful magic they learned how to cross over into the other world and they left this one behind, not knowing if they would ever be able to get back. Sometimes they managed to cross back over and visit their dead, lonely for the valleys they once knew. It was said the men and women wore headdresses made of antlers and were fleet as deer. If they encountered Dakota warriors or maidens they would lure them away with the secrets of this other world and those people would never be seen again.

In this haunted place, they set up camp. On the hill above them, clearly visible in the twilight, Hazel saw the tall, whitewashed buildings of the Upper Agency. A brick warehouse was flanked by a schoolhouse with a pretty steeple. Hazel felt herself standing between two worlds. On one side there were the mounds of a people long since passed away; on the other, all that remained of her own people, the empty buildings they had left behind.

WEDDING
NIGHT

BLUE SKY WOMAN was waiting for her when she came back to the teepee, a blood-red woolen blanket folded in her lap. Hazel went to arrange her grass sleeping mat and saw that this was rolled up and tied with a sinew along with Winona's awl. She looked back at Blue Sky Woman who held out the blanket silently. "Tonight," she said as she rose and folded the red blanket around Hazel's shoulders, "will be your *wowinape*."

It was late and the only sounds in the camp were distant gunshots, some of the braves drunk now with liquor taken from agency stores. Here and there the half-wolf curs took up their wolf song.

Blue Sky Woman drew a hot needle through Hazel's earlobes, her voice soft as breath, saying, "Yes, it will be like that, pain and joy together." Then Winona's tin earrings, bells and crosses, were hanging from Hazel's ears. She felt the weight of them, felt the dull pain that remained even after Blue Sky Woman dabbed the blood spots with balm. She felt somehow that her disguise was completed. She was transformed.

The violent winds of the night before had died down. Her wedding night was nothing like other Dakota weddings. There was no pony for

her to ride to her suitor's teepee. There were no crowds of people waiting on either side to watch and cheer the bride. Most of the village was
sleeping. There was no nearest relative waiting to greet Hazel at the
entrance of the teepee, to fire off a gun over her head and signal that
the ceremony was complete. Only Blue Sky Woman was there and
Otter as she walked through a damp summer night, the blood-red
bridal blanket around her shoulders. Hazel turned to look back at the
woman who had been her protector for these last few weeks, and then
ducked under the *teopa* to meet her husband.

Wanikiya sat across from her, his braids undone, his hair coppered
by the near firelight. He looked composed and otherworldly, as though
he shared none of her fears. His eyes didn't meet hers at first. The air
was so damp out that she could see her breath in the room. Was it really
completed now? Is this all it took for her to become a bride? Despite all
she had seen and done, she was still only a sixteen-year-old girl. But her
mother had been a child bride; Hazel remembered the daguerreotype
portrait and the sense of her mother's fierceness. What would her pa do
when he heard she had married an Indian?

Swaying on her feet, the wool blanket itching her shoulders, she
waited for her groom to speak. At last, he said, "Sit," so quietly that he
had to repeat himself.

Hazel let her eyes fall. He was looking at her intently. "I remember
the first time I heard you speaking English the night when you stopped
my wound. You whispered in my ears and I could hear the unwinding
of your life story, a thread somehow I could follow. Your story has been
threading into mine ever since, as tightly as those that make your
blanket. Even when I was away from you I went on hearing your voice.
All these winters that I have been with Tatanyandowan, learning how
to be brave, I haven't stopped thinking of you. You said you do not know
me anymore. It is true. I also do not know you. But your cord is bound
with mine and so now you are here."

Hazel's vision blurred with sudden tears. Until this moment she
had never heard him speak at length. Their relationship was based on
glance and gesture, touch and quiet. He was no longer the boy she knew.

She was overcome with the sense that she had made a mistake; maybe this ceremony could be undone. She did not belong here with him. She would go back to Blue Sky Woman.

"Where are you going?" he said as she ducked under the door and went out into the dark.

In the distance she heard the continued chucka-chucka sound of the drunks firing their shotguns at shadows in the trees. A lone dog howled at the outskirts of the camp. The ponies, in a corral of loose brush, stirred restlessly. The planet her father called the Shepherd's Star, Venus, was low on the horizon. She heard Wanikiya's voice behind her. "You can't go back," he said. "Blue Sky Woman can't keep you safe any longer. You're with me now." He was close to her now, his breathing audible. He touched her arm and she allowed herself to be led back into the teepee.

He unfolded one of the buffalo blankets and stifled a yawn. Was she expected to sleep with him this night? Hazel hesitated. How did a man and woman fit together? Would it be violent like with Tatanyandowan at the river? If Emma had lived would she have told her such things so she would not have to be afraid?

"Come," he told her. "I am tired."

She knelt on the blankets and then felt his hands touching her sore ears as he took off the tin earrings and lay them gently to the side. Wanikiya undid her tightly wound braids, the ribbons that Blue Sky Woman had woven through her hair. He laid her back against the softness of the blankets. His fire had dimmed to ashes. He folded a blanket over her and then moved away. In this way only did he touch her the first night.

She lay awake for a long time, looking at his back in the shadows, thinking: *This is what it means to be married?*

She didn't meet his eyes when he returned. She had their fire going, and had placed cedar flatboards near the heat on which she was baking mashed cornbread, the sweet smell filling the enclosure. His hair was dark and wet and he smelled of the river. He wore a doeskin bag around his throat, his medicine bag she knew, something she wasn't allowed to touch because a woman's menstrual blood could strip away a warrior's power. The doeskin bag was beaded with the shape of an owl's watching yellow eye. She knew that it contained owl's down and a few pebbles darkened with pictograms. She knew as well that the pebbles had belonged to his father, Seeing Stone, who spoke the language of stones. Hazel wondered if he had come to understand his father's magic in the time they had been apart or if the stones were still silent when he held them in the palm of his hand. She remembered the second time she had seen him, crouched above the tiny body of an owl he had killed, grief raw in his voice. While she watched him, Wanikiya went to his corner and cast aside the rumpled blankets.

What he uncovered horrified her. It was a totem figure carved of knobby cottonwood bark. The feet were made of severed raccoon paws, webbed for swimming. The face looked like the skull of some creature, a baby possum with bared teeth, but the carved torso was that of a man, its phallus elongated and distended. Glued to the skull was black hair—human, she realized—perhaps cut from an Ojibwe scalp. The figure was both crude and disturbing.

"Do you know this?" he asked her.

She shook her head.

"I took it from Tatanyandowan's teepee. It's the Canotina. The tree-dweller. Sometimes he danced with this totem strung around his throat."

The cornbread had begun to smoke and blacken at the edges. She took it from the fire and passed one of the boards across to him. The bread had burned along the bottom but it tasted sweet and warmed her throat on the way down.

"My first memory is of my mother and sister drowning. I should not remember it; maybe it is only that I have heard the story so many times, how I was left tied to a tree in my cradleboard and saw them break through the ice. You see, the Canotina gives power to warriors like Pretty Singer, but in turn it asks the names of those you love and it takes their lives. The Canotina is one of the most terrible spirits."

"I know," she said. "You told me once. Would you really want such power?"

He pinched away a thumbnail of crumbling cornbread and swallowed it. She watched him to see if he was pleased. He said nothing and washed the bread down with a swig of water. Was it too dry, had she left it to cook too long? "Last night the Canotina came to me in a dream," he said. "It spoke about my brother's death."

"Wanikiya. . . ."

"I know what you did," he said. "I am not sorry." He set down the cedar board that held the bread. "After Winona died, Hanyokeyah left with Tatanyandowan to search for Inkpaduta. He never returned. I knew when Tatanyandowan came back alone that the old man was dead. I waited for my brother to kill me too. But that is not what he wanted. What he wanted was for me to become like him."

"You're not him," she said, thinking of the emptiness in Tatanyandowan's eyes.

"In the moon when the wind shakes the leaves from the tree, Tatanyandowan took me north. We were not hunting deer to provide for our camp. We hunted Ojibwe. We found what we searched for when one old man and a boy left their camp. The old man went down trying to shield the boy. Though the boy had only a knife, he did not run. He stayed near his dying grandfather until Tatanyandowan gunned him down. My brother cut the old man's scalp from his head while he was still alive and then we fled. I counted coup with my brother. I touched the dying man and dead child, wishing that one day I would be as brave as that boy."

"You are," she said, "though you don't know it yet."

From the gathered belongings he also took his headband with its two feathers that he'd earned from counting coup. "The canotina," he continued, "promised me even greater power than my brother, power to destroy. In my dream he looked just like this figure that Tatanyandowan made. I've been wanting a dream of power for so long. Twice in the past summers I have gone alone in the woods for four days as the Zuya Wakan instructed and dug a hole and listened in the clouds and winds. Twice, no vision has come to me. And now I saw the canotina and it told me I will be a great warrior. But one of the names it asked for was yours."

Hazel felt the corn bread go dry in her throat.

"I told it no and it attacked me and drove me from the woods, laughing the whole time. And it said that you would cause my death. It said that you would kill me just as you had killed my brother."

Hazel sat back on the blankets and buried her face in her knees. She remembered Pretty Singer at the river and the dream she had had later.

When she looked at him again she saw him through a blur of tears. "Then you should stay away from me."

"I can't," he said. "I tried in the beginning, after I brought you here, just as I've tried in each battle to be faithful to my people without hurting any more of the whites. I've seen enough killing. It doesn't change things. Tatanyandowan said that when we drove the whites from the valley, my father's stones wouldn't be silent anymore. The old magic would be alive again. He said the buffalo would return to the prairie. He said there would be no more sickness. But he lied."

"Will you still go with them to fight?" Hazel couldn't stand to think of making more bullets for him that might be used against her own people.

"I don't know," he said.

The entire camp was alive and stirring, morning turning into a bright afternoon. Wanikiya stood and put the Canotina totem into the fire. Its black hair curled around the skull, yellowing, then darkening in the flames. The fire hissed around it. They watched it burn together. Soon all that remained was the charred skull and the heart-shaped embers of the torso.

"Come, Caleb," Noles encouraged. "I wouldn't like to be caught out here alone."

Caleb paused and wiped the sweat from his brow with a kerchief. It was late afternoon, the cicadas humming electrically in the tallgrass, their insect song reverberating in his eardrums. He ran the palms of his hand along the hickory shovel handle, felt the smooth wood against his coarse and blistered skin. Beside him, Noles took a long swig from the canteen. "'Tis deep enough," he said, "for your brother to have his rest."

The two men had joined the Cullen Guards to help buttress Sibley's Sixth Minnesota Volunteers. Most of the volunteer guards had left immediately to gather what harvest they could this late in season, but Caleb and Noles followed after the burial detail and crossed the river with Captain Anderson and his cavalry. It was grim work. Caleb had lost track of the men, women, and children they'd put under the ground in shallow, quickly dug graves. *They'll never know for sure how many were slaughtered.* The corpses bloated in the heat, blackened under the sun. *Not something you'll ever forget, this stench.* And the small animals, maggots, huge bluebottle flies spinning in funnels, and most terribly, the monarch butterflies fluttering in the open wounds. *Why God allows such a thing I'll never understand. Children. Do you think He's weeping up in Heaven? Lot of good that does us down here. Shut up, you. He's right. Noles, be quiet for once. You're not helping things.* But when they were alone, Noles started again with his one-sided diatribe against God. As far as Caleb was concerned, you might as well spend the day wondering about the lost annuity payment. *Can you blame God for what a man does to another man? Free will, some will say. Ach, I say.*

Truthfully, as irritating as Noles was now that his facial wounds had healed, Caleb was glad not to be alone. Noles could have left with many of the other Cullens to harvest his fields. Instead, there was this dark harvest. He stayed with Caleb, bringing the one mule he owned, becoming his shadow, one that was never quiet and reeked of bitter English tobacco. He'd even crossed the river, leaving the rest of the detachment back at the Lower Agency to help search for Caleb's family. They had less than an hour remaining. Once the sun fell below the trees they had to get back to the rest of the men, recross the river, and make camp for the night. Scouts said the Indians had gone far north to the Yellow Medicine country, but Noles was nervous, stopping his shoveling often to cock his head and listen, his nostrils flaring as if he might smell them in the wind.

They found Matthew partly buried in the vegetable garden. The grave had been unearthed by small animals, feral dogs likely, and the boy's face was gone. The sight sickened him, but he did not mourn this strange child. Touched by God, Hazel would say, a boy with one foot already in heaven. Caleb hoped his death had been quick. In the turned soil of his makeshift grave Caleb had found one broken, bloody fingernail. "She's still alive," he told Noles, knowing who had dug this grave with her bare hands. "My stepmother."

They had searched in the prairie, found bent tunnels in the bluestem, and bloodstains, turned to rust by days of sun, in the golden grasses. Caleb called his stepmother's name but there was no answer. In the garden there had been more signs of her, carrots uprooted, a woman's large bootprints crossing and recrossing the furrows. "She may have been alive once," Noles agreed. "But she was wounded bad if she's the one who made them tunnels."

They had reburied Matthew and afterward Caleb knelt beside the grave. When it became clear that Caleb wasn't going to speak, Noles cleared his throat and then began to sing some somber Welsh tune in his gravelly voice:

> To all, life thou givest, to both great and small;
> In all life thou livest, the true life of all;
> We blossom and flourish like leaves on the tree,
> And wither and perish, but naught changeth thee.

Afterward it was silent. Nothing remained of the cabin but a burned husk, the timbers fallen into the root cellar. Caleb lowered himself into the mess, casting aside heavy charred logs. Noles, standing over the gaping hole, called down to him. "Leave it, lad. You'll not find anything worth our lives. It's time for us to head back."

He searched at first for bones, thinking that some of his brothers might have been burned alive here. Underneath a scattering of blackened shingles, he found the crate of wine intended for his and Cassie's wedding. The ashes were thick in his lungs. Sweat stung his eyes. When he moved aside the shingles and wood, it was all there, bottles packed carefully in hay. Caleb dusted one off and held it up in the light, the wine ruby-red in the sun.

"Glory!" cried Noles. "Why didn't you tell me what you were after?"

Caleb coughed again and before he knew it he was weeping. The tears carved channels in his grimed, sooty face. He held the bottle, cool glass against his chest, and knelt beside the crate. His weeping was convulsive and cleared the ashes from his lungs, even as it dropped him to his knees. He was ashamed to be caught like this, the first time he could remember crying since the war began. And it was not the finding of his dead stepbrother, the bodies lying in the fields, or the condition of his fiancée, still in the fort's hospital two weeks later, that churned his insides. It was the wine and everything it stood for. The wine intended for his wedding. All of that life, lost now. For this he allowed himself a moment of self-pity and he wept until he felt Noles's hands in his hair and then the two raised the crate of wine and loaded it onto the mule.

It was the first of September and night was coming on. The whippoorwills that had haunted the children's imaginations one month before had already fled south to escape the coming cold. The two men walked beside the lumbering mule hearing the clink of the bottles in the crate. As they came through the tallgrasses they did not see a woman's hand, the fingernails shredded from digging, raise itself above the grass. Kate had been crawling across the prairie ever since she'd heard Caleb call her name, waking her from a near-death stupor. She called after him now, her voice so hoarse that it carried only a little distance. Only the searing pain in her back—where a scattering of buckshot still burrowed under a layer of weeping skin—told her that she was still alive.

Caleb paused once to listen. A feral dog howled out on the prairie. Her voice had just strength enough to make him wonder what he was hearing and pause for a few seconds. Then he continued on beside Noles who was talking again about God's will. Neither of them turned back to see the hand, just above the tip of the bluestem, waving to call them back.

Wanikiya brought her plums from the forest, the fruit past its prime but still satisfying. They ate the plums together in the teepee after a dinner of roasted corn and beef braised over the fire. When the juice spilled down her chin, Hazel's mind turned back to the night the uprising began and Asa coming from the river with his strange warning. She wiped her face with a cloth and looked across the fire at Wanikiya. They had spoken very little that night. The other warriors had ridden out, one contingent with Little Crow heading for the Big Woods, another following Gray Cloud, hoping to gather more plunder in towns further down the river. But he was still here and she was afraid to ask him why. He must have seen how she was looking at him, because he stopped eating, letting his half-chewed plum roll into the fire. He settled against his backrest and studied her.

"You did not go?" she said at last.

He shook his head.

"Why?"

He thought for a long time before speaking. She had always liked that about him, the careful way he considered his words. "There is nothing brave in what they do," he said. "At first I went because Tatanyandowan said I would be killed if I did otherwise. When it began they were going to kill all the farmer Indians and half-breeds along with the whites. To purge this valley with blood."

Hazel shuddered. When she looked at him again, he was gazing intently into the fire, watching the embers blaze and darken to ash.

"The blond one . . . Cassie? She told me that the Creator made the red man dark on the outside because our hearts were dark inside. She said we were children of darkness and had no soul. That the Our Father prayer you taught me was a sin from my lips." He spoke the words *soul* and *Our Father* and *sin* in English.

"She was wrong."

"Hanyokeyah taught me that each of us has two souls. One soul must travel a perilous journey after death. Even in death the Dakota must face enemies and cross a great river to reach the afterworld. But the other soul stays here, close to earth. Like Winona."

Hazel was quiet, thinking of that sense she had had, down at the river.

"I did not think I would be sorry to have killed Asa." He told her of seeing Asa beneath the tree where Winona hanged herself and knowing he'd had something to do with her death. He'd told Tatanyandowan, who said that Wanikiya would be haunted by the girl's ghost unless he avenged her. "Winona did not deserve to have her spirit roaming, never able to rest."

She already knew this and wondered that she could accept it and not hate Wanikiya for what he had done. "Did you kill others that day?"

Wanikiya went on to tell her about the Stolten's farm and how he'd come across it with his brother and found Mr. Stolten in the hay meadow impaled by his pitchfork, lying next to a dead son. The Stoltens lived near the Sengers, and were known to both Hazel and the Indians. Mr. Stolten had begged Wanikiya for mercy. Then the youngest girl, Aschendel, had come up from the cellar where she had been hiding and Tatanyandowan had gone to kill her. Wanikiya was left alone with the man, made sick in his soul by the very sight. And so he had done it, drawn his tomahawk and buried it in the skull and somehow Mr. Stolten had not died even then, but continued to scream and Wanikiya had to work to free the blade from the ridged bone of the skull and buried it again, this time ending the man's life. Then Tatanyandowan returned from the cabin and Wanikiya had looked up to see a white face watching from a near grove of trees, another son, and he'd looked away hoping his brother would not also see the last remaining child.

That son, he told her, must have seen the entire thing happen, including what Wanikiya did. Had he known it was for mercy? "Next we saw a wagon on the road, the oxen slow and stumbling. That was you. The world was on fire. Tatanyandowan was already running and I did not want him to be the one who caught you first. I regret ending Asa's life. Revenging Winona has not brought me any peace. I keep on seeing the way you held him."

"Please," she said. "I don't want to talk about such things anymore. I would not be here tonight, alive and whole, if you had not carried me from the cornfield. Sometimes I wish that I wasn't, but then tonight, eating these plums, being with you near a warm fire, I'm glad you saved me. I'm glad that you did not leave that man to suffer."

He nodded at this and rolled over, so that his back was to her again. Hazel climbed under her own blankets. What he wanted, she thought, was absolution. The quiet boy she had known had been replaced by this young man who let words spill from him in a breathless rush. He had no one else to talk to, to tell these things. He wanted to be forgiven for shooting Asa. Hadn't they each killed for self-preservation? *But I don't have that power*, she thought.

Several times she heard him turn over and knew that he too was restless. "Wanikiya?" she said after a long time had passed. She had to call his name twice before he would answer. "I'm cold," she said. "Come over to my side."

The fire had dimmed to ashes. She could smell the sage braided in his hair, and rolled over so that her body was pressed against his and she felt his bony, boyish hips joined against hers and his breath on her neck. The other captives would hate her when they learned what she had done. Maybe even her own family. But she was thinking about that day in the cave and the storm that swept over the valley and how she had longed for it to carry both of them away. She felt his heart beating close to her breast. He breathed in time with her. She ran her hands along his hips, along the sharp jut of his ribcage and the lean muscles of his torso. When she touched her face against his she felt that his cheeks were warm and damp and she knew that he had told her all that he had because he was wounded inside. She knew that she could offer him healing just as she had a long time ago. She pressed her lips to his cheek and tasted his salt, the way he'd done after first bringing her here but she continued, kissing his mouth and throat and when she did speak at last her voice sounded husky in her own ears. "Husband," she breathed, her hands continuing to touch him.

Outside a keening wind began to blow through Yellow Medicine country. The wind seeped under the teepee skin where the lovers touched and pressed together until they were sated and in this mutual heat did not feel the falling chill. Only when they were finished could they hear the horses whinnying from the corrals down by the river.

Wanikiya raised himself on his elbows to listen carefully.

"Is it a storm?" she asked, pressing her face close to the hollow in his throat.

"No," he said. "It's the lost ones. They are crying because they can't come back to this valley ever again. The horses sense them in the wind."

She clung to him and drew one of the buffalo furs over them as though to hide their nakedness from the spirits coursing outside. They didn't sleep that night, limbs entwined. They traded stories, Hazel describing her father, Wanikiya telling her how Hanyokeyah had protected him throughout his childhood. Her body ached sweetly where he had entered her. Her blood had dried on the robes beneath them, one more thing that joined them. Outside the maple hardwoods lining the river began to change color a month early so that in the morning they found the leaves in red drifts, dappled spots against the goldenrod.

BIRCH
COULEE

INSIDE THE CIRCLE of wagons, Noles bid Caleb stay close. They had joined the other men after sundown and crossed the river to rejoin Captain Grant's infantry. More than 160 men and a dozen wagons, the horses restless and whinnying in the dark. The men talked loudly and joked to forget the sights they had seen on the prairie. Each seemed grateful for this darkness, but was afraid to go to his own bedroll, afraid of what he'd see when he shut his eyes. A few had found what they feared, their wives or sons and daughters. These sat in the short grass, holding their knees to their chests, rocking back and forth while they stared vacantly into the dark.

Caleb was nervous about his wine. If the men found it, they would drain the entire crate full of bottles in no time. He must bring it back for Cassie, who was not speaking to him. She'd stopped eating, would only allow water to be poured down her throat. Her skin was clammy to the touch. "I can't feel the baby anymore," she'd told him. "It's gone quiet inside me." The next day she still would not eat and the skin began to shrink around her dark blue eyes. If he could bring back the wine, the bottles whole and shining, then she might see that child or no child, they still had a future together.

He kept the crate close to him while he unrolled his blanket. Noles was smoking in the dark.

"Stick close," he said again, "there's a man from the Cullens who said he's seen signs of Indians. A half-breed named Joe. Can you trust even the half-breeds now?"

"Joe?" Caleb said. "That man is missing his two daughters. He's desperate as the rest of us."

"Well, this Joe says he's seen bark shaved from a tree, kinnikinnick, that they like to smoke. If it's true, and we get surrounded, what a pretty spot this will be. Idiots. To camp on the open prairie. Why, look at that treeline where the moon hovers. All around us there's place for murderous braves to take cover. We don't have the howitzers, nor any big guns. Dead, that's what we'll be if the half-breed speaks true. They'll overrun us in a minute."

Noles coughed and hacked up phlegm. His throat had gone raspy from talking too much.

"I'm tired," Caleb told him. "If the Indians come and kill us, so be it."

"Aye. You're a fatalist. How I fell in with such as you I don't understand."

Caleb grunted and pillowed his shirt under his head. Prairie grass poked through his wool blanket and itched his skin.

"O Most High," Noles continued, taking up his monologue again since Caleb had proved a poorly conversationalist. "Raise up officers with some sense in their noggins. Your creation is overrun with idjuts, and if there's killing to be done, let the bullets find *them*. Let not your children's fates be determined by imbecilic . . ."

"Noles?"

"Yes, Lord? Oh, it's only you."

"Listen. If we get out of this, I want to marry that girl I left behind at the fort. I'll need a best man."

"I'd be honored," Noles interrupted. "I'll start composing my speech right away. It must have the right blend of humor and solemnity. Matrimony, after all . . ."

"There's one condition."

"What's that?"

"Be quiet, so's I can sleep."

"Oh," Noles said. He tapped out the ashes of his pipe, muttering under his breath, and still muttering climbed into his bedroll. Caleb's thoughts turned to the broken fingernail they'd found by Matthew's too-shallow grave. Grant's men had found a woman in the tallgrass, a survivor after all this time. Krieger, was her name, or something like it. Half-dead, she slept now in the bed of one of the Conestoga wagons. *I should have stayed longer out there. They can't all be dead like Matthew. All those countless others. I wish I had the sight back.* He tried to find it within him, to get some sense of his sister and brothers out there in the broad darkness. Straining, he thought he heard something beyond the wind in the grass. He pictured Kate, her dress worn to rags, crawling on bloodied hands toward him, a curse on her lips that he had left her behind.

All the night birds had gone quiet. Noles had rolled over in his sleep, snoring like a wounded moose, his breath rancid. Caleb jabbed a hard finger into the man's ribs and forced him to roll back. He burrowed into his blankets, trying to find what he had been thinking about, his mind too restless for sleep.

Wanikiya had left to fight with the rest. It was important he stay near the other braves. He knew that Cut-Nose and others, like Running Rattler, had spoken of killing all the captives if things went poorly in battle, that if they must die they would take as many whites as they could along with them. He knew that Little Paul and the Upper Sioux were trying to offer a safe haven in their side of the camp, hoping to rescue as many whites as they could. Wanikiya feared that before all the fighting was done the Dakota would turn against one another. *Another civil war*, Hazel thought, when he told her. *Men in this age find such simple reasons to kill one another.* Even the Tetons, when they heard of this uprising, had fled further out on the prairies, not wanting any part of the destruction. And so it was important that he stay close to the Medewakanton and Wahpekutes who trusted him because of his brother, Tatanyandowan. If they planned something, he would hear of it first. Wanikiya went forth to the battles and loaded his gun. But he would not kill.

He had fled that dream of the tree-dweller.

Caleb woke before first light in the early gray of morning, the hiccup of a single shot startling him from the dregs of his dream. He reached for his rifle, tucked near his blanket, and tried to stretch a kink of out of his neck. He had little time to dwell on his discomfort.

Noles, caught out by the perimeter of the sentries relieving his bladder, was running back through the tallgrass with his pants still around his ankles. He tripped and went down while still fifty yards away. The single rifle shot called down a rain of gunfire. A raveling cloud of blue smoke erupted from the treeline Noles had pointed out the night before. Where had Noles gone? He'd disappeared in the grass. Two sentries raced back toward camp, screaming about Indians as they came. One of them sat down in the grass a second later, as if pausing to catch his breath, his mouth falling open in surprise while a scarlet blot spread out on his white shirt. His boyish face contorted; his hands touched the dark spot and then he fell forward into the grass.

Caleb quickly forgot the fallen sentry as the first gunshots were followed by war whoops and shrieks from the coulees and ravines and woods. The air *boiled* with lead. Horses, hobbled to wagons, screamed and fell, blood frothing from their mouths. The lead shredded white-topped wagons and dropped men where they stood around the ashes of their night fires, tin cups of steaming coffee held in their hands.

"Down," an officer screamed. "Take cover!" Caleb pressed his face against the dew-wet grass until he heard a rustling directly in front of him. He cocked back the hammer and prepared to shoot. The short grass parted to reveal Noles, breathing hoarsely, as he spidered his way back into camp, his breeches left behind on the prairie. Noles rolled to a spot beside Caleb and fumbled for his own rifle. Bullets thunked into the crate of wine and scattered wood splinters around them. "Hellfire and damnation!" he crowed. "Must be the entire Sioux nation come for us." He checked the priming of his rifle, climbed onto his knees, and squeezed off a shot. Smoke and the familiar, acrid stench of gunpowder roiled the air. "What are ye waiting for?" Noles called to him. "If we don't shoot back we'll soon be overrun."

Caleb shook free from his paralysis and crouched beside him. He sighted down the rifle and picked out one spot of grass moving in the gray light, the dark grass-entwined headband of an Indian just peeking above the crest. The head vanished seconds after the shot, but Caleb had no idea if he'd hit him. Noles took cover to reload.

Behind them chaos reigned in the camp. Captain Grant, his shirt-tails untucked, was shouting hoarsely for the men to assemble in a line. Spittle was flung from his mouth with each shout of "Here," and "To me!" while he waved his saber. A group of men responded, but when Caleb tried to rise he was pulled down by Noles. The men never had a chance to form their line. They were priming their rifles one moment and cut down the next, five falling like saplings before an ax, and Grant, still shouting, still untouched by gunfire, was left waving his saber at nothingness.

"Stay down," Noles hissed in Caleb's ear. "I mean to hold ye to yer promise of a wedding." A bullet shattered the spoke of a wagon beside them and Caleb was blinded by a hail of splinters, live hot spikes of oak burrowing into his cheekbones and forehead. Noles, caught by the same explosion twisted around with a hoarse cry. Caleb couldn't see for the blood that streamed over his eyes as he clawed at the hot splinters burrowing into his face, pulling each out along with patches of skin. He was stumbling, crawling through the melee, hands still clutched to his smoothbore musket, when he felt Noles pull him down again. Caleb cleared his eyes to see Noles beside him, beard scarlet, spitting blood and teeth and wood fragments into the prairie grass. The ricocheting bullet had ripped a fresh gash in one of his wounded cheeks. The Welshman shook his fist at the howling mass on the outskirts of the camp, shouting "Sons o' bitches!" and then scrambling, half-dragged Caleb to better cover.

All around camp the soldiers scurried to find a decent position from which to return fire. The most terrible sound was the horses screaming as the bullets and buckshot ripped into their hides and shattered bones. Officers hurried men into groups behind horse carcasses. Other men went from wagon to wagon, overturning them with a clatter, to provide protective cover. The air was thick with blue gunpowder smoke. Men who had passed a sleepless night in horror, remembering the dead they had encountered face-down in ditches and sloughs, now scrambled to avoid a similar fate. The surrounding Indians were firing a withering barrage of buckshot and heavy trader's balls from their double-barrels.

Noles hauled Caleb through this carnage until they found cover behind a screaming horse, an immense percheron whose intestines spilled in greasy coils on the grass before it. Caleb affixed the bayonet to his rifle in case they were overrun, pausing every few seconds to wipe blood from his eyes. Once the bayonet was affixed he ran the heaving horse straight through the neck, throwing his full shoulder into the strike. The blade pierced the horse's throat. Man and horse were impaled together. The horse shrieked and then gave its death rattle. Caleb yanked the blade out quickly, wiped another sheet of blood from his eyes, and crouched beside Noles. More bullets thunked into the heavy horse-flesh, but could not reach the men in their hiding place.

Noles shook his head, stuffing wads of cotton stripped from his shirt into either side of his mouth, soupy with blood. Splinters bristled from his face like a hedgehog, but when Caleb tried to pull them out, Noles screamed, "Leave them!" and shoved him away. His skinny, hairy legs were tucked under him and his eyes bugged out as he grimaced and stuffed the cloth into his cheek. The initial barrage had diminished and become more scattershot; the men were in a better position to cut down any Indian who left cover to attack. Somehow they had reached a stalemate.

"How long do you think we have?" Caleb asked.

Noles shook his head and pointed at the rags stuffed into his wounds. His cheeks were inflamed and swelling. Caleb tore another strip from his own shirt and tied it around the bleeding gash in his forehead. He laughed then, in spite of his terror. Noles looked so piteous without his pants, the recent wound finally silencing his monologues. Noles turned a questioning stare on his new friend. *Probably thinks I've lost my marbles*, Caleb thought. *Oh friend, that happened long before now.* The cloth around Caleb's forehead soaked up enough of the blood that he could see clearly. He raised himself above the horse from time to time to fire at fluid shapes moving in the treeline a hundred yards away.

The sun rose and through the dust the carnage was apparent all around them. Wagons splintered. Every horse, and there must have been near ninety, dead or barely breathing. The men raising tiny clouds of dust as they scraped up thick prairie roots and tried to dig trenches using tin plates. The wagon that held Justina Krieger was the only one that had not been overturned; its white-topped canvas fluttered in shredded bits from the hoops and the siding was marred with bullet holes and gashes. *She must be dead inside there*, Caleb thought, her life leaking out from a hundred wounds.

Captain Grant, moving from entrenched group to group, his saber clattering in its sheath, ducked over by Caleb and Noles.

"Jesus!" he said, shaking his head at Noles. "This man needs a doctor."

"Mmph!" said Noles through his bloody teeth.

Caleb coughed out dust. "Do you think they've heard us at the fort, sir? How long before we can expect reinforcements?"

Grant shrugged. He had a long, aristocratic nose and a high, needling voice. "We'll be here the afternoon at least. Unfortunately, the wagon that holds our supplies is outside our circle. It'd be suicide to go to it now. And there's more bad news," he added, calling for a man at a near barricade—an overturned wagon—to bring them fresh ammunition. "We brought along .62 caliber bullets for .58 caliber rifles. You'll have to whittle them down. Make every shot count."

"Mmph!" Noles said again, glowering darkly at the man. Through the bloody gauze Caleb heard him cursing, *You shit-for-brains*.

"Yes, sir," Caleb said, speaking quickly. "Used to it by now."

"And there's another thing," Grant continued. "We have only one canteen of water and one head of cabbage. It will be around shortly. Each man gets a leaf of cabbage and one swallow. No more than that."

"Mmpher!" Noles said, preparing to raise his rifle.

Grant put his hand atop Noles's greasy black head. "God give you strength. And remember, make every shot count!" He was already ducking and running to the next group of men, his saber clattering behind him in the dust.

Noles made the sound in his throat again.

"I know," said Caleb. "But it would be a waste of a bullet with so many Indians coming to kill us."

His head felt light and he wondered faintly if one of those splinters had gone straight into his brain. Last night he hadn't cared whether he lived or died. Now—beside this grotesque, wounded figure, this strange friend whose life had become bound with his—he no longer felt afraid. He would fight until the end.

Noles gave Caleb his extra swig, since the water would have done the gauze in his mouth little good, but Caleb refused it. There were men dying not far away, gut-shot, and crying for water. Leave it to them. A sheen of dust and blood and sweat covered everything. Through the passing clouds of acrid gunpowder, Caleb lifted himself up on the haunches of the dead horse and shot at the Indians trying to establish sniper positions from higher ground. Noles whittled the bullets and crammed in fresh powder and rags with the ramrod, trading rifles with Caleb after each shot.

Morning turned to afternoon and the sun climbed to its apex and turned a harsh light on the camp. It was too hot to think, too hot even to fight. The Indians seem to have lost interest, retreating, Caleb imagined, to their own well-fortified positions to drink spring water and eat red meat dripping from sticks and ladles full of stew. The saliva pooled at the back of his throat just thinking of it.

The day turned brilliant with white heat. The huge horse they crouched behind swelled with fly larvae and gases as the afternoon passed. Across the camp horse carcasses bloated in the September sunshine, empty cavities inflating and filling like balloons. The heat grew so intense, the carcasses so swollen, that some cracked open, the dead lungs breaking the rib cage with an audible noise, and filled the air with fetid, boiling gases. Men retched in the trenches they had dug and held useless handkerchiefs over their mouths and noses to try and stifle the smell.

Occasionally this suffering was broken by moments of terror as Indians from different positions—the southern ravine, the western woods near Caleb and Noles—launched a yipping attack and charged toward the camp. They turned away again while still out of range, but not before the men had fired a few useless shots to stop the charge. Immediately, the Indians would spring up in the grass, taunting, and calling them women and children in their own tongue.

"Fill it with a double load of powder," Caleb said, watching one brave caper near the edge of the woods. Noles did as he asked. Each time Caleb leaned on the horse they huddled behind he forced heated air from its nostrils, the horse continuing to breathe in death. The Indian pounded his chest and then whirled around. Caleb watched him from the end of his barrel, his blood leaking down again, freckling the edge of the rifle. He squeezed off a shot and the double load of powder actually kicked him off his knees and spilled him over backward.

Noles made an appreciative sound in his throat. Caleb climbed back up and looked over at the distant woods. The Indian he had shot at was gone. It was difficult to tell whether his aim had been true, but at least no more of them approached close enough to taunt.

Afternoon climbed into evening and the men heard cannonfire in the distant ravines. A few began to shout encouragement, knowing this was their reinforcements, but as the hours passed the sounds came no closer.

They lay in a miasma, a dense odorous film of foul-smelling dust. Caleb's throat was raw and thick. Noles napped beside him, his cheek inflamed and festering. The man had dabbed his wounds in gunpowder to stave off infection, but it seemed to do little good. Caleb had an image of the two of them bloating like the horses until their ribcages opened with a crack and spilled out their innards. Such a fate had happened over and over again across the prairies, for those that they had buried had lain in their own filth, in intense heat and showers of rain, in vortexes of bluebottle flies. It filled his heart with hatred to think of it. Each passing second was a torment. Caleb's skin was peeling and sunburned beneath his wounds and coating of dust. His tongue, like some great slug, grew until he wheezed for breath. Hatred filled him. He wanted every Indian dead. *If I live past this moment, Lord*, he vowed, *I will live to see my suffering paid for in full.*

Before dark the Indians sent one white-flag draped brave asking them to surrender the half-breeds, promising that they "were as many as leaves on trees" and that they would finish their work the next morning. The men had amused themselves by calling back hopeless insults at the brave, even shot out his horse from beneath him when he tried to retreat.

Then darkness fell, releasing them from the burning eye of the sun. The wounded continued to cry for water in parched voices. Caleb's uneasy mind slouched toward sleep and backed away again with each renewed scream. His brain felt heavy and drugged. Noles was feverish beside him, his forehead blazing like a forge. *Water. The man is dying for a glass of water.* If Caleb had a single container to store it in he would have left the protective circle and run the gauntlet of the guns to bring him water, but he had nothing. He stayed where he was, drifting between alertness and his own fevered dreams of a wounded woman crawling toward him in the grass.

Caleb could see it in their faces when they came. The reinforcements arrived in the morning, a full thirty-one hours after the battle was joined. The men gagged and held camphor-laced handkerchiefs close to their mouths. Caleb lay where he was, beside the decaying horse and his dead comrade. He'd woken earlier and called to his friend, but Noles had quit breathing sometime in the dark. Caleb was given a swig of water and helped to his feet, but he promptly collapsed again. "Leave me!" he cried, but the hands would not. They pulled him to his feet.

One of Caleb's eyes was webbed shut with dried blood. He looked on the scene, the dead, Noles among them, being dragged into the same trenches where they had sheltered earlier, the officers on horseback riding through the camp, the horrified soldiers, sunstruck and delirious, eyes void of color and feeling. There was no hoarse shouting of men glad to be alive. Thirteen dead out of a hundred and seventy. *Oh it could have been far worse. And have you heard? That woman they rescued, she lived too! The wagon shot full of holes, even the cup of water she held pierced. But she's alive and well. It's a providence amidst such suffering.* Caleb kept walking until he could kneel in the grass to vomit, spilling out the water he'd just been given, his chest dry and cracking. Then he wept for Noles. And he wept to be alive. And when he was done he heard the guns being fired off, a salute in their honor. He tried to recall the song Noles had sung at his stepbrother Matthew's grave. Something about leaves. Something about not changing the mind of God.

Back at camp, he heard a wounded man asking the chaplain who'd ridden along with the cavalry, a man named Joshua Sweet, for wine. He was dying, he said, and he wanted communion. "I don't have any," the chaplain told him. "I'm sorry."

Caleb heard the man's quiet weeping and knew then what he had to do. He walked forward and touched the chaplain's shoulder. "I know where there is wine," he said.

CAMP
RELEASE

SHE THOUGHT OF red leaves on snow, of a cleaved apple. Her skin was so pale against his. Snow on copper. Water and earth. By night they were one breath and she clung to him as though they were falling from a great height, a hole that had opened in the center of the clouds, down and down, and he within her, and she within him, his breath her breath, lips, hands, touching and kissing until they were sated with the smell and salt of one another. The fire burned down while they lay together in the red bridal blanket. Stars swirled above in the smoke hole's opening. A north wind breathed against the canvas. It was early September, she thought. The Long Trader, Colonel Sibley, was coming with his army to end the war.

After their first night together, the entire camp had awakened to a changed world, leaves turning red a full moon before their time. The old ones said it was a sign the spirits were angry. It was a mistake to leave their homes and come here. Some said it was the white captives' fault and they should be killed to keep from slowing the Dakota down. The spirits were angry because the whites had polluted this valley.

. . .

Each day that passed the scouts came back with reports of troop movements, a great river of men and guns and horses that would come for the Dakota. "But Little Crow is not afraid," Wanikiya told her that night as they lay together, naked beneath a blanket. "He thinks that he will surprise them as they did the soldiers at the river. Like what happened at the prairie. He has nothing but scorn for the way the *wasicun* fight." He'd come back from Birch Coulee. Wanikiya was sure that he'd seen Caleb there from a hiding place in a tall tree. "Your brother fought well," he told her, the admiration apparent in his voice. "He did not tire."

Caleb. Her blood brother. Hazel was so filled with joy to hear that he was alive. And yet it was bittersweet. For seeing her brother again meant the end of this life. She ran her hands through Wanikiya's hair, one long unbroken sheen. It fell in his eyes and veiled his expression. She brushed it away, kissed his cheek, the center of his forehead. He had smooth skin, smooth and supple and always smelling of the river and crushed leaves. A leaf child. But he was no elf out of Old World folklore. A man the same as any other, naked except for the medicine bag that hung by a cord around his throat. Her hands found the old wound in his side, the delicate web of flesh, and his breathing quickened. "When I carried you from the corn," he was saying, "I thought that made us even and that you would no longer hold a place in my heart. But I did not stop thinking of you. And now, when you are gone, I will continue still."

"Gone?" she said. Both had been too frightened to speak of the future. She had hoped that together they could make a family, something that would be safe from the destruction sweeping the world they knew. That they could go someplace, maybe to the far North where the Metis hunted the buffalo, and not live in fear.

"When it comes to the last battle you must go to Little Paul and the Sisseton. They will keep you safe. We have already spoken."

"But you?"

"I will go to fight, but not like Little Crow thinks. I will not allow him to surprise the soldiers. I will make sure a shot comes to warn them. This war must end."

"They will shoot you down. Either the white soldiers or your own people."

He touched her hair. "I am not afraid," he said.

"Let us run away," she said, "where no whites or Dakota will find us."

He scoffed at this. "Where would we go? Among the Tetons?"

"I will be a good wife for you."

"You are that already. No. I must stay and fight now. "

Her fingers continued to circle around his abdomen and then descended lower, touching his bony hip, the smooth skin of his buttocks. She gently pulled him toward her. "Stay here," she said.

He responded to her touch, beginning to slide his fingers along her backbone, his hands coming up to caress her arms, fingertips circling her nipples. His face was close to hers and she saw herself below him in the opal mirrors of his eyes, her black hair fanned around her, her tongue touching the tip of her parted lips. She felt him stiffen and felt the damp heat in her own center longing for him. They stopped speaking in words for a long time and it was strange to her how familiar his body had already become, how naturally he fit within her, gliding in and out, while she placed the backs of her heels against his buttocks, ran her fingers up and down his spine. With her feet and hands she pulled him closer, slowed his rhythm. His mouth parted and his eyes went cloudy and she brought her hands around and touched his face at this moment of release, telling him, "Look at me. Be lost within me as I am within you."

Afterward he lay with his face pressed to hollow of her throat, his breath warm against her breasts. His face was damp. She loved him even more for that. How afterward each time, his eyes would glisten as though the moment had so filled him that he overflowed. As though to hold her so was both joy and sorrow.

That night while he lay beside her, the stones within his medicine bag grew light as the feathers that surrounded them. In his dream, the bag tugged at the cord around his throat and pulled him out of the blankets, the bag flying out before him and he rising with it out into a country of tallgrass pulsing in the night wind. There was no moon, only a multitude of stars as far as his eyes could see. While he watched, one of those stars flew closer, swimming down and taking shape as it approached the grasslands, growing white wings until he saw again the bird he had sacrificed so long ago. The burrowing owl perched on his shoulder and studied him with its great yellow eyes.

"Hinyan?" he asked it. "Why have you come back now?"

The bird did not speak but spread its wings and flew out over the grassland. He had to run quickly to keep up, his feet light, the grass swishing as he passed through it, parting like water. He ran by places he'd known as a boy, the river where his mother and sister drowned, the dark center of it where his brother had overturned the canoe. In his dream, his mother and sister were running beside him, fleet as does. Then they passed the spine of rock where Tatanyandowan had bound him and the blackbirds that came down from the stars were there again, one of them larger and darker than the others. "Hanyokeyah," he said, knowing that he was alive because the old man had come as a spirit and unbound his ropes. They went further into the past, to the winter encampment where his father, Seeing Stone, struggled against the speckled sickness, further back to when the people lived beside the great waters. Other things came out of the stars. Unktahe, a great coiling serpent, brown as the river it came from. Stones rising up from their furrows. The tree-dweller in his cottonwood home. Thunderbirds and riders from the clouds. "Why?" he asked the bird. "Why are you showing me all this?" For a moment he was part of one great story, a river of spirit flowing out through the grassland to the place where it joined the stars.

He couldn't run fast enough to keep up and the figures around him began to grow indistinct. They were fading back into the darkness. His breath turned to fire in his lungs. The stones in his medicine bag grew heavy again. "Come back," he called to them, but they were gone and there was only the wind in the grass. Then he knew why the bird had appeared to him, knew that he had one thing left to do. He must make a sacrifice before it would end. Only then would his spirit be allowed to enter the same country where those he loved had gone before.

. . .

In the morning a crier moved through the camp warning that Long Trader and his many wagon guns and soldiers had come to Yellow Medicine country. Every warrior would be needed to fight. Men painted themselves and sang their death songs.

Within their teepee, Wanikiya knelt beside her, braiding her hair, as was custom. "Remember," he was telling her. She loved the feel of his hands smoothing out the snares in her hair, the way her own mother had brushed her hair. "Remember to go the Sissetons when the fighting starts."

"Will you come then? Will you come and find me when the battle is done? Turn yourself in. Turn yourself over to the soldiers. When I tell them how you have protected me they will not hurt you."

Her braids were finished. He painted the stripe of vermilion down the center of her parted hair, but could not dab her cheeks because her face was wet with tears. He squeezed her hands and then rose to fetch his rifle and the parfleche filled with dried meat. "Turn yourself in," she repeated. "I won't let them hurt you."

His adam's apple bobbed up and down and his eyes were bright. He nodded once at her and then ducked under the teopa and was gone. Hazel forced herself to watch him walk away, across the river running quick through the woods, a red rain of leaves coming down around him and the other Indian soldiers. There was a blue-gray light in the east, but the sun was not up yet. *False dawn*, she thought, not knowing if she would ever see him again.

She found Otter near the river, his skull crushed by a large stone. His body had been covered with a hasty matting of wet maple leaves. She knew him only by the mouth harp strung like a medicine bundle around his throat. The impact of the stone had caused him to bite through his tongue and the leaves around him were reddened. Hazel held him as though he were her own Daniel, the brother she missed most. She did not care if his blood darkened her broadcloth skirt. Her mind was filled with the memory of him that first day in the teepee, trying to shush her so she would not be hurt further, a goblin-child whom she had bitten in her anger and sorrow. Wanikiya's messenger boy. The one he had sent to warn the Sengers of what was coming. Otter had been full of mischief, but there was not a harmful bone in his body.

Hazel heard the crunch of footsteps in the newly fallen leaves at the same time that she realized who had done this. Henrietta. The woman loomed over her, fist still wrapped around a blood-soaked grinding stone. Her face was streaked with grime, leaves and twigs jutted from the wires of her hair. Arms red to the elbows, face mottled in the tree-shadows. The calico blouse she wore draped loosely, exposing one heaving, muscular shoulder. "I told them," she said, breathing heavily, "I told them I would break them like twigs."

From miles distant the sound of the battle drifted their way and Hazel turned involuntarily toward the sound. There were more cannons and howitzers than at Fort Ridgely. Even here Hazel felt the faint reverberation of their explosions in the ground beneath her. When she looked again at Henrietta, the woman was smiling. "Our day of deliverance," she said, her eyes blazing. "We are free."

"I will tell them," Hazel said. "I am going to tell what you did."

Henrietta advanced toward her with the stone gripped in her fist. Hazel held her ground, crouched over Otter. "He was harmless," she said, words that Henrietta repeated back to her in a mocking tone.

"None of them are harmless. We will cull the children before they can become adults. A weed must be taken from the furrow before it puts down roots. Cull them like weeds. It's their way. It's the reason I no longer have children of my own. I will have vengeance. Don't you know how we have watched you with that warrior? Disgusting. You're a traitor to your own kind. To bed a with murderer. You, a little whore."

The woman blocked out the sunlight leaking through the canopy of red leaves. Hazel flinched from her words. What could she say to defend herself? Everything the woman said was true. She had forsaken her own kind and now must face the consequences. Wanikiya would not come back from this battle. The guns would shred the warriors, no matter how fleet their ponies. If the whites did not kill him, his own people would for his betrayal of them. Henrietta raised the stone, saying, "I've waited for this moment, ever since I first saw you."

Hazel sensed the stone rushing toward her, and then heard a crackling split, the sound of a maul cleaving a stump. Her eyes were shut against the impact. In her mind she saw her skull caving in like Otter's, saw in that one moment the leaves continuing to come down in a red rain. *And they will never find me here*, she thought, *neither Caleb, nor the soldiers, nor anyone. I will be left with this leaf-child, in this valley of spirit.*

There was no blinding light, no flare behind her eyelids. She opened her eyes again and saw Henrietta still looming above her, the stone loose in one hand, swaying back and forth, her mouth locked in a snarl. Her eyes fluttered as a seam of blood appeared on her forehead and began to pour down. Then the earth shook again and Henrietta fell onto a crushed heap of leaves.

Hazel saw Blue Sky Woman holding Tamaha's tomahawk. The woman came over and knelt beside her to take the boy, holding his ruined skull in her palms and wailing. Together they raised his body and left him in the limb of a low-hanging oak tree. They found one more child, his skull also crushed in. Blue Sky Woman took a lock of hair from each. Hair to keep in a medicine bundle so she could pray for their journey through the afterworld. It would be a hard journey for boys so small.

When they were done, they cleaned their hands and arms in the river and walked back toward camp, Hazel pausing over the crumpled form of Henrietta. "She still breathes," Blue Sky Woman said. "What strength she has."

Henrietta's broadcloth skirt had ripped as she fell, exposing two solid stumpy legs bristling with hair. The woman's tresses were dark with blood, her breathing husky. For a moment, Hazel considered asking for the tomahawk pipe. Hazel could make sure that she didn't kill again. But how many other Henriettas were out there? How many survivors, certain that the only thing that would bring them rest at night was to answer blood with blood? Hazel had seen enough killing.

She left Henrietta in the woods and walked beside Blue Sky Woman into the camp of the Sisseton. There they dug entrenchments along-side the other captives, working with tomahawks and stolen hoes to make deep holes where Paul and the so-called band of "friendlies" could take cover if Little Crow tried to steal the captives back. Her face close to the earth, Hazel went on hearing the sounds of the battle until late afternoon when the artillery went silent. Far off, she heard what sounded like fife music. Infantry. The Long Trader, here at last.

But Sibley had not come that day. Ever-cautious, even after he crushed the Dakota at the Battle of Wood Lake, he took his time com-ing for the 170 or so captives at the Indian camp.

Like the rest of the women, Hazel's braids were taken out. She cried when they unplaited her hair and washed the sacred paint from her face. They were erasing the memory of him as they did so. Hazel was given a plain green gingham dress, and a slat bonnet. All the captives were dressed in the best clothing the Dakota could find to show that they had been treated well. Inside the bonnet, she felt blind. Only a child again, returning to blinded existence and a world where her voice did not matter.

It took Sibley ten days to come for them at Camp Release, the infantry playing fife music and marching in formation. The new cloth-ing she had been given was infested with fleas and she scratched her-self until she bled. The other captives kept clear of her. Henrietta had staggered back to camp and taken charge. Every hour more Indians came to them, hoping to ingratiate themselves and prove they had been friends to the whites all along. The Indians had learned that the color white meant surrender and so everywhere in the camp strips of white canvas fluttered from the tips of teepees. Men tied frayed cotton through their headbands and along the tails of their ponies. All sem-blance of native pride was banished as they sought mercy. The worst of them, the Indians who had started the killings up north in Acton, the reluctant leaders like Little Crow, escaped out onto the prairies. True friends like Blue Sky Woman, Spider Woman, and Tamaha stayed in the camp, uncertain of their fates.

Even the soldiers kept clear of the captives after they arrived, as if they might have been infected by their close association with Indians. Hazel was not certain of time, had lost all perception of days, weeks, months. She woke nauseous each morning, felt the world spinning around her, and could not keep her breakfast down. No blood stained the petticoats she had been given, though she was certain the time for her monthly had come and gone. She began to hope.

On the eleventh day, Caleb found her. His wheat-blond hair had darkened in a single month. She was at the edge of the encampment, looking not in the direction of home, but toward the great western oceans of grassland. She was touching the flat of her stomach, her hands smoothing the cloth down, before she felt his eyes on her. She turned, a name rising in her throat. It was not the name she had been hoping to speak, and he knew that, too. He couldn't bring himself to touch her; his features were set into a hard mask, the light brown eyes drained of emotion.

"They told me where to find you," he said. He hesitated before approaching her. Had she been violated? He didn't know if he was afraid for her, or of her and the knowledge she might carry. "Is it true that you married one of them?"

She had not stopped caressing the flat of her stomach. Instinctively, Caleb knew why. He tore her hand away. "Look at me," he said. "Don't you want to know about the others?"

"Oh, Caleb." She wrapped him in her arms, felt him shrinking from her. But she would not let go and eventually the rigid muscles along his back and arms softened. He raised his hands, allowing himself to hold her too.

"Kate won't let you keep it when she finds out. Those herbs that Cassie's mother knows about. It's not for her midwifery that women came to her." As he said this he realized that Cassie's mother was likely dead for they had not found her after she ran away. And the names of all the dead rose up inside him. Would he ever see Daniel or Ruth again? What news did Hazel have of Asa? An entire town, he wanted to tell her, Milford, gone as though it never was. Liza and

Traveler's home. The Stoltens. Herr Driebel. And our own dead and wounded. Matthew. Noles. He must tell her about Noles. About what happened with the wine. *Why?* He wanted to ask her that. *Why are we two alive and they are not?* When he found his voice again, he told her about Kate. "She sleeps at night on her stomach because of the suppurating sores in her backside. Every morning the flesh spits out a new hunk of buckshot. She's living with Cassie and a few others in a canvas tent on our property." He went on speaking, patting her back, his voice hoarse. "I'll build over the old place. I'll try to make things like it was before. But she won't let you keep it, so don't get attached to what you're carrying inside you."

HEROD'S
JUSTICE

Even the Christmas story found in Matthew, chapter two, failed to bring Hazel peace. She read of Joseph and Mary fleeing to Egypt with baby Jesus, warned by an angel of what was to come. All around Bethlehem, Herod ordered the slaughter of any child under two. He did this because the magi, following a star in the east, told him that a king had been born and Herod was frightened of losing his power. He did it because it was prophesied that Rachel shall weep in Ramah, and not be consoled, for her children were no more. Each time Hazel read this passage, she had to set the Bible down again, unable to read any further, the cries of all those wailing mothers filling up her mind, rising up out of time, rising up even to God.

Ashen sunlight sifted from a high attic window where Hazel sat listening to the brief roar of the crowd, ascending from Mankato public square two blocks below. A cloth bandage coiled around her dark hair to conceal a savage head wound. Now she had seizures; she was epileptic. Locked in this room, she could not see what was happening.

She knew about the gallows—a massive medieval structure built to hold thirty-eight men at one time. A perfect square, a feat of engineering, it was surrounded in concentric rings by rows of soldiers with bayonets. The lines of the soldiers also formed perfect squares, rippling outward, evenly spaced. A few horsemen rode between the rows of men standing at attention. The last row was cavalry, their sabers drawn, the heads of their mounts bobbing in the cold. Flagpoles stood at either end, the flags whipping in an icy wind. All around the men in martial dress were milling crowds, thousands of white onlookers dressed in greatcoats and cloaks and Sunday finery. Clouds of their breath rose to the slate-colored sky. Except for the horses clattering over the stones, the wind quickening the flags, it was a picture of absolute stillness.

She could not see any of this, and yet her mind was filled with images. Hearing the warriors singing their death songs, she imagined them mounting the gallows. Only later would she see a picture of this in *Leslie's Illustrated Newspaper*, and understand how much courage it took for the thirty-eight to keep singing their death songs, known to them as songs of terror, even as the soldiers dishonored them by hooding their faces with white cloths so that the men dropped to their deaths shamed and blinded. Hearing the drumbeat, she thought back to that first night lying out under the stars when Otter came to warn them. When the drum rolls ended, a man whose own family had been killed at Lake Shetek, William Duley, cut the ropes, and the planks opened. The roar of the crowd caused even the high window of her room to shudder. Hazel felt it inside her, a brief lurch that dropped her to her knees. Their roaring stopped as quickly as it began, the crowd now stricken by the spectacle of so many bodies dangling before them in a keening wind.

Hazel rocked back and forth on her knees, holding her belly, willing a prayer to travel to the child inside her. *Do not fear*, she prayed. *There is yet a place for you. I will not let them harm you.*

Already a winter's worth of snow lay between her and the surviving members of her family out on the prairie west of New Ulm, their homestead just past where the town of Milford once stood. Four more months would pass before the ice broke on the Minnesota River and her stepmother bought steamboat passage to come for her. The day of the hanging Hazel wished for her father, Jakob Senger of the *Bohmer-wald*, for one of his dark stories, the *Marchen*, that carried them to the edge of destruction but did not leave them orphaned there. She did not know that he was already dead, shot through the throat while crossing Miller's cornfield at Antietam on September 17, half a world away. If he were there he would have kissed the center of her forehead and whispered some tale from his childhood land, perhaps of the god Woden who carried two ravens on his shoulder, Hunin and Munin, understanding and memory. Each morning he released the birds into the world and waited for the news they brought. When she was a child her father would heft her onto his broad shoulder, a dizzying height near the nest of his dark beard. "Hazel," he would say, "You are my raven." The ground spread out below her while he spoke those words. "I will send you out, but you must always return."

Noah, too, had his ravens and they failed him as surely as she had failed her father, forgetting to think of him during her own summer trials, forgetting to name him in her prayers. Sometimes she pictured herself like one of those birds circling and circling the dark sea below. Jakob's *nacht vogel*, night birds, the ones who fluttered down to the blind soldier tied to the gallows and spoke of healing rain, of a world where he was still needed. Birds of prophecy in the old stories.

Hazel did not take the laudanum the doctor's wife, Ida, brought for her each night and morning. Each evening her wrists were tied to the bedstead with loose cloth sashes to still her nightly thrashing. Hazel would stretch forth her tongue so Ida could deposit the bitter liquid there. While Ida tied her she held the opiate tincture within her mouth and did not swallow. When she was left alone, she spit it out onto the wooden planks beneath the bed. She did not wish to lose hold of her memory, her sense of being, and let her body become a poison well for the baby inside. Ida was a small wrenlike woman with light brown hair. She came and went from the attic room in which Hazel was held with the swishing of a long, black silk dress with a worn silver chatelaine that clinked at her waist while she worked.

Morning appeared in the triangle-shaped window, the sun plaiting into a single focused beam of light that touched the girl where she lay in bed. Ida unlatched the door and brought her usual breakfast of salt-rising bread, a single boiled egg, and a glass of sarsaparilla to cleanse her corrupted blood.

"Good morning," she said, her breath pluming in the cold of the room as she settled the tray on the nightstand without looking at the girl. She touched a chill hand to Hazel's forehead and then scrutinized her wrists for bruising. "Open," she said, while deftly hooking her fingers into the girl's mouth to check for blood. Satisfied that no fit or delirium had come upon her during the night, she untied the cloth sashes and fed Hazel laudanum. Hazel rubbed her wrists, still yellow from past bruising, until the pain lessened and circulation was restored. While Ida turned aside, Hazel hoisted her cotton chemise and crouched low over the bedpan, her long black hair fanning down before her eyes while she spit out the black opiate she had held under her tongue and let it mix with the rising steam of her urine.

If there was blood, Dr. Kolar was summoned for further examination. Only two patients were boarding at this house, she and a gravel-voiced man named George who lived below her. Each morning she woke to the sound of him hacking gobs of phlegm into a bedpan by his side. Each of them was here because of Dr. Kolar, a specialist in mental disorders and paralysis, who paid house calls by day in a black carriage decorated with advertisements for cure-all elixirs. Kate had sent Hazel here at the behest of Dr. Weschke of New Ulm.

Dr. Kolar questioned her in a toneless voice, his gray eyes dreamy and distant. He had long, delicate fingers which felt like the extension of something cold and metallic as they prodded the tender places of her body. He was very concerned with Hazel's menstrual patterns prior to the pregnancy and her amorous experiences with Wanikiya in late summer, both of which he believed responsible for the nervous condition she suffered from.

When Ida latched the door behind her, Hazel was left to roam the small attic room. The furnishings were Spartan: one rush-bottomed chair in the corner, a rope-spring bed that sagged in the middle and was topped with a straw tic, and a nightstand of light oak. Hazel was not to be trusted with tallow candles or a lamp. The roof was low and slanting and she had to crouch while dragging the chair into the shaft of light lacing through the window. She passed her days reading the Psalms in the King James Bible and writing in a journal on mornings when the ink had not frozen in the inkwell. When she was first brought here, Ida washed her hair in kerosene to kill the lice. Still on some days, Hazel felt a phantom itching beneath the bandage on her head. A restlessness there, like a persistent memory rising to the surface.

Her head wound did not come from the war. The last time she had seen Wanikiya was early November when the army transferred the Dakota prisoners from the walled enclosure at the Lower Agency to Camp Lincoln. Weeks had passed without rain and the land was drained of color, the earth cracking as the river narrowed to a thin artery. The wind painted the leafless trees and dry bluestem grasses pale brown with soil as fine as talcum powder.

The procession passed through New Ulm on the way, raising a cloud of dust Hazel saw from their homestead. The billowing cloud gave birth to soldiers in soiled blue uniforms, autumn sunlight flashing on brass buttons and Sharps rifles, marching in step, while their Indian prisoners huddled low, shackled, in creaking mule-driven carts. From the hill above Goosetown, this procession seemed to stretch in the shape of a vast blue-brown serpent winding a half mile through the river valley. There were no drums or bugles, the only sound the tread of boots, a mule braying here or there, the groan of the wagon axles.

She came down the hill as fast as she could, hoping for a glimpse of Wanikiya. She wanted to touch her hand to that single lock of silver in his hair, have him turn to regard her with his dark eyes and understand her condition—for him to know that she was determined to obtain his release. They had not allowed her to speak at his trial, before the five-man commission charged with separating the guilty from the innocent. Henrietta had been there at the tent door, elegant in a blue delaine dress, a queen presiding over these ceremonies. The woman hooked one of her large hands under Hazel's throat, saying to the others, "This is the one I told you about. The traitor." Hazel had fled. She carried a child after all. She was torn between the guilt she felt over what her family endured, renewed with each hateful glance Kate cast toward her swelling stomach, and her desire to still be with the Dakota, with her husband, a prisoner like him. She was no longer certain who her people were.

That day she had run, but she wouldn't run anymore. Hazel would not let him die; she had promised to protect him if he turned himself in. She hobbled from cart to cart, but the Indians kept their heads low, and she did not recognize a single familiar face. She had given up hope when his cart trundled past. His head was bowed and the two feathers were gone from his headdress. She was out of breath and could not have cried his name even if she wanted to. Her attention was so fixed on him, willing his head to lift and look at her, that she did not see the mob until they were upon them.

The crowd parted the veil of dust the procession raised. They came fresh from reburying their own loved ones. At the head of the mob, Hazel saw Henrietta leading a phalanx of women in dark dresses. They came armed with brickbats and stones which they hurled at the shackled Dakota. The cart drivers hollered and lashed their mules in a desperate attempt to push forward. "Hah! Giddup!" they called. Low, bellowing moans erupted from the frustrated beasts, a sound lost in the high wailing of the descending mob. The soldiers ducked the rain of missiles and advanced with their rifles held out like fenceposts in a futile attempt to restrain the crowd. This mob, women mostly, chests heaving beneath the armor of steel corsets, their wide skirts jouncing over whalebone hoops, surged past the soldiers as though they were a line of scarecrows, a blank unseeing light in their eyes, mouths contorting as they howled and threw stones. A mustached colonel cantered past Hazel on a panicked sorrel, the horse's nostrils flaring in fright, yellow teeth gritted around a foam-lathered bit. He drew his saber and shouted orders while the horse tried to retreat. "Affix bayonets!" His voice came out reedy and thin amid the clamor. "Fix your bayonets!"

Hazel tasted the grit of the dust billowing around her. She smelled the sweat of the mules and the sour fear rising from dark places in men and women. She could hear the keening cries as stones whistled past. A cart overturned in front of her and spilled prisoners in a heap. The mob fell upon them and a screaming child was raised above their heads and then dashed upon the ground. Its mother, bleeding from her scalp, arms shackled but held aloft, pleaded, *"Me chonk she, me chonk she!"*

Wanikiya's cart was lost to her sight. Across the roadway she spotted Henrietta at the same moment as the woman saw her. Henrietta stood beside a girl in pretty French braids, a small girl screaming while she threw pebbles and debris at the Indians. Hazel's eyes fixed on the girl, frightened for her, thinking she might be crushed beneath the hooves of a maddened mule. No more than six years old, the child was snarling like the rest of them while she threw what her tiny fists could hold. Too late Hazel looked back to Henrietta, saw the woman heave a brickbat, all her strength behind the throw. The last thing she remembered was her own arms rising up, far too slowly, as the missile struck her forehead.

A light tap came at the door. Hazel heard someone fumbling with the latch outside and knew it was Leah again. The door opened and Leah, with one last gaze down the stairs to make sure her mother had not heard her, stepped into the room. She regarded Hazel impishly with her strange mismatched eyes, one dark green, the other a copper penny. Her hair was pinned on top of her head in a style Leah called "cat," and her large pointed ears jutted below the intricate braids. Hazel raised a hand in greeting and then made the sign for *cold*, both hands bent close to her body and shivering. Leah mimicked her perfectly and then settled her hands on the frame of the whalebone hoops beneath the skirt. Leah understood that Hazel no longer spoke out loud, and so when she was with her she did not speak either.

Hazel stopped talking again after she had failed Wanikiya at his trials. What had words mattered then? She knew she was reverting, recalling the long four-year silence that followed her mother Emma's death.

But sign language had been her first language with Wanikiya. As her hands carved patterns in the air, she could remember him beside her.

Leah waited for a moment to see if Hazel would show her any more signs and then came forward and lay her head against Hazel's belly to listen for the child. Hazel did not mind this. If there was a thump or kick Leah would squeeze her hand. She would stand again and make the sign for baby, a right closed fist across a left hand, palm up, as though holding something fragile, like water sifting through fingers. Leah's mother would not like it if she knew she was here, for she suspected that seizures were contagious, perhaps demonic in origin, and that Hazel should be locked away from the world for her sake and others. To suffer from both an indelicate condition and "nervous instability" made her troublesome.

"Leah," her voice sang from below. "Leah, we are going now, come here at once." Leah left the door open as she tiptoed down the narrow stairwell. Hazel watched the light seeping through the open doorway for a long time, listening to the bustle of the family getting ready, and then the house was silent except for the raspy breathing of George.

It was the morning after the hanging. Hazel had been a ward of Dr. Kolar for two months and had not left this room. She had thought herself as a prisoner for so long, first with the Dakota, and now here, a girl in a high tower surrounded by thorns, that she was afraid for a moment of venturing outside. She slid the worn carpetbag that contained her belongings from under the bed and put on the clothes her stepmother had sent with her: the green gingham dress, a scarlet cape, a homespun lavender shawl, and a bonnet trimmed with roses. Hazel's swollen feet would not fit into her narrow black leather boots and she had to strain to pull them on. She could not see over the rise of her belly to tie the boots so she limped out the room and down the stairs with her laces trailing behind her. She knew where she had to go.

Before she left, Hazel stopped to look in on George. She had heard him all this time and wondered what he looked like. The old man turned over on his side and regarded the girl with gunmetal blue eyes.

Beneath a cotton shift his great barrel chest rose and fell with each breath. His right eye winked uncontrollably and that side of his face was sealed in a rigid grin. Hazel didn't know what to do now that she was in the room with him. He struggled to open his mouth, to make his lips form words. "Go," he said. "Go and don't come back."

Hazel went out the back door and made her way through a side garden stripped clean in winter and sheathed in potato sacking. She clopped unevenly down the street, avoiding long patches of ice that glimmered in the frozen, cratered muck. She came down Front Street to the square where they had hanged Wanikiya and thirty-seven other Dakota.

In her left hand she carried with her the beaded moccasins she had embroidered during the summer of her captivity in Blue Sky Woman's teepee. She meant to leave these as an offering at the grave, a gift meant to help him cross over into the other world. She had seen his name listed in the *Leslie's Illustrated* Leah brought her. The account said that one of the Dakota had prayed the Lord's prayer instead of a death song. If he was being called to account for his deeds before the white God, he would go to Him speaking their tongue. This knowledge twisted cruelly inside her; when she taught him that prayer their first summer she had not known he would remember so well, had never envisioned him speaking it at such a moment.

The wind streamed out of the north and hurled sharp flakes of ice that chased away the few stragglers still gathered around the spectacle of the scaffold, a huge structure of pine clapboards with severed ropes swinging in the wintry wind. One of those ropes had held Wanikiya. She could not bear to look at the scaffold for long. People hunched past, unseeing, hats pulled low over their eyes, cloaks and coats cinched tight.

Hazel wandered down toward the river and there she found the remains of the mass grave where the thirty-eight had been buried. It was a gaping mouth that breathed steam in the cold. There were dark scattered impressions in the sandy ground, like snow angels left behind by children. The soil smelled fresh and damp, even a day later.

"They're gone." When the boy spoke it startled her so badly she almost fell into the grave. She turned a questioning gaze toward a tow-headed

child clad in long woolen shirts and patched pantaloons. A boy of thirteen perhaps, fists clutching a hidden object, grimy toes poking out of
undersized, handmade boots.

"The doctors took them," he said in a high, piping voice. "They cast
dice for the corpses. Dr. Mayo won the body of Cut-Nose." He leaned
over and spat into the grave. "When they catch Little Crow I hope they
leave him hanging so's the birds can peck out his eyes." It was then that
Hazel noticed what he clutched in his hands, a small leather bag the
size of a coin purse, embroidered with yellow beads in the shape of an
owl eye. Before he could tuck the object away, she seized his wrist with
her right hand and squeezed with her long fingernails. "Ouch!" he
hissed, dropping the tiny bag. It was a cruel thing to do, but she knew
if she had asked for it the boy would have dashed away with his stolen
treasure. She plucked the object from the ground.

"That's mine," he said. "I found it at the bottom. There's nothing else
left." He rubbed his wrists where tiny droplets of blood began to bead and
drop to the snow. "The others took everything." His jaw trembled with
anger, this boy who had nothing. "Give it back," he said. "It's mine."

Hazel held the leather bag close to her and turned away from him.
The bonnet shadowed her face and she was grateful he could not see
her tears. *He was here*, she thought, *there can be no doubting it now. He's
dead and it's my fault for not speaking up for him. My fault he turned himself in.* It was forbidden that she should show any sorrow for the Indians, even to this child. The prairies west of here were littered with the
countless shallow graves of settlers. Two of her brothers had gone
under the scalping knife, their bodies bloating and blackening under
the August sun. A few on each side did evil and the rest of them had
been left to struggle through the wreckage. All those Dakota hanged.
All those in filthy, measles-infested prison camps who had risked their
own lives to save whites like Hazel. *I will not lay blame. The word for
anger and sorrow is similar in Dakota,* woiyokisica, *and I will cling to that
dark energy. I will keep my sorrow, because I was there and I was one of the
few who understood what was lost. I know this bag, the smooth stones
within a pocket of owl's down, just as I knew the owner and his longing for*

a previous age. She looked up once more at the boy in time to see him kneading a rock-sized hunk of snow and ice.

"Witch!" he shouted. "You dirty thieving witch." His eyes watered with anger and he wiped them with his shirt before cocking his arm. Hazel took a halting step back as he unleashed the ice ball. It caught her square in the forehead, tearing loose the bandage and knocking off her bonnet. She felt needles of ice and grit explode in the wound as her head whipped back. Stumbling, she caught herself at the lip of the shallow grave, dropping the moccasins, but keeping the bag sealed in her fist. Another fit began to flicker like heat lightning inside her. These seizures started with just a faint tremor behind her left eyelid, an innocent twitch that spread to the left side of her face when she clamped her jaw down. *Oh no,* she tried to say as the shuddering possessed her body, but the words came out as vapor that passed before her and dissipated.

"Lady, what's wrong with you?" she heard the boy say, his anger turning to concern, before he saw the whites of her eyes rolling back. Dimly, she heard his cry and the footsteps stamping away and that's the last thing she remembered.

The sign for *forget* and *night* is the same: a still left hand, palm downward with the right hand sweeping over it. She would forget the next two months if it were in her power. They found her rolled inside the grave, the leather bag of stones knotted in her fist. The sandy soil that had briefly held her husband's remains had to be picked out of the reopened wound with tweezers. She woke to that sensation, like wasp stings on her forehead, as Dr. Kolar cleaned the wound. Her eyes followed the rise and fall of his arm to the stained apron he wore, white cloth dappled with yellow blood. A butcher's apron. She sat up in fear and looked at her swollen belly.

"Easy now," the doctor said. "You've had quite a shock. What did I tell you about leaving here? Any change in surroundings is likely to produce delirium and fits of apoplexia." Hazel's hands were trembling. She reached out and touched the soft fabric of her chemise where the smooth hill rose. Deep within her she sensed the child, a silent, waiting hum of energy. Beyond the doctor she saw her gingham dress hanging from the rafters, the material darkened and dripping clots of bloodlike soil to the floor. Ida was cleaning the cloth with a brush, sweeping fragments into a pan. Her slender beaklike nose wrinkled as though she were a bird pecking at unsavory crumbs.

She sensed the girl watching her and set her pan down to join the doctor and pat Hazel's hair. "You poor, dumb thing," she said. "The things you must have seen." Hazel felt a knot forming in her chest, for even this touch was a kindness she craved. "They say the lucky ones are those that died. A woman shouldn't let herself be captured alive by those red devils." She held Hazel in the gaze of her fierce brown eyes. "We'll take care of you now, dearie," she said. Hazel wondered why the woman did not mention the child inside her. Ida continued to stroke her hair, smoothing out the tangles while Dr. Kolar brought forth a hollow, wooden cylinder tapered at the end.

"To listen to your heart," he said when he saw the fright in her eyes. He moved the scope from the girl's chest and then listened for a time at her belly. Hazel watched his expression carefully, but his pale features betrayed nothing. He turned his back to her and it was then that she realized where the blood on his apron came from. He was one of the doctors who had been at the grave on the night of the hangings. In the cool darkness of his basement some warrior had been carved up and would have to carry those mutilations with him into the afterlife as his spirit traveled the path across the Milky Way. Hazel pictured Wanikiya stripped of his beaded breechclout, the sacred paint washed from his face, soft flesh of his neck serrated with rope's imprint, while the doctor hovered over him with a toothed saw. She pictured the wound in his side, the pretty hollow where his throat joined his chest, a place she would lay her own head and listen to the drumming of his heart.

Horrified, she tried to sit up again. Ida's caressing hands turned instead to talons, pinning Hazel back to the bed. Her mind flickered with blue fire, the remnant of her seizure. She was too weak to fight them, too weak to do anything but lift her arms, his name in her throat. Dr. Kolar carried over a long-needled syringe filled with milky fluids. It entered her skin and she stopped thinking for a time.

Two lost months. She did not run. Ida became kinder, stopping each morning to brush out the tangles from her hair. The seizures stopped as though Hazel had emerged from the grave a new creature, and they did not tie her to the bed each night. The nausea passed, too, and she felt the child moving about within her. How would she keep it safe once it breathed the cold air of this world alone? "A boy," Ida said. "Only the boys cause this much trouble. A little savage doing a scalp-dance in your tummy right now." Hazel's hands and feet swelled with water weight, fingers and toes becoming fat, throbbing sausages as though the child's liquid environs had leaked into her blood. The baby within her was restless, pressing down on her bladder at night so that Hazel stained the bedsheets. Her belly was not round exactly, more oblong. She should have run, she knew it in her heart, but where could she have gone in a strange town in the middle of a Minnesota winter?

Listen. The old ones spoke of stones raining from the firmament at night and plowing furrows in the earth. This was the spirit who moved in all things, even rocks, and the stones traveled between heaven and earth, and knew the language of the sun and moon and could teach it to a few. These were the stone dreamers who carried round pebbles wrapped in swan's down and could send out the tiny stones to find missing children, lost treasures, the impending future, for the stones were everywhere and could see all things. Wanikiya's father was such a medicine man, but died before passing the knowledge on to his son. Wanikiya carried the embroidered bag, a relic of the vanishing past, but the stones were inanimate in the palm of his hands.

Hazel passed her days reading the Bible again, especially Old Testament stories of captivity. She heard Job crying out, "Where is God, my Maker, who gives songs in the night?" She thought, *What song will my Maker give to me?* She took out the smooth stones from their bed of down and imagined them bringing Wanikiya back. When the child kicked and tumbled inside her, she soothed it by running a hand over her belly, pretending that it was his touch on her skin. The low slanting roof of this room became their shared teepee, the window an aperture above the lodge poles where stars swam, her steaming breath in the cold, smoke from the fire to warm them. A part of her knew these were delusions, but they allowed her to forget what went on in the lower regions of this household, his body, or perhaps another's, being diced up, his journey no longer possible.

But skin and bone were only a vessel for the eternal. He had been converted by Father Ravoux, the Black Robe who came among them before the hanging. God would know him for his heart. If there was such a life beyond this one, she would be able to find him again. It was Wanikiya who brought her out of silence; for him she began praying again.

For a few words he might have been saved, but the commission in charge of separating the guilty from the innocent, deciding who among the Dakota was guilty of the 485 recorded whites dead on the prairies, would not hear her speak. She was a girl. Henrietta had told them what she had done. If anything she would be tried beside him.

Wanikiya was no innocent and there was blood on his hands. The Stolten boy remembered him, testifying that Wanikiya was there the day his family was massacred, his father run through with a pitchfork. And Wanikiya said nothing in response, even though he knew enough English to answer their charges. So many whites had died, he must have intended to offer up his own death, life for life, a balance, as it was in their ancient conflict with the Ojibwe. There was no record of him saying a single word in Dakota or in English. In that room of killers, white and red, he was called to account with no one to speak for him. She believed he meant himself to be a sacrifice, but she was not there, and perhaps could not have changed things if she had been. She could pretend to send out the stones, but she could not bring him back, could not unmake the lies that broke his neck.

When her child was born she heard it cry before it was carried from the room. She never held him.

Ida had run cool, damp cloths across her forehead, the water dribbling into her mouth. Hazel crumpled the sheets in her fists, gritted her teeth, and pushed. She was sitting all the way up, her face near her kneecaps, when she saw that head crown, a circle of dark hair emerging, and she felt a rush of renewed strength and lay back and pushed. She swore she heard it cry, but later Ida told her the child was born dead, strangled by the umbilical cord. A death like its father's. Dr. Kolar held it muffled against his chest as he carried it from the room. Hazel's dark hair was pasted to the healing wound on her forehead and her vision clouded. She felt she was looking down a swirling tunnel narrowing to a pinprick of light. At the end of the tunnel she saw Leah in the doorway; the girl flashed the sign for good, the sign for baby, and then the tunnel closed.

A fever burned in her afterward and she dreamed that dark circle of hair was a raven she had birthed, a bird out of legend. It perched there on her knee, waiting for her die, a night bird slick with her own fluids.

Leah stopped coming, either forbidden or because there was no more child to listen for. Hazel could no longer hear George below her and wondered where he had gone. She passed in and out of the fever, once imagined her stepmother Kate in the room looming over her. "It's better this way," Kate was saying. "The child would only have reminded you every living day what you had been through." Hazel blinked and she was gone, a feverish phantasm.

During a warming spell in April, Ida and Dr. Kolar took her to her child's grave. A drenching rain lashed the cobbled streets and rinsed wet snow in gritty funnels down the hill. Hazel was still too weak to walk without the support of their arms on either side, Dr. Kolar on her left holding a small umbrella that only partially shielded them from the rain. Ida pointed out a cairn of stones beneath three oak trees, told her that Leah had made the cross of woven willows. They heard her sob, a choked sound as though a corset was binding her too tightly. When they relaxed their grip, Hazel lunged forward and began to throw the stones aside.

She slipped in the mud, her fingers clawing at slick rocks, exposing packed solid ground beneath. Ida was shouting; Dr. Kolar had hooked his arms around her waist and was pulling her away. Hazel strained with all her might, arms outstretched, a high-pitched wail escaping her throat. She fought them all the way back down the street, her blows landing without any force, until Dr. Kolar carried her back up the narrow stairwell to the attic room where she was kept.

Locked in the room, she continued to wail. Her voice was the voice of those mothers in Matthew, chapter two. At first it was wordless, but then that passage swam into her head, the memory of what happened after Christmas, and she was furious with God. She raged in the low-ceilinged attic room, her blood throbbing in her temples, the dress plastered to her shivering skin. All her remaining strength was channeled into her scream. Her hands curled into such tight fists that her fingernails pierced her palm. In the midst of her outcry, as she was pacing, her boots clacking the floorboards, chewing her lip so hard that she tasted blood inside her mouth, she was upright one moment, and then brought to her knees. The answer came to her like the prairie fires that sweep through the tallgrass in high summer, sucking the air from the lungs of any creature caught in its path. It put her on her knees, her palms against the floorboards. Rising up in her chest she felt her guilt over Wanikiya's death, her sorrow over the lost child. These dark feelings were rooted in her belly one moment and then torn out of her, as though a hand had literally reached down her throat to yank them out, held each thing up to the fire, one by one, each ugly as chaff, until they were charred away and she was emptied out. A purgative flame. She was emptied out and yet there was still this presence inside her, speaking, undeniable.

Hazel wept. When she was done weeping she saw the ragged edges of her fingernails against the floorboard, saw the black dirt beneath them. And had her answer. *He is alive. My child lives.* She began to pray again.

The Great Sioux War. The Sioux Uprising. Little Crow's Revenge. The Indian Massacre. These are the names history assigned to what she endured. That evening Ida entered the room after Hazel had quit making such terrible noises. She brought tincture of laudanum, a hairbrush. Ida let the door creak open, warily, as if afraid that Hazel would assail like her some demon. But the girl was lying quietly on top of the sheets, dressed only in her chemise, humming something under her breath that sounded like a hymn. The girl let Ida put the tincture in her mouth and she swallowed as she bid. There was something different about her. Her dark green eyes flickered with pale fire. Ida wiped away blood at the corner of the girl's mouth.

Had the girl gone mad? She was changed, though Ida couldn't put her finger on it. Hazel's forehead blazed. She looked like a picture Ida had once seen of Joan of Arc, a stylized portrait, a peasant woman in a rude shift in the midst of the fire. Then she realized what she was seeing. The girl lay with her arms rigid at her sides. She would endure these things, her eyes told Ida. She would outlive Ida, all of them. Even when laudanum mellowed her facial features, unlocked her jaw, she looked no less fierce. *I hold something,* her eyes said, *you will never touch, never have yourself.*

When I dreamed I dreamed in Dakota. Eventually, the Kolars decided they could do no more for me and I was released in late May. Ida gave me a few dollars to buy passage back upriver and find my family. Instead I went looking for the Dakota, but their winter camp south of Mankato had been abandoned, the Indian prisoners transferred down the Mississippi to Davenport, Iowa. I wanted to find Blue Sky Woman, to have her braid my hair, sing to me, heal me.

I lived hand to mouth as I made my way downriver. The foxes have holes, the birds have their nests, but the Son of Man has no place to lay his head and rest. I made it as far as Winona, Minnesota, where, half-starving, the seizures began to afflict me again. Someone found me, dirty, convulsing in the street, and took me to the Langley Home, a makeshift hospital. They could not coax a single word from me in English. The Civil War raging in the east consumed their attention. One madwoman was of little concern and so I was kept fed and cleaned and confined by four walls, an unlocked door. With nowhere to go, I retreated so far inside myself I lost even my name for a time.

When the St. Peter Hospital for the Insane opened in 1866, I was among the first patients. Ten years of my life. But inside there, no one looked at me any differently, or cared about my history. I had a room that overlooked a garden. I learned I had a talent for growing things, could show them how to sprinkle hay among the tomato vines to keep down weeds, singing softly in Dakota against the blackbirds that came to thieve the corn. Long periods passed when it even seemed they forgot I was one of the patients.

Always the seizures came like heat lightning flickering just behind my eyes. Oh, they left my physical body ravaged. But in a way I have missed them. Most of what we know of God in this world is His absence. Don't think that I mean any sacrilege. If faith were easy, it would have little worth.

There is a place inside us beyond blood and breath. Picture rolling grassland spilling over the edge of a cliff in a green wave. The other side of the cliff is molten with rivers of light winding toward the jaws of the mountains. All around you smell the rain, and in the wind there are voices of those you lost.

You are afraid of this edge inside you, of what will happen when you step over. Maybe in your ordinary days you forget it even exists. Children know it, and the elderly.

I go there just before each seizure. I step over, but it is not like in one of those dreams where you fall and fall and wake just before impact. A warm wind courses beneath me and I move like a cloud. There are ridges and ridges of mountains and beyond them a place of energy, lightning boiling inside thunderheads. The backbone of the world. A place of both fear and awe. Even the animals glimpse it when they feel their deaths rising up inside them and shamble off to be alone. But I am never afraid. For what I feel then is His presence. And I know that I will pass over unharmed. I know I shall not be cast down.

I long for this place. There was only one thing that kept bringing me back to this world. The story was not finished. Jakob, Daniel, Asa, Matthew, Wanikiya, all the banished Dakota. They had passed from this world without leaving any trace. I was haunted by my own history. So, I made a book of my own, a book like my father once made in Missouri, patching it together from the few pages the doctors parceled to me each month.

Why? Because I knew my child was out there, alive. I pictured him, a fleet runner, dark as his father, but shy and thoughtful like me. I knew that he was growing up with a space inside him he did not understand. One day I would meet him again. I knew it as surely as my father Jakob knew that escaped slave was running his way. Life would bring us together again. "Who am I?" he will say to me when he comes. "Please tell me who I am."

I set this down now for him, for the day of his return. This was all foretold long ago. A time I saw the world end and walked through the wreckage to witness its rebirth. "This is where you come from," my book will say, "this is what you are."

KINGDOM TOWNSHIP

1876

THE
GOOD ROAD

IT HAD BEEN dark for a few hours. The rain beat a steady rhythm on my slicker. When I glanced up at the roof I saw a pool forming in the center and the whole shelter preparing to collapse. My fire had dimmed to ashes. I threw on more dead limbs and blew on the embers until it flared up again. Rivulets of rain rinsed down the steep slope to join the swelling river. Some huge thing, a snapper turtle I figured, went into the water on the opposite shore. For a moment I considered dismembering my shelter and using the prong to spear the turtle. Hadn't the Indians eaten turtle flesh, cracking open the shells on sharp stones? But it was a cold rain and once my clothing got soaked it would be a long while before I got warm again.

I lay back, puzzling over the end of Aunt Hazel's story, which raised as many questions as it answered. I knew why my papa never stepped forward to take communion, why he didn't raise his pleasant voice during hymn singing. But that feverish phantasm of Kate, had she been real? These were just a few things I needed to talk over with Aunt Hazel. I had to make it to Mankato. I wanted to touch my hand to the sandy soil where they buried the thirty-eight. I wanted to find medicine so my aunt would go on living with us.

The fire sizzled and complained when the rain grew heavier. Storms had been rare in the years of the locust, arriving with sudden violence, carving streams in the cracked earth, before they gusted away and left the ground as bare as before. From the corner of my eye I saw a finger of lightning on the horizon. I counted to four before I heard thunder. The world was about to get a whole lot wetter and here I was camped at the bottom of a slope beside a surging river. More thunder reverberated through the barren woods. I started to take down my shelter, figuring I would wear the oilskin slicker and crouch next to the fire, when I heard hoofbeats drumming along the shallows of the river. Smoke mushroomed around me and rose up to meet the rain. I hesitated. It could be anyone out there. The man had said that the whole countryside had turned out in search of the James gang. I heard one of the riders shout something as he smelled my smoke. It didn't sound like more than two horses out there in the night. Six outlaws had escaped the firefight in Northfield, so this couldn't be them.

I drew up my knees to my chest and waited for them to find me because there wasn't anywhere to run. The best I could do was pull out the rusty pocketknife from the pillowcase and unclasp the blade. One of the men dismounted and slogged through the muddy shallows. "Who's there?" he called to me. "Show yourself." His voice, that easy southern twang, froze me in place. I knew that voice. Jordan, he had called himself when he stayed at our farm. Of course they would come back this way. They had mapped it going north. Maybe the other four were dead. Maybe they had split up. I only knew the voice calling to me now belonged to Jesse James, a known murderer.

All those thoughts flashed through my mind seconds after he spoke. Then I heard him draw back the hammer on his pistol. "I'm gonna count to three and then I need to see you standing by your fire, hands held high. If you don't come out, I'll start shooting."

I tucked the pocketknife within the drawstring of my pants and did as he asked. I knew they could see me clearly standing beside the flickering

fire, a boy trying not to shudder in the rain. Beyond the smoke and circle of light they were only shadows on horseback. Jesse dismounted and
approached my fire, moving through clouds of smoke as he led his horse.
A few feet away he paused to study me again and then laughed. "Well,
if this don't beat all," he said. Jesse didn't seem bothered by the smoke
that touched him and rose up to meet the rain. He stood there, his
slicker smoldering, before calling to the man still down in the river.
"Frank, get your carcass up here. I told you this was the river to follow.
It's a boy here. The boy from the farm."

Frank stayed motionless, slouched over his horse, while the shallows
coursed around his mount. Thunder crackled downriver and Jesse's
horse whinnied softly but did not try to pull away. When Frank didn't
respond, he turned to study me again. "Who else is out here with you,
son? Speak quick. Your pa. Is he up in those trees?"

"No, sir," I said, "I'm by my lonesome."

The barrel of Jesse's gun was trained on me while he scanned the
woods around us. He tipped his hat and let rain dribble from the brim
then smiled. I saw the glint of his teeth reflected in the firelight. "I have
a good sense for people," he said. "So I think you're telling the truth.
While I'd like to conversate about what brings a boy out to camp in
such weather, I've got bigger concerns. Has the news spread this far . . .
what was your name again?"

"Asa," I said, drawing a deep breath to steady my voice. "And yes,
the whole countryside is turned out to look for you."

"That's fitting," Jesse said. "Well then, we don't have much time." A
sudden gust scattered sparks from my fire all the way down to the shore.
Lightning slivered into the river somewhere close, outlining the quick
silhouette of the other rider. For a moment, I thought he was dead.
Then came roaring thunder, though this time neither horse stirred.
Jesse's eyes never left me. "Asa," he said softly. "I'd rather not have to
kill you. You seem a good boy. My brother down there is hurt bad. He's
shot in the leg and the bullet has burrowed inside. Riding this far has
been a torture. The bullet's got to come out, and it's gotta come out
tonight before infection sets in. Do you understand me so far?"

I nodded. "I think so."

"Good," he continued. "Because I'm going to need your help. I'm going to go fetch my brother from his horse and carry him to your shelter. You're going to hobble these horses, though I don't think they'll be going anywhere soon. If you try to run away, you just might escape. But I know where your live, and in my rage I would find your family and hurt them. I am capable of this."

I swallowed.

"So, I'm going to make you a deal. If Frank lives, you live. If he dies, you die with him. You see that I'm a fair man. Take care of these horses now," he said, handing me the reins of his mount.

Away from the fire, I recognized the bay I had helped Jesse brush down in my stable, though all the shine had gone out of her fine coat and brimming black eyes. Her teeth frothed with pink blood around the bit. Each breath gurgled wetly. Underbrush had scoured long gashes along her hide and when my hands passed over her flank I touched something wet and warm that was not the rain. I led her to a thicket of willows and hobbled her. Jesse had already helped his brother to my shelter, so I went for the other horse, a large gray charger whose hooves were implanted in the sandy shallows. The horse was rooted there and I had to stroke its withers, gentling it with touch and talk, before it awakened to follow my lead. Both mounts had been ridden beyond exhaustion. I came away from hobbling them smelling of horse and blood and the deeper sorrow of an animal that will soon give its life for spur and master.

For a passing moment I thought about running, but I understood instinctively that I would have to think quickly to live through this night. Jesse or Frank had killed that bank teller because he hadn't followed instructions. Running might be the very thing that got me killed. Jesse's voice quenched all such thoughts. "Bring me the saddlebags," he called, "and be quick about it."

I felt the rain soaking into my shirt, spreading icy fingers down my spine. I wasn't ready to die. Then I felt the medicine bag within my shirt, close to the hollow of my throat. The light weight of the stones against my skin reassured me. There was medicine in here to guide me; I was not alone.

I brought over each saddlebag while Jesse put more wet wood on the fire. Frank was stretched out on his back on the muddy ground beneath my shelter, his lean face and bushy goatee glistening in the firelight, his eyes flickering open briefly to take me in. Jesse had stripped off Frank's jeans, an operation that involved much cursing and exposed the man's pale, hairy legs. "Jesse," Frank said hoarsely. "You were supposed to find a doctor. The plan was to kidnap a doctor."

Jesse drew out a whisky bottle from the saddlebag and passed it to his brother. "You take a good long drink of this," he said. "I'm the only doctor you need."

Frank sat up and took a slug of the golden liquid, his adam's apple dancing. "I feel better now," he said. "Let's take care of the boy and then keep riding. I don't want your dirty hands mucking around inside of me."

All the blood drained out of me when I heard those words. I realized that even if I did everything they asked of me, I might not live. Jesse took off his hat and slicked back his hair. "No, Frank. Those horses won't go another step. They need rest. Besides, I'm not the one to fetch out that bullet. The wound was made for smaller hands. Someone stronger needs to hold you down."

Frank sat all the way up. His beard was black with rain, his eyes flashing. "You're a crazy bastard. This whole goddamn plan might as well been hatched up by monkeys. Too goddamn far, too many goddamn things that could go wrong."

"That's three times you took the Lord's name in vain. You got enough to answer for in the hereafter for blowing out another man's brains."

"The dumb son of a bitch died for other people's money. I would shoot him all over again if I had the chance. I can't abide stubbornness in people or animals." Frank took another slug of whisky and sat back again, still grumbling.

"Asa," Jesse said, "do you believe in fate?"

I shook my head, too stunned to say anything. While Frank knocked back more whisky, Jesse passed a filleting blade through the flames and then gave it to me, handle first. Then I found my voice. "Sometimes," I said. "But other times there isn't a reason in the world for things happening."

"A philosopher," Jesse said. Frank grumbled something wordless and Jesse turned toward him. "I know. Such talk makes you impatient." He ran a hand through his thin, boyish beard and looked back at me. "Well, fated or not, I like to believe there's a reason we ran into you tonight. I can't dig out this bullet on my own. He's a big fellow, meaner than a hellcat, and if he jerks the wrong way, I'll cut too deep. Besides, he has no tolerance for pain. This won't be easy."

"You want me to cut him?" I said. "I don't think that's such a good idea."

Jesse smiled. The firelight winked in his pale eyes and I saw my own reflection in the middle of the flames. The image brought my heart up into my throat. "That's the thing about fate, you don't get to choose." He lowered his voice. "I'd sooner wrestle a grizzly bear then hurt my brother. I'll hold him down. You cut carefully, hear? I don't think the bullet hit bone. It'll be there, nestled in muscle. You pluck it out like a pearl. The pearl of great worth."

Once, as a young boy, I reached under a log where I'd seen a garter snake dart a moment before. My hands found cool, wet mud and slick root and then there was a pain so sudden and sharp it felt like a thousand fangs had pierced my searching hand. I yanked it out and saw yellowjackets boiling over the skin. A cloud of them erupted from the hole and enveloped me, one hellish cloud of stinging rain closing all around. I screamed and ran for the creek.

I expected the insides of a murderer to feel like that, to sting the one foolish enough to reach inside. Frank had drained most of the whisky before Jesse fell on top of him and pinned his arms. Frank's good leg lashed out, narrowly missing me. Then the pain must have over-whelmed him. He stopped kicking. Smoke from the fire saturated the air. I felt this great stillness all around us, watching. In my hands I held a wicked filleting blade, useful for gutting fish. Despite what Jesse said about fate, I knew I had a choice. Jesse's back was to me and his brother was unconscious. I could have leaped forward and stabbed Jesse and kept slicing with the knife until they were both dead. Would that have made me a coward or a hero? Neither man had harmed me yet. My hands shook, but not out of fear. And then inside me, I heard Hazel's voice unrolling a long story, the healer touching her throat and saying, *Even demons believe in the Son of Man. If belief is powerful enough to destroy nations then surely it might command the blood in its narrow travels from heart to wound.* I knew then that I wasn't capable of any violence. The soul and sinew that made me what I was rebelled against bringing harm, even to someone who deserved it.

What I remembered later is the absolute lack of fear in this moment. I had been raised up for such things; the entire summer had trained me for it. The skin was swollen and taut around the wound. I touched it gingerly with the edge of the blade. I made only one incision to allow my fingers to reach inside, marveling at the steadiness of my hand, how I cut into a man's leg as though it were no more than thick gristle. There was too much blood for me to see the wound's opening now and so I searched it out using my hand and then hooked an index finger inside. What a lot of stew and grease is the human body. I shut my eyes and pictured soup bubbling on the stove, soup with a hard layer of lard casing the surface. The more I probed the more the wound widened until I went knuckle deep. I was not surprised when I found the black ball of steel buried in a web of meat, not far from bone. I hooked inside a second finger and pinched it out, like a parent removing a sliver from a child's hand. Then, I held it up in the firelight, saw my red hand, and the bullet no bigger than a marble. My own voice sounded distant, lower than, and echoing within me. "Here's your pearl," I told the outlaw Jesse James.

After Jesse stitched the wound shut, I wept for my own cowardice. "I wish you would go ahead and shoot me," I said. "You probably will anyway." Red-hot embers pulsed like hearts in the remains of the fire. The storm had lifted and there were stars between the shredded clouds. I lay on the wet ground near the fire, exhausted.

"No," Jesse said. "I made a promise. Besides, I like a good story. Imagine what the newspapers will print."

"No one will ever believe it."

"No, I suppose not." Jesse was quiet for awhile. "What were those words you were muttering while you searched for the bullet? That was a fine bit of doctoring for a boy. I couldn't have done it. You were whispering something about blood. 'When I saw thee and past thee,' you said. I didn't hear the rest. It sounded like witchery."

"A prayer," I said. "One from Missouri."

"Sounded far older than Missouri."

"I'm just as wicked as you," I said. I was thinking on the dream I'd had after they left the farm, the feeling that I'd done something terrible. Now these men, if Frank lived, would be free to ride again, to kill again, and I had helped them. What would Hazel say if she saw me now? Would she be ashamed? How could anyone find the good road, when every choice was bad? "You ought to take me with you."

"No, you don't belong with us."

I shivered, cold even by the fire. I drew my knees up to my chest. Jesse's voice often sounded far away when he spoke. He was watching the east where in a few hours the sun would rise. It's always coldest right before dawn. "Why do you do what you do?" I asked. "Why did you kill that man in the bank?"

"He got in the way," Jesse mused. He cast something out into the river, the bullet from his brother's leg, I guessed. "You know I wasn't much older than you when the Union militia came into my yard. Frank had joined up with the Raiders and it was him they were after. None of the rest of us had done any wrong, but that didn't stop them from stringing my stepfather up by a rope and torturing him until he almost breathed his last. He wasn't right ever after. They damaged him forever. I fell in with Quantrill's Raiders after that. Been trying to set the world right ever since."

"By murder?" All of this talk made me weary. I felt chilled to the marrow.

"Yes, I've seen and done terrible things. We had a taste of it just a couple of days ago. We aren't anything before what's coming. An age of machines. The great plains tribes will fall before the Gatling gun. Wires will whirl a voice across mountains and deserts in a blink. The railroads and steamships will go on reducing ocean and distance into nothing. I stand in the way of such an age. I want to throw a cog into the churning wheels of these machines. Such things will consume us.

"There's more money out there than I could ever steal. The tracks will cross buffalo country, the herds vanish. And I can't go back to being what I once was, a boy on a clear morning standing in the knee-high corn while riders approach on the trail. To come up from the fields and not let my heart be turned to hate. I long to ride into the past, but that's a lost territory. I can't go back. Now, I suppose, neither can you."

I never even saw the pistol. He said those words and then he brought the butt of the gun against my skull and I saw a quick imprint of light and then nothing.

EPILOGUE

J ESSE JAMES DID what he did so I wouldn't see the direction they rode off in. Still, it about killed me. He hadn't needed to tie my hands and feet. The blow to my head left me dizzy and the rain had soaked into my soul. I woke the next morning fast in a fever, my hands bound behind me. He'd taken out my knife and buried it blade up in the soil, a few feet away. I only needed to crawl over and saw away the ropes. Galloping consumption, people called it in town. You could catch it from getting chilled and be dead within a day's time. I liked the name of it. Galloping spoke of hard journeys and horses crossing vast territories, like the journey Indians said we take after we breathe our last and must find the good road.

But I don't like what it did to me. I don't remember sawing away the ropes that bound me. I don't remember climbing the steep slope up to the trail, dragging the pillowcase behind me. I only remembered waking to find my papa, Caleb, standing over me. He reached inside my shirt and pulled out the doeskin pouch that Hazel had given me. I opened my mouth to tell him about the James gang, everything I had seen or done the last few days. Then I remembered the whole reason that I was out here.

"Aunt Hazel," I whispered.

Papa said nothing. His eyes seemed to glisten in my feverish vision. "She told me where I might find you," he said. Then he gave me water and slung me over the saddle of our draft horse and led me home.

I believe I galloped through a whole landscape during my illness. Once I saw a man coming toward me, crossing no-man's land. Dust devils skirred around him. He was not like the Indian Papa and I had captured earlier that summer. His face was a boy's face, dark and serious. A lock of silver shone in his hair. He wore the same pouch Aunt Hazel had given to me, and he took out the stones from inside it and loosed them into the sky. They changed shape as they lifted into light, growing dark wings that fanned them out over the prairie. Two crows dipped on a hot breeze and whirled toward me. They swooped so close I felt the touch of their feathers on my cheeks and then they rose into the hot sky and were gone. The countryside that had held a man moments before was empty and I was alone again in a barren place. But I didn't feel afraid because I knew this barren territory was inside me and I knew I'd be seeing the man again.

Daniel had carried Ruth all the way down the Minnesota River. A sixty mile journey, on foot. A seven-year-old boy carrying a baby. They lived off what the birds left behind, leaves of wild grapevine, hazelnuts, crabapples, and green corn from the unharvested fields. At the end of his journey he didn't weigh any more than a bag of leaves. His skin was livid with insect bites. He'd walked sixty miles through hostile country, chewing the fruits he found and spitting them into the baby's mouth. In bustling St. Peter he handed Ruth into the stunned arms of the first woman he found and then sank down on a plank walkway and fell into a coma. His breath grew shallow and then stopped. Kate read about his story in the paper and left to find Ruth in November. A year or so later Kate took Ruth and went back to Missouri. She lives there still. Her father Josiah was killed by vengeful Jayhawkers after the war.

. . .

I have often thought of journeying there to see the town where the Sengers came from. I have no desire to see Kate, however.

I didn't make it as far as Daniel. Papa later told me that I had only walked six miles north of Kingdom Township. Had I made it to Mankato, it wouldn't have mattered. In my absence, my mother had already arranged to have Hazel sent back to St. Peter. I didn't get the chance to tell her goodbye.

The first day the fever broke, my room felt like the lonesomest place in the world with Hazel gone. I stood holding the doeskin bag in my hand and remembering dimly the vision I had seen. I knew it contained owl's down and two stones. There would be figures of birds etched into their surface. When I clutched the bag in my palm it felt warm, as if the stones had been heated. I shut my eyes, the way Hazel told me the stone dreamers had. What was it I had lost?

My papa's voice surprised me. I hadn't heard him climb up the ladder. I wiped my eyes with my sleeve. "Your father would want you to have that," he said.

"What?" I was puzzled.

"That's the second time I've found you in the woods," he continued. "The first time, you were only a baby. When Kate came back from Mankato after visiting Hazel, she told us the baby and Hazel had both died. I didn't believe her. I had seen the way she watched Hazel touch the growing mound of her belly. Cassie had already lost our baby and the doctor told her she would never have another. Those two women watched Hazel with murderous eyes. Each had died a little during the war. Then Hazel was wounded in the New Ulm riots and had to be sent to the doctors. I had the feeling I wouldn't ever see my sister again.

"It was April, in a spring of warm rain. The very day Kate told me Hazel and her baby were dead, I left to see for myself. I had to see my sister once more, or her grave. Halfway past New Ulm I camped in the woods. I had only my bedroll, some jerky to chew on, flint and puck to start a fire. A family came along in a Conestoga wagon. Settlers moving in to take the place of those who had died. The mother held up a child, dark as a prairie nigger, saying some Indian must have left it as they fled the army. The baby had been bundled in a blanket and placed in a crate that was left in the woods. I begged them for the child and they were glad to give it up since they had too many mouths already to feed. You see I knew who the child was, this swaddled boy with a crow's dark hair. My knack for finding things had worked once more. I recognized the crate the child had been left in. It was an old wine crate, one that I had kept to remind me of Birch Coulee. One meant for a wedding. You were inside it. You, the baby who Kate had left either to die or to be rescued by someone happening along. You. Hazel's boy."

Light filters through a stained glass window at an old stone church named for St. Joseph. The window was paid for by Indian children picking berries and selling them in town. Within the stained glass you see lambs lying in the tallgrass, the picture dedicated to the memory of all those children who never made it to this place. I sometimes wonder what the Indians must think of the lambs, for they have never seen such a creature on the reservation. I do not know if lambs would fare well drinking from the alkaline streams above Sisseton, but I have often been surprised in this life. I am told the man who founded this church, Bishop Whipple, was called Straight Tongue by the Dakota. It is said they sang him into the ground with Christian hymns in their own language. Like the saints of old he was entombed beneath the altar.

I am called Tun-kan-wan-ya-kapi, after my grandfather, Seeing Stone, by those who still wear-the-blanket and follow old traditions in the privacy of their homes. I have kept the medicine bundle, though so many have cast their own into the fire to appease the missionaries. Like my mother, I am Christian, but it would feel wrong to destroy something sacred to my ancestors. Nothing I read in the Good Book calls for such a sacrifice; the God I serve is not half so jealous. Like my mother, I also have a knack for healing, though there is nothing magical in the doctor's bag that I carry from home to home, the crude, square sod houses the Dakota have come to inhabit. There are things inside this bag she would not recognize: the stethoscope made of metal and rubber, the bottle of synthesized aspirin. She would not recognize me either, for I have let my hair grow out, and wear it in two braids, one down either side.

The Sisseton Reservation is a hard country of wind and bitter salt streams. Even the cattle are thin. Before the turn of this century, many Dakota followed a chief named Good Thunder back to Minnesota where they bought land around Birch Coulee with long overdue money from the government.

I pass through Yellow Medicine country every year when I travel to St. Peter, bumping over dusty roads in a Model T. I pass the new Dakota settlements in the river valley. I pass through a country she came through as a captive, follow a river my uncle Daniel followed in his own flight.

Kingdom Township is not along my way. I lived with Caleb and Cassie until I went off to school. I remember one particular afternoon when Caleb and I took the scalps from his jail out onto the plains and made a bonfire. He wept when we burned them and told me these were all that were left of a band of Winnebago that had been luckless enough to pass through the territory after the uprising. There is no smell worse than smoke from burning skin. It is the smell of hatred. The smoke from the fire obscured the sun. Then we walked away from the remains, Caleb leaning on my shoulder. My uncle, who saved me. He went on going to church, refusing communion. But there were always tears in his eyes when he was done praying. And I like to think he found some forgiveness there, even without blood or bread. As for Cassie, she and I were never close, before or after.

Jesse James was killed by Bob Ford in 1882. I can't speak to the legends that grew up around the man, except to say that there was a charm about Jesse that made you like him, even though he might kill you. His brother Frank turned himself in to the Missouri governor, was acquitted, and went on to live a long life hosting a Wild West show with the former outlaw and partner Cole Younger.

Today, in April of 1908, my own son Jakob White Bear Senger rides besides me in the motor car. He is ten years old. His head tilts back to watch the screel of dust following us in a low cloud. We pass farmers driving teams of draft horses through wet black fields, harrowing the ground with loud metal machines in preparation for the planting. Jakob is a quiet child. His mother, Cloud Woman, gave him his high cheekbones and shining black eyes. The German measles nearly carried him away last winter and he has come through a long season of sickness with a new reckoning of this world.

We pass through canopies of ancient burr oak forests, the tree limbs gnarled and tangled above us, through light which dapples the roadway. When I halt on a high place overlooking the St. Peter Hospital, at first the boy does not follow me into the graveyard. He has fallen asleep with his face against the window, so I quietly remove the gardening trowel and small shovel I have brought with which to tend grave number 121, the small fist of granite that marks where she went to rest. It's a hot spring afternoon, the kind of humid day that will crack open the seeds in their hard shells, causing them to reach up through the dark soil toward light.

A year's time is enough for the weeds to collect and obscure the stone. Sometimes, I don't know whether I come here out of habit or to do penance. That same winter Hazel returned to St. Peter in 1876, she contracted tuberculosis from another patient. Three years later, on my way to Carleton College to begin my studies, I found a nurse who remembered her. She told me Hazel was often seen holding the sick patient's hand, kneeling by her bedside and praying with her. The other patient survived the winter; Hazel did not. I had been angry at her before I came and heard this story. She had responded to none of my letters that told her how much I longed to see her again, how unbearable my life seemed without her. In April of 1877, when Governor Pillsbury exhorted Minnesotans to fast for four days and pray for release from the locust scourges, Hazel was already gone. She was not there to feel the late frost that stole down from the north, killing the larvae where they waited in their furrows, turning them into so much dust. She was not there to know that she had spoken truly.

I wonder when I am here if she would be satisfied with the life I lead now, tending to the Dakota that she longed to return to. I have become fluent, as she once was, in their tongue. I am regarded as *tioysape*, a medicine healer. Usually when I am here I hold long conversations at her head-stone. I tell her about the book I am writing that records stories the blanket-Indians tell me during long winters. I tell her about my wife and my son. I tell her that I have begun to try and remake the book of her stories I accidentally burned that summer. Page by page, I am bringing the book back. This is what you hold in your hands now.

"Papa?" a voice calls behind me.

I turn toward my boy, seeing his winter-pale skin. "Where are we?"

I point down toward the hospital where there is smoke rising from the chimneys of white buildings and from the stovepipes of the tin shacks along the ravines outside it. Like a citadel unto itself, she once told me.

"Did I ever tell you about your grandmother?"

"A thousand times," the boy replies. "You kept telling me about her all winter long."

But when I am quiet, he urges me on, "Papa, I suppose I wouldn't mind if you told me once more."

"That is where she was sent after the hangings."

He sets his hands on his hips and peers down into the valley, chewing on his lower lip. "It looks scary," he says. "She must have been brave."

"It isn't such a bad place," I tell him. "From up here, the view is nice. It's not far from where Daniel ended his journey."

The boy kneels beside me and pulls out a dandelion growing in the devil grass. He doesn't ask any more questions, just takes the trowel and begins to work cleaning this spot of land. His face is still speckled with scabs from old measles sores. I can see his grandmother rising up in his eyes, stripping away his sickness.

Two crows come down and land in a nearby burr oak to watch us work. The boy picks up a stone and balances his arm as if to throw it, but something stops him. He kneels back in the grass, watching the birds warily. I smile at him. "Hunin and Munin," I say. "Like brothers, they return. Or so your great-grandfather Jakob would say."

"Yes," my boy says. "I remember their names. Memory and Understanding."

AFTERWORD

FIVE YEARS AGO, while preparing to
move to *Little House on the Prairie* country—where I was to join my wife
Melissa for the first year of our marriage—I happened upon a children's
book about growing up in pioneer America. This book touched upon the
Dakota Conflict and the hangings in Mankato. The scope of the blood-
shed staggered me. Growing up out West I had never heard of this piv-
otal historical event, since it is so often overshadowed by the Civil War.
The book mentioned two things that triggered my imagination. I read of
Sarah Wakefield, who married a warrior named Chaska to protect herself.
Later, Sarah was vilified in the press for trying to save him from hanging.
The book also told of Snana, a grieving Dakota mother who adopted
Mary Schmidt and cared for her like a daughter throughout the war. Both
stories fused in my brain and I felt compelled to set something down on
paper. Then I discovered that the congregation where my wife—a
Lutheran pastor—accepted her first call was a mere five miles from the
Lower Sioux Agency which was burned to the ground in 1862. I felt this
story reaching for me from out of time and knew I had to tell it.

That first summer of exploration was a glorious time. Green fields spread out under a July sun. I was newly married and had two months' freedom before I started work teaching high school. My wife tolerated my newfound obsession, as I went down to the basement to start work on a novel, not knowing what I was getting us in for. She read that first middling draft, forty pages later, and saw something there to encourage me to keep going. A year later, I enrolled in MSU, Mankato, where I went on to earn my MFA in creative writing. There I met professors and lifelong friends who shaped how I write. Terry Davis instilled in me the principle of narrative generosity. Roger Sheffer helped me learn to sculpt my prose. Friends like Roger Hart and too many others to mention read early drafts over the summer and provided constructive criticism. This book wouldn't exist without their help.

Though this is a work of fiction, it also would not have been possible without research. I am indebted to the hard-working historians at the Lower Sioux Agency who opened up their archives and shared their gathered knowledge. Certain books in particular sparked my imagination and their truths are woven into the text of my narrative. I highly recommend these sources for further exploration:

Lucy Leavenworth Wilder Morris. *Old Rail Fence Corners: Frontier Tales Told by Minnesota Pioneers*. This book was my constant companion in the early drafts. Though pioneer accounts are spare in detail, read together the texture of a lost world emerges. What do whippoorwills sound like to a woman missing her husband? Do cows get homesick? How do you make sour-emptying bread or soap from ash and lye?

Charles Eastman. *Indian Boyhood*. This Boston University–educated doctor, present at Wounded Knee, grew up Dakota and fled with his people after the conflict. His memories of his boyhood are both nostalgic and haunting. His *Wigwam Evenings* also includes many fine folk tales. The story of Eya the Destroyer, which Hanyokeyah tells Wanikiya, is adapted from this work.

Vince Randolph. *Ozark Magic and Folklore*. This is the single most entertaining collection of folklore on water-witches and "Holy Rollers" that I have ever read. Randolph traveled through the Ozark region interviewing soothsayers and collecting their lore. Sometimes, it seems these country folk were pulling his leg. I found Hazel's blood prayer in this book, along with many of the tidbits from Jakob's *Book of Wonders*.

Kenneth Carley. *The Sioux Uprising of 1862*. This is considered the most balanced accounting of the conflict. A must-read for any interested in this history.

Alan Woolworth and Gary Clayton Anderson. *Through Dakota Eyes: Narrative Accounts of the Minnesota Indian War of 1862*. This book offers a collection of thirty-six narratives from the Dakota perspective. Joe Coursolle's story, mentioned in passing in the novel, is stunning.

Sarah Wakefield. *Six Weeks in the Sioux Teepees: A Narrative of Indian Captivity*. Sarah's accounting is remarkable for its compassion. She was pilloried by society for speaking out on behalf of her protector, Chaska.

Amos E. Oneroad, Alanson B. Skinner, and Laura L. Anderson. *Being Dakota: Tales and Traditions of the Sisseton and Wahpetons*. A wonderful book for lovers of folklore. It was here that I first encountered the tree-dweller, Canotina.

Duane Schultz. *Over Earth I Come: The Great Sioux Uprising of 1862*. Some consider Shultz's compilation of narratives the most exciting of the historical accounts.

Frederick Manfred. *Scarlet Plume.* Every fiction writer who approaches this time period does so in the shadow of Manfred. Manfred was inspired by the letters General Sibley wrote to his wife. He begins his narrative in the fictional Skywater, based on the Lake Shetek massacre.

Samuel L. Pond. *The Dakota or Sioux in Minnesota As They Were in 1834.* Samuel Pond spent twenty years as a missionary among the Dakota. His work, while occasionally condescending, provides numerous ethnographic insights.

There are too many other great books to list here. When people in our community heard I was writing a novel about the conflict, many stepped forward with stories passed down to them. History, I found while researching, is very much alive.

One day in particular stands out in my memory. While attending an event at the Lower Sioux agency, I ran into a descendant of a German settler in the parking lot. When he heard about my novel, he squeezed my arm and told me the story of his grandfather witnessing his family's massacre while hiding in the trees. "They don't tell it how it happened anymore," he said, his eyes bright, nodding toward the agency. That same afternoon I met a Dakota Indian who lowered his eyes when he heard about my project. "Be careful how you tell the story," he told me in a quiet voice. It seemed to me then, as it does now, that if I told the story right neither man would be happy. I have been as faithful as possible to historical fact while writing this novel, but my ultimate loyalty has always been to the characters who found a voice in my imagination, as I hope they have in yours.

READING GROUP GUIDE

THE NIGHT BIRDS

1. *The Night Birds* centers on the Senger family, who live across the river from a small band of Dakota. Famous leaders such as Little Crow or Colonel Sibley do not appear as characters. Does the novel gain by focusing on ordinary individuals rather than people most often written about in history books?

2. The novel alternates between two time periods, 1876 and 1862. Why did the author choose a dual narrative structure? Do the alternating stories echo each other in unexpected ways?

3. "I was born in the shadow of the Great Sioux War," Asa tell us in the first line of the story. Is the first person voice compelling? When Hazel begins her narrative of the family's journey from Missouri the writing switches to the third person. What effect did this change have on you?

4. On page 23, Hazel tells a story about children gathered in a castle where the king has forbidden speech. Why does she tell this story in response to Cassie's question? Does the theme of silence resonate throughout the novel?

5. In a summer of war, Hazel survives by attempting to shed her German-American identity, seeking to become Dakota. Is she successful? How did you respond to her character as a young woman and the choices she makes? When she returns, how has she changed?

6. How does place impact the people in *The Night Birds*? Did the narrative transport you into the past?

7. Discuss the title of the novel. What are the night birds? Why are they a motif?

8. "The mystic fatalism that suffuses *The Night Birds* comes from both sides of a cultural frontier and it is often beautifully expressed," Madison Smartt Bell wrote in a *Boston Globe* review. Do you agree? How do German and Dakota folklore traditions inform the characters' lives? What are the spiritual dimensions of this story?

9. The Dakota Conflict, once known as The Sioux Uprising, is considered a lost or forgotten episode in national history. Why do you think this event is not widely known today? How does the novel illuminate history? Did the author achieve balance in his portrayal of German and Dakota relations?

10. Did you find the ending satisfying? Why or why not? What scenes or images will linger in your imagination?